THE BRIDE OF
IVY GREEN

Books by Julie Klassen

THE BRIDE OF IVY GREEN

JULIE KLASSEN

BETHANYHOUSE
a division of Baker Publishing Group
Minneapolis, Minnesota

Published by Bethany House Publishers
11400 Hampshire Avenue South
Bloomington, Minnesota 55438
www.bethanyhouse.com

Bethany House Publishers is a division of
Baker Publishing Group, Grand Rapids, Michigan

Printed in the United States of America

Library of Congress Cataloging-in-Publication Data
Names: Klassen, Julie, author.
Title: The bride of Ivy Green / Julie Klassen.
Description: Minneapolis, Minnesota : Bethany House, a division of Baker
    Publishing Group, [2018] | Series: Tales from Ivy Hill ; 3
Identifiers: LCCN 2018020664| ISBN 9780764218170 (trade paper) | ISBN
    9780764218187 (cloth) | ISBN 9780764233043 (large print) | ISBN 9781493416042
    (e-book)
Subjects: | GSAFD: Christian fiction. | Love stories.
Classification: LCC PS3611.L37 B75 2018 | DDC 813/.6—dc23
LC record available at https://lccn.loc.gov/2018020664

Scripture quotations are from the King James Version of the Bible.

This is a work of fiction. Names, characters, incidents, and dialogues are products of the author's imagination and are not to be construed as real. Any resemblance to actual events or persons, living or dead, is entirely coincidental.

Cover design by Jennifer Parker
Cover photography by Mike Habermann Photography, LLC
Map illustration by Bek Cruddace Cartography & Illustration

Author is represented by Books and Such Literary Agency.

18   19   20   21   22   23   24   7   6   5   4   3   2   1

To Karen Schurrer,
So thankful for your skill, love of story, support,
and encouragement for so many years of my writing journey.
I'm blessed to count you as a friend as well as editor.

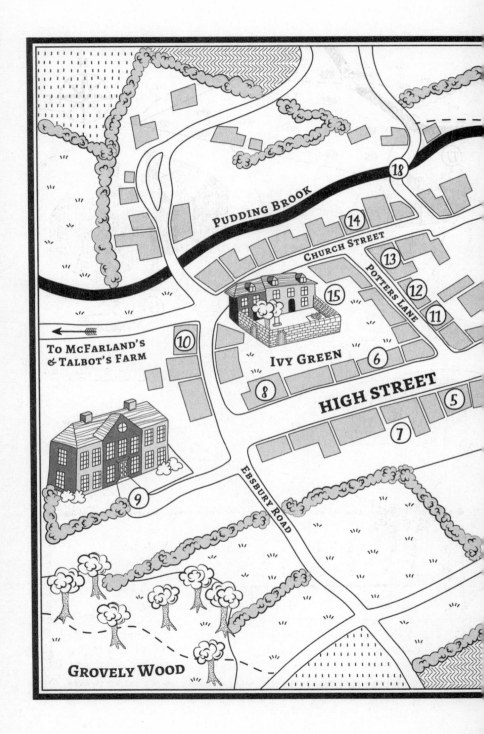

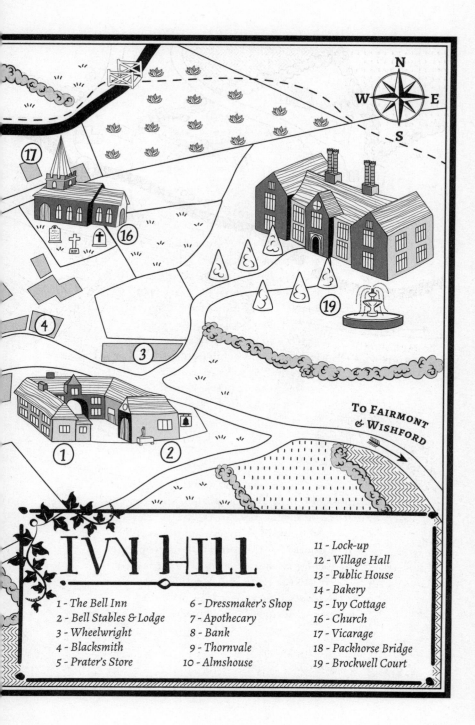

IVY HILL

1 - The Bell Inn
2 - Bell Stables & Lodge
3 - Wheelwright
4 - Blacksmith
5 - Prater's Store
6 - Dressmaker's Shop
7 - Apothecary
8 - Bank
9 - Thornvale
10 - Almshouse
11 - Lock-up
12 - Village Hall
13 - Public House
14 - Bakery
15 - Ivy Cottage
16 - Church
17 - Vicarage
18 - Packhorse Bridge
19 - Brockwell Court

To Fairmont & Wishford

MADAME VICTORINE
(from Paris)
Milliner & Dress Maker
4 Stratford Place, Hastings

—*West Sussex Advertiser, circa* 1850

E. CLAPHAM,
Fancy Dress and Mantua Maker,
Begs Leave to inform the
Ladies of Leeds, and its Vicinity,
That she has just received a Variety of
Fashionable Fancy Models from London,
Which may be seen by those
Ladies who please to honor her
with their Commands, and hopes
through her strict Attention,
to merit their future Favors.
Two Apprentices Wanted.

—*The Leeds Intelligencer,* 1798

POLITO'S MENAGERIE
Indisputably the most grand, rich, and complete
collection of rare and beautiful living animals ever
known to travel in any part of the world,
is now offered for the inspection of the public.
By the very last arrival from India, was received the
HORNED HORSE OR NILGHAU,
Universally acknowledged the most
elegant quadruped of the Hindustan. . . .

—*Perthshire Courier,* 1816

CHAPTER
ONE

February 1821
Ivy Hill, Wiltshire, England

Mercy Grove could no longer put off the painful task. Her brother had recently married and would soon return from his wedding trip, ready to move with his new bride into Ivy Cottage—the home Mercy and Aunt Matilda had long viewed as their own.

Mr. Kingsley and one of his nephews had already relocated the bookcases to the circulating library's new location in the former bank building and helped return the drawing room to its original purpose. It was time for her schoolroom to follow suit.

The Groves' manservant had carried the desks, globes, and schoolbooks up to the attic, and now all that was left to move was Mercy's prized wall slate.

Resigned to the inevitable, she asked Mr. Basu to take down the slate for her, but the manservant stood, knuckle pressed to his lip, uncertainty written on his golden-brown face. He sent her an apologetic look.

"If it breaks, it breaks," Mercy said, more casually than she felt. She reminded herself she was no longer a teacher, but rational or not, she wished to save the slate intact. Just in case.

She recalled her father's consoling words. *"I know you will miss your school. But if nothing else, you might help educate George's children one day."* But as George had just married, it would be several years at least until she had a niece or nephew to teach.

As the two stood contemplating the framed slate, the sound of knocking on the front door reached them. Mr. Basu hurried off to answer it, clearly relieved for an excuse to postpone the task.

A few moments later, her aunt poked her head into the school-room. "Mercy? Mr. Kingsley is here."

"Oh? I did not know we were expecting him."

"I happened to mention you were unsure how to remove the slate in one piece, and he offered to help."

"Aunt Matty, we have asked too much of Mr. Kingsley already. He—"

Before Mercy could complete her objection, her aunt opened the door wider, revealing tall Joseph Kingsley standing behind her, hat in hand. His sandy hair looked damp from a recent bath.

"Morning, Miss Grove."

Mercy's hand went to her throat. Could he see her pulse beating there? She fiddled with the fichu tucked into her neckline. "Mr. Kingsley. Thank you for coming, but are you not needed at the Fairmont?"

He shrugged his broad shoulders. "Oh, my brothers will get along without me for one morning. Besides, work has slowed to a trickle with Mr. Drake away so much."

Mr. Drake had taken Alice home to introduce her to his parents. Mercy had yet to see them since their return. How she missed the dear girl.

Aunt Matilda backed from the room, eyes twinkling. "Now that Mr. Kingsley is here, Mr. Basu and I will see if Mrs. Timmons needs any help in the kitchen."

Not very subtle, Mercy thought, cheeks self-consciously warm.

When the door closed behind him, Mr. Kingsley stepped forward. "You traveled after the holidays, I understand. I came to call once and found only Mr. Basu in residence."

Mr. Kingsley had come to call? Mercy had seen him on a few occasions since then, and he'd never mentioned it, although his nephew had been with him at the time. "I am sorry to have missed you. Was there . . . something you needed?"

"Nothing in particular. Just to see how you fared and if you'd had a happy Christmas."

"That was kind of you. Aunt Matilda and I spent some time with my parents in London, and then we all traveled north to attend my brother's wedding."

"You traveled with *only* your parents and aunt?" he asked.

"Yes. Why?"

He looked down, twisting his hat brim. "I recall that you planned to give your suitor an answer by Christmas."

Embarrassment heated her face once more. Why had she burdened poor Mr. Kingsley with all her woes?

"I did, yes."

"And may I ask what your answer was?"

She gestured around the empty space. "I should think that obvious, as we are dismantling my schoolroom to make way for the new master and mistress."

He winced, and Mercy instantly regretted her sharp tone.

"Forgive me," she said. "I know bitterness does not become me. I thought I had accepted the situation, but apparently not."

"I understand. I did not want to assume. The professor must have been terribly disappointed."

"I don't know. He wrote back to tell me he postponed his retirement for another term. I suppose you think it was foolish of me to refuse him. My parents certainly do."

"Wise or not, I cannot say. I am not sorry to hear it, only surprised. Your mother described him as perfect for you. Educated, well-read, an Oxford tutor. Not many in this parish have such qualifications."

She looked down. "I am not so exacting, I assure you."

"You should be. You deserve the best, Miss Grove."

Mercy was taken aback by his earnest tone. Was he applying for the position? But when she found the courage to look into his face, he quickly averted his gaze.

Mercy swallowed. "And you, Mr. Kingsley?"

"Me? I would never presume to be worthy, uneducated as I—"

"I meant, did *you* have a happy Christmas?"

"Oh." A flush crept up his fair neck. "I . . . yes. I spent Christmas with my parents and brothers, and Twelfth Night with . . . in Basingstoke."

"Basingstoke? With your wife's family?"

His eyes flashed to hers in surprise.

She hurried to explain. "You mentioned that was where you met your wife." And, Mercy recalled, where she had died in childbirth only a year after they wed, their child with her.

He reached up and rubbed the back of his neck. "Right." He turned abruptly to the slate mounted on the wall. "Let's see about taking this down, then."

Seeing his obvious discomfort, Mercy was sorry she had mentioned his wife.

He walked closer and ran his fingers over the frame. "I'll do my best, but slate is fragile. There's a high risk of cracking."

"I understand. I trust you. You can do it if anyone can."

"I'll try to live up to that, but I haven't much experience with slate. I will need help lowering it once I begin prying the frame from the wall. Perhaps Mr. Basu?"

"Yes. I will go and ask him to join us."

Mr. Basu reluctantly followed Mercy back up to the schoolroom, padding quietly on his pointed leather slippers. He stood at the other end of the slate, awaiting instructions. Curiosity and keen intelligence shone in his dark eyes as he glanced from Mr. Kingsley to her and back again.

From his toolbox, Mr. Kingsley extracted a crowbar. Then both men looked at her once more.

"You're certain?" Mr. Kingsley asked.

The two simple words meant so much more.

She made do with a nod, fearing if she spoke, her voice would crack, and she wanted no cracks today.

Mr. Kingsley held her gaze a moment longer, then nodded to Mr. Basu.

"Just hold that end steady as I pry around this edge."

The two men worked in silence, communicating with looks and small gestures.

Mr. Kingsley pried slowly and carefully, and Mercy held her breath. As he levered up the last corner, a sickening *snap* rent the air, and a jagged line snaked up one side.

"Dash it," he murmured.

Mr. Basu muttered something in his mother tongue.

Mercy pressed a hand to her mouth. She felt that crack run straight through her heart.

Mr. Kingsley looked at her over his shoulder, crestfallen. "I am sorry, Miss Grove."

"It isn't your fault. Besides, it is not as though I have any plans for it."

He carefully extracted the loose piece, and then the men lifted the frame. "Where shall we put it?"

"Let's store it in the attic for now." *With the rest of my hopes and dreams.* Mercy reminded herself that God did not promise ease and happiness in this life. But He did promise peace and joy, and she was determined to hold on to both, somehow.

The next morning Mercy and Matilda helped the servants begin an early spring cleaning to prepare Ivy Cottage for its new residents. There was a great deal to do and only a few of them to accomplish it.

Becky Morris offered to paint the walls of the former schoolroom, which showed signs of fading once the large slate had been removed. To spare Mr. Basu the task of washing the outside windows—he was not as young as he used to be—Mercy borrowed a tall ladder from Becky and hired one of the Mullins boys to do so. The strapping boy, who was always looking for extra work, also helped Mr. Basu bring down her grandparents' old bedroom furniture stored in the attic these last ten years.

Needing to stretch their household budget after so many added expenses, they economized with simple meals and scant meat while planning a more extravagant dinner to welcome George and Helena home. At her mother's suggestion, they had engaged a kitchen maid to assist Mrs. Timmons. Her father had said he would increase their allowance accordingly but had yet to do so. Mercy hoped he would, especially now that she no longer received any income from her school to help make ends meet.

They worked steadily until the day of her brother's return. The new-married couple was due to arrive at four. By half past three, old Mrs. Timmons was perspiring and red-faced from her extra exertions over a hot stove, and the new kitchen maid, Kitty McFarland, looked about to weep. Agnes Woodbead ran between kitchen and dining room, laying out the best china and silver and arranging flowers from Mrs. Bushby's greenhouse on the table.

Mercy and Matilda scurried about as well, straightening and adding finishing touches to the newly restored master bedroom. Mercy set a vase of hothouse flowers on the bedside table, checked to make sure freshly laundered hand towels were folded neatly at the washstand, and smoothed the lace cover, purchased from the Miss Cooks, on the dressing table.

Soon the room was fresh and tidy, but a passing glance in the mirror told Mercy *they* were not.

"Aunt Matty, do take off your apron. They shall be here at any time."

Matilda surveyed Mercy as she did so. "And you ought to change your frock and comb your hair, my dear."

"Perhaps we had both better change."

Matilda readily agreed, and in the jerky nod and distracted gaze, Mercy realized her aunt was as nervous about the new arrivals as she was.

The two women retreated to their rooms, helping each other into gowns more suitable for receiving guests. Then Mercy quickly brushed and repinned her hair and turned to her aunt for approval. "All right?"

"Very nice, my dear. Me?"

Mercy regarded the thin flushed face, out-of-fashion primrose yellow gown, and wispy grey curls. She extracted a stray cobweb from her aunt's hair and smoothed an errant tuft. "Perfect. Remember, we must be on our best behavior. We are the visitors now."

Matilda nodded. "I shall try."

When the hired chaise arrived, Mercy and her aunt waited in the vestibule while Mr. Basu went out to meet it, looking smarter than usual in a crisply ironed high-colored jacket over his traditional loose trousers. As always, a soft cotton cap covered his black hair.

They watched through the window as a groom hopped down to lower the chaise step and open the door. Then he returned to the boot to unfasten trunks and valises and hand them to Mr. Basu.

Mercy's tall brother alighted first, reaching back to help his dainty wife down. Helena looked regal in purple-and-gold carriage dress and fashionable hat. She glanced up at Ivy Cottage and, if Mercy was not mistaken, was not overly impressed with what she saw.

Mercy's stomach tightened. She silently asked God to help this first encounter go well and for Helena to approve of the Ivy Cottage servants, who were worried about their future employment if they failed to please their new mistress. A second woman, dark-haired and dressed in serviceable black, emerged next, a stack of bandboxes in hand. Helena's lady's maid, Mercy guessed. She hoped Agnes had remembered to ready the room next to hers as well.

Mercy's heart pounded. *Foolish girl, it is only your brother and his wife.* There was nothing to be frightened of. Beside her, Aunt Matty clutched her hand.

Mercy reached out to open the door, but Matilda kept hold of her hand, gesturing with a nod for Agnes—in her best dress and freshly laundered apron—to open it. Mercy supposed her aunt was right. First impressions mattered. A woman like the former Helena Maddox would expect a servant to open the door. She would no doubt prefer a tall liveried footman, but short Agnes Woodbead or silent Mr. Basu would have to do. At least for the present. Mercy wondered if, and when, Helena would begin making changes. It was her household to manage now as she saw fit.

As he entered the vestibule, George stretched out his arms, a charming smile dimpling his face. "Well, here we are."

"Welcome home, George." Aunt Matty returned his smile.

George kissed his aunt's cheek and Mercy's, then turned to his wife. "You remember my darling wife, I trust?"

Helena said coolly, "Of course they do, George. We met at the wedding. And I have a name, you know."

"You do indeed, Helena. Although I prefer *Mrs. Grove*." He winked at his wife, but she ignored his teasing.

"A pleasure to see you again, Helena," Aunt Matty said.

"Yes, welcome to Ivy Cottage," Mercy added. Noticing Mr. Basu still carrying baggage through the side door, she said, "Here, let Agnes take your things."

Helena's gaze swept over Agnes's plain form with a small wrinkle between her brows. Mercy reminded herself not to be prejudiced where her new sister-in-law was concerned. Just because Helena was raised in a wealthy home did not mean the woman would be critical or difficult to please—she hoped.

Mercy smiled at Helena. "Dinner will be ready soon, and I imagine you will want to freshen up first?"

"Dinner . . . so early? Ah yes, we are in rural Wiltshire now, with its charming country manners. We are accustomed to dining later. I will need time to rest and change."

Mercy felt her smile falter, thinking of Mrs. Timmons's exhausting efforts to prepare an elegant meal and to have everything ready at just the right time.

Helena directed her next comment to Agnes. "And a hot bath, if you please."

A hot bath—now? When every inch of the stove was covered with cooking pots and simmering sauce pans, and their small staff stretched thin as it was?

George glanced from woman to woman, then spoke up. "My dear, might your bath not wait a bit? I can smell our dinner, and my mouth is watering already. It has been far too long since I've tasted Mrs. Timmons's cooking. Come, my dear. We can alter meal times in future, but if everything is ready now . . ."

Mercy's heart warmed to her brother, who at that moment seemed less like the stranger she had felt him to be at the wedding and more like the sibling she recalled.

His wife's eyes shone icy blue. "Heaven forbid you should miss a meal, my dear. If the bath must wait, so be it. But I will need an hour at least to rest and dress." She patted George's waistcoat and looked at Mercy. "Married life agrees with your brother, as you see, Miss Grove. He has gained a stone or more since we became engaged. He ate his way through every city on our wedding trip."

An uneasy smile lifted her brother's handsome features. "And why not? What a delicious opportunity to sample the cuisine of several different regions."

"Sounds wonderful," Matilda agreed. "We look forward to hearing all about your travels."

While the newcomers went upstairs to rest and change, Mercy hurried to the kitchen to inform Mrs. Timmons to delay the meal. Mrs. Timmons grumbled, doubting it would look or taste nearly as good after being kept warm for an hour, predicting the new mistress would send her packing for serving fallen Yorkshire puddings, reheated meat, and congealed sauces.

"She will understand," Mercy said, trying to reassure her. "After all, she was the one who postponed the meal."

At least Mercy hoped she would understand. Kitty and Agnes were still young and could likely find new employment, but if Helena dismissed Zelda Timmons or Mr. Basu, both would struggle to find new positions—Mrs. Timmons because of her age, and Mr. Basu because he was a foreigner in a land sometimes unwelcoming to darker-skinned people. Both were dependable and hardworking. She hoped Helena would come to think so as well.

An hour later, Mercy reached the dining room first and watched as her sister-in-law descended the stairs in a vibrant indigo gown with a high lace collar. The petite woman possessed fair skin and delicate patrician features. Cool hauteur pinched her small mouth, but she had likely been an angelic-looking child with a halo of blond curls. Now Helena wore her hair in an ornate style, with braids from ear to ear and tight pin curls fringing her forehead like curtain tassels.

Mercy felt large, awkward, and ill-dressed in her presence, especially as Helena's gaze traveled over her inelegant form with silent censure, or at least pity.

When they had all gathered and taken their seats, Helena surveyed the table with its soup tureen, fish course, and more dishes to follow. After two weeks of sparse meals, Mercy's stomach growled in anticipation.

Helena said, "Quite a feast. Do you two always eat so well?"

"No, but we wanted your first meal here to be special."

"I see."

Mercy added, "Mrs. Timmons has been with us for years. And we recently hired a new kitchen maid, as Mother suggested."

"I trust your father has increased the household allowance?"

She was surprised Helena would raise the topic in company. "He plans to, I know."

"George, you will have to write to him. I won't see my dowry spent on the butcher's bill."

"Yes, my love. Straightaway."

As they began the next course, Matilda changed the subject. "Now that you have returned to England, George, what will you do?"

Helena smiled. "Oh, we expect great things. Parliament, perhaps."

"Ah," Matilda murmured doubtfully.

Helena prodded a limp puff of dough with her fork. "Is this meant to be Yorkshire pudding?"

"Yes. Made in your honor."

Helena did not appear impressed, and even less so when she lifted a ladle of lumpy gravy.

Mercy's enjoyment of the generous meal was diminished by

the tense atmosphere of the room. Aunt Matty, she noticed, also ate sparingly.

Surely things would improve after everyone grew more accustomed to one another. After all, they had weathered many changes in recent months, and hopefully they'd endure this one as well. *Peace and joy*, Mercy reminded herself. *Hold on to peace and joy.*

CHAPTER

Two

On the first of March, Mercy wrapped a shawl around herself and slipped out the back door. She nodded to Mr. Basu, preparing the kitchen garden for spring planting, and then opened the gate onto the village green. The world was awakening from winter— ivy and moss beginning to green, tree branches overhead starting to bud, and wrinkly rhubarb sprouting along the sunny wall. In the distance, she heard a lark singing for the first time that year. Ivy Green was transitioning to springtime before her eyes. She paused to fill her lungs with fresh, cool air, feeling as though she was transitioning too.

Ahead of her, a man and a little girl stepped onto the green. With a jolt, she recognized Mr. Drake with Alice, the former pupil and ward she had once hoped to adopt as her own daughter. The two walked hand in hand in coats and hats, talking companionably, Alice laughing at something he said. For a moment, Mercy stood still, holding her breath, taking in the poignant scene with equal parts pleasure and aching loss. But she loved Alice too much to wish her to be anything but completely happy in her new life.

Alice turned her head and a smile broke across her face. "Miss Grove!" she called, waving. With a quick look at Mr. Drake, Alice tugged her hand from his and ran across the green to her. Mercy glimpsed barely a shadow of the girl's former reticence, her dimpled cheeks a little rosier than Mercy recalled.

Mercy bent low of old habit to bring herself to eye level with the eight-year-old—though she did not have to bend quite so low now.

"Alice, my dear. How lovely to see you. You are looking well, and so tall."

"I grew over the winter, Mr. Drake says."

"You have indeed. I like your redingote. I have not seen it before."

"It's new. My dress and hat too. Grandmother had them made for me."

"Grandmother?"

"My mother," James explained, reaching them. "She asked Alice to call her that and insisted on taking her to a mantua-maker while we were there."

"Well, you look lovely," Mercy assured her.

From the opposite direction, two girls entered the green, walking arm in arm.

Seeing them, Alice's eyes brightened. "There are Sukey and Mabel. How I have missed them! And Phoebe, of course."

Phoebe and Alice had been Mercy's youngest pupils and were close friends. But after her school closed, Phoebe's father, a traveling salesman, had enrolled his daughter at a different school along his route.

Alice asked, "May I go and speak with them?"

"You may . . ." Catching herself, Mercy glanced at James Drake. "That is, if Mr. Drake doesn't mind."

"Not at all. Go and greet your friends. Invite them to join us for tea and cake at the bakery."

Alice hurried away eagerly. For a moment, Mr. Drake watched her go, a smile on his handsome face. His smile lingered as he turned to Mercy.

"Speaking of invitations, Miss Grove, I would like to invite you to the Fairmont to see Alice's new room, and perhaps have dinner with us. I know Alice would enjoy that, and . . . so would I."

Mercy hesitated. The words he had spoken back in December

echoed again through her mind: *"I hope you and I might spend more time together, Miss Grove. And Alice, of course. I think it would help her to see that you and I are not enemies, but friends."* But so many weeks had passed without him calling again—except to pick up Alice and her things—that she'd begun to think he'd changed his mind.

He lowered his head, then looked up at her from beneath golden lashes. "I realize you might have expected an invitation before now, but I hope you will understand that I wanted to give Alice time to grow accustomed to her new surroundings, and to me. Selfishly, I did not wish to try to compete for her affections—a contest you would still win, I'm afraid."

"I don't know. . . . Alice seems very happy in your care."

"I am glad to hear you say so."

Mercy asked, "How did it go with your parents? Did you have a pleasant time over Christmas?"

"We did, yes, once they got over their initial shock. My mother especially took quite a liking to Alice."

"I am glad to hear it. Alice has never really had grandparents before. At least not doting ones."

"Well, my father is not the doting type, but Mamma is generous and affectionate enough for the both of them." His gaze sought Alice across the green, and he lowered his voice. "I know you hoped Alice's origins would remain secret, but neither of my parents believed the pretense of Alice being the daughter of friends. They saw too much resemblance to me, and even more to my sister."

Mercy's smile faltered. "And have you told Alice?"

"She overheard our conversation and asked me directly. I decided to tell her the truth."

Suddenly cold, Mercy drew her shawl more closely around herself. "You will acknowledge her openly, then?"

"Yes. I think the truth is easiest."

"Easier for Alice to be known as your illegitimate daughter than the orphan of respectably married parents?"

His jaw tightened. "That was a fiction, Miss Grove. A fiction I don't feel compelled to perpetuate. In fact, I have begun legal steps to make Alice my heir and change her name to Drake."

A stew of conflicting emotions churned through Mercy. "Was Alice upset? She must have been, after thinking herself the daughter of Lieutenant Smith all her life."

"At first, perhaps. You may ask her yourself, if you like. But in my view, she seems to have adjusted well to the news."

Perhaps it is for the best, Mercy thought. Better to be a daughter than a mere ward. How Mercy hoped Alice's beginnings would not bring rejection later in life.

He changed the subject. "And how are you, Miss Grove?"

Mercy hesitated. "I am well, thank you."

He tilted his head to the side. "Come, you needn't pretend with me. You must be sad about closing your school."

"I am a bit at loose ends, I admit. The school was my focus for many years. Now that the girls have gone, we have changed the schoolroom back to a bedchamber for my brother and his new bride." Her chest ached at the words.

"And have they arrived?"

"Yes, a fortnight ago." Eager to divert attention from herself, Mercy asked, "And you, Mr. Drake? How goes the Fairmont?"

"Not well, truth be told. I have been preoccupied with more important matters, as you might guess. I gave the Kingsleys time off to spend with their families in December and January. And outside work had to be postponed during the last cold spell, which Alice and I happily spent in more temperate Southampton."

He inhaled deeply. "Now that there is a hint of spring in the air, progress will hopefully accelerate. We are accepting post-chaise traffic now, but I hope to soon open the remainder of the rooms and advertise for more business. When you visit, you will have to judge the accommodations for yourself. I am sure Mr. Kingsley would be willing to give us a tour of his many improvements."

Mr. Kingsley . . . Mercy grinned. "Then I shall look forward to visiting the Fairmont," she said. "Just name the day."

THREE

Jane Bell rode her horse down the long tree-lined drive to Lane's Farm, now the home of Gabriel Locke. The old farmhouse gleamed with a fresh coat of whitewash and green trim. New slate shingles capped the roof. Two hired men were hauling straw into the barn and stables across the yard, while a drystone man skillfully arranged stones to close a gap in the low wall around the paddock.

Nearby, Gabriel worked with wire and pliers, securing a long pole to three evenly spaced trees, where he could tie horses being saddled or groomed.

His dark head lifted, and noticing her, a smile split his handsome face. "Morning, Jane. How is Athena today?"

"She is well." Jane rode toward him, teasing, "And so am I. Thanks for asking."

"I am glad to hear it."

He tied Athena's reins to the new post and raised his hands to help Jane down. She leaned into his arms, thrilled at his strength and the warm light in his eyes as he lowered her to the ground. He took her gloved hand and kissed it, and she wished away the leather. He bent closer, his face nearing hers. Her heart rate accelerated in anticipation. But one of the hired men hailed her from the barn, and Jane stepped back to return the man's greeting.

"Morning, Mr. Mullins."

Then she returned her gaze to Gabriel. "The house looks well. Everything is much improved already."

"Not everything." He nodded toward a sagging shed and chicken coop. "The woodshed and coop will have to wait. I plan to first build a forge, so I can more easily shoe my own horses. Then we plan to build a few small cabins for the hired men—the single ones, at any rate. Mr. Mullins walks over every morning."

"How is he doing?"

"Better. I admit I was surprised he took the job, considering a kick from a horse is what put him out of work before. I understand he wasn't expected to walk again."

Jane nodded. "Dr. Burton's son studied medical massage and stretching under an East India Company physician. Apparently, he showed Mrs. Mullins how it was done, and she took it from there. At all events, thank you for giving him a chance. I know his whole family appreciates it."

"He works hard. Still skittish around the horses, but I can't blame him for that."

Jane nodded. "What else is on that long list of yours?"

He gestured toward a murky green pond. "I plan to dredge the old duck pond and stock it with fish, extend the stables, and . . ." He went on, listing off projects and needed repairs.

Jane said, "Your long list reminds me of what I faced when taking over The Bell."

Gabriel looked at her. "Speaking of The Bell, how are things going with Patrick gone?"

Jane shrugged. "Colin and I are managing, for the most part. And Patrick seems happy. He and Hetty have begun renovations on their lodging house. A great deal of work to do, much as you have here."

He nodded. "I am enjoying it, actually. I wake up each morning ready to tackle another project."

"I can understand that. After all, you are no longer working for your uncle or for me. This is your farm now."

He stepped closer and took her hand again. "It could be our farm, Jane. In fact, I very much hope it will be one day soon."

She ducked her head, cheeks warming with pleasure and uncertainty. She recalled the day he announced he'd bought Lane's Farm, right after Rachel and Sir Timothy's wedding. The words he spoke to her in the churchyard echoed through her mind. *"I'm not going anywhere, Jane. I love you, no matter what the future brings, and I will wait."*

True to his word, he had been content to wait—not pressuring her or raising the topic of their future. Until today. Was she ready to take the next step, even if marriage meant more miscarriages?

Not sure how to reply, Jane instead asked, "Will you be able to manage all the repairs between you and your men?"

"Most of them. I'll likely hire the Kingsleys to help with the cabins and stables. Although my uncle is threatening to visit, and he's handy himself."

"Has he come round to the idea of your managing a farm of your own?"

"Yes, I have his full support."

"And your parents? I remember you told me they once hoped you would go into the law."

He nodded, crossing his muscular arms. "They are pleased, actually. More financial security than working for my uncle all my life—or the risky business of horse racing. I would like you to meet them, Jane." He looked at her closely, gauging her reaction.

"I . . . would like to meet them as well," Jane said, hoping he had not noticed her momentary hesitation. She did want to become acquainted with the people who had raised the man she had grown to love. But did agreeing to meet them signal her intention to join that family through marriage? They would certainly assume Gabriel was settling here in Ivy Hill and introducing her to them for a reason. Two more people to disappoint. People who no doubt longed for grandchildren, as Thora had.

She asked lightly, "Have you told them about me?"

He nodded. "I told them there was a woman I wanted them to meet. Someone very important to me."

A puff of dry laughter escaped her. "Did you happen to mention I am a thirty-year-old who has been married before?"

"I am not so ungallant as to mention a woman's age, Jane." His brown eyes twinkled, but then he sobered. "I did tell them you were John Bell's widow. They met him once, so had heard your name in passing."

"Oh."

"Don't worry. They will love you. As I do. You will be the daughter they never had."

Pleasure warmed her heart even as fear lingered.

Then she thought of something. "Gabriel, there is something I should tell you. About my own father. He——"

"Mrs. Bell." Mr. Mullins walked over, a humble smile on his face. "I've been meaning to thank you for putting in a good word for me with Mr. Locke here. Much obliged."

Jane was quick to deflect the gratitude to Mercy Grove, who was better acquainted with the Mullins family than she was. By the time the man had returned to his work, Athena was stomping her hoof, anxious to continue their ride.

Gabriel's brow furrowed. "What about your father, Jane?"

"Another time," Jane said. "Athena's patience is wearing thin, and I have to get back to The Bell before the midday rush." She had waited this long to tell him; a few more days wouldn't matter.

"Very well. But you will visit again soon, I hope?"

"I shall."

He helped her back into the saddle, hands lingering on hers as he returned the reins. "Don't be a stranger."

"Same to you. You are always welcome at The Bell, you know."

His mouth tightened, and his eyes glittered with some unexpected emotion. Irritation? Frustration?

"I know. I'll get away when I can." He lifted his hand and waved her on her way.

As she rode back into town, Jane found herself thinking about her brother-in-law and Hetty Piper. After becoming engaged to Patrick, the former chambermaid had seemed nervous about posting the banns for a church wedding and suggested they elope instead. Patrick had at first tried to persuade her to marry in Ivy Hill, especially for his mother's sake, but after a private talk, he had silently supported her preference, without really explaining why.

Swallowing her disappointment, Thora had offered to care for their daughter, Betsey, while they traveled. The two had returned as man and wife a week or so later, eager to begin work on an old lodging house they'd purchased in Wishford. Though Jane missed Hetty's cheerfulness and Patrick's steady presence at the inn, she was happy for them and wished them every success. Nothing about the couple's relationship had followed the traditional pattern, but at least they were married now.

Would she and Gabriel ever work out their differences and marry? And how in the world would Mercy find happiness now that she had lost Alice and her school? At least Rachel and Sir Timothy—married three months now—showed every sign of being blissfully happy together. That was something. Hopefully there would be more happy endings to come.

When Jane returned to The Bell, she noticed Colin and Ned carrying a large trunk up the stairs. A second waited in the hall.

Curious, she stepped to the reception desk and turned the registry toward her. One new guest had registered. She peered at the hard-to-read feminine scrawl and made out *M. E. Victore*, or something like it.

A few minutes later, Colin and Ned returned to the hall, Ned huffing and puffing.

"Those were large trunks," Jane commented. "As heavy as they looked?"

"Not too bad," Colin replied.

"Yes they were," Ned panted, heading down the passage. "I'm for a drink of water after that. . . ."

Jane watched him go. "A female guest, I take it?"

Colin nodded. "Yes. A pretty one too."

"Traveling alone?"

"Apparently. Though she said she visited Ivy Hill years ago with her family."

"Did she happen to mention her business here or how long she plans to stay?"

"No."

It was uncommon for a female, especially a gentlewoman, to travel alone. "Did she seem . . . respectable?" Jane asked.

Colin shrugged. "I think so. Well spoken. Well dressed. Are you worried about her sneaking out without paying her bill?"

"Not with two trunks that size."

"True." Colin started toward the office, then turned back. "Oh, she did ask where she might find the property agents. I directed her to Arnold and Gordon's office down the street."

"Very well. Thank you, Colin." Jane wondered what the woman's business was with the property agents but kept that question to herself.

CHAPTER

FOUR

The next day, Jane and Rachel sat in the coffee room, chatting over tea. For their wedding trip, Rachel and Sir Timothy had traveled to Scotland's Loch Lomond and the Trossachs Mountains, made famous in Sir Walter Scott's *Lady of the Lake*. Not long after their return, Rachel had resumed her former habit of coming to The Bell weekly to talk with Jane.

Jane was pleased that marriage had not dampened Rachel's interest in keeping up their friendship and listened with interest as she read aloud part of a recent letter from her sister, Ellen, describing her new baby. "*Your youngest nephew is bald and toothless and always hungry. He reminds me of Papa. . . .*"

The two laughed, and then Rachel asked, "Have you talked with Mercy lately? I saw her brother and his new wife at church and wondered how that is going."

"I have only seen her in passing myself, but she said she would stop by today if she can."

"Oh good." Rachel sipped her tea, then leaned near to ask, "Anything new between you and Mr. Locke?"

Jane had told her about Gabriel's proposal soon after their return, as well as her reasons for hesitating.

Jane nodded. "He did raise the topic yesterday. He said he would like me to meet his parents."

Rachel's eyes brightened. "Oh, Jane, it's perfect. A handsome husband and a horse farm. You shall be surrounded by horses every day and may ride and jump to your heart's content. You will have everything you've always wanted."

"Not quite everything."

Rachel pressed her hand. "I'm sorry, Jane. But is it possible it will be different this time? There is always hope, is there not?"

Jane sketched a shrug. "With God, all things are possible. With my body? I think not, but I appreciate your well wishes. If I do marry Gabriel, I hope it will not create a new barrier between you and me—your being married to a baronet while I'm married to a farmer."

"Of course not. Timothy already esteems your Mr. Locke. You know the two share a passion for horses. They get on splendidly. And Lady Brockwell is appeased by the fact that Mr. Locke is a landowner now. So while she doesn't exactly encourage his invitations to Brockwell Court, she is at least polite to him."

Jane said gently, "You are Lady Brockwell now, you know."

"I know, but I find it difficult to refer to my mother-in-law as Lady Barbara. She has asked me not to call her *Mother Brockwell*—says it makes her feel ancient. She is not fond of the term *dowager* either."

"And how is Justina?" Jane asked. "I have not seen her in some time."

Rachel considered. "She is well for the most part, though conflicted over her future. She likes the idea of pleasing her mother by marrying Sir Cyril and being mistress of his fine house one day. But I don't think her heart is in it. And for his part, he's as nervous as a cat around her."

"What does Timothy say?"

"Not much. He agrees with his mother that Sir Cyril is a man of excellent character, and if the match would make both his mother and sister happy, then he is for it. Thankfully, Timothy asked Sir Cyril to wait until Justina is a year older before proposing."

Rachel raised her teacup partway to her lips, then set it down. "Oh look, here's Mercy."

Jane turned and waved to her. "Come and join us."

Mercy walked toward them, a small parcel in her hands. "I stopped at Fothergill's on my way here."

"Fothergill's?" Jane echoed. "You are not feeling poorly, I hope?"

Mercy shook her head. "My sister-in-law is complaining of indigestion, so I asked the apothecary for advice. He prescribed hiring a new cook, but I settled for peppermint and lemon verbena tea instead."

Jane chuckled. "Well, we are glad to see you. May I offer you tea or coffee?"

"None for me, thank you. I took tea with Aunt Matty and Helena before I left the house." Mercy sat down and smiled at each of them in turn.

Rachel said, "I have been thinking about you, Mercy. How are you faring now that your brother and sister-in-law have moved in?"

Mercy hesitated, then replied, "I am enjoying my brother's company, and I know Aunt Matty is too. I'd almost forgotten how amiable and amusing George can be. His years in India have matured him to a degree. When he was young, he could not wait to escape Ivy Cottage. Now he looks upon it as a comfortable home."

"And his wife?" Jane asked.

Again Mercy hesitated. "Helena is . . . growing accustomed to the house and the village. I trust in time she shall settle here happily."

Rachel's eyes glinted knowingly. "You are quite magnanimous, Mercy."

Mercy shrugged. "Having seen the grand house she grew up in, I can understand her . . . disappointment. She probably feels she has come down in the world. Not a pleasant feeling, as I can attest to."

Jane tucked her chin. "Have you come down in the world, Mercy Grove?"

"I only meant . . . Never mind. I have no right to feel ungrateful. I have a roof over my head, family, food, friends. I am blessed. I am."

Jane wondered if Mercy said it to reassure herself or them.

Rachel said, "Thankfully, I am enjoying living with my sister-in-law. I hope you and the new Mrs. Grove will become friends as Justina and I have."

Mercy nodded. "Me too." Then she changed the subject. "By the way, Mamma has written to ask Aunt Matty and me to visit them in London again."

"Oh?"

Mercy nodded. "The tone of her letter was so uncharacteristically warm that I was touched. She rarely invites us, except at Christmas, though I know their door is always open, if need be."

Rachel asked gently, "You don't think she is planning on matchmaking again, do you?"

"I don't think so. She gave no hint of any particular reason for the invitation. She mentioned we might attend the theatre or a few routs. But she wrote nothing of new gowns or any single gentlemen who will be in town for the season."

"That's a relief, I imagine. So, will you accept?"

"I am not sure. I will see if Aunt Matty wants to go. If we do, you two would be more than welcome to come with us. I'm guessing you won't be so inclined, Rachel, being newly married, but what about you, Jane?"

"I couldn't get away either," Jane said. "But it is kind of you to offer, and to consider going for your aunt's sake."

"Not at all. I would enjoy the diversion as well."

They went on to discuss other village news, including James Drake's return and his invitation for Mercy to visit Alice at the Fairmont.

The three talked a few minutes more, and then Mercy rose to take her leave. "I had better get this tea to Helena. But thank you for listening, dear friends. I feel better already."

As they watched her go, Rachel sighed. "So sad about her school." She gestured out the coffee room window. "And sad to see Mrs. Shabner's shop is still closed. I feel guilty for not buying any new dresses from her recently. I had hoped she might change her mind about retiring."

Jane nodded, glancing through the window to the building across the street. A *For Let* sign hung on the dressmaker's door. The bow window had been papered over to conceal its empty state, or some renovation work in progress.

Jane had been surprised when Mrs. Shabner finally retired and moved to Wishford after years of threatening to do so. *Good for her*, Jane thought. But sad for the women of Ivy Hill, who would now have to travel farther for the services of a milliner or dressmaker.

Mr. and Mrs. Prater were taking advantage of the dressmaker's absence, stocking more ribbons, gloves, and fancy wares in their windows in place of the baskets, brooms, and brushes that had been arrayed there before. A year ago, Jane might have disparaged the wily shopkeepers, but now, as a fellow business owner, she begrudgingly admired their swift action to increase profits.

Just as Jane was about to return her gaze to her friend, Mr. Gordon came striding down the High Street and stopped in front of the shop. "Rachel, look."

As they watched, the property agent took down the *For Let* sign, and out in the street, a commotion arose. As if they had been lying in wait, Mrs. Barton emerged from the butcher's and the two Miss Cooks from their shop to converge on the man, shooting questions at him like grapeshot.

With budding smiles of unspoken agreement, Rachel and Jane hurried over to join the inquisition. News in Ivy Hill usually passed quickly along the village's many connected vines, but Jane had not heard a word about the shop's future.

"Who is the new tenant, Mr. Gordon?" Mrs. Barton demanded. "Pray, don't keep us in suspense."

Charlotte asked, "Is it a dressmaker or perhaps another lace maker?"

"You must prepare us." Judith's fingers fluttered nervously around her lace collar. "Are we to have competition?"

The man lifted a quelling hand. "Ladies, ladies, I am not at liberty to say just yet. But when my client is ready to open her shop—"

"A her, is it?" Judy said. "Well, that is good news."

"Is it?" Charlotte frowned. "A man might be less likely to be a lace maker."

The agent looked kindly on the Miss Cooks. "I think it safe to tell you that the new tenant is *not* a lace maker, ladies. You may ease your mind on that score."

Charlotte Cook expelled a relieved breath, and her sister clutched her heart. "Thank you."

Mrs. Barton, however, was not appeased. "Is that all you are going to tell us? I call that unfair, Mr. Gordon. I have known you since boyhood. I promise we would keep the information to ourselves."

The agent gave the dairywoman a grin. "And I have known *you* since boyhood, Mrs. Barton, so you will excuse me if I doubt that."

She huffed but could not deny her penchant for gossip. The only women more known for gossiping were Mrs. Craddock of the bakery and Mrs. Prater of the Universal Stores and Post Office, who was, moreover, Mr. Gordon's mother-in-law. Typically, the shop-keeper enjoyed her role as bearer of the latest *on-dit*, but perhaps Mr. Gordon had been as reluctant to confide in his mother-in-law as he had been with Mrs. Barton.

Rachel whispered, "I would wager my last farthing that a new dressmaker has let the place, and that's why he won't tell us. His in-laws want to sell their inventory before people hear about the new competition."

Jane nodded. "You are probably right." She thought of the guest at the inn who had asked to be directed to the property agents. It seemed too much of a coincidence to be unrelated.

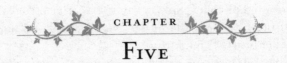

On the agreed-to day, Mercy walked across the turnpike and through the Fairmont gate. From a window above, a flash of movement caught her eye. Alice waved at her before the lace curtain fell back into place. It took Mercy back to her childhood, when she had come to visit young Jane Fairmont and had seen her waving from that same window.

As Mercy walked up the drive, Alice came bounding out the front door and across the lawn to greet her.

"Miss Grove!"

Mercy held out her arms, and the little girl ran into her embrace.

For a moment, Mercy closed her eyes and relished the sweet affection. Though the ache of loss lingered, she adopted a light tone. "Now, that is what I call a proper welcome! Thank you, Alice. I gather you are eager to show me your new home?"

The girl vigorously bobbed her head, blond hair swaying.

James Drake appeared on the threshold, the door still open from Alice flinging it wide.

He greeted her warmly. "Welcome, Miss Grove. We have been looking forward to your visit."

"I have as well."

"I would have been happy to send a carriage, you know."

"No need. I like to walk."

"Well, what would you like to see? I will give you the grand tour myself."

Mercy swallowed a lump of disappointment. He had said Mr. Kingsley would be the one to show her his work.

She smiled anyway. "Everything, I suppose. I have not been inside since I was a girl—other than my brief visit to your office that day. . . ." She winced at the memory of their horrid argument over the guardianship of Alice.

"I promise you today's visit will be far more pleasant." He gestured for her to precede him around the side of the house. "Did you visit Jane here when you two were girls?"

"I did, yes. Many times."

"Then allow me to show you the recent additions." He pointed out the new stable block, repaired after a fire had damaged the timber-framed building he'd first built, and an impressive masonry-and-brick carriage house.

They walked around the house, where he gestured to the rose garden, leaves beginning to green, and then the gardens at the rear.

Inside, he led her through the hall, which had been converted into a reception room and sitting room with sofas and chairs clustered around tea tables and inlaid game tables for chess or draughts. Next, he showed her the new coffee room, as well as private dining parlours and a formal dining room that looked completely different than Mercy remembered.

He explained, "This is the old library."

"Ah! This is where all those bookcases came from—the ones you donated to Rachel's circulating library."

"Just so. Have you any interest in seeing the kitchen and work-rooms belowstairs?"

When Mercy hesitated, Alice said eagerly, "Let's go upstairs so I can show you my room." She looked at Mr. Drake. "Is that all right?"

"Of course."

He gestured across the hall to the stairway. "We'll see the guest rooms while we're up there."

Reaching the next floor, James opened a door with a flourish. "Here is one of the finest rooms. It has a private water closet. We have also added a bathroom and water closet on each floor to be shared by other guests."

"Impressive. You have been busy!"

"Yes, or rather, the Kingsley brothers have been busy." He grinned. "Though I've been kept busy paying them."

"But you directed the work."

He shrugged. "I hired an architect to determine what structural changes were needed to accomplish the plan I had in mind. Countless decisions and details, but very little muscle or skill on my part, I'm afraid. Thankfully, the Kingsleys have a great deal of both."

"Yes . . ." Mercy murmured. She had noticed Joseph Kingsley's muscles and skill on more than one occasion.

Alice tugged her hand. "Come and see my room."

Mercy and Mr. Drake exchanged amused smiles as they allowed Alice to lead them down the corridor.

Alice opened a door at the far end and waited for Mercy to join her. Mercy noticed a sheepishly proud tilt of the girl's chin and a dimple of suppressed pleasure.

Mercy surveyed the carved half tester bed with its new rose print bed-curtains, the dressing table, and a freshly upholstered window seat. An armchair and footstool sat in front of the fireplace where Jane had once liked to sit and read. The chair was now occupied by a large doll with a fine porcelain head and dressed in a fancy gown.

"This was Jane's room," Mercy observed.

"Yes," Mr. Drake said. "I slept here originally, but I wanted Alice to have this room. I've taken one across the passage."

Mercy nodded her understanding. She looked at Alice and saw the girl waiting expectantly for her reaction. "It's lovely, Alice. Do you like it?"

She nodded. "I love it. How could I not?"

"Very true."

Alice opened the dressing-room door, where bandboxes were stacked and colorful fabrics poked from gown drawers. She pulled out one long drawer after another. "Look at these, Miss Grove. Have you ever seen so many gowns in your life?"

"Goodness. No indeed."

His tone almost apologetic, James explained, "My mother's doing. She does love a project—and any excuse to visit her favorite modiste."

Mercy grinned at him. "Sounds like my mother."

Back in the corridor, he opened the door to a commodious shared bathroom, and then a second, smaller guest room, before suggesting they go back downstairs for tea.

He escorted them into the coffee room, which was brighter than The Bell's, with its low beams and shadowy corners, but somehow less inviting. Coachmen occupied a few of the tables, and there was Mrs. Burlingame, talking with a woman Mercy didn't recognize. Mercy decided she would not tell Jane she'd seen one of her regulars here.

Mr. Drake ordered tea from a waiter, and as they sat back to wait for it, a young man stepped eagerly into the coffee room. A groom, Mercy guessed, from his clothes and the smells of hay and leather he brought with him.

His expression brightened upon seeing Alice. "Miss Alice, there you are. The striped tabby has had her litter of kittens. Six! I thought you'd want to know." His glance shifted to his employer. "Forgive the intrusion, Mr. Drake."

"That's all right, Johnny."

Alice's eyes widened in delight, and she turned to Mr. Drake. "May I go and see them?"

"Yes, you may. I will keep our guest company while you do."

Alice rose. "I hope you don't mind, Miss Grove. I won't be long."

"Not at all." Mercy smiled at the girl. "Who can resist kittens?"

James watched Mercy with a knowing expression as Alice hurried away. "I suppose you think I ought to have insisted she stay since you are here."

Mercy waved a dismissive hand. "I am hardly some important guest."

"Of course you are. I am simply glad for a few minutes to talk with you about Alice in confidence."

Concern flashed. "Is anything the matter?"

"No. Alice is well. A bit lonely, I think. Which is no wonder, with only my company after living in Ivy Cottage with five other girls, along with you and your aunt. She often spends time in the stables under the guise of visiting the horses and cats, but I think she likes to talk to Johnny, who treats her like a little sister. She also follows Joseph Kingsley around like a loyal pup whenever he's near. Though he's had to gently ask her to leave a few times to keep her out of danger while he's working."

At the mention of Joseph's name, Mercy found her gaze straying into the hall, hoping for a glimpse of him. She forced her attention back to her host. "And how are you and Alice getting along?"

"Well, I think. We take our meals together. Spend the evenings talking or reading. And I am teaching her to ride. I've asked Gabriel Locke to find a suitable gentle horse for her for when she outgrows a pony."

"Sounds like heaven for a little girl," Mercy allowed.

"I think it would be . . . if there were more children about. Or someone to keep her company when I am occupied with some business matter or other."

Mercy said, "It does no harm for a child to spend some time alone, reading or playing. It is good for the imagination. She needn't be entertained every waking moment."

"That's a relief. Well, enough about us for now. How goes life in Ivy Cottage, Miss Grove? Is your new sister-in-law amiable?"

Mercy hesitated. "We are not all that well acquainted yet, but I hope we shall become fond sisters in time. I have never had a sister before."

"I have one, and you are welcome to her, if you like." He winked. "Only joking. We sparred as children but are friends now, thankfully. And your brother? Are you two alike?"

Mercy shrugged. "We are both tall and dark-haired but quite different otherwise. He is not bookish at all. He is far more gregarious and likable, and makes friends easily."

"I cannot imagine anyone more likable than you, Miss Grove."

Mercy blinked in surprise.

"And as far as making friends easily," he added, "I believe a truer measure of a person's character is how well he keeps his friends. And I know from talking to Jane that you are the most loyal and valued of friends."

"Thank you." Mercy shifted uneasily and was relieved when the tea arrived. "Was there anything else you wanted to discuss about Alice?"

"Yes." Mr. Drake poured and handed her a plate of sandwiches. "I wanted to ask what you would suggest for her education. I cannot abide the thought of sending her away to school when we have so recently found each other."

"Very understandable." Mercy sipped her tea, then said, "I suppose a governess is the traditional choice."

He nodded and set down his cup. "In all honesty, I once thought of asking if you would like to be Alice's governess. But I hesitated because I feared it might be confusing to Alice as to who her guardian was."

Me . . . a governess? Mercy thought. She felt a retort rise, but it lodged in her throat. After all, that was the fate of many impoverished spinsters.

He lifted a consoling palm. "Don't worry. I quickly dismissed the notion. I thought, why would a person who has capably managed an entire school want to educate only one pupil in someone else's home? A governess's lot is a lonely and thankless one, I gather."

"So I have heard," Mercy murmured. It was a lot she had never wanted for herself, never thought she would have to consider. How the mighty schoolmistress had fallen!

"But perhaps you might help me choose a qualified candidate?" he asked.

Mercy smiled. "Of course. I would be happy to."

She took another sip and was relieved when Alice returned, happily describing each and every newborn kitten, and asking Mercy to come out and see them before she went home.

Mercy agreed, sad to realize her visit with the sweet girl was almost over.

A short while later, Mercy walked back to Ivy Cottage. On her way, she passed the Kingsley Brothers' workshop. As she did, she glanced though the broad double doors and felt her stomach drop. No wonder she had not seen him at the Fairmont, for there stood Joseph Kingsley talking to the petite blonde she had seen him embrace on the green a few months before. He'd said her name was Esther, and that was all he'd said about her.

A group of tall Kingsley brothers and several of their wives emerged from the house across the lane. The beautiful blonde smiled into Joseph's face, pressed his arm, and walked over to join the others.

Joseph noticed Mercy then and stepped out to greet her. "Miss Grove, good day. You are . . . in good health, I trust?"

"I am, thank you. And you?"

"Yes, quite. I rarely take ill."

Mercy glanced at Esther across the lane. "Your friend is visiting?"

"Hm?"

"I believe you said her name is Esther? I saw the two of you on the green last autumn, remember, when Mr. Hollander was here."

"Oh, that's right." He lifted his chin in recollection, then looked over at Esther talking and laughing with his brothers and sisters-in-law. "Esther is more than a friend. She's one of the family. Or soon will be." His warm gaze lingered on the blonde.

"Oh." Surprise washed over Mercy. Did he mean . . . ?

One of his nephews ran across the lane, a ball under his arm. "Can you play with us, Uncle Joseph?" Noticing Mercy, he said, "Oh, sorry, ma'am."

Mercy managed a quick grin for the lad. "That's all right. I was just going. Well. Good-bye, Mr. Kingsley."

"Good-bye, Miss Grove."

Mercy walked away, uncertainty plaguing her. Was Mr. Kingsley engaged? Or soon to be? Disappointment filled her at the thought.

CHAPTER

Six

The following day, as Jane swept the front walkway, she again looked across the High Street to the dressmaker's former shop.

The ground-level windows were still papered over. Jane gazed up at the windows of the apartment above, where Mrs. Shabner had lived. The curtains up there were now open, though Jane couldn't see inside. *Hmm . . .* The woman with two trunks had left The Bell without Jane meeting her. Had she let the property and moved upstairs?

Idea striking her, Jane set aside her broom, crossed the street, and cut across the green toward Ivy Cottage. Matilda Grove was an old friend of Mrs. Shabner's and might know the identity of her new tenant. Besides, it would give her an excuse to talk to Mercy again.

When Jane reached Ivy Cottage, she was pleased to see Louise Shabner sitting with Matilda at the small table in the front garden, although the day was quite chilly.

"I am surprised to see you two out here. Are you not cold?"

"Temperatures inside are not much warmer at present," Matilda replied, hugging her shawl around herself.

"Oh?"

"Never mind. With Louise visiting, I decided we would be more comfortable chatting out here. Mercy has gone for another walk for much the same reason, I suppose."

"I am sorry to miss her. I won't keep you. I've only come shamelessly begging information about your new tenant, Mrs. Shabner. I thought Miss Matty might know, but how much better to ask you directly since you're here."

"Louise just came from Wishford to tell me the news." Matilda pattèd the chair beside her. "Come and sit for a few minutes."

Jane did so, glad for her long, warm pelisse.

"Ivy Hill is to have a new dressmaker," Mrs. Shabner said. "Mr. Gordon conducted the actual negotiations, so I only met the woman briefly when signing the lease. I thought her a pretty, pleasant young woman. Her name is French—Victorine something— and she has just a hint of an accent. She objected to the amount of rent I asked for, so I agreed to reduce it. I am just glad to have someone in the shop after all this time. If she is able to make a go of it, we will renegotiate the terms later."

"A French modiste here in Ivy Hill?" Jane breathed. "My goodness. I fear there will not be enough demand for such fashions in our humble village. If we could not keep you busy, I doubt this new dressmaker will be satisfied with our small budgets and simple tastes."

Matilda considered. "There are always the Brockwells."

Louise scoffed. "Bah. The Brockwells rarely darkened my door."

"I am sorry, Mrs. Shabner," Jane said gently. "But you must admit, a French modiste might secure their patronage. And perhaps Mrs. Ashford's? I imagine even Miss Bingley and her mother might come from Stapleford at the prospect of French fashions so much nearer than Bath or London."

Matilda nodded. "And don't forget George's new wife. What a boon for the new bride to have such an establishment at hand in what she judges to be a rustic hamlet. But poor George's purse!"

Jane nibbled her lip. "I wonder why the modiste would choose Ivy Hill of all places. Has she friends or family here that you know of?" Jane remembered Colin mentioning that their pretty guest had visited Ivy Hill years before.

Louise shook her head. "I know nothing more than what I've told you."

Matilda Grove's eyes sparkled. "Nor do I. But I shall happily be among the first to visit her shop in hopes of satisfying my curiosity."

Jane grinned. "Let's go together as soon as it opens."

When Jane walked home, she saw Becky Morris, house-and-sign painter, exiting the dressmaker's shop, shoulders slumped.

Jane waved to her, and Becky stopped to talk, a book of sample lettering under her arm.

Becky jerked a thumb toward the door. "I was hoping she would hire me to paint a nice big sign, but she politely declined my services. Said she'll make do with the small one she made herself for now."

"That's unfortunate for you both. A good sign is so important."

"I agree, but of course *I* would." Becky grinned, then added, "I gather she is letting the shop on something of a trial basis and doesn't want to invest the money until she is sure she will stay."

Jane nodded. "What is she like?"

Becky considered. "Dark-haired. Lovely smile. Far younger than our last dressmaker. A bit nervous, maybe. Though I suppose you can't blame a newcomer for that. Well, I'll see you later, Jane."

Becky walked away, but Jane remained long enough to survey the shop again.

A handwritten *Closed* sign hung on the door, and she noticed a discreet sign tacked to the wall beside it. Jane walked nearer to read the fine calligraphy on heavy card stock:

Madame Victorine's
Millinery & Dressmaking
~Offering a Variety of Fashionable, Fancy Models~

Madame Victorine . . . It was very like the name Jane had seen scrawled in the guest register. She walked back across the street to ask Colin what else he recalled about the mystery woman who'd stayed at The Bell.

But Colin reported little more than he had before. He thought she *might* have been French but was perhaps making an effort to conceal it, the French not being popular after the war.

When Jane asked Cadi about the woman, the chambermaid seemed surprised to hear that Colin had described her as French. "I didn't think so, ma'am. Nor did she seem like some fine, high lady to me. She was polite and friendly, not demanding as some are."

"Did she ask you about the property agents or the dressmaker's shop?"

Cadi nodded. "Now you mention it, she did ask if I was acquainted with our former dressmaker. I told her about Mrs. Shabner sending over that lavender dress, though you had not ordered it, wily woman. Earned a sale though, did it not? And she was right, for that dress suits you perfectly. I hope you don't mind that I told that story."

"I don't mind. Well, I will let you get back to work." Saying the words reminded Jane that she had her own work to worry about. It wasn't like her to pry so. Leaving Cadi to her tasks, Jane walked to the office to review the latest receipts.

Mercy walked to the new home of the Ashford Circulating Library to select another book. That was one benefit of losing her school—she had more leisure time to read. She was trying to focus on the good. Yet how she missed her pupils—even obstinate Fanny—and the purpose she'd felt as their teacher. Again Mercy prayed a silent prayer for each girl.

Inside the library, she looked around the open main room with its large raised desk at the center and shelves of books against the outside walls. An attractive arched doorway led to a separate reading area with comfortable chairs and lovely paintings on the walls, all featuring books or reading in some form. She didn't see Rachel anywhere about, but there was Anna Kingsley across the room, helping Mrs. O'Brien locate a title.

Seeing Mercy, Anna's pretty face broke into a sparkling smile, and as soon as the candlemaker took her leave, the young woman came over to greet her.

"Miss Grove!" Anna took her arm in a friendly squeeze. "What a pleasure to see you. I miss you. I hope you are well."

"I am indeed, Anna. Thank you for asking. And you? How go things here in the library's new location?"

"Very well. Though I miss having Mrs. Timmons's kitchen to dart into for a cup of tea between patrons. I miss your aunt's biscuits, too, more than I thought possible."

Mercy chuckled. "I am sure Aunt Matty would be happy to deliver some of her famous baked goods if she knew you were longing for them. I shall tell her."

"Thank you. By the way, if you were looking for Miss Rachel— the new Lady Brockwell, I should say—she is busy at present. She is leading a discussion of the Ladies Book Club that meets here."

"Oh, where?" Mercy looked around her.

"We've set up chairs in Mr. Blomfield's old office for the purpose." Anna gestured to a closed door. "The meetings disturb other patrons less that way. Some of the women are quite . . . passionate . . . in their opinions about books."

"As they should be." Mercy bit back a grin, for even now she could hear Mrs. Barton's voice rise in disagreement and Charlotte Cook's vociferous rebuttal through the closed door.

Anna added, "Lady Brockwell comes in a few days every week to help with shelving and record keeping and such, as well as leading the book club."

"And does Colin McFarland still come to you for lessons?"

The girl blushed. "I do see Mr. McFarland fairly often, though I confess we don't talk about arithmetic much anymore."

Mercy returned the girl's dimpled grin. "I see." Mercy looked around the library. "Everything looks organized and tidy. Rachel made a good choice when she selected you to manage the place. I hope you are enjoying it?"

"I am. The best part is introducing people to my favorite authors. Which reminds me, have you read Frances Burney's *Evelina* yet?" She handed Mercy the novel, and Mercy decided to take the girl's suggestion and borrow it.

Anna wrote down the title, then added, "I also enjoy helping reluctant readers find something to interest them. I even convinced my uncle Matthew to read a book. A miracle in itself, my father says." Again Anna's smile appeared, as bright and appealing as sunlight on water.

A similar smile flashed through Mercy's memory. Esther's smile.

Feeling slightly guilty, Mercy said, "You have so many uncles, Anna, I struggle to keep track of them all. Nor am I acquainted with all of their wives. I recently saw a young woman named Esther, but—"

"Oh yes!" Anna enthused. "Miss Dudman is delightful! We are all fond of her already."

"Miss Dudman? She is not married?" Mercy asked, hoping her expression gave nothing away.

Anna grinned. "Not yet. Though we have reason to believe there will be another Mrs. Kingsley soon."

"I see." Recalling their affectionate embrace and the admiring way Joseph looked at the woman when he'd said *"Esther is more than a friend,"* Mercy's stomach cramped.

She opened her mouth to ask another question, but the front door opened and Colin McFarland stepped inside. He greeted Mercy politely, and then his fond gaze quickly settled on Anna.

"I have some free time before the next stage is due. Just thought I'd walk over and ask how you were, Miss Kingsley."

"Thank you, Mr. McFarland. I am well."

His eyes lingered on her face. "As I see . . ."

Mercy decided it was time to take her leave. Seeing the two young people staring warmly at each other suddenly stung more than it should have.

CHAPTER

SEVEN

Two days later, Jane went out to plant spring flowers in the pots flanking the inn's front door. Glancing across the street to the dressmaker's shop, she noticed the paper had been removed from the glass, so she set aside her gardening tools and walked over to investigate. The same dress forms and hat rack had stood there in Mrs. Shabner's time, but the forms now held fashionable gowns, complete with accessories like long redingotes, tippets, and feathered hats. The *Closed* sign had been replaced with a handwritten notice: *Opening Soon*.

Later that afternoon, Jane was standing at the booking desk when Matilda Grove entered the inn, dressed in her favorite yellow gown, a shawl, and a bonnet whose drooping feather had seen better days. She greeted Jane, then asked, "Shall we go and meet our new dressmaker?"

Jane cautioned, "I don't think the shop is open yet."

"I know." Matilda's eyes sparkled. "But I can't wait. Let's go over and introduce ourselves."

Jane smiled. "Very well."

Together, they crossed the street. A woman was now standing outside the shop, polishing its front windows.

Slightly above average height, she possessed an enviable figure accentuated by a dark blue gown, well-made and elegant. Her black hair was secured in a knot at the back of her head. When she turned at their approach, Jane saw she was in her mid-twenties and had a pretty oval face with dark brows and a straight, if somewhat pointed, nose.

"Good day, ladies," she greeted, her bright blue eyes glinting in the sunlight.

"Madame Victorine?" Jane asked, studying the woman's face. Who did she remind her of?

"That is the name of my shop, yes. I am afraid I am not quite ready for customers. Might you return later?" She spoke excellent English with only a trace of an accent.

"We simply wanted to introduce ourselves," Matty said warmly. "And to welcome you to our community. I am Matilda Grove, and this is Jane Bell, who owns the coaching inn just there." She pointed across the street. "You are practically neighbors."

The woman turned to Jane. She did indeed have a lovely smile.

"Ah. A pleasure to meet you, Mrs. Bell. I stayed there two nights and found everything and everyone most congenial."

"Thank you," Jane replied. "I was sorry I didn't have a chance to meet you then."

The woman shrugged easily. "No matter. Thank you for coming over to introduce yourselves now."

Matilda said, "My friend Louise Shabner used to be the dressmaker here."

The woman nodded. "Yes, I met her briefly. I do hope her retirement was voluntary and not because the shop was failing." She chuckled dryly. "If such an experienced dressmaker struggled, then I . . ." She shook her head and let her words trail away.

Jane asked gently, "Is this your first shop, then?"

"Yes, my first time on my own. I worked with another woman before, but she recently passed on."

"I am sorry to hear it," Matilda said. "But we are all glad to see the shop open again and another woman of business added to our numbers."

"In fact," Jane said, "we have something of a club for women managing businesses here, called the Ladies Tea and Knitting Society. I hope you will join us."

"Knitting?" The woman's brows rose.

"Don't let the name discourage you. We meet to discuss business concerns and to support one another—Monday nights, at the village hall, just around the corner. You would be very welcome."

"Thank you. I shall join you when I can, though I shall be busy arranging things here for some time."

"I understand. Is there anything we can do to help you?"

"Nothing right now." She grinned and gestured to the window. "Except to tell everyone you know to come and buy these dresses."

Jane returned her grin. "I shall be happy to spread the word. If you think of anything else, don't hesitate to stop by the inn."

At the sound of a door closing across the street, Jane glanced over and saw Gabriel talking to Mr. Prater outside his store. Noticing her, Gabriel waved, his smile causing Jane's heart to flip, as usual. Jane waved back, then looked again at her companions.

Miss Matilda's attention had been caught by the gowns displayed in the window. "These are lovely," she breathed.

"Yes, I . . . thank you," the dressmaker said. "Perhaps you might return and try them on, madame?"

"I am afraid I have little occasion to justify such a gown," Matilda said. "But they are beautiful. I especially like the gold with the blue overdress. Is that silk?"

The woman looked at the gown in question. "I believe so. I can verify, if you like."

"That's all right. I was only curious."

Jane supposed the dressmaker made a great many gowns in her profession and could not recall the details of each. Deciding they had importuned the woman long enough, Jane slid her arm through Matilda's. "Well. We shall return another time. Again, a pleasure to meet you."

"And you, ladies. Thank you for calling."

As Jane and Matilda walked away, Jane glanced back over her

shoulder, then mused softly, "There is something about her. Something familiar . . ."

"Do you think so?" Matilda said. "I am quite certain I have never seen her before in my life. Perhaps you visited a shop where she once worked?"

Jane felt her brow furrow, trying to grasp at the fleeting impression. Had she seen her before? If so, where?

"It's possible. I will have to ask her where she lived before coming to Ivy Hill."

After walking Matilda back to Ivy Cottage, Jane returned to The Bell, pleased to find Gabriel waiting for her.

"Morning, Jane. Just came into town for a few things. Left my horse and gig in your stables; I hope you don't mind."

"Of course not. I am glad to see you. I was afraid you'd left after I saw you on the street."

He shrugged. "You seemed occupied with Miss Grove. I did not want to interrupt."

"We were only meeting the new dressmaker."

"Very neighborly." He gave her a wry grin. "I doubt I shall have occasion to call on her."

"How are things at Lane's Farm?" Jane asked. "Or have you changed its name?"

"Not yet." He stepped nearer and lowered his voice. "Jane, will you join me for dinner at the farmhouse? I'd like you to see the improvements I've made inside as well. And we could talk more then, just the two of us."

Jane hesitated. She reminded herself that she was a thirty-year-old widow, not some innocent young miss whose reputation held the key to her future happiness. But still . . .

As if reading her mind, he said, "I have taken on a maid-of-all-work, Susie McFarland. So we will not be alone and even better, you shall not have to suffer my cooking."

She smiled. "Very well. That sounds lovely. I will accept if you will allow me to bring dessert or something."

"Susie makes a decent roast and potatoes, but that's about all. Bring anything you like." He smirked. "Will you prepare it yourself?"

"Hardly. I am afraid I probably have less cooking ability than Susie. Though I can clean fish and make an interesting chicken-and-egg soup."

His expression puckered. "Chicken and egg?"

"Never mind. I'll see what I can wrestle from Mrs. Rooke."

When Jane rode into the farmyard the following evening, Gabriel took the basket she held and helped her down. Together they settled Athena in the stable, and then Gabriel led Jane to the house, entering through an enclosed front porch that served as the office for his farm and stables. Inside, the room and desk were tidy and professional, and paintings of proud horses decorated the walls.

"Oh, I love these! Did you buy them recently?"

"I have collected them over the years, but this is the first time I've had a proper place to hang them."

"They are perfect."

Gabriel set her basket in the kitchen. From there he led her on a brief tour through the rest of the house—the comfortable informal sitting room, paneled dining room, and new indoor water closet.

"The main bedchamber is down here." He led the way along a dim passage, and Jane felt self-conscious being alone with him there. The shadowy space seemed private and intimate.

He opened the door. "This is my room. For now."

She stood at the threshold but did not enter. She glanced around the masculine room, with its handsome oak furniture and rich russet bedclothes.

"Very nice," she murmured, her heart beating a little harder than it should.

"Mrs. Locke may furnish it however she likes, of course."

Jane swallowed. Would she be Mrs. Locke? "It is wonderful as it is."

"I am glad you think so."

They returned to the front hall. "There are two more bedrooms up there." He pointed up the stairway, illuminated by a window at the top, where two doors opened off a narrow landing. "They are smaller and simply furnished."

Rooms for the children he hoped to have? Jane wondered.

Noticing her reserve, he said, "I will . . . show you those another time."

They returned to the dining room, where Susie was adding the finishing touches to the table.

"Evening, Mrs. Bell."

"Good to see you, Susie. I hope you are enjoying your new situation?"

"I am. A lot to learn, but Mr. Locke is patient and not particular, thankfully. I hope the same is true for you, ma'am."

"I am no great cook myself, so I am sure I will enjoy whatever you make."

"Thank you, ma'am. And thank you for bringing the jam tarts for dessert."

The girl bobbed a curtsy and returned to the kitchen. Gabriel pulled out a chair for Jane and, when she was seated, took the chair across from her.

He lifted a pitcher of lemon water and poured for the two of them. "The well water here is excellent. But if you would prefer tea or wine . . . ?"

"No, water is perfect. I am suddenly thirsty."

Susie brought out a tureen and set it before them. From it, Gabriel ladled out a rich soup of chicken and leeks.

Jane tasted it. "Mmm . . . Much better than chicken and egg."

They ate in silence for a minute, then Gabriel said, "Jane, I have been thinking. I know you're concerned about The Bell, especially without Patrick there. When we marry, perhaps we could keep two residences for a time."

Jane looked at him in surprise. "The Bell is a few miles from here. Would you really ride into town every night to . . . sleep? What if a foal came in the night or fire broke out or—"

"Or you could ride out to me."

"And what if a guest had an emergency? Or Colin needed me? I can't leave."

"We could still marry."

She frowned. "We would be a strange couple indeed, if you lived here and I lived in the lodge. Is that what you want?"

He shook his head and set aside his spoon. "No, Jane. If I'm honest, what I want is for you to share my house. Share my bed—"

Susie came in with the main course. Jane sent him a warning look, and Gabriel waited until the girl left the room again before leaning near and continuing in a lower voice.

"I want to wake up in the morning and see you beside me. I want to put my arms around you and hold you close. Kiss you one more time before chores force me to leave you. I want to sit with you on the porch in the springtime and watch it rain. And in the winter, sit with you by the fire and talk about our plans for the future. I want to pray together, work together, and ride together. And I want to make love to you. Often. Not be miles away from you."

Heart pounding and cheeks flushing at his words, Jane looked down, appetite fleeing. "I know."

He reached for her hand, and she felt his steady gaze on her profile. "Don't you want that too?"

Fear and longing twisted through her.

When she hesitated, he continued, "If your father were alive, I would ask him for his blessing, but—"

"He is alive," she blurted.

"What? Is he?" He sat back, staring at her in disbelief. "Last time you were here you mentioned there was something you wanted to tell me about your father, but I never guessed this. I thought he was gone."

Jane felt sheepish that she had not explained earlier. "He is *gone*, yes, and has been for years, but not dead—at least, as far as I know."

"But you let me think . . . or at least I assumed, both of your parents had passed on."

She inhaled a shaky breath. "My mother died many years ago. My father, however, walked out of my life right after I married John. He sold Fairmont House and left the country."

"But you almost never mention him. I thought it was because his loss was a painful subject."

"It is."

"Why, if he is alive?"

Jane pushed a few peas around her plate. "Right or wrong, I felt abandoned when he sold everything—including Hermione—and left, intending never to return."

"Where did he go?"

"India. He was in colonial service as a young man and eager to return."

"But surely he has written to you?"

"He did write a few letters soon after he left, but I . . . I did not answer them, and so the letters stopped."

He stared at her soberly. "Jane . . ."

"I know it seems harsh. It probably was unfair of me. But I felt that he betrayed me and my mother's memory. I have written to him once now, to let him know John died and to thank him for the marriage settlement he arranged for me."

Gabriel frowned. "How did he betray your mother's memory?"

"He left as soon as he could to return to a woman he had known as a younger man and had never stopped pining for. I realize it was probably irrational of me, but it seemed that he was relieved my mother died and eager for me to marry, so he could go back to the woman he truly loved at long last. I suppose I was overly emotional around the time of my wedding. Losing my station in life, my horse, my childhood home, and my last living relative all in the same month."

Jane thought back. "I remember being amazed at how readily

he approved my decision to marry an innkeeper, when he had assumed for years I would marry a baronet, as did most everyone else. When I learned *why* he was in such a hurry to dispatch his last responsibility in England—me—I resented it all the more."

Saying the words aloud made Jane squirm in discomfort. Did her behavior seem as petty to him as it was beginning to seem to her?

Gabriel watched her carefully, eyes boring into hers. "Jane, do you feel to marry me would betray John's memory as your father betrayed your mother's? Is that the real reason you hesitate to accept me?"

Surprised he had drawn that conclusion from her confession, Jane hurried to assure him. "No, Gabriel. I don't see it as the same at all. I didn't even *like* you until John had been gone a year." She attempted to soften the words with a grin. "But *if* I had admired and pined for you all the years of my marriage; wished I were with you instead of my husband . . . ? Been making plans to join you before he was in his grave? Would that have been right?"

"Of course not. But are you sure all that is true, or just assuming the worst?"

"It is how I saw it at the time. You were not there, so please don't judge me too harshly." She heard the defensive barb in her voice and inwardly cringed.

"I don't judge you harshly." He took her hand again and squeezed comfort into his reassuring grip. "But I hope you will forgive your father, Jane. For your sake as well as his."

His words were similar to what Mercy had said when Jane told her about the settlement she'd discovered and admitted she might have misjudged her father.

"He isn't here to forgive," Jane said. "And as I have yet to receive a reply to my letter, I fear it may be too late."

"Then perhaps it is time to write again."

Jane dipped her head, feeling chastised and embarrassed, a young girl caught in misbehavior. This had certainly not turned out to be the romantic dinner she had imagined.

Half serious, she said, "And I suppose you have been the perfect son who has never done wrong and has always treated his parents with unwavering respect?"

"No. I only wish I had been. I told you my father was disappointed when I did not pursue the law—and worse, when I became embroiled in horse racing and gambling. But those days are over, thank God."

Would they also be disappointed in his choice of wife? Jane wondered. A woman who had already been married and could not bear children? How could they not be?

CHAPTER

EIGHT

The next day, half an hour before the posted opening time, "Madame Victorine" unlocked the shop door, then walked back to the workroom to gather her composure and check her reflection in the mirror. She wore a simple but elegant gown that had belonged to her mentor, Martine, hoping to look the part. It was one of the few gowns in her possession that fastened in the front. That and her wraparound stays allowed her to dress herself. She had taken in the gown quite a bit, but she thought it looked well on her now.

Poor Martine. She had waited too long to pursue her dream, but her older friend's death had spurred her to act.

She smoothed her hair, a plain coiffure without curls or fuss. Professional, or so she hoped. As she did so, she noticed her hand tremble. She took a deep breath, and then another. *I can do this. . . . Or can I?* She could almost feel her mother's hands on the sides of her face and hear her warm voice saying "*Ma fille*, all will be well."

She and her mother had dreamed of opening a dressmaking shop together one day. Instead, she was about to open a shop on her own. *Oh, Mamma, if only you were here.* Out front, she heard a door open and close. Her first customer? Her heart beat hard, as it always did before a performance.

Mercy and Matilda met Jane at The Bell, and together they walked over to Madame Victorine's newly opened shop. Outside,

Mrs. Prater and the Miss Cooks stood at the dressmaker's window, gaping and pointing at the fashionable gowns on display.

"Can you imagine how fine we'd look in those gowns, Char?" Judith Cook murmured dreamily.

"I doubt we could afford one between us, Judy."

"Very true, Miss Cook," Mrs. Prater said. "But I will be happy to offer you reduced prices on all *our* fancy goods today. Do stop by."

Poor Mrs. Prater, Jane thought. Left with inventory she would now be unable to sell for her usual high profit.

Inside the shop, they found Justina and Miss Bingley already there, trying on bonnets.

The interior—including the shelves, counter, long mirror, and chairs—was the same as before. Apparently Mrs. Shabner had let the place fully furnished and the new dressmaker had added nothing of her own, save the gowns themselves.

Madame Victorine emerged from the back workroom and drew up short at finding so many people in her shop. "My, my. Quite a crowd." A smile warmed her startled expression. "Welcome, ladies." She handed Miss Bingley a bonnet with a cluster of artificial fruit adorning it. "Here you are, miss. I added the cherries, as you requested. I thought this pink satin trim would set them off well, if you like."

Miss Bingley put the bonnet on and regarded her reflection in the mirror. "Oh yes. Very smart indeed, madame. I shall wear it on Easter next month. Thank you."

Matilda spoke up, "It isn't likely I shall have occasion to purchase the gold-and-blue gown, but might I try it on anyway?"

"Of course you may, Miss Grove."

Jane said, "You have such a fine assortment of model dresses, madame. Are they to demonstrate what you can make?"

The woman nodded. "I could sew something new, if you prefer. But I am happy to sell these gowns as well. I can alter them to suit."

Miss Bingley murmured, "How . . . unusual."

"How convenient," Matilda insisted with a smile.

Madame Victorine removed the gown from the dress form and led Matilda to the back room to try it on.

"Do come out when you're ready," Justina called after them. "We want to see it on you!"

While they waited, Jane looked at hats and bonnets.

Mercy joined her, browsing halfheartedly, and sent Jane a pained look. "I almost hope it does not suit her, for I hate to disappoint either Aunt Matty or our new dressmaker when we fail to buy it."

Several minutes later, Matilda emerged, wearing the gold-and-blue gown. It suited her very well indeed, bringing out the color of her eyes and lending vibrancy to her softly lined cheeks.

"What do you think?" Matilda swayed this way and that, the full skirt swishing over her ankle bones.

Madame Victorine came out behind her. "I had to pin up the waist, but I could easily take it in."

"Is it not too short?" Mercy asked hopefully.

"Another flounce at the hem would take care of that."

"Yes, I suppose that would do it." Mercy's eyes shone wistfully. "It is lovely on you, Aunt Matty."

"Thank you, my dear. I shall begin saving my pennies. Perhaps I could sell a few cakes."

Jane guessed it would take more cakes than Craddock's sold in a year to pay for such a dress.

"Oh! And this hat would be perfect with it." Justina fetched a gold-and-blue hat from the rack and carried it to Matilda, helping to arrange it over her silvery hair.

"More cakes to make," Matilda teased.

She admired her reflection in the shop's long mirror for a minute, then, with a resolved nod, turned to the dressmaker. "Thank you, Victorine. May I call you that?"

"Yes, if you like. And the rest of you as well."

Matilda removed the hat. "I shall take off these lovely things now, in hopes that someone else might buy them from you very soon. We want you to be successful here, so you stay for many years to come."

"You are kind, ma'am."

"Matilda. Or Miss Matty, if you like. It is what most of my friends call me."

"Thank you . . . Miss Matty." Victorine smiled almost shyly and helped her out of the dress.

Justina picked up a long fur tippet from a shelf and draped it around her shoulders. "You have such beautiful things. I should love to have you make a new gown for me."

"Thank you. I would be honored to do so."

Miss Bingley smirked. "I should warn you, madame, that receiving such a commission would be something of a poisoned chalice. Miss Brockwell's brother is a baronet, and her mother *most* exacting."

"A baronet. Really . . . ?" Victorine's eyes shone, though Jane saw her swallow hard.

"Don't frighten her off, Miss Bingley," Justina protested mildly. "Yes, my mother can be fastidious, but Madame Victorine need have nothing to fear. French modistes are much in demand in England. From Paris, I imagine? Mamma cannot disapprove."

Oh, but she could, Jane thought, holding her tongue.

Victorine hesitated. "I . . . have not been to France in years, truth be told. And never to Paris, I'm afraid."

"Is that why you haven't much of an accent?" Miss Bingley asked. "I did wonder."

"Yes, I suppose it is."

Jane admired her honesty. She said, "Where are you from, Victorine, if I may ask?"

"I was born in France. But for many years now I have lived in England."

"Where?"

"In many places, Mrs. Bell."

"Jane," she insisted.

"In many places, *Jane*," she repeated. "And now I look forward to living in Ivy Hill . . . if all goes well."

"I have lived here all my life. Mercy too." Matilda assured her, "You will love it."

Victorine turned to her. "And you, Jane?"

"I grew up closer to Wishford, just east of here."

The dressmaker looked from her to Mercy. "Have you two been friends long?"

Mercy nodded. "Oh yes, since we were girls."

A wistfulness shone in the woman's eyes. "How wonderful."

Jane tilted her head and regarded Victorine more closely. "Have you been to Wishford before?" she asked. "When I first saw you, I thought you looked familiar."

"Do I? I don't recall Wishford, but my family did visit Ivy Hill once, when I was young. But you would not recognize me from then, I don't think."

"Probably not," Jane agreed. "Especially as I only came to Ivy Hill to visit friends in those days. Ah well, I must be mistaken."

Justina brought them back to the subject at hand. "Well, I shan't mention to Mamma that you've never been to Paris. I don't care a fig about that, but it won't help my cause. Have you a card I could give her?"

"I am afraid not. Not yet."

Justina blithely shrugged. "Never mind. I shall bring her to meet you."

"Thank you."

In the woman's bright eyes and clasped hands, Jane saw both eagerness and nervousness. A commission from Justina Brockwell, a young lady from Ivy Hill's most prominent family, was certain to secure her future. Unless she failed to please her affluent customer. And knowing Lady Brockwell, that was a distinct possibility.

Jane could relate to a fear of failure. She recalled her own worries and struggles when she took over management of The Bell. Hoping to encourage their new dressmaker, Jane decided she would buy something in a show of support. Perhaps one of her lovely bonnets.

At the next meeting of the Ladies Tea and Knitting Society, the conversation revolved around Ivy Hill's new dressmaker.

"Has anyone bought anything from her yet?" Mrs. Burlingame asked. "She won't stay here long if none of us patronize her shop."

"Oui, oui! Ooh la la!" Becky Morris exclaimed in an exaggerated French accent, winding a colorful scarf around her neck. "I bought zis just today from *Madahm Veectorine*."

Jane grinned at the comical accent.

"Can you not fancy me in one of those gowns in the window?" Judith Cook asked wistfully. "I like them all."

Her sister nodded. "Me too."

Young Miss Featherstone wrinkled her nose. "I looked at the gowns, and they are striking to be sure, but a bit . . . matronly, I thought."

Charlotte Cook frowned. "Are you calling us old, Julia?"

"No. Just more . . . mature . . . in your tastes."

"Humph."

The laundress, Mrs. Snyder, sighed. "I doubt I could afford anything there, her being French and all."

Mercy said, "Jane, you bought something."

"Only a bonnet," Jane demurred. "Though I thought the price very reasonable. Less than Mrs. Shabner would have charged, truth be told."

"Really?" Mrs. Snyder's eyebrows rose. "Then maybe I will stop in tomorrow."

"Me too," Mrs. O'Brien said. "I could use a new pair of gloves."

The vicar's wife spoke up. "Has she hats as well?"

"Yes, a nice variety."

"Then I shall visit her too."

"Please do, Mrs. Paley," Mrs. Barton said. "I have been meaning to say something to you about your old hat."

"Bridget!" Mercy exclaimed.

"What? It's nothing to be ashamed of. We can't all have as many fine hats as Mrs. Klein."

The piano tuner blushed. "Mr. Klein, God rest his soul, did like seeing me in new hats."

The vicar's wife smiled sardonically at the dairywoman. "Thank you, Bridget. I *shall* buy a new hat. And if Mr. Paley gives a long sermon on thrift and self-denial, we will have you to thank for it."

Several groans went up at that, and Jane hid a chuckle behind her hand. Then she gave her own gloves a second look. Perhaps she could use a new pair as well.

CHAPTER

NINE

Rachel spent the morning in the Ashford Circulating Library, reviewing the accounts and subscriber lists, and giving Anna a few hours leisure, as she did each week.

Her mother-in-law, Lady Barbara, would have preferred that she wash her hands of the place, but Rachel enjoyed spending time among her father's books and visiting with some of her favorite patrons.

The book club gathered to discuss an autobiography, diverting from their usual choice of novels. They read *The Interesting Narrative of the Life of Olaudah Equiano*. Equiano was a young African sold into slavery. He traveled the world on several ships, became a skilled sailor, and eventually bought his own freedom. The account of his struggles and suffering brought the women to loud lamentations and even tears. And his conversion to Christianity and efforts to end the slave trade inspired them all.

When Rachel walked home afterward, she saw her sister on the street ahead of her, looking in the modiste's window.

"Something catch your eye, Justina?"

"I like that hat. I didn't notice it when I was here before." She pointed to a blue silk hat with silvery veil and ostrich plume. "But I wonder if it is too matronly for me. What do you think?"

The jingle of a door opening caught Rachel's ear. She turned and saw Nicholas Ashford step out of the apothecary shop across the street.

"There's Mr. Ashford." She waved him over.

With an answering wave, Nicholas waited until a farmer's cart passed, then crossed the street to them.

"Hello, Miss Ash . . . That is, Lady Brockwell. Still getting used to that, I'm afraid."

Rachel replied, "So am I."

He bowed to her companion. "Good day, Miss Brockwell." A teasing light warmed his eyes. "It is still Miss Brockwell, is it not? Or have you also acquired a new name lately?"

Justina's pretty smile faded. "No, not yet."

Doubt flickered over his face. "Forgive me. I did not intend to raise an unhappy topic. I was only trying to be amusing—and bumbling it, as usual."

"Not at all," Justina said. "Fear not, Mr. Ashford, I am not pining away for a new surname, though others in my family might do so for me."

Dark eyes flashing, she turned away and feigned interest in the window display again.

To bridge the awkward moment, Rachel asked lightly, "What do you say, Mr. Ashford? Justina likes the blue hat but fears it might be too matronly for her. What do you think?"

Nicholas glanced at the hats, but his focus quickly returned to Justina's profile.

"I think Miss Brockwell would look charming in anything she wore."

Justina turned toward him at that, her pique evaporating and replaced with warm interest. "You are too kind, Mr. Ashford."

"Not at all, Miss Brockwell."

Rachel looked from one to the other, mischief tingling her stomach. Dare she? Lady Barbara would not be pleased. "Mr. Ashford, perhaps you might join us for dinner at Brockwell Court sometime soon? We would enjoy that. Would we not, Justina?"

"We would, yes." Justina beamed up at the tall young man, a rosy glow in her cheeks.

Nicholas held her gaze, then, realizing he was staring, looked down and cleared his throat. "I thank you for the kind invitation and will wait upon you to name a date at your leisure." He bowed and doffed his hat. "For now, I shall bid you good day, ladies."

As he turned and walked away, Justina watched him go, her eyes soft and thoughtful. "There's something about that young man. His diffidence only makes him more appealing. I . . . believe Miss Bingley admires him."

"And you like him as well?"

Justina turned to her. "My dear sister, are you playing matchmaker?" A dimple appeared in her cheek. "Mamma won't like that, you know. She does not want anyone interfering with her plans for me."

"I am more concerned about what you want, Justina."

Tears brightened the young woman's eyes, but she blinked them away. "I want Mamma to be happy. Is it selfish to wish I might be happy too?"

"Not in the least."

Justina shrugged and lifted her chin. "It's too late anyway. Mamma is already anticipating the wedding. Just this morning she said, 'These pastries are delicious. We should serve them at the wedding breakfast.'"

"But you are not yet engaged to Sir Cyril."

"No, but my birthday will soon be here. The days are flying by much too fast."

"Justina, if you don't want to marry him, you need to tell your mother that in no uncertain terms."

"I've tried, gently. But I hate to disappoint her." Justina took her arm. "Come. Let's go home. I want to be there when you tell Mamma you've invited a single man to dinner."

"You stay by my side, then. I shall need reinforcements," Rachel teased.

To be fair, Lady Barbara had been kind and gracious to Rachel since she'd joined the family. She'd set aside her former objections to Timothy marrying her, but that did not mean the dowager was ready to relinquish her plans for her daughter's marriage as well.

Before Rachel could seek out her mother-in-law, her husband greeted her and asked her to join him in his study.

"How was the library today, my love?"

"All seems well. The ladies were enthralled by the autobiography you suggested—except for Mrs. Barton, who complained that it kept her up so long reading that she was late milking her bossies this morning."

He grinned.

"By the way," she added, "I spoke to Justina on the way home. She does not seem happy about your mother's plans for her to marry Sir Cyril."

"Does she not? She was reticent at first, I know. But I thought she had warmed to the idea of marriage, after our sterling example." He winked, sliding his arms around Rachel and drawing her close.

"She might be enamored with the idea of wedding gowns and wedding trips but not with the man himself."

"No? Well, there is no hurry for her to decide."

"But your mother pressures her. And Justina—like her eldest brother—has always wanted to do the right thing, for the honor of her parents and the Brockwell name."

"That is to her credit."

"But likely not to her happiness."

Timothy kissed her forehead, then lowered his mouth to her cheek. Her ear. "I will talk to her later. Right now, I don't want to talk about Justina or anyone else. Only you. And me." He leaned down and kissed Rachel's lips, turned her to face him more fully, and kissed her again.

The next day, the three Brockwell women sat together in the morning room. Lady Barbara read the newspaper, Justina flipped through a ladies magazine, and Rachel embroidered.

When Carville brought in the post on a silver salver, Justina looked up eagerly. "Anything for me, Carville?"

"I am afraid not, miss."

He extended the tray to the other two women in turn. Rachel was pleased to receive another letter from her sister.

Lady Barbara accepted the one addressed to herself. "Ah, from Richard. How nice." She opened the letter and read the few lines with the aid of her quizzing glass. Her younger son wrote but rarely, Rachel knew, and usually when he needed more money.

Rachel took a deep breath, steeling herself.

"Lady . . . Barbara, I have invited Mr. Ashford to join us for dinner sometime soon. I hope you don't mind. Is there an evening that works better for you?"

"Mr. Ashford?"

"Yes. Nicholas. You have met him and his mother several times, I believe."

"I have, yes. At church, and at the Awdrys' concert. But it never crossed my mind to invite them here."

"I thought it would be a nice gesture."

"Would it not be awkward for Mr. Ashford to be here, now that you are married to Timothy? The young man admired you, after all."

"That is in the past."

"Would it not be salt in his wound to see you and Timothy happy together as man and wife?"

"I don't think so. Mr. Ashford and I have agreed to remain friends. And we are distant relatives, so I hope to maintain warm relations between our families."

"But why would he want to come?" Lady Barbara's eyes narrowed. "Tell me you are not trying to encourage an interest in Justina? She is all but engaged to another man! Do you really want to raise that young man's hopes only to be the means of disappointing him yet again?"

Rachel had not thought of that. No, she did not want to cause Nicholas more heartache.

"You had better make sure he knows Sir Cyril is courting Justina. So that his expectations—and his mother's—are in line with reality. If not, I will certainly make it clear when next I see them."

"Very well."

Perhaps dinner was not the best idea after all. Rachel decided she would postpone the invitation for now.

CHAPTER

TEN

A few days later, Rachel and Justina accompanied Lady Barbara to Madame Victorine's shop.

"Remember, Justina," Lady Barbara said, "I have only agreed to hear what the woman might suggest, how much time she requires, and so on. I have not agreed to actually hire her to make your wedding dress."

"Of course not, Mamma. That would be premature, as I am *not even engaged*."

"It is only a matter of time, so it does not hurt to start considering our options. But I still say we should go to my favorite modiste in London for your wedding clothes, as we did for Rachel's."

Rachel offered, "It would be a kind gesture to support Ivy Hill's new dressmaker."

"We shall see."

Reaching the shop, they paused to look at the fine gowns on display. Lady Barbara did not admit it, but Rachel thought she looked impressed.

Inside, they greeted the pretty dressmaker and introduced her to Lady Barbara Brockwell.

Victorine curtsied and then tightly clasped her hands. Rachel could not blame her for being ill at ease. The dowager was an intimidating figure.

In her excitement, Justina plunged ahead, "I have decided, madame, that *if* I marry a certain gentleman, *you* must make my wedding dress! Mother would prefer we go to London, but I want you to make it right here in Ivy Hill." She beamed at the woman.

Victorine blinked. "A *wedding* dress. For you, miss? How . . . unexpected."

"Let us not get ahead of ourselves, Justina." Lady Barbara looked pointedly at her daughter. "Remember, we are only here to discuss ideas at this point."

The four sat down together, and Justina handed Victorine a ladies magazine, opened to one of its hand-painted fashion plates. "I am thinking of something like this. I like the lower, more defined waist, and less fullness in the hips. I also like this Anglo-Greek bodice with puff sleeves, don't you?"

"Anglo-Greek," Victorine echoed. "Yes, I see."

Justina opened another magazine, *Ackermann's Repository*, to a page with square fabric samples glued to the paper, as some of the more expensive magazines did.

"Isn't this fabric breathtaking? I love the idea of sheer netting over satin. So much more interesting than plain ivory."

"It is beautiful," Madame Victorine agreed, tentatively fingering the fine fabric.

"Could you acquire it? Perhaps from the linen draper in Salisbury?"

"I can certainly ask if they carry it. But this material is very delicate, and no doubt very expensive."

Justina looked at her mother. "Do you mind the expense, Mamma?"

"No. It is lovely fabric. *If* we decide to proceed, I will advance the funds needed to purchase the material."

Justina spread one more magazine before Madame Victorine. "And a veiled bonnet like this one, I think."

Victorine bent to study it, then nodded with more confidence. "I could make that, yes. The Miss Cooks have many excellent pieces of lace we might use."

Justina closed the magazines. "Well. What is the next step?"

Victorine answered slowly, "I think I will make some drawings first, if you don't mind. One can only see so much detail in these fashion prints. I will show you some options, then we can go from there, if you approve them."

"Very well. How long will you need for that?"

"A few weeks."

Lady Barbara asked, "And how long to make such a dress once approved?"

"Oh, um . . . a month, perhaps? Six weeks?"

"You don't seem certain. Are you up to the task, madame?"

"If we can agree on the design and acquire the materials, then yes, I will be . . . anxious to proceed."

The dowager narrowed her eyes at the qualified response. "May I ask where you took your training? Were you apprenticed to some dressmaker I might have heard of?"

"No, my lady. Not . . . officially."

"Then how did you learn?"

"I learned a great deal from my mother, who trained as a dressmaker. And when I grew older, I worked with another woman, Madame Devereaux. She taught me how to take the simplest materials, even castoffs, and create the most beautiful pieces."

"Castoffs?" Lady Barbara's nose wrinkled.

"Not everyone has a large budget, madame. If funds were scarce, she could take apart an old dress, perhaps two, incorporate some leftover trimmings, and create a whole new costume."

"By *costume*, I assume you mean a riding costume, or a bathing costume, or the like?" the dowager asked.

Victorine nodded. "Whatever was needed. Everything she touched turned out beautifully. She had many other talents as well."

Lady Barbara sniffed. "Then perhaps we ought to pursue this Madame Devereaux instead."

"Impossible, I am afraid. She died very recently."

"Pity." The dowager Lady Brockwell rose to her full, imperious height. "Well, make your drawings for now. And we shall let you know when the engagement becomes official."

"Very good, my lady. I shall begin at once."

Rachel held her tongue. She did not want to disappoint the new dressmaker, but she privately hoped that the engagement would never take place.

Jane rode over to the farm to see Gabriel again. She regretted how their recent dinner had ended and hoped to suggest a more pleasant evening to make up for it.

Seeing her ride down the lane, he stepped away from his hired men and walked over to greet her.

"Hello, Jane. I didn't expect you today."

"I have come to ask a favor."

"Of course. Anything."

"I am afraid you may find it rather shocking."

"How intriguing." He grinned. "Shall I help you down first?"

"Yes, thank you."

He reached up to grasp her waist and eased her down.

"There, you see?" she lamented as her feet touched the ground. "That is just it. It's too difficult to mount and dismount on my own."

He tightened his arms around her. "I don't mind helping you."

"Well, I admit it is far more pleasant when it is *you* doing the helping. But to be dependent on a groom, or at the very least a mounting block or stile every time I want to ride?" She shook her head.

He sent her a sidelong glance. "What are you suggesting?"

With a glance toward the men near the barn, she stepped from his embrace and lowered her voice. "I would like to try riding astride, as you do. I imagine the control would be far superior. Just once I'd like to experience the freedom of galloping without a sidesaddle."

He nodded. "I can understand your curiosity. I have often wondered how you do it, riding so fast and so well like that."

"The newer sidesaddles with double pommels do help."

Gabriel considered. "I imagine if you had grown up with a brother, you would have conspired to make it happen long ago."

"Then will you act as my accomplice instead? Not that I think of you as a brother."

He smirked. "I should hope not."

"I thought perhaps it would be wisest to try it in the evening when I'd be less likely to encounter a neighbor. Or even Talbot and Thora."

Gabriel rubbed his chin. "Evening might suit the purpose. Though it stays light later now that spring is almost here."

He thought, then added, "Since Athena is primarily trained to sidesaddle, and Sultan has experience with both, perhaps you might ride him astride. I know you like him anyway."

"Indeed I do. Though Athena is first in my heart. So . . . tomorrow evening? The almanac calls for a full moon."

"You are eager. Yes, I don't see why not."

"There is no other man I would trust with such a request, I assure you."

He gazed fondly into her eyes. "I am glad you know you can trust me, Jane." He winked. "You rebel."

The following night, Jane wore her old riding habit, the brown one with the long frockcoat-style jacket and separate skirt. Under it, she wore a pair of John's old breeches, a sash tied at the waist to keep them up. Beneath those, she wore opaque stockings and her boots.

She rode past Thora and Talbot's place, feeling strangely ill at ease. When she reached the farm, Gabriel came out to greet her, dressed in his riding clothes. Sultan and a second horse she did not recognize were already saddled and waiting at the post.

He dubiously regarded the long, full skirt. "Mounting in all that will pose a challenge."

"I know. I'm wearing breeches beneath. I thought I'd tuck up the skirt just until I'm in the saddle, then spread it out again."

He pursed his lips, eyes twinkling. "I think I'm glad the men have left for the day."

Together they stabled Athena. Then, feeling self-conscious, she tucked her skirt hem beneath her sash, which shortened it to about half its length, exposing the breeches. The jacket of her riding habit covered her hips, so she hoped she was still modest enough.

Her face heated. "I suppose I look ridiculous."

"On the contrary. I appreciate this glimpse of your figure usually hidden by billowing skirts." He grinned impishly. "Are you ready?"

Jane looked at the tall chestnut with a white blaze on his forehead. "You know I never pass up a chance to ride Sultan." She stroked his forelock. "I don't believe I've seen this other horse before. Is he new?"

"Yes. I bought Spirit at the auction in Salisbury. I prefer to buy from breeders directly, so I can see where and how a horse was raised. But the man selling him couldn't handle him and let him go for a low price. I could not resist."

Gabriel stepped to Sultan's side, shortening the stirrups. "With or without mounting block?" he asked.

"Without."

"Very well. To mount, put your left foot in the stirrup, then swing your right leg over his back. If you can."

His eyes glinted with playful challenge and Jane rose to it. "I am sure I can manage." She wasn't sure. The horse was tall and broad, and she had never swung her leg in such an unladylike manner in her life.

Riding crop in one hand, she took the reins, grasped saddle leather, and pulled herself up, trying to swing her leg up and over. She didn't quite clear Sultan's back the first time and he shifted uncertainly.

"There, there, boy," Gabriel soothed. "She'll manage next time."

Jane tried again. And this time, Gabriel gave her a boost from the rear. Her leg cleared the horse's back and settled on his other side. She smiled down at Gabriel. "I think you enjoyed giving me that hand up a little too much."

His only answer was a grin.

Jane wiggled the toe of her boot into the other stirrup and shifted in the saddle. "My goodness. How different it feels."

She untucked her skirt and spread it over her legs. Only a few inches of her stockings showed over her half boots. Noticing his admiring gaze linger on her calf, she tugged the skirt a little lower.

When she was settled, he mounted his new horse, who jigged to the side.

"Are you sure he's ready?" Jane asked, studying the animal with concern.

"I can handle him."

As twilight fell, they trotted out the farmyard gate and started across the adjacent field under a full moon.

With a glance at her handsome companion, Jane took a deep breath and expelled a contented sigh. If she married him, their life together would be full of evenings like this—though probably with only one of them in breeches.

As they rode, Gabriel said, "You asked me if I had changed the name of the farm yet. I have not. But I do know what I'd like to call it."

"Oh? What?"

"I was thinking . . . Locke and Locke."

Jane flinched and looked away. There it was again. The stumbling block between them. He might as well have said Locke and Sons. Sons she could not give him. "Gabriel, I told you. I cannot have children."

"Who said anything about children? Locke and Locke, as in Gabriel and Jane Locke. Husband and wife. Partners in the horse business, or at least I hope we shall be."

"Oh. But I already have a business."

He huffed. "Jane, do you want to marry me or not?"

"I . . . do. But—"

"Not very reassuring." Gabriel turned his horse's head. "You said you wanted to gallop, so let's go." He started off across the field.

For a moment, Jane remained where she was, watching him ride away, regret filling her. Sultan strained against his bit, eager to follow.

Then a flash of movement startled Sultan and Jane both. A brown blur leapt from the thicket and shot across the field. A large dog, fangs bared, chased after Gabriel's new horse, growling and snarling.

Spirit lurched to the side, head turned, eyes and nostrils wild with terror.

Jane saw Gabriel react, choking the reins up tight. He yelled at the dog, which startled the spooked horse all the more.

Then the dog lunged and snapped at the horse's foreleg.

Jane sucked in a breath. *No . . .*

She rarely used her riding crop, but she now touched Sultan's side, calling, "Hyah! Get up!"

The well-trained horse leapt forward, and Jane gripped tight with her legs as he galloped onward. She bent low over Sultan's neck, willing him to catch up with Gabriel's runaway horse.

Nearing them, Jane stretched out her riding crop and tried to strike the dog—deter it, if she could.

At the same time, Spirit reared up violently, sending Gabriel flying.

Jane gasped, fear seizing her. He fell, landing on a mound of some sort. Startled, Sultan lurched away. Jane almost lost her seat as well, but she hung on with a mighty press of strength and desperate grip on saddle and mane. "Whoa, boy. Whoa."

Sultan begrudgingly halted, while the other horse ran on, kicking its hooves to forestall its attacker, the dog still at its heels. Struggling to dismount and nearly falling herself, Jane ran toward Gabriel's fallen form, pulse beating wildly.

She fell to her knees beside his prone body, expecting him to rise up on an elbow and yell at the dog in his commanding voice, his first concern for the horse and not his own bumps and bruises. Or to rub his head, grin sheepishly, and say, *"That's what I get for being overly confident."*

Instead, he lay unmoving, eyes closed, legs sprawled.

Closer now, Jane saw that the mound was not a molehill or a gorse bush, as she had at first thought, but a rock. *Dear God, no!*

Jane gently touched his shoulder. "Gabriel, are you all right?" She took his hand. "Can you hear me? Gabriel!" Her throat burned, and tears swamped her eyes. Why had she put him off? She should have married him months ago. She loved this man more than she had ever loved anyone. And if she lost him now . . .

She circled her fingers around his wrist and closed her eyes to focus, feeling his pulse with ecstatic relief.

"Gabriel, I am going to get help." Jane rose, relieved to see no sign of the dog. "If you can hear me, try not to move. I'll be back as soon as I can."

With a prayer, she pressed a hand to her bosom and ran to Sultan's side. She clumsily remounted and galloped the short distance to Thora and Talbot's farm.

CHAPTER

ELEVEN

Jane sat in a chair pulled close to Gabriel's bedside, her fingers entwined with his, stroking his arm with her free hand.

Walter Talbot and his men had borne Gabriel into his bedchamber at Lane's Farm. Dr. Burton had come and gone. No bones were broken as far as he could tell, but Gabriel had several nasty abrasions and bruises. He'd briefly regained his senses— long enough for the physician to ascertain he had a concussion. Dr. Burton was also concerned about possible injury to his neck and spine but said they would have to wait and see.

In the meanwhile, Jane continued to pray, and to thank God that the man she loved still lived.

Dawn brightened the sky. Through the bedroom door, she could hear Thora's hushed voice and the occasional clatter of pots and pans. Helping Susie make breakfast, she guessed. Thora and Talbot had spent the night in one of the spare rooms, just in case their help was needed.

A rooster crowed in the distance, and Gabriel opened his eyes. He blinked and blinked again, as though having difficulty focusing. He mumbled, "Why do I feel so groggy?"

"Dr. Burton gave you laudanum for the pain."

He frowned, dark brows bunching. "I can't feel my legs. Are they broken?"

Jane's heart raced. Would the paralysis last? She replied evenly, "Dr. Burton doesn't think so."

"Then why can't I move them?"

Jane bit her lip. She longed to reassure him, but she knew Gabriel would want the truth. "He says you've likely injured your spine."

"God have mercy. I am paralyzed?"

She chose her words carefully. "He said when the swelling abates and your body heals you will most likely regain the use of your legs."

"Most likely? Not a certainty?"

"It is too soon to tell, but he didn't seem overly concerned. He had several other patients to see, but he will return as soon as possible. I'm sure he will answer your questions then."

She added, "And you will be glad to know that your new horse has been found and returned, thanks to Walter Talbot and his men."

"How is Spirit?"

"He'll be all right. Talbot treated a bite wound and will ask Tom Fuller to come out, although you will no doubt want to look at it yourself . . . when you can."

He tried to shift his upper body. "I should go see him now."

She laid a restraining hand on his shoulder. "Don't worry about your horse. He is in better condition than you are at present." She managed a grin.

Gabriel didn't return it. "And the dashed dog?"

"Disappeared. Talbot suspects the creature is the same one responsible for an attack on his sheep a few months ago."

Gabriel frowned and averted his gaze. "What foul timing. This is what I get for thinking I could tame that horse when others failed."

"Oh, you will tame him yet. I don't doubt that for an instant. You could not have foreseen an attack by a wild dog."

They fell silent for several moments. The exertion of cheerful banter wearied her.

She squeezed his hand. "I am just so thankful you're alive."

That evening after dinner, Rachel sat in the drawing room, reading the next book to be discussed at the library while Justina idly played a few halfhearted measures on the pianoforte.

When her mother-in-law joined them, Rachel glanced conspiratorially at Justina, then began, "I have been thinking, Lady Barbara, and you are right. A dinner with Nicholas Ashford as our sole guest would not be quite the thing."

"I am glad you agree."

Rachel nodded. "I think, instead of dinner, a house party would be far superior."

"A house party?" Her mother-in-law's face lengthened in dismay.

"Yes, we would invite Sir Cyril and his sisters, Miss Bingley, her brother, and Mr. Ashford. And of course, Timothy and I would act as chaperones."

"Oh yes, I long for a house party," Justina cooed.

Rachel went on. "Most of the time Justina has spent with Sir Cyril has been in formal occasions, family dinners, and the concert. Not exactly conducive to fostering closer acquaintance or affection. I think that is part of the reason she remains undecided. She has had insufficient interaction to truly sketch the man's character. But a few days together, with diversions and dancing? Time to stroll the grounds and talk at their leisure, even steal a few minutes alone in the garden . . . ? I think it would do her a world of good. Help her compare and contrast the qualities of the eligible men in the area."

"Oh yes, Mamma," Justina enthused. "I think it an excellent idea."

"I see your point," Lady Barbara allowed, "and approve of the plan, except for the guest list. Why include Nicholas Ashford?"

"We must have enough young men to even our numbers," Rachel replied. "Even with him, we are short one man."

The dowager considered. "Perhaps we could invite Richard to come home for the party." She frowned. "Though I doubt he will accept."

"Oh, I wish Richard would come," Justina said. "I haven't seen him since my London season."

Lady Barbara narrowed her eyes in thought. "What a boon if he might take an interest in Arabella Awdry. Although she might be reluctant to consider another Brockwell after her recent disappointment with Timothy."

Rachel and Justina exchanged a look at that, but Rachel said only, "Well, we can invite Richard and see what happens."

After dinner that evening, Rachel shared the plan with Timothy as they crossed the hall together. "And as the lone married couple, we would act the part of chaperones." She grinned ruefully. "How matronly that makes me feel!"

"You look anything but matronly to me, dear wife." In the quiet passage, he wrapped his arms around her and nuzzled her neck. "You look altogether enticing, truth be told."

Hearing two maids chatting as they came around the corner, Rachel whispered, "I don't think this is the best place, my love."

"I quite agree." He took her hand and led her upstairs.

The following morning, Dr. Burton returned to reexamine Gabriel. Tom Fuller arrived about the same time to look at the injured horse's leg, so Jane went out to thank him, knowing Gabriel would want a report on Spirit's recovery.

When she returned to the farmhouse, Dr. Burton had already left, but Gabriel relayed his report, which repeated much of what he'd told her initially. It was too soon to know for sure, given the mysterious nature of the spinal cord, but Dr. Burton was as confident as he could be that Gabriel would regain the use of his legs.

Eager to encourage him, Jane said, "Tom Fuller has just been here. You will be glad to know he thinks Spirit will heal thoroughly and the wound will leave no lasting damage."

"At least physically," Gabriel added with a grimace. "Poor creature. It will take months to regain his trust. I can't believe I lost control of him. I haven't fallen from a horse in years."

"Well, your fall knocked some sense into me."

He looked at her warily. "You? What do you mean?"

Remembering her fear and regret when he lay there unresponsive, Jane's throat tightened all over again. She whispered hoarsely, "Gabriel, will you marry me?"

He gingerly turned more fully toward her, grimacing in pain as he did so.

"Jane, don't ask out of pity. Let's wait and see what happens. If I am able to walk and regain my strength, then we'll—"

"No!" she exclaimed, leaning forward till her knees touched the bed. "When you lay there, unmoving, I feared I'd lost you. Everything became clear to me. I love you, Gabriel Locke, more than I've ever loved anyone. And I am so sorry I've put you off, that I let fear hold me back." She squeezed his hand. "No more. I don't want to wait any longer."

"Jane." He shook his head. "Yes, you let fear hold you back, but don't make a rash decision now to accept me out of another kind of fear."

"I don't want to marry you because I'm afraid to lose you. I want to marry you because I love you with all my heart and don't want to waste any more time. Life is precious and short, as I know from experience."

"Jane, slow down. Take time to consider. If the worst happens and I am unable to walk, that means it's highly unlikely that working with horses is in my future. I would have to sell the farm. Find some . . . alternate profession. Something at a desk, which I would not relish. There are not a lot of jobs like that in Ivy Hill."

"The worst did not happen. You are alive and here with me. And as far as giving up horses, let's not worry about that until we must. Remember, Dr. Burton is quite certain this"—she gestured to his blanket-covered legs—"is only temporary."

"But if it's not . . . Jane, I would not blame you if you had second thoughts."

Indignation flashed through her. She released his hand and straightened in her chair. "Gabriel Locke, you expect me to believe you have no reservations about marrying me with *my* physical limitations, yet you dare suggest I would reject you because of yours?"

He held her gaze, and a slow grin warmed his somber expression. "Touché, Jane Bell. Touché."

She released a tense breath, then teased, "In fact, I rather like the idea of you having a limp or something, so I am not the only one in this union with a physical flaw."

"You are perfect as you are, Jane. As I've told you countless times."

"And so are you, regardless of the outcome." She rose and leaned over the bed, bringing her mouth to his in a sweet, lingering kiss.

CHAPTER
TWELVE

Later that morning, Thora and Talbot brought over their trusted maid, Sadie Jones, to help Gabriel convalesce, since the woman had been such a capable nurse to Nan Talbot. Thora quieted Gabriel's protests, assuring him they could spare her and that Sadie was happy to help.

While they were there, Jane shared the news of their engagement. Talbot shook Gabriel's hand, and Thora embraced her. "I am so happy for you, Jane," she whispered. "For you both. Truly."

Then, confident Gabriel was in good hands, Jane returned to The Bell. She reassured the staff who gathered around her that Gabriel would be all right, thanked them for their concern, and gently urged them to return to work. She admonished herself in similar fashion. After all, she had been the one to insist she had a business of her own to manage, yet she had fallen behind on several overdue tasks. *Time to get to work, Jane,* she told herself, already planning to ride back out to the farm that night to see her intended.

When Jane visited Gabriel again that evening, she found his condition unchanged. She helped Susie tidy the kitchen and relieved Sadie for an hour, sitting with Gabriel while he alternately talked and slept.

The next day, James Drake came to the inn to see her. "Jane, I was sorry to hear about Mr. Locke's accident. Will he be all right?"

"We are praying so. Dr. Burton predicts a full recovery."

"That is good news."

Jane hesitated. She didn't relish saying the words to this particular man. "Speaking of good news, I would like to share mine. Mr. Locke and I are engaged to be married."

A shadow curtained his face and quickly cleared. "Ah." He gave her a small smile. "Then allow me to congratulate you both. I wish you happy, Jane. I sincerely do."

"Thank you. I hope I may have the opportunity to wish you happy one day as well."

He looked down, rocking back on his heels. "Oh, I think my chance at happiness, at least romantically speaking, has passed me by."

"James, no. Don't say that."

"Never fear. I am far happier with Alice in my life than I deserve to be. I doubt I am very good at being a father, but I am striving to rise to the occasion and make her happy."

"You don't need to *strive* to earn her affection and make her happy. Just be yourself and she will love you."

James shrugged, sloughing off the idea like itchy wool. "I never liked that admonition. Just be myself—which one? The self-centered, ambitious self? The resentful son, estranged from his own father and fearful of becoming just like him? I want Alice to have a better father than I had, a happier childhood."

Jane laid a hand on his sleeve. "Then you're well on your way to becoming a good parent already." She squeezed his arm and released him. "But I don't think you give yourself enough credit. I'd say you turned out remarkably well."

He ducked his head, then looked up at her. "But not well enough to earn your favor."

"James—"

He held up his hand. "No, Jane. You made the right decision. I don't know Mr. Locke well, but by all accounts, he's an excellent fellow. He will make you far happier than I ever could have." His eyes glimmered with humorous resignation.

"Thank you." It was all she could think to say.

He cleared his throat, then crossed his arms and looked up in thought. "Would you like to marry from the Fairmont? You would be very welcome. I don't offer with any thought of profit for myself. It simply occurred to me that you might like to hold your wedding breakfast in your old home."

"That is very kind of you. Truly. And it would certainly be a more elegant setting than the one I have in mind. But I would like my wedding breakfast to be here at The Bell. If the weather is fine, we might extend out into the courtyard as we did during the party Thora and the others gave me when I acquired my license. Otherwise we shall all squeeze into the dining parlour instead."

He smiled. "Are you not glad you heeded my advice to expand that room?"

"I am indeed. I am glad of so many things where you are concerned, especially that we have become friends. I hope that will remain the case . . . ?"

"I hope so too," he said, but he did not look convinced.

Not long after James left, Mercy and Rachel came to call on Jane, having heard the news of Gabriel's accident. The three sat in the office together, her old friends expressing their concern and asking if there was anything they could do to help.

"Nothing besides pray."

"What does Dr. Burton say?" Rachel asked.

"That he has every confidence in Gabriel's full recovery."

Mercy asked gently, "And if he is wrong?"

"Then we will deal with that possibility if and when the time comes."

"What does Gabriel think?"

"He wants to wait until he is walking again to set the date."

"Set the date?" Rachel echoed. "Does that mean you've accepted him at last?"

"Yes. In fact, I asked *him* to marry *me*." Jane shook her head. "I still dread another miscarriage, but I love him, and I'm through waiting. He is to be my husband, and I don't want to have to leave him at night with only a maid or chamber nurse to care for him."

Mercy nodded. "Understandable. You know, we still have my grandfather's wheeled chair in our attic. He could use that to move around . . . for now."

"Thank you. I will ask him about the chair. And thank you both for your concern."

Rachel squeezed her hand and repeated, "You will let us know if there is anything we can do?"

Jane nodded. "I shall."

Jane went to visit Gabriel again the next evening, bringing him a book from the library.

She said, "Rachel and Mercy send along their prayers and congratulations."

"Thank them for me."

"How soon shall we marry?" Jane asked. "Mr. Paley needs a week's notice, then he'll begin publishing the banns. So probably four weeks from now, at the earliest. Though a few months might give us more time to—"

"Let's wait to set the date until I am walking again."

Jane shook her head. "Gabriel, we've been through this. I don't want to wait."

"How will you marry me when I am stuck in this bed?"

"Don't be stubborn, my love. Mercy has offered us the use of her grandfather's wheeled chair."

"How romantic." He shook his head. "I don't want to sit in a chair. I want to stand beside you in church like a man."

"You are a man. My man—standing or not. And before the summer is out, I will vow to love and honor you in front of all my friends and neighbors. Talbot and your men will deliver you and the chair to church, where I shall be awaiting you, looking charming in my lavender gown and new bonnet."

He crossed his arms, lower lip protruded, and for a moment he looked like a petulant little boy. "I don't want an invalid chair," he repeated. "And I don't want you to marry an invalid."

She put her hand on her hips. "Good thing it's my decision, then, and not yours."

He tilted his head to the side as a thought struck him. "Why would you not order a new gown? If things at The Bell are tight financially, I can—"

"No. I just don't think I need one. It's hardly what's important right now, considering everything else that's going on."

"But what about your new friend the dressmaker?"

"To tell you the truth, I think she has all she can manage with a gown for Justina Brockwell." She shrugged. "Besides, I like my lavender gown."

Jane stepped to the side table and filled his water glass. "By the way, I think we should hire Mrs. Mullins to put you through the same course of massage and exercise that helped her husband."

"I don't know, Jane. I don't want to raise false hopes. Just because it worked for Mullins doesn't mean it will work for me. What has Dr. Burton said about it?"

She returned to his bedside. "He agrees it may help your legs and back but said it will do nothing to cure your stubbornness."

His dark eyes glinted. "No? And what does he suggest for that ailment?"

Jane leaned near and pressed a kiss to his mouth.

Gabriel kissed her back, then murmured, "Mmm . . . very effective indeed."

Mercy visited the almshouse to talk to Mrs. Mennell and see what she could do to be of use there. Mostly, she wanted an excuse to get out of the house for a while.

When she returned to Ivy Cottage an hour later, she slipped through the side door into the library and headed toward the stairs.

As she passed the double doors, she overheard her sister-in-law and brother talking within the drawing room.

Helena's falsely sweet voice reached her ears. "How pleasant to have a few moments to ourselves, my love. This quiet is blessed relief after so much female chatter, as I am sure you agree. Your aunt is certainly . . . loquacious. They are both dears, of course, but I never imagined myself living with a cluster of spinsters."

"I hardly think two amounts to a cluster."

"You forget the cook and maids, my dear. But you are right, of course. At least we haven't a gaggle of schoolgirls to contend with as well."

"True."

"I wonder why your parents tolerated the school for so long," Helena added. "Did Mercy need the funds so desperately?"

"I doubt my sister was motivated by gain. Though I suppose a bit of spending money of her own was welcome. In fact, perhaps we ought to do something for her, now that she hasn't any income."

"Surely your father will give his daughter whatever allowance he deems best?"

"He may not think of it."

"You are the most generous of men, my dear. But I hope you don't intend to spoil her. What would a single woman possibly spend money on . . . ?"

Mercy continued upstairs, heart thudding in her ears and muffling George's reply, whatever it might have been.

She decided then and there that, if Aunt Matty was amenable, she would write to accept her parents' invitation to spend time with them in London.

CHAPTER

Thirteen

Jane returned to Lane's Farm the next afternoon, bringing a jar of calves' foot jelly. Gabriel regarded the gelatinous grey mound with suspended shards of fatty meat, his distaste poorly concealed. "It is . . . kind of you, but I am not on my deathbed, nor an octogenarian."

"I know, I just thought it would help strengthen you. I have to do *something*."

He set aside the dish with a sigh. "Jane, as you have often reminded me, you have a coaching inn to manage. You don't need to come here every day to coddle me."

"I don't mind. I like taking care of you."

"But I . . ." He ran a frustrated hand over his face. "Jane, I don't want another nurse. Sadie is more than enough. Listen, I've given some thought to what you said about Mrs. Mullins, and I agree. She may come and put me through her regimen, but please, go about your own business until I am well."

Hurt nipped at her. "Are you saying you don't want me to visit you?"

He reached for her hand. "Of course not. But I want you to be a normal bride-to-be, preparing for her wedding. I want you to go and buy wedding clothes and whatever else it is engaged females do."

She considered. "Perhaps Victorine has something suitable in her shop."

"Jane."

"I don't like leaving you alone here."

"I am not alone. I have Susie, Sadie, and soon Mrs. Mullins. And with the hired men on the farm, I shall be very well looked after."

"I don't know . . ."

"And of course Dr. Burton stops by regularly, as do Talbot and Thora, the best neighbors a man could ask for."

Jane studied his earnest eyes and admitted, "I suppose a new gown would be nice. As it happens, Mercy and her aunt are going to London soon and have invited me to join them."

"There, you see? Perfect. Go and enjoy every minute." He leaned forward and kissed her cheek.

Still, Jane hesitated. "Are you certain? It doesn't feel right to leave you now."

"Perfectly certain. And why not? You heard Dr. Burton. I am in no imminent danger. I shall not die while you are away, except perhaps of boredom." He winked.

"Then I should stay and read to you, or—"

"No, Jane. I can read for myself." He squeezed her hand. "Please. I know some men might like their wives to baby them, but not me. I don't like you seeing me so weak. I want you to see me as strong and capable."

"I do."

"Then prove it by leaving me for a time."

Jane finally relented. She reluctantly agreed to go, but only after confirming with Mrs. Mullins that she would tend to Gabriel during her absence and instructing Cadi to deliver a meal every day from The Bell kitchen, which Mrs. Rooke was surprisingly happy to prepare. Jane would try to do as Gabriel admonished and go about her own business and even go to London, but her heart would remain on Lane's Farm.

After church on Sunday, Aunt Matty stopped to talk to Mrs. O'Brien, so Mercy walked out with Jane alone.

Jane took her arm and said, "If the invitation still stands, I will go to London with you. Gabriel thinks I should go and buy wedding clothes. He seems to want to be rid of me for some reason."

"I am certain it is not that, Jane. But whatever the reason, I am glad. Aunt Matty is eager to go as well. In fact, I have already written to Mamma to accept. I will write again with the happy news that you will be joining us."

"She won't mind?"

"I am sure she won't. And between you and me, I have decided to buy Aunt Matty a new gown for the trip from Victorine's—if I can scrape up enough money. She has not had anything new in years."

"That gold-and-blue dress looked so pretty on her."

"I agree. It will likely cost a pretty penny too. But I will see what we can do. I have a little money left from the school."

"You are a kind and thoughtful niece, Mercy Grove."

"Thank you. But going to London is not a selfless decision." Mercy had her own reasons for wishing to be absent from Ivy Hill at present.

The next day, Mercy and Matilda went to the dressmaker's shop together. After naming the day of the proposed trip, Victorine agreed that there wasn't time to make a new dress, so she offered to sell them the model from the display window. She had to take it in quite a bit and add an extra flounce on the bottom to accommodate Matilda's height, but she did so quickly and even gave Aunt Matty a matching turban at no additional cost. Mercy thought the price exceedingly reasonable. She hoped Victorine had not taken pity on them as two poor spinsters and charged them accordingly, but her aunt was happy, and therefore, so was Mercy.

Jane had seen the Miss Groves enter the shop across the street and walked over to join them just as they were finishing up. She congratulated Matilda on the new gown and again thanked the two for including her in the upcoming trip.

Victorine said, "I have just heard your good news, Jane. Congratulations on your engagement."

"Thank you." Jane added a little sheepishly, "I hope you don't mind, but I plan to have a dress made while we're in London."

"Not at all. I am still working on a design for Miss Brockwell." She added, "One wedding gown is enough pressure for now, believe me."

Jane bid them all farewell and left the shop. She was just crossing the street back to The Bell when Jack Gander walked through the tall coach archway, stretching his legs, she guessed, while the ostlers changed the horses. He braced his hands on his hips and leaned back with a grimace of pain.

"Morning, Jack. Are you all right?"

Another grimace. "Weary of being on the road, truth be told. Especially this year, with all the foul weather we've had. Spending all day on the back of that coach takes a toll."

Jane had never seen the gregarious Royal Mail guard anything but cheerful. The vulnerability on his handsome face touched her, but a moment later it vanished behind one of his mischievous grins.

"But don't tell the coachman I said so. He'll call me a mollycoddled milksop."

She returned his grin. "Your secret is safe with me, Jack. Is there anything I can do to help?"

"Not unless you can control the weather." He winked. "No, I'm all right, Mrs. Bell. Helps just talking to you."

"Any time, Jack."

Something caught Jack's attention across the street. "Who is that?"

Jane turned to look, and saw Victorine standing before her shop, bidding farewell to the Miss Groves, then pausing to greet Mrs. Snyder.

"That is our new dressmaker, Madame Victorine."

His brow furrowed. "I have seen her somewhere before."

"Do you know, I had that same feeling when I first met her. I've decided she must just remind me of someone."

He shook his head. "I have seen her. I know it. A man doesn't forget a beautiful woman like that. Where is she from, do you know?"

"She mentioned she was born in France but has lived in England for many years."

"Where did she live before coming here?"

"She didn't say. Apparently, she has lived in many places. Perhaps you have seen her on your route somewhere."

"I suppose, but it is going to bother me until I figure it out."

"You could simply ask her, you know."

He looked at her, brows quirked. "I always knew you were a clever woman, Mrs. Bell. I believe I shall take your advice. But right now—duty calls." He doffed his hat. "The mail must not be delayed."

CHAPTER
FOURTEEN

The eve of their departure, Mercy packed her better dresses and helped Aunt Matty pack hers, along with the new gown from Victorine's.

At the appointed time the following day, they met up with Jane at The Bell's booking desk, where Colin McFarland helped them purchase seats for London.

He glanced at Mercy and teased, "Look sharp. Teacher on the premises. Heaven help me figure her change correctly."

Mercy gave him a grin and assessed the coins on the counter. "Perfect. You have come a long way, Colin. I'm proud of you."

"Thank you. You ladies have a pleasant journey now. Don't you worry, Mrs. Bell, I shall send for Thora if any problems arise."

"Very good, Colin. And don't forget the brewer's bill is due today."

"Oh. Right." Colin headed for the office.

When Aunt Matty stepped to the side door to keep watch for their coach, Mercy whispered to Jane, "Are you worried about leaving The Bell, with Patrick living in Wishford now? I hope Colin is up to the challenge."

"Colin has improved, as you see. And Thora has offered to help out as needed while we're away."

"Good, then you can relax and enjoy yourself."

Jane smirked. "I can try."

After a tedious, jarring journey made more pleasant by conversation between friends, they arrived in the city. Reaching the Mayfair townhouse, they were greeted warmly by Mercy's parents and shown to their rooms. Even Jane was made to feel very welcome.

"What a delightful time we shall have," said Mrs. Grove. "It has been too long since we've all enjoyed the season together. We shall go to the theatre and a concert. And we have been invited to several parties at the homes of old friends."

Mercy pressed her eyes closed and asked, "Mamma, please tell me you haven't any matchmaking schemes in mind?"

"No, my dear. Not a one."

Her father gave her a significant look and nodded his agreement.

Apparently her mother was in earnest, for they attended the parties over the next few days, and there was not a single suitor in sight.

After a concert the third night, Mercy and Jane sat on the bed together in their nightclothes and curling papers. It was as if they were girls again, spending the night at one of their houses, sharing biscuits sneaked from the kitchen and staying up too late talking. If only Rachel might have joined them, but she was Lady Brockwell now, and soon Jane would be married too. Their lives were changing. Though in Mercy's case, it seemed, not for the better.

"I am relieved, of course," Mercy said. "Though at the same time, it is slightly depressing to realize that even my mother has given up on me and is resigned to leave me on the shelf." She gave a self-abasing chuckle and popped the last butter biscuit into her mouth. "You have to fit into a wedding dress. I don't."

The next day, Jane and Mercy joined her mother for tea and conversation over several new ladies magazines. Her father was out at his club, and Aunt Matty was enjoying an afternoon nap.

Jane said, "The alto last night was wonderful. Thank you for including me."

Mercy nodded. "Yes, thank you, Mamma. The whole visit has been lovely."

Her mother replied, "Of course I was happy for you to visit, but truth be told, it was Helena's idea."

Mercy blinked in surprise. "Oh?"

Her mother nodded and turned to another page of fashion plates. "She wrote to hint that such an invitation would be a great personal favor to her. Apparently, she longed for some time alone with George in their new home. I am only sorry I did not think of it myself."

Mercy noticed Jane's sympathetic look, but said evenly, "I suppose I can't blame her, though after their long wedding trip and time with all her relatives, I had hoped that having Matty and me in residence would not be too much of an imposition."

"Now, Mercy, she didn't say you were an imposition. Although I remember the early days of my married life, and it was a little uncomfortable having my sister-in-law at every meal. But we grew accustomed to each other, and so shall you. And hopefully there will be a child or two soon, which will give you something to distract yourselves. You can help Helena with the children as Matilda helped me. It did a great deal to improve our relationship."

"Yes, Aunt Matty said something similar. I shall keep that in mind."

"There, you see?" Her mother blithely turned another page without looking up. Would she even have noticed Mercy's despondent expression if she had?

When they were alone, Jane pressed her hand. "Are you all right?"

Mercy sighed. "Yes. And truly, I cannot blame Helena. For I confess it is a relief to be out of her company for a time. Having to be polite and tread carefully, to constantly guard my tongue. Never to feel perfectly at ease. I should not be offended that she feels something of the same. And I have the benefit of friends and neighbors to distract me. She does not even have that. I should try harder to be more kind and accepting."

Jane slowly shook her head. "Mercy Grove, you are one of the kindest people I know. Hopefully Helena will come to realize that as well."

On their last night they prepared to attend the theatre. Jane had a final fitting on her dress scheduled for the next morning, and then they would begin packing for the trip home.

As Mercy dressed, her mother surprised her by saying, "You know you may stay longer, if you wish. Your father and I have quite enjoyed the company."

"Thank you, Mamma. We have enjoyed our time here too. But Jane must get back. And I miss my neighbors and snug Ivy Hill, where I know each winding lane and bend in the brook like the lines of my own palm."

"I shall never understand how you can prefer tiny Ivy Hill to the great city of London, but"—she raised an expressive hand—"to each her own. Do promise to visit again, won't you?"

"I shall."

During the intermission at that night's performance, Mercy, Jane, and Matilda left their seats in the overly warm box and ventured into the crowded hall, hoping for a breath of fresh air.

A woman wearing a nearly identical blue-and-gold dress stopped to stare at Matilda. After a moment, she spoke. "Madame Roland admitted she'd made another gown like mine, but assured me it was bound for France. She promised me mine would be the only one like it in all of London. Apparently I was deceived."

Matty chuckled awkwardly. "I am not acquainted with anyone by that name. I purchased this dress from a Madame Victorine in Wiltshire."

"Really?" The woman raised a skeptical brow.

Mercy regarded the woman uneasily and added her assurance, "Yes, truly. I was with her at the time."

The woman studied Matty's bodice. One bony finger touched a sleeve. "Dupioni silk, I believe. With muslin lining?"

"I . . . believe so," Matty replied. "I did not look that closely."

"Yours has an extra flounce."

Her aunt looked down at the skirt. "Yes. I rather like it."

The woman's beady eyes sparked with ire, and for a moment Mercy feared she would yank the gown's neckline to look for an identifying mark. But then the woman seemed to notice the curious looks they were drawing from passersby.

She said, "Well. What a remarkable . . . coincidence. I shall have to speak with Madame Roland and see what she has to say about it. Good evening."

With that, she turned on her heel, stalked away, and was soon swallowed up by the milling crowd.

"Well, that was strange," Mercy said.

Matilda watched her go. "Yes . . ."

Jane spoke up. "The second act is soon to begin, so we had better return to our seats."

As they walked back, Mercy whispered, "What do you think, Jane? You don't suppose Victorine is selling another dressmaker's gowns, do you? Or secondhand gowns?"

Jane whispered back, "I wouldn't think so. Though I recently read in the newspaper about a lady's maid who sold her mistress's clothes for profit and was transported for her crimes."

"Stolen gowns?" Mercy looked at her askance. "Surely not. At least I hope not."

Jane said, "You're right. Magazines are full of fashion plates of the latest French gowns, and no doubt many dressmakers copy them in their shops. I did the same myself once. I took a fashion plate to Mrs. Shabner and asked her to make the gown pictured—to disappointing results, I can tell you. I'm sure that's all this is. A case of similar gowns made from the same pattern. A coincidence, as the woman said."

Mercy winced. "I have never been a big believer in coincidences, Jane."

Jane sighed. "Nor I."

"What should we do?"

"We don't want to accuse anyone on such flimsy evidence. But perhaps we ought to mention it to Victorine when we get home and see how she reacts?"

Mercy nodded. "I'll talk to Aunt Matty. See what she wants to do."

Jane had enjoyed the rare trip to London and time away with her dear friend, but she'd missed Gabriel terribly and worried about him during her absence. She had smiled through the parties, performances, and fittings, but as the days passed, she had begun to almost wish she had insisted on shopping in much nearer Salisbury instead.

Finally, they returned to Ivy Hill with bandboxes, glove boxes, and sundry parcels in hand, and the gown to be delivered a fortnight later. Jane remained at The Bell long enough to stow her purchases, greet the staff, and make sure there were no pressing matters to attend to, but then she rode Athena out to Lane's farm.

It was after five when she arrived, so she expected Susie and Mrs. Mullins might have left for the day. But she assumed Sadie or someone else would be there.

Jane knocked softly, in case Gabriel was resting. When no one came to the door, she tried the latch and found it unlocked, then remembered Gabriel saying he never locked his door. She quietly eased it open and let herself in, wondering where everyone was. Perhaps Sadie had not heard her knock. Jane tiptoed down the passage to the master bedchamber and found the door open. Inside she saw Gabriel lying atop the bedclothes, dressed in his shirtsleeves, lap rug over his legs, but otherwise much as she'd last seen him, a book open over his chest, eyes closed.

For a moment she simply relished the sight of him. The thick hair falling over his brow. The fan of dark lashes against his cheeks, already shadowed with whiskers this late in the day. The rise and fall of his broad chest.

She slipped inside, quietly crossed the room, and leaned over the bed, her fingers itching to touch him. Reaching out, she brushed the hair from his forehead.

His eyes opened. "Jane," he said, voice groggy from sleep. "I must have drifted off. Only meant to rest a bit."

"I don't like finding you alone. Where are Susie, Sadie, and Mrs. Mullins?"

"Susie has gone to her family's for the evening. Sadie as well. Mrs. Mullins was here earlier but was needed at home."

"But *you* need help, stuck in bed as you are. I hope you haven't been left alone for long?" She sat on the corner of the counterpane. "I realize it isn't perfectly proper for me to be in your bedroom with no one else in the house. But in your current state, I suppose it's all right."

One black brow rose. "And what current state is that?"

"I only meant that you're harmless now. No one would think you were going to carry me off in your arms as you are. You are still a patient, after all."

"No one would think that, would they?" he said, a dangerous glint in his eye. He pushed himself up into a sitting position, pulled her close, and kissed her.

Not so harmless after all.

When he released her, Jane rose a bit breathlessly. "Well, I . . . guess you're feeling better." She smoothed her mussed skirts. "May I bring you anything? Tea or something to eat?"

"I am not . . . Actually, yes. Thank you. A glass of water would be welcome."

She smiled. "I'll be right back."

Jane went to the kitchen, filled two glasses from the pitcher, then returned to the room. A few feet inside the door, she drew up short, water sloshing from the glasses. The bed was empty.

A creek of floorboards brought her head around. What she saw caused her to whirl full about, sloshing more water onto the floor.

There stood Gabriel, fully dressed except for shoes, standing on his own power.

"Gabriel!"

He gave her a lopsided grin. "Welcome home, Jane."

"But . . . ! How . . . ? When?" With trembling hands, she set the water glasses on the bedside table.

"Sensation began to return the day you left, but I didn't mention it. I didn't want to raise your hopes or mine. But Dr. Burton and Mrs. Mullins have been working with me to help me regain strength. I wanted to surprise you."

"You did!"

"The doctor still wants me to take it easy. To rest every day—which is what I was doing when you came in."

"You might have said so straightaway."

He sheepishly rubbed the back of his neck. "I . . . thought it best to put on trousers first. Besides, it's more fun to show than tell."

He picked up a walking stick and gingerly took a few steps toward her. "Still a little weak but getting stronger every day."

Jane clasped her hands and pressed them to her lips, tears of joy heating her eyes. *Thank you, God!*

Gabriel held out his arms, and she walked into them. They held each other close in a long, warm embrace.

Welcome home, indeed.

That night Jane slept fitfully and dreamt of her father. In the dream, she was stunned to learn that he had been living alone and forgotten in dilapidated Fairmont House all these years, and not in India as she'd thought. The house was falling down around him, but still he sat there amidst the rubble, alone.

Gabriel discovered the truth and glared at her. "He's been alive all these years and you never told me? Never visited?"

Remorse swamped her. "I'm sorry!"

Jane awoke, breathing hard, the apology on her lips. How relieved she was to find it had only been a dream. Even so, the dread of it clung to her like acrid smoke.

Then she recalled Gabriel's recovery and their happy reunion of the evening before, and the dread began to dissipate. She rose, dressed in her riding habit, and rode back to the farm to see him.

He sat in his office drinking coffee and perusing an auction bill when she arrived, but he rose gingerly when she entered, surprised and pleased to see her again so soon.

She stepped into his embrace. "I just had to make sure last night was not a dream."

"I know exactly what you mean." He nuzzled her cheek and neck, enveloping her in the tangy smells of shaving soap, coffee, and cinnamon. He whispered, "I had the strangest dream that you finally agreed to marry me. Better kiss me, or I'll never believe it's true."

She chuckled and raised on tiptoes to kiss him.

A short while later, Jane rode back to The Bell, filled with joy over Gabriel's love and warmed by his kisses. But as she groomed Athena in the stables, she found her thoughts returning to Gabriel's earlier admonition that she needed to forgive her father and write to him again. She was not sure about the first, but after her horrid dream, she decided she would at least write to him to share the good news of her engagement.

On her way to the office for pen and paper, Jane passed the coffee room and jerked to an abrupt halt.

Mercy and her aunt were sitting at one of the tables. Matilda Grove leaned forward, all animation, laughing and talking to a man with tan, leathery skin, silver-and-brown hair, and a startlingly familiar profile. Her stomach lurched. *Papa . . . ?*

Surely the man only resembled her father. Jane had been thinking of him just moments before, so he was in her thoughts and evidently was now appearing in her imagination.

"You look the same as ever, Matilda," the man said in a voice that stole Jane's breath.

"Then you've lost your eyesight, Win. And you are as brown as a berry, except for your hair. My goodness—we've both gone and got old."

"I own that charge, but you should not. You are a sight for these poor sunburned eyes, I can tell you."

As Jane stood there, stricken into stillness, Mercy glanced up and noticed her there. Her smile fell away. She looked concerned, almost guilty. "Here is Jane."

The man turned to glance over his shoulder, and Jane's heart hitched. The eyes in that tanned face were as familiar to her as her own.

Her father's expression transformed from tentative pleasure to wariness. He might very well wonder about her reception after their parting, almost nine years ago now.

"Jane." The single syllable sounded like a question and an answered prayer rolled into one.

He rose and turned to her. And for a moment they stood like that, a few yards apart.

Miss Matty's voice broke the awkward silence. "Can you believe it, Jane? There were Mercy and I walking along the High Street, and whom should we see? The nabob himself, back from India at last."

"We were only keeping him company until you returned, Jane," Mercy added gently.

Matilda's eyes sparkled as she looked at Winston Fairmont. "Don't just stand there, Win. That's not a proper greeting. Go on and kiss your daughter. Don't hesitate on our account." She gave his arm a little nudge.

He stepped forward and, when Jane didn't pull away, pressed a kiss to her forehead.

Mercy stood and turned to her aunt, sending her a significant look. "Come, Aunt Matty. Let us leave these two to their reunion."

"Oh, very well." Matilda rose. "But you must promise to visit us at Ivy Cottage while you're here, Win. How long do you plan to stay?"

"My . . . plans are not yet definite. But I will pay a call soon."

Matilda beamed at him. "We shall hold you to it!" She paused to put on her bonnet, but Mercy took her arm and led her from the room, murmuring something about a mirror in the hall she could use.

Dear Mercy. Mercy understood.

When the Miss Groves had left them, Jane sat down and gestured for her father to reclaim his seat.

"I am astonished," she began. "I thought to never see you again."

"Did you not receive my reply to your letter?"

Jane shook her head.

"Apparently I reached Ivy Hill before it did." He sighed. "I was surprised to receive a letter from you at last and should have guessed it contained bad news. I was sorry to hear about your husband, Jane. It is why I am here. At least in part."

"Thank you. But as I wrote, I am well. I never intended that my letter should force you to travel all this way." Jane looked around the empty coffee room. "Is your . . . wife . . . not with you?"

He grimaced. "No. I'm afraid not. She died in September."

Her gaze flew to his. "Oh, Papa. I am sorry."

"Are you?"

"Of course. I would never wish her any harm."

"Although you were angry with me for marrying her."

"I *was* angry with you, yes. For many things." Jane felt her defenses rising. "But that was a long time ago."

He flinched. "It sounds as if you are still angry."

"Can you not understand? That you still esteemed and longed for another woman, after all those years married to Mamma . . . It seemed like a betrayal."

"Yes, I always remembered Rani fondly. And a mutual friend mentioned her in his letters from time to time, so I knew she had not married. When your mother died, I thought I might have a second chance at happiness."

"Logical or not, it felt like you abandoned me. Abandoned us all. Selling everything without notice and with no intention of returning."

"I waited until you married, Jane," he said gently, "until you were settled."

"I know you did. It seemed as if you were glad to have me off your hands."

"I thought you were happy with John. Was it so wrong for me to wish to be happy as well?"

When she did not answer, he leaned across the table and touched her arm. "I am sorry, Jane. But after your mother's drawn-out illness and death, I wanted to escape the pressing grief—be anywhere but here."

Jane clenched her hands in her lap. "And were you happy in India?"

"I was, yes. Eventually. Rani's family was against the match, insisted she needed to marry one of her own countrymen. Finally they agreed, though reluctantly. We had several happy years together, thank God. I only wish it could have been more."

Noticing Bobbin return with bottles from the cellar, Jane lowered her voice. "How did she die?"

With a glance at the barman, her father grimaced. "Cholera. But that is not a conversation for a public coffee room."

"I am sorry." Her poor father had lost two wives, Jane realized, her heart beginning to thaw toward him.

They sat in silence for several moments, then Jane changed the subject. "Have you just arrived?"

"Yes. Reached the coast a few days ago and arrived in Wiltshire yesterday."

"You must be exhausted. I hope you were not thinking of staying in Fairmont House?"

"Of course not. I sold that years ago. Why? Is it empty?"

"No. It is a hotel. So, actually, you probably could stay there, if you wished."

His face slackened. "A hotel? How did that come about?"

"The admiral you sold it to died soon after you left, and his heir put it up for sale. It never sold, until a hotelier bought it recently."

"You can't have liked that."

"No. But at least the new owner is a kind and helpful person. Though I admit seeing all the changes stung."

"I can only imagine. What do they call it?"

"The Fairmont."

"You don't say. . . . Never dreamed of having a hotel named after me."

"But you can stay here in The Bell, if you like."

"Thank you, Jane, but I have already taken rooms in Wilton."

"Have you? Why?"

"I did not wish to presume. Or be a burden."

"You would not have been." Did she truly mean that? She hoped so. "Well, then . . . I see you've had tea, but you must be hungry from your journey."

"I long for good English food, I don't deny."

Jane smiled. "That we have. And plenty of it."

He rose. "But tomorrow, Jane, if that's all right. The morning grows late, and I should catch the stage back."

"Are you sure? You could quit your rooms in Wilton and stay here, you know."

"I am . . . content where I am for now. But perhaps later. Thank you, Jane. I shall see you tomorrow." He reached toward her, hesitated, and let his hand fall back to his side.

After her father left, Jane saddled Athena for the second time that day, eager to tell Gabriel the astounding news of her father's return. As she rode back out to the farm, she realized she'd completely forgotten to mention their engagement, so stunned she'd been to see him. She would tell her father the next day, she decided, and bring him out to meet Gabriel as soon as she could.

After Mercy and Matilda returned from London, George and Helena welcomed them warmly and treated them more cordially than before. Mercy began to think she had been wrong to feel herself unwanted.

But at dinner the next evening, her misgivings returned.

It was only the three of them at the table. Matilda had been invited to spend the evening with the Miss Cooks, who were eager to hear about her time in London.

"I have had a letter from my parents," Helena began. "They are coming to visit. Of course they will need a place to sleep."

"They may use my parents' room," George replied.

"But did you not tell me, Mr. Grove, that your parents' bedchamber is sacrosanct?"

"Well . . . I think we may justly put your parents in that bedchamber when they come. I shall simply write to Mamma and Papa and ask them not to visit at the same time."

"There are also my younger brother and sister to consider. We cannot ask them to share a room. They are not children any longer."

George sawed his roast, unperturbed. "Lydia may have my old room now that Miss Ashford . . . that is, Lady Brockwell, has moved out. And Alistair is a strapping boy of—what—fourteen now? The old governess's room in the attic shall serve him well, I imagine. He'll clamber up all those stairs without trouble. Probably like being far away from the adults."

"But, my love, the housemaid keeps a room up there, as does my lady's maid."

"Why yes, but at the opposite end of the attic."

"Still, I don't know that it would be proper to put a guest with servants."

Mercy resolutely set down fork and knife. "Don't trouble yourself, Helena. I shall move my things upstairs."

Helena tipped a pert chin in her direction. "I was thinking your dear Aunt Matilda might like the solitude, but if you prefer it . . ."

"That would be a great many stairs for Aunt Matty, but I am young and strong."

Helena said, "Relatively speaking, of course."

George frowned. "Mercy, no. That room has been yours for as long as I can remember. My dear, we cannot put Mercy out of her own room."

"No one is forcing her! She volunteered, quite graciously. Thank you, Mercy."

For a moment, George held his wife's gaze, mouth tight. But whatever he saw in her icy eyes dissolved his objections. "Well, then. Yes, thank you, Mercy," he echoed with an apologetic smile. "And it's only temporary. I am sure they don't mean to stay more than a week or so."

"True." Helena nodded. "The arrangement will ease my mind about this particular visit. But when our own children arrive . . ." Her words trailed away on a vague little gesture of her pale hand.

George said, "The old nursery upstairs has become little more than a storage room, but it could with some alteration be made up into a fine nursery again. It is where I slept as a child, after all, until I was breeched and given my own room on this floor."

"Our beloved infant so far away from its mother? I could not abide it, Mr. Grove."

George rose, stepping to the decanter to pour himself a glass of port. He murmured, "You may change your mind when said infant cries its lungs out at three in the morning."

"What was that?"

"Not a thing, my love. You know best." With a wink at Mercy, he returned to the table, where he bent and kissed his wife's forehead.

Helena's brow remained furrowed. "You realize, my dear, that with an event like a christening, both sets of parents will want to attend, and then where shall we put everyone?"

George said mildly, "Shall we not wait and cross that bridge when the blessed event arrives, my love?"

"I am only thinking ahead." Helena chuckled, but it sounded derisive in Mercy's ears. "It sometimes seems that I must do the thinking for the both of us."

George frowned again. "That was uncalled for, my dear."

"I only mean it is difficult for you to see the situation clearly, being so entrenched in the past and how things have always been in Ivy Cottage. Far easier for a newcomer to have a clear perspective on the future. You do see that, I trust?"

She bestowed on him her most charming smile, and it worked its magic.

George's chest puffed out with pride. "What I see is a beautiful woman, and clever in the bargain." He grinned at Mercy. "Am I not blessed, sister, in my choice of wife?"

Mercy obliged with a nod. "Yes."

"It is a pity you have missed the blessing of matrimony, Mercy," Helena said, not unkindly.

Again Mercy nodded, but made no reply.

The next day, Jane's father returned to The Bell as promised, driving a hired fly from Wilton. Over an early dinner of pea soup, roast, and spring salad, he looked around the busy coffee room and said, "I suppose John's family stepped in to keep the place going after he passed?"

"They have helped, yes. Thora has recently married, as has John's brother, so they are busy with their own homes now. Thora and her husband stop by regularly and help out during busy times. But John left the inn to me, Papa. I am an innkeeper, if you can believe it. I hope that is not too shocking."

"Surprising, yes. But surely you have a manager who does the actual work?"

"We all share the work. I do employ a clerk who is learning and coming along well. Perhaps in time, he might step into a manager's role."

He slowly shook his head. "My goodness. My daughter, land-lady of a coaching inn."

She nodded. "By the way, Papa. The settlement you arranged for me helped a great deal after John died." She did not explain the loan, the gambling, the debts. "I know I mentioned it in my letter, but again, thank you for making sure I had some security, should the worse happen. As it did."

"It was the least I could do. I am glad it was helpful."

Jane hesitated, then asked, "When you left, Papa, did you tell anyone else of your plans to remarry? I didn't know what you had told people, or if you had left me in the awkward position of doing so. I am embarrassed to say I took to mentioning you as little as possible. In fact, at least one newcomer to Ivy Hill has assumed both of my parents were dead, and I did not correct them."

He ruefully shook his head. "I told almost no one of the par-ticulars of my decision to return to India. Thought it would cause less talk that way. I confided in Alfred Coine, my lawyer. And my old friend Sir William. Sorry to learn he died, by the way."

He considered, then added, "Jane, I know I could have handled things better, but please try to understand. Had my elder brother not died, leaving me heir, I would have remained in India the first time I lived there. Rani was just a girl when I met her. But I planned to wait a few years and marry her then. Instead, when my brother died so young, my parents begged me to return. How could I refuse my grief-stricken mother and father? Once here, I was persuaded to remain."

"Was Mamma always second choice? Did you even love her?" Jane wondered if he had wished all along he was back in India with Rani, raising a family with *her*.

His face fell. "Need you really ask that, Jane? You who saw us day in and day out?"

Jane lowered her head. "You can't blame me for wondering." *For wanting reassurance.*

"I came to love your mother too, Jane. You know I did. The fact that I returned to Rani after your mother's death does not negate our marriage. The human heart is more complicated than romance novels would lead you to believe, as you may find out for yourself one day. You can love more than one person in this life. Sometimes you have to. And that is a blessing, especially when a spouse dies young."

Jane could not deny her father's words. She had once loved Timothy. And had come to love John. And now she loved Gabriel with her entire being. Nine years ago, she had been young and idealistic. Fiercely loyal to her mother's memory and so harshly judging. *Oh, God, forgive me.*

"You are right, Papa. I have discovered that for myself. In fact, I am engaged to be married."

His mouth parted. When he hesitated, Jane added quickly, "John has been gone nearly two years. I hope you don't think it wrong of me."

"Of course not. How hypocritical would that make me? I am only surprised. But I am happy for you, Jane. Who is the fortunate man?"

"Mr. Locke. You would not know him. He came here long after you left."

"May I meet him?"

"Of course. I would like that. And he wants to meet you too. Perhaps after our meal?"

Later, after her father had eaten his fill of Mrs. Rooke's cooking, he sat back with a contented sigh.

John's brother, Patrick Bell, strode in and waved to her. "Good afternoon, Jane. Just rode over to pick up a novel for Hetty at the library. Thought I'd stop by and see how you were." His gaze flicked to the man beside her and back again.

Jane said, "Patrick, do you remember my father, Mr. Fairmont?"

Her brother-in-law frowned. "Your father? I thought he was dead."

Jane felt her neck heat.

Patrick grimaced. "Sorry, sir."

"An understandable misapprehension," he replied. "I have been gone a long time."

Jane explained, "My father has been in India these last nine years or so."

"Ah." Patrick nodded. "I have never been to India, sir, but have done a fair amount of traveling myself. I am here to stay now, however. Are you?"

Winston Fairmont hesitated. "That depends."

"Oh? On what?"

He glanced at her, and then away. "Well, of course I must stay long enough to see Jane married. After that, only God knows."

Jane and her father rode out to Lane's Farm together to meet her intended. When they arrived, Gabriel came out of the farmhouse, still supporting his leg with a walking stick.

"Papa, I'd like you to meet Gabriel Locke. Gabriel, this is my father, Winston Fairmont."

"An honor, sir."

"Likewise." Her father's gaze landed on the stick in Gabriel's hand.

Noticing, Gabriel said, "Don't mind this, sir. I am only recovering from a recent accident."

Jane added, "And regaining strength daily, God be praised."

Her father's expression remained sober. "I understand you are engaged to marry my daughter."

"I am, sir, and count myself blessed to be."

"And will you be able to support her?"

"Papa!"

"It's all right, Jane," Gabriel said evenly. "A valid question. We plan to establish a horse farm here together. Raise thoroughbreds, riding horses, and private carriage horses, as well as train and board them. I admit the majority of my funds are tied up in the purchase of stock at present. This injury has been a setback, but I hope in time to be successful."

"Fell from a horse, did you? Doesn't exactly give one confidence."

"Papa . . ." Jane repeated, shifting uncomfortably. "Gabriel is an excellent horseman. And we don't need a great deal of money."

"But it sure came in handy when your inn was failing."

"True," Jane allowed. "As I said, the settlement you arranged was a godsend."

Her father sent Gabriel a challenging look. "I trust you won't object to another marriage settlement, Mr. Locke?"

In her father's confident posture and profile, Jane saw remnants of the Winston Fairmont of old. Respected gentleman, proud landowner, determined father. She also recalled Gabriel telling her that John had been offended when her father insisted on that first marriage settlement. His pride pricked that Mr. Fairmont assumed a *lowly* innkeeper might not be able to provide for the privileged gentleman's daughter. Now Jane glanced at Gabriel, wondering if he would be offended as well.

For a moment, Gabriel held her gaze, then turned humbly to her father. "No, sir. Though I have every hope of supporting Jane in the manner she deserves."

"Hope is one thing, insurance another." His eyes glinted. "We have to look no further than Thornvale or The Bell to see the truth of that."

"I can't disagree, sir."

Her father's tone softened. "Have you family, Mr. Locke?"

"I have, sir. Parents, uncle, cousins. It would be my pleasure to introduce them to you at the wedding. Assuming, that is, we have your blessing?"

"You do. And I shall look forward to meeting your family on the big day. But for now, I'd like to see more of this farm of yours."

Jane released a relieved breath, and Gabriel smiled. "With pleasure."

CHAPTER
SIXTEEN

The next night, Mercy lay on a narrow bed tucked beneath the eaves of Ivy Cottage's top floor. The small chamber was adjacent to the larger room that had formerly served as her pupils' dormitory and before that the nursery for several generations of Grove children. The narrow bed had been occupied by a series of governesses, some who took advantage of the distant room rarely visited by parents to neglect their duties, and one to exact harsh punishments. Finally, there had arrived Miss Dockery, who was everything good and caring. Mercy would have liked to keep her forever, but eventually her father replaced the young woman with a tutor in the hopes of preparing George for university. At least he had allowed Mercy to be educated alongside her brother, and in many ways, in spite of her non-scholarly sibling.

Now here she was, the former mistress of the Ivy Cottage Girls School, relegated to this small, drafty room, far from the family, sleeping in a chamber meant for a governess but with none of the benefits of actually being one—no pupil to teach, no wages, no position of respect. She recalled the momentary affront she had felt when Mr. Drake mentioned he'd considered asking her to be a governess. The irony washed over her. She had never thought herself vain, but was this God's way of humbling her even further?

Or was it a sign?

She pushed away a kernel of bitterness and forced herself up and onto her knees beside the small bed. With her body in the posture of submission, she surrendered her heart as well.

The next time Rachel came to The Bell for coffee, she told Jane about an upcoming house party she was hosting.

"We have sent invitations to several single people near Justina's age, including Richard, the Awdrys, the Bingleys, and Nicholas Ashford."

Realization flashed through Jane. "Ahhh . . . I recall you mentioning Justina's reluctance where Sir Cyril is concerned. Are you doing a little matchmaking of your own?"

"Perhaps. Though you shall not hear me admit that to Lady Barbara." Rachel's eyes sparkled with mischief. "Just trying to be a good sister to Justina, you know. And everyone has replied in the affirmative, except for Richard. He sent a few lines to his mother, and some flimsy excuse about an important meeting at his club. Lady Barbara sighed and said it was as she expected, but I could tell she was disappointed. My heart goes out to her. How sad to have a son disconnected from the rest of the family. It is little wonder Lady Barbara is so attached to Sir Timothy. It makes me appreciate my thoughtful husband all the more."

Jane nodded her understanding. "What do you have planned for the party?"

Rachel described the activities—archery and shooting and hopefully a dance. "That reminds me. May we hire The Bell musicians for one evening? That way none of the women will have to play instead of dance."

"Yes, assuming it is not our busiest night, and the men are willing."

"We will pay them well, of course."

Jane smirked. "Then they will definitely be willing."

After discussing the details of the party, Jane told Rachel about her father's surprising return.

"Oh, Jane, how wonderful! And in time for your wedding. I cannot believe you let me prattle on about an inconsequential party when you had such news to share!" Rachel leaned close and embraced her.

The two talked a while longer, and then Rachel took her leave. Jane returned to the paperwork awaiting her in the office.

Later, while Jane sat writing orders at the desk, her father appeared in the office doorway. "Jane? Sorry to disturb you." His gaze traveled over the paper-strewn desk. "You look busy. Never mind."

"Not too busy for you, Papa. I am glad to see you again."

"Thank you. I have asked Matilda to meet me here for coffee. But she won't be arriving for a few minutes. Could you join me for a bit?"

"Of course." Jane put her quill back into its holder and rose.

The two sat in the coffee room and talked of generalities, their conversation at first a little stilted. Grasping for a topic, Jane told him about her struggles to save the inn and acquire a license in her own name. "Your old friend Lord Winspear gave me rather a hard time, but he acquiesced in the end."

"Dear old Winspear. Always did like to be difficult. Still, a good man deep down. I shall have to visit him while I'm here."

Jane nodded, and another awkward silence stretched.

She knew she should ask more about his wife, show some interest. Doing so made her uncomfortable, but she reminded herself that the woman had been very important to her father—as important as Gabriel was to her.

She swallowed and asked, "You and Rani were not blessed with children?"

He pursed his lips. "She was late in her childbearing years, so we knew it unlikely from the outset."

"I see."

He swirled his fingertip in the salt cellar. "How would that have made you feel, Jane? If I had written to tell you we'd had a child?"

"I am not sure. How strange to imagine a half brother or sister half a world away."

"Considering how you felt about my marriage, I assumed you would feel resentful. Would you spurn a child of a union you disapproved?"

"How shrewish you make me sound! I suppose I would have felt a whole flurry of emotions, truth be told. But how could I hold any negative feelings toward an innocent child?"

He watched her carefully but did not look convinced.

Matilda Grove entered the coffee room, and her father stood. "Miss Matilda, thank you for coming. Sit with me and tell me everything I have missed in all these years."

"That could take all day!"

His expression and voice softened. "Yes, I hope it does."

"And that is my cue to get back to work." Jane rose to let the two old friends talk in private.

Matilda gently grasped Jane's arm as she passed, forestalling her exit. She drew near and whispered, "Are you terribly busy?"

The woman's troubled eyes sent needles of alarm through Jane. "What is it, Miss Matty?"

The older woman hesitated. "I just thought you might, em, stop by Ivy Cottage when you have a spare minute and visit Mercy."

"Is something wrong?"

"I . . . just think she could use a friend right about now. I had already promised to meet your father today, or—"

"Of course I will go." Jane laid her hand over Matilda's. "You know I am always happy to see Mercy." And at the moment, curious to see her and a little worried as well.

After putting on a bonnet and slipping a long-sleeved spencer over her dress, Jane walked directly to Ivy Cottage.

When she knocked, Mr. Basu came to the door to let her in, and Helena Grove stepped out of the drawing room to see who had come to call.

They had met briefly at church, but knowing the woman had met many new people, Jane introduced herself again, adding, "I am a friend of Mercy's. Is she at home?"

"Yes, I believe she is upstairs in her room."

Jane nodded. "Then I shall just pop up, if you don't mind."

Helena gestured her assent, and Jane started toward the stairs.

"Oh, you won't find her in her old room," Mrs. Grove called after her. "She has taken a different room on the top floor."

Jane turned back, brow furrowed. "Oh? Why?"

Helena smiled. "Why, to make room for our expanding family."

"I . . . see. Are you and Mr. Grove to be congratulated?"

"Not yet. But I do like to be prepared. And my parents, brother, and sister will soon pay a visit. Mercy was so kind in offering up her old room. Between you and me, I think she prefers it up there. So much more solitude, which bookish people seem to like, don't they?"

"I . . . wouldn't know," Jane murmured. She turned and continued up the stairs, concern for her friend fueling her steps.

Reaching the attic floor, Jane walked down the passage, looking into open rooms. She found Mercy sitting atop a narrow, neatly made bed, dressed and wearing a wool shawl, reading a book.

Jane knocked on the doorframe. "Mercy?"

She lifted her head, eyes wide. "Jane! What a surprise to see you up here."

"I could say the same of you."

"Oh, I don't mind. Not really. I almost feel closer to my former pupils here. Feel sorry for them too. I never realized how drafty it was."

Jane sat on the edge of the bed. "Are you sure you're all right? Your aunt is concerned about you. But when I arrived, your sister-in-law told me you prefer it up here, as 'bookish people like solitude.'" Jane smirked.

"Good heavens. She'll paint me a hermit in my lonely tower."

"An exaggeration, I'm guessing?"

Mercy shrugged. "I truly don't mind, Jane. Except . . . the stairs are a bit hard on Aunt Matty. We were so accustomed to being across the corridor from one another, borrowing this or that, helping each other with fastenings or pins. Ah well, I am taking more exercise, going down to her and back up again, and that is not all bad."

Jane studied her. "You needn't pretend with me, you know."

"I know." Mercy nibbled her lip. "Jane, may I ask you something in confidence?"

"Of course."

"Tell me honestly. If I were to become, say, a governess, would you think less of me?"

"Of course not. Did you think less of me when I became an innkeeper?"

"Not at all. I admired you for it. But we can't pretend it didn't cost you something in terms of social position and friendships."

"True. Marrying John strained—even broke—some relationships. With Rachel, Sir Timothy, Lord Winspear, the Bingleys. . . . But never with you, Mercy. And thankfully, relationships with many of my old friends have been restored."

"Was it worth it?"

"Yes, I think so. But, Mercy, this is different. I married into innkeeping. Becoming a governess . . . that's a single state."

"Which I am resigned to."

"Are you?" Jane sent her a challenging look. Mercy lowered her eyes.

Jane considered and then said, "I always assumed gentlewomen who became governesses did so when they had no other choice—as a way to keep body and soul together."

"My family is not insisting I earn my own bread, if that's what you mean. I have little money of my own, but I will not starve."

"After managing your own school, I can completely understand your desire for some independence and an income of your own, the ability to purchase what you need without having to ask your brother or father for every penny."

Mercy nodded. "Yes."

"But a governess's lot is not exactly known for being one of independence or significant means," Jane pointed out. "Would you not be constrained to live in some small remote room like this one, with only a pupil or two for company, taking meals with them or by yourself? Not allowed to befriend either the family or the servants?"

Again Mercy nodded.

Jane asked, "Are you sure it would be an improvement over your current circumstances?"

"No, except . . ." Mercy met her gaze. "The pupil would be Alice."

Jane's mouth parted, and she leaned back, realization dawning. "Ah. . . . I should have guessed. Still, I am surprised Mr. Drake would ask you to take such a position, knowing your background."

"He didn't. He admitted he'd thought of asking me earlier, as a way to ease the sting of losing Alice."

"How did that make you feel?"

"At first, affronted. But that quickly faded. Why should I be offended? Am I not a gentlewoman with no other income? But then Mr. Drake asked me to help him choose a qualified candidate instead."

Jane watched her carefully. "But you want to do it?"

Mercy looked down. "My parents would not approve. And I don't want to leave Aunt Matty."

"What does she say?"

"I haven't discussed it with her yet. Besides, it's probably too late. He has already advertised the position."

Jane took her hand. "I can't tell you what to do, but I know your aunt wouldn't want you to remain in an unhappy situation for her sake. If I were not getting married, I would invite you to come and live with me, but—"

"Oh, Jane. Don't let me spoil your happiness. You are about to marry a wonderful man and raise horses together. It's perfect for you. God is good."

Tears blurred Jane's vision. "I know. I am blessed. But I would be happier if my dearest friend were happy too."

Later that evening, Mercy set aside her book and sat up, almost hitting her head on the low sloped ceiling. She looked out the room's small window, lost in thought. As the sun lowered in the sky, casting shadows across the room, Mercy sat there, perched on the edge of the governess's bed. It was not a bed she had made for herself, nor would have chosen. But perhaps it was time to lie in it. The fading light felt almost tender, and she sensed the nearness of God, calming her fears. *Lord, help me make the right choice.*

Her aunt Matilda's voice interrupted her reverie. "Mercy? What are you doing sitting up here in the dark?"

Mercy glanced over, surprised to see her aunt standing there, candle lamp in hand. She hadn't realized it had grown so late.

"Here, let's light your candle . . ." Matty lifted the glass dome and lit the lamp on Mercy's side table.

Then she sat beside her niece and took her hand. "A penny for your thoughts?"

Mercy told her what Mr. Drake had said and confessed she was contemplating becoming a governess.

"Oh, Mercy, why didn't you tell me straightaway?"

"I didn't want to worry you."

"Too late. I am already worried about you, my dear."

"And I am worried about you, Aunt Matty. I wouldn't want to leave you."

"Oh, my dear. You think a young chit like Helena can keep me low for long? I shared a house with your mother for years and lived to tell the tale." She winked. "Don't you dare stay here for my sake. I would miss you terribly, of course. But it is not like you would be moving to the other side of the world."

"You truly wouldn't mind?"

"Not if you think you would be happier."

Mercy hesitated. "You know my parents wouldn't approve. It would embarrass them."

"Let them be embarrassed. When I think of how you have been embarrassed here. . . . Oh, Mercy. I wish I had the money to set up housekeeping for the two of us somewhere."

"So do I."

"Are you sure you would not prefer to live in London with your parents? They did offer, you know."

"How lonely I would be in London, so far from you and all my friends. Unless you were to come with me?"

"No, my dear. Ivy Hill is my home. I am too old to start over in a big city like London."

"I feel the same. My friends are here. You are here. My heart is here."

Matty patted her hand. "Then do what you think best." She leaned her shoulder into Mercy's. "Are you sure Mr. Drake does not need a baker? Or an old woman to sit at the door and lend elegance to the place?" She grinned.

"You would indeed do so, Aunt Matty."

The humor in her aunt's eyes faded. "My dear . . . one word of caution. You were hard hit when Alice was taken from you. You do know that if you pursue this course, Mr. Drake would be engaging you only temporarily. A governess does not stay forever. Would not teaching and caring for Alice again, day in and day out, make it that much more painful when you must part a second time?"

"I suppose so."

"I know you are stoic, my dear. But it will not only be painful for you, but also for Alice."

"Your point is a valid one. I would be more concerned about Alice, except she is not pining for me any longer. She has clearly become attached to Mr. Drake. And he, in turn, dotes on her. In fact, he plans to make her his heir and change her name to Drake, to be her father in every sense of the word."

"I am glad to hear it. I hope you are glad as well. I know it might be difficult to find yourself replaced in the girl's affections."

"Aunt Matty, I promise you, I am not considering this course to try to win back Alice's heart. I would not do that—to him or to her. But does that mean I must deprive myself the joy of teaching her and being a part of her life for another year or two, or as long as they'll have me?"

"I don't know, my dear. A part of me hates to see you postpone your own life any longer, your chance to marry. To give years to someone else's child—years you won't get back—that might have been spent raising your own children."

"Aunt Matty, you speak as though I have several promising offers of marriage to choose from. You know I already wrote to Mr. Hollander to release him."

"What about Mr. Kingsley?"

Mercy shook her head. "I think he admires another woman. I have seen him with a pretty blonde a few times now. Saw them embrace. And when I asked, he said, 'Esther is more than a friend. She is one of the family.'"

Her aunt's brow furrowed. "One of his brother's wives, perhaps?"

"No, she isn't married. And if you had seen the way he looks at her . . ." Mercy slowly shook her head, sadness lancing her heart.

"Perhaps she is an old family friend or a cousin?" Matilda suggested. "I am sure there is an explanation."

Feeling weary, Mercy sighed. "Perhaps. But even if the woman is merely a friend or relative, I have given Mr. Kingsley every encouragement. And nothing has come of it."

"My dear, knowing how soft-spoken and modest you are, I imagine you were very subtle in expressing your interest."

"I don't know." Mercy shook her head. "But there is no point in waiting or in wishful thinking. His affections clearly lie elsewhere."

Aunt Matty chewed her lip, then offered, "I could ask his mother if—"

"No, please don't. She would guess why you were asking—how embarrassing for us both. And please don't say anything to anyone about what I'm considering doing either. Not yet. I need to talk to Mr. Drake first. He may already have engaged a governess, or may prefer someone less attached to Alice. Nothing may come of it."

"Very well." Aunt Matty took her hand. "Then I will pray for God's will to be done, my dear, whatever it is."

Mercy nodded. "Me too."

CHAPTER

SEVENTEEN

Mercy's heart pounded, and her palms perspired as she sat waiting in Mr. Drake's office the next day. The booking clerk had gone to find him.

The door opened, and James Drake strode in, well-dressed as always. His deep blue frock coat was exquisitely tailored and, paired with his confident posture, made him the picture of a competent gentleman of business. Intimidating as well.

"Miss Grove, what a pleasant surprise. I did not expect you. I hope you have not been waiting long?"

"Not at all."

His green eyes narrowed in concern. "Is everything all right?"

"Yes, I . . ." Mercy swallowed. "I was wondering if you have already engaged a governess for Alice."

He winced and took a chair across from hers. "Not yet. I have received letters from two candidates, but neither seemed promising enough to summon here for a personal interview. I may have to advertise farther afield." He raised a hand. "Never fear. I won't forget my promise to include you in the selection. Nor shall I neglect Alice's education for long."

"I am not worried. Nor did I come to criticize. I have come to ask for the position myself, if you have not changed your mind about my suitability."

He leaned back, brows rising. "Not at all. But . . . I thought we had decided the position was beneath you."

"You decided that. And my family would no doubt agree with you. But I . . . I need to be doing something. Something worthwhile. I miss teaching dreadfully. And I miss Alice, of course. But you mustn't worry that I would try to usurp your role in her life. You would remain her parent, and I only her teacher."

He tucked his chin. "Come, Miss Grove. We both know you feel more for Alice than a mere teacher would, and vice versa. After all, you once cherished the hope of being her guardian. I am not a religious man, as you know, but I thank God that Alice has come to trust me, to care for me. Would it not be painful for you to witness that?"

"I confess initially it stung a little to see Alice shift her affections to you. But that was a selfish, petty reaction on my part, and thankfully short-lived. With all my heart I want Alice to be loved and part of a good family. That is what I see happening between you, and I am sincerely happy for you both. But I will understand if you think it would be too confusing for Alice, or feel it would upset the relationship you have. I would never want to do that."

He studied her a moment, and Mercy barely resisted the urge to squirm. He crossed one leg over the other. "I believe your intentions sincere, Miss Grove. Though you cannot control the outcome, or how Alice will react to your presence."

"That is true. So if you think it not worth the risk, just say so."

He rose. "Excuse me a minute, Miss Grove." He stepped out into the hall, and she heard his muffled call. "Alice? Could you come here, please?"

A moment later, Alice came in, and when her gaze landed on Mercy, her pretty face split into a smile. "Miss Grove! I am so happy to see you."

"And I you."

Mr. Drake asked, "Alice, how would you feel about Miss Grove becoming your governess?"

She whirled to him, mouth open wide. "Truly?"

He nodded.

"I would love nothing better!"

Mercy's heart squeezed, but she kept her tone even. "I should tell you, Alice, that if I become your governess, I shall take my responsibility seriously. I would expect you to study hard and to listen and behave just as you always did in Ivy Cottage. I am not here to be your . . . friend, alone."

"But you will still be my friend, won't you?"

"Of course."

"And you would really come to live here, in the Fairmont with us?"

"That is the idea, yes. At least, temporarily."

"Why only temporary?"

"You shan't need a governess forever. You are growing up. Your fa—Mr. Drake might decide to send you to school one day, or hire a tutor or . . ."

Alice turned to Mr. Drake. "You would not send me away, would you?"

"Only if you wished it. Some young people like to go away to school, you know."

"I shan't."

"You would have more friends. I know you miss your former classmates."

"Yes. But with you and Miss Grove here, I shall be perfectly happy."

"Then it is settled." Mr. Drake looked at Mercy and held her gaze. "That is, if you have not changed your mind?"

"I am more resolved than ever."

Alice beamed. "I must go and tell Johnny!" The girl dashed out of the room, eager to tell the young groom the good news.

Mr. Drake gave her a sheepish smile. "She has all but adopted the lad as one of the family." He partially closed the door Alice had flung wide. "Now, I suppose we must discuss salary and other arrangements. Does forty pounds per annum seem reasonable?"

"Very generous."

"And how soon will you move your things here and begin?"

"I won't need long to pack."

He rubbed his chin as he considered. "Why not give us a week or so to prepare a room for you. It shan't be one of the hotel's finest, I'm afraid."

"I would not expect it. A small room is all I need, either near Alice or up with the servants. And I believe I recall a schoolroom upstairs, from Jane's day?"

He nodded. "Yes, I had planned to fit out the old schoolroom and tidy the room next to it for the governess. But now that I know it is you, I will see what can be done to make it more comfortable."

"You needn't go to any trouble or expense on my account."

"Oh, but I want to. I want you to be as well cared for and content here as Alice was in Ivy Cottage."

Mercy's heart warmed, and her doubts faded. "Thank you, Mr. Drake."

After dinner that night, Mercy and Matilda relaxed in the sitting room, enjoying the evening together—just the two of them. George and Helena were entertaining her parents and siblings in the drawing room. Helena preferred the formal room, while Mercy and Matilda favored the humble sitting room with its cozy but worn upholstery and patched seat cushions, framed needlework samplers on the walls, and a fireplace screen embroidered by Mercy's great-grandmother.

Mercy rose and moved to the desk she had once used for school correspondence. She said, "I suppose I must write to my parents. Any advice in phrasing my decision? I hope they won't forbid me."

Aunt Matty replied, "I've been thinking about that, my dear. Let me write to your father first, remind him of the tension between his wife and sister in the early days of his own marriage. Would he not have preferred a peaceful home and more privacy, especially while still in their honeymoon period?" Matty grinned. "And might a happier daughter-in-law speed the arrival of hoped-for grandchildren?

"I will convince him that your becoming a governess will be worth a small amount of . . . awkwardness. I shall also praise Mr. Drake—how respected and successful and admired he is in the county—and emphasize that he wanted none other than their learned and accomplished daughter to teach his prized ward."

"My goodness, Aunt Matty. People sometimes tease me by saying *I* should have been a reformer or politician, but I could say the same of you."

"And no wonder." Matty winked. "Where do you think you learned it?" She nudged Mercy from the chair and took her place at the desk to write the dreaded letter.

Mercy waited until Helena's family had departed several days later before sharing her news. After dinner, Mercy joined George and Helena in the Ivy Cottage drawing room and announced her plan.

Her brother and his wife stared at her, mouths parted, eyes turned downward in matching expressions of stunned dismay. It might have been comical were Mercy not so nervous.

Mercy had thought Helena might appear exultant to hear she was leaving Ivy Cottage. But she saw no barely suppressed grins or sly looks of triumph exchanged between husband and wife. Mercy guessed, however, the pair's shocked silence had more to do with what Mercy planned to do upon leaving rather than the leaving itself. As their silence stretched, Mercy swallowed a queasy lump of dread. Was she making a mistake?

"My dear sister," Helena finally began, fixing her with an apologetic little smile. "I do hope nothing I have said or done has caused you to think we wished you to leave."

George gave his wife a fond look and patted her hand. "Of course not, my dear."

Uncertainty and guilt lanced Mercy. Had she misjudged Helena?

Her sister-in-law added, "Now, if you had decided to live in London with your dear mama and papa, then of course, we would understand and support your decision. But this . . . ?"

Her brother's brow furrowed. "It does seem a rash course, Mercy."

"Why rash? I miss teaching. I believe it is what God fashioned me to do. And now I have an opportunity to teach one of my favorite former pupils. It is not as though I am moving to some remote and dangerous land as you did, George. Only to the Fairmont."

"That almost makes it worse!" Helena exclaimed. "Everyone will know, and think you are in desperate circumstances. It will reflect poorly on us—and on your parents. They can't have approved of this."

"Aunt Matilda and I have written to them to explain."

Helena threw up her hands. "You are both determined to embarrass us! Mr. Grove, do talk some sense into your sister."

George leaned forward imploringly, elbows on his knees. "Mercy, I realize you may miss your school and the income from it. Helena and I have even discussed doing something for you, an allowance or modest annuity. I am sure if I spoke to Father and explained, he would agree."

"You are all generosity, my dear," Helena said. "And when you write to your father, remind him the household allowance still needs to be increased as well."

Mercy said, "There is no need to ask for more money on my account. With me taking my meals at the Fairmont, there will be one less mouth to feed here, which will help with household expenses." Hoping to dispel the tension, Mercy joked, "The savings in candles alone from all my late-night reading should save you a small fortune!"

Neither of them smiled.

"Mercy, I must ask you to reconsider," George said. "As your only male relative currently present, I think I have some say in the matter."

Irritation flashed. "George, I am one and thirty years old. I have managed a household and school and made my own decisions for more than a decade now. I am also capable of making this decision. I don't make it to hurt or embarrass anyone. I make it because I believe it is the right choice for me at this time in my life. I will be happier, and I think the two of you will be happier as well."

Helena twisted her hands, casting about for another argument. "Mr. Drake is an unmarried man, is he not? What will people say?"

George replied, "I wouldn't worry on that score, my dear. I hear only good reports of Mr. Drake, except perhaps that he isn't much of a churchgoer. I understand the girl is the orphaned daughter of friends of his and he plans to raise her as his own. Nothing untoward in that."

It was what most people thought, and as it was to Alice's benefit, Mercy would not contradict it.

"There is nothing between the two of you, I assume?" her brother asked.

"Of course not," Helena murmured.

Mercy hesitated only a second. "No."

Mr. Drake had been friendly to her, yes, but there was nothing romantic in his behavior toward her.

"What about Aunt Matilda?" George asked. "You would leave her?"

How unfair to bring up her beloved aunt. *Oh, that I could take her with me.*

"I will miss her, of course. But I will see her at church every week. Good heavens, I am only going to the Fairmont!"

Indignation mottled Helena's pale complexion. "If you insist on doing this, I trust you will take full responsibility for your decision and not let anyone believe we drove you to it? For we shall certainly tell everyone you chose this course without our approval or compunction."

"I will," Mercy replied. She had no intention of blaming anyone. What people concluded on their own was beyond her control.

Rachel, Justina, and Lady Barbara returned to Madame Victorine's to see the drawings of the proposed gown. When they arrived, Rachel looked once again at the gowns displayed in the window. As much as she wanted to support their new dressmaker, she had acquired a whole new trousseau just before her wedding and could not justify another dress. She turned to her mother-in-law. "Lady Barbara, this emerald gown would suit you very well. Perhaps for the house party?"

The dowager paused to look at it. "It is lovely, I own. But I have no need of a new dress. You will be the hostess for the party, Rachel."

Rachel studied her face and was relieved to see no resentment in her expression.

When they entered the shop, the dressmaker spread a series of sketches across her worktable. She had drawn not only the gown, but also Justina in it. She included full-length front, back, and side views, as well as inset drawings of some of the details close up, like the bodice, sleeves, and neckline.

"Mamma!" Justina exclaimed. "It looks just like me! Well done, madame. You are quite the artist."

"Thank you. I enjoyed drawing these, but they are merely sketches, to help me better understand what you have in mind and give you options to choose from."

Victorine pushed a page forward. "For example, you mentioned an Anglo-Greek bodice, but I wonder if it will lend an unnatural breadth to the chest. Might this Gallo-Greek bodice be more to your liking? It will accent your slender waist."

"Yes, I see your point. I do like this one."

"And here are the puff sleeves you requested."

"Very nice."

"And a back view . . ."

Lady Barbara lifted her quizzing glass to inspect the drawing of the back of the gown more closely. "I am confused about the detailed drawing here. You propose ties for the waist and bodice closure?"

"Yes. Would not ties be the most convenient? The quickest way to dress and undress?"

"I hope you are not suggesting my daughter will have need to disrobe quickly, madame."

"No! Heavens, no."

"My daughter will have a lady's maid and has no need of ease or convenience when dressing or undressing, I assure you. Old-fashioned lacing, tiny buttons, pins . . . all of these are perfectly appropriate for her station in life."

"Of course, my lady. I do apologize. I will make the necessary adjustments."

The shop door opened, and Mrs. Barton, the dairywoman, entered.

Victorine said, "I shall be with you shortly, Mrs. Barton."

"No hurry; just looking."

On her heels, a second woman entered. Rachel had seen her pointed out in passing and knew she was lady's maid to the new Mrs. Grove.

The maid began speaking to the dressmaker in rapid-fire French. Victorine held up her palm. *"Je regrette, mademoiselle. Pouvez-vous parler plus lentement, s'il vous plaît?"*

Rachel knew enough French to understand the gist of Victorine's request: *I'm sorry. Please speak more slowly.*

The smaller woman threw up her hands. *"J'ai pensé que vous étiez française!"*

I thought you were French!

"Ma mère, oui. Mais je parle rarement français maintenant."

My mother yes, but I rarely speak French now.

"Dommage." The French woman huffed, then switched to ac-cented English. "Too bad. I have zis list from my mistress, Madame George Grove. Stockings and such. I shall leave it with you. You deliver, I trust?"

"Yes, if you like."

The woman turned on her heel and swiftly exited. *"Au revoir."*

When the door closed behind her, Lady Barbara said, "You did not understand that woman?"

Victorine rocked her hand from side to side. "Some. She spoke too quickly. I'm afraid I don't speak French very often anymore, since my mother passed on."

"And your father?"

"An Englishman."

"I did not realize." Lady Barbara frowned. "You are not from France?"

"I was born there but have lived in England most of my life. Is that a problem?"

"I suppose not. Perhaps a disappointment, when one thinks one is viewing fashions popular in Paris, only to learn one's modiste has not been to France in years."

"You are welcome to take your custom elsewhere, my lady, if you like. I will understand completely."

"No, Mamma," Justina interjected. "If I marry, I want Victorine to make my dress."

Lady Barbara looked again at the sketches. "Very well. If she can sew half as well as she draws, it should be a lovely gown."

EIGHTEEN

Mercy and her aunt went to that night's gathering of the Ladies Tea and Knitting Society together. Mercy wasn't sure she would be able to attend meetings once she began working as a governess, so she was determined to enjoy this one.

She considered how best to frame her news. She wanted the women to hear it from her, to see it as a good thing and *not* feel sorry for her. But before she could form the words, Mrs. Barton launched into another topic.

"Such a disappointing discovery. Remember how excited we were to have a French dressmaker in Ivy Hill?"

"Yes . . . ?" Mercy glanced at Jane across the room. Beside her, Aunt Matty dug an elbow into her side. Preoccupied as they had been with Winston Fairmont's return and Mercy's move, they had let the issue of the look-alike gown drop.

Bridget continued, "I happened to be in the shop when your sister-in-law's maid came in. *Hortaahhnse*, something or other. On an errand for her mistress. Well, she tried to converse with the dressmaker in French, but Victorine couldn't make out half of what she said. It turns out she hasn't been to France in years. And her father is a plain old Englishman."

"Yes, I know," Mercy replied. "She told us that weeks ago."

Undeterred, Bridget went on. "We did wonder why she would settle in our little hamlet, and now we have our answer. Probably driven out of some other place as an imposter. *Madame Victorine*, indeed. She likely has no idea what is truly fashionable."

"And you do, Bridget?" Charlotte Cook tartly asked. "I did not realize you were a fashion *connoisseur*. Learned that from your prized cows, did you?"

Mrs. Barton lifted her chin. "If you must know, I am one of the most frequent patrons at the Ashford Circulating Library. I read not only books but all the ladies magazines with their fashion prints as well. I know more than you do, Charlotte Cook, with your lace thirty years out of style."

Charlotte gasped. "You take that back!"

"Lace is classic!" her sister, Judith, protested, face crumpling. "It never goes out of style."

"Your lips to God's ear, Judy," Charlotte breathed, and the two Miss Cooks clasped hands in solidarity.

"Ladies! Ladies," Mercy soothed. "Let us not devolve into insults and arguments. It isn't like us."

Mrs. O'Brien asked, "What has Mrs. Shabner to say about our new dressmaker?"

Matilda spoke up. "I don't believe she has visited the shop, as she didn't want to intrude. But I could ask her to take a look, if it would make everyone feel better about Victorine's skills."

Bridget humphed. "It's not only her skills I'm questioning. She's so secretive-like when you ask her where she came from or anything about her family."

Mrs. Klein nodded and said apologetically, "I'm afraid I agree with Bridget. And she isn't that much more forthcoming when you ask about the dresses in her window. She doesn't seem very familiar with the fabrics used or details of their construction. In fact, I almost don't believe she made them."

"Oh, come now," Becky Morris defended. "If she didn't make them, where did they come from?"

That was the question. Noticing Jane trying to signal her, Mercy interrupted, "Ladies, we are not here to gossip or to judge anyone on hearsay and supposition. Let us give Victorine the benefit of the doubt. Now, moving along, I have some news of my own to share . . ." Mercy went on to announce her new position. The women reacted with a mixture of surprise, pity, and halfhearted congratulations, but at least the topic of Victorine's gowns was forgotten. For the moment, at any rate.

The next morning, Mercy, Jane, and Matilda visited the dress-maker's shop together.

Mercy began, "Good day, Victorine."

"Good day, ladies. I have not seen you since you returned from London. How was your trip?"

"We enjoyed ourselves. And Auntie's gown drew a great deal of notice."

"I am glad to hear it."

With a tentative glance at Mercy, Matilda said, "Yes. In fact, one night at the theatre a woman wore a dress almost exactly like it, even down to the lining. She was most adamant that it had been made by someone named Madame Roland. Although, in the end, she allowed that perhaps it was just a coincidence."

A stillness settled over Victorine, her pupils widening and nos-trils quivering, reminding Mercy of a cornered hare.

Victorine slowly shook her head. "I am not personally acquainted with anyone named Roland."

Jane offered, "Are not many dresses made from the same pattern or fashion plate . . . ? Might that explain the identical dress?"

"I believe so," Victorine murmured. "I never claimed the design originated with me."

For a moment longer, the three of them stood there, hands clasped awkwardly, looking at Victorine. If they expected some revealing confession, they were to be disappointed.

"Was there anything else, ladies?" Victorine opened the door for them. "If not, I thank you for your call."

When the door shut behind the women, guilt swamped Victorine. Should she have told them the truth—that she had not made Miss Matty's gown, nor the others in the window? Instead, fear had closed her lips. Even now, second-guessing herself, she struggled to think of a way to explain it without giving away her past, without revealing where she and Martine had worked together.

The thought of Martine brought an ache to her chest. Martine had become a second mother to her after her own mamma died. To lose them both like that, and her sister too . . . She pressed a hand to her throbbing heart.

After Martine passed away so unexpectedly, her husband, Pierre, had given her the gowns, insisting she take them. "Martine would have wanted it," he said. "Use them to start your own shop, as you and your *mère* once hoped to do. That way, Martine will be a part of it as well, in a small way. And something good will come from this horrid loss."

And so she had accepted them and determined to set out her shingle as a dressmaker. What else could she do with two trunks full of gowns and things that did not fit her and were styled for an older woman? Besides, if her younger sister could create a new life for herself, then so could she. She had decided she must at least try.

But she had told the ladies none of this. She knew people would not want to engage someone with her background to make a fine gown. So she resolved to keep her past secret. At least for now.

A silent Mr. Basu helped Mercy move, carrying down her small trunk, valise, books, and bandboxes. Mrs. Burlingame waited outside with her cart. Mr. Drake had offered to send a carriage from the hotel, but Mercy declined. She would feel less self-conscious riding through the village with her friend the carter.

When all was loaded, Matilda, Mrs. Timmons, Agnes, and Mr. Basu came outside to bid her farewell. Mr. Basu bowed low, his solemn eyes communicating more respect than words could have. Mrs. Timmons thrust a cloth-wrapped pudding into her hand and then wiped her eyes on her apron.

"We shall miss you, my dear." She lowered her voice. "I'm too old to make a change, but if you hear of anything for Mr. Basu, let us know, won't you? She wants him to start wearing livery. I think it will kill him."

Mercy nodded. "I shall."

Agnes embraced her. "God bless you, Miss Grove. You will come back and visit us, I hope?"

"Of course I will."

Aunt Matty walked with her to the cart, arm in arm.

"Am I doing the right thing?" Mercy whispered.

"You are."

Mercy implored, "Tell me you shall be all right."

"I shall be all right."

At the gate, Matilda halted. She bracketed Mercy's shoulders with determined hands and looked her full in the face. "And so shall you be, Mercy Grove." She squeezed all the confidence and affection into her niece she could muster, then released her, eyes bright with unshed tears.

"I will see you on Sunday," Mercy reminded her.

Aunt Matty pressed her lips together to stop their trembling and silently nodded, sending a tear down each cheek.

Alice and Mr. Drake were waiting in the Fairmont hall to greet Mercy when she arrived. He introduced her to Mrs. Callard, the housekeeper, who in turn introduced her to the rest of the house-hold: chef, kitchen maids and chambermaids, clerk, porter, waiters, potboy, and boot boy.

Mercy concentrated during the introductions, trying to remember every name. She glimpsed Joseph Kingsley crossing the hall with his toolbox, and he paused, raising a hand in greeting. Determined to guard her heart, she nodded in his direction but did not wave or smile back. Instead, she quickly returned her attention to the housekeeper as she explained the daily schedule.

"Mr. Drake suggests that you and Miss Alice take breakfast together in the schoolroom and have your other meals with him in the coffee room."

Mr. Drake interjected, "If that is agreeable, Miss Grove? I rise early and often make do with coffee, but I would enjoy your company later in the day."

"Whatever you think best. I don't mind eating my other meals alone, if you prefer."

"Not at all. I would like to hear how Alice's studies progress."

"Of course."

Did the others think it strange that their master wished to take meals with the governess? Mercy was glad to see no censure in their expressions.

Horse hooves and the jingle of harnesses heralded the arrival of a customer, and Mr. Drake stepped to the window as a grand post chaise arrived, flanked by two outriders. Alice skipped after him.

Mrs. Callard dismissed the assembled servants, who hurried off to return to their duties or meet the chaise.

Mercy asked the older woman, "Mrs. Callard, were you not housekeeper when the Fairmonts lived here?"

"Indeed I was. Good of you to remember."

Mercy's gaze swept the compact, tidy woman. She had dark hair with only a few strands of silver and a remarkably smooth face. "How is it you have not aged a day in all these years?"

"Kind of you to say so, miss, however untrue. I will ask Theo to deliver your baggage up to your room as soon as he's seen to the chaise. And one of the maids, Iris, will help you dress. Anything else you need, just let me know."

"Thank you, Mrs. Callard."

The housekeeper began to turn away, then paused to add, "It will be good for Alice to have you here, Miss Grove. The sweet child is lonely, I think. Everyone is kind to her, don't mistake me, but we are all busy with our work."

Mercy smiled. "I will keep her happily occupied with studies for several hours each day, though she will still have time to wander and play. And to spend with Mr. Drake, of course."

The woman nodded approvingly. "As it should be."

Alice hurried back to Mercy's side. "Come up and see your room," the girl enthused. She then turned to Mr. Drake, who was still standing at the window. "May I show her?"

"You may. I must stay here and greet the new arrivals, or I would go up with you. I hope you approve, Miss Grove. We've made some improvements."

"I am sure it will do very well. Thank you."

Alice tugged her hand, and Mercy allowed the girl to lead her to the top floor.

When they arrived, Mercy drew up short at finding a man inside the bedchamber. He turned, and seeing who it was only made her more uncomfortable.

"Oh. Mr. Kingsley. I . . . did not realize you were up here."

"Hello, Miss Grove. Alice."

She saw a level on the mantelpiece and his toolbox on the floor nearby. "Don't tell me Mr. Drake has pulled you from your more important projects to work on my room?"

"I volunteered."

Mercy looked around. The narrow room had mullioned windows at one end overlooking the gabled roof. A single bed, dressing chest, washstand, armchair, and footstool filled the small space. There was no bookcase, however. Oh well, a minor inconvenience. The room was light, pleasant, and thankfully had a fireplace, which would be welcome on cold mornings.

Alice walked to the window and peered out. "There's Johnny. He looks so small from up here!" She pushed opened the window and called down to him.

Mercy walked toward the hearth, studying the carved oak shelf with interest. "This mantelpiece . . . it looks brand new."

"It is. Used to be only a plain pine board. I thought something finer was in order."

"It's beautiful, but you needn't have done that. It's too fancy for a governess's room."

"Not at all. I doubt this hearth has been used in years. But I've laid your first fire, just in case." He gestured toward the wood, coal, and kindling. "Nights can still be chilly."

"Thank you."

He pointed to a mirror hung on the wall. "I found this mirror in the storage room. Thought it might come in handy for combing your hair and whatnot."

Mercy was not especially fond of mirrors herself, but she dutifully thanked him anyway. Catching a glimpse of her reflection, she self-consciously smoothed a loose strand of hair.

"Johnny!" Alice called again. "I'm up here!" She stuck her hand out the window and waved.

"Alice," Mercy said mildly, "perhaps we ought not shout from windows, hmm?"

Mr. Kingsley took a step nearer and lowered his voice. "I was surprised to learn you'd taken a position here. But knowing how you feel about Alice, I suppose I shouldn't have been."

Mercy felt her defenses rise. "You disapprove?"

"Of course not. Why would I? I'll see more of you, working here so much as I do."

"That is not why I took the position."

He frowned. "Of course not. I would never think that."

Alice closed the window and turned to them. "Is it not wonderful, Mr. Kingsley? Miss Grove is to be my governess! Now we shall see her every day."

He regarded Mercy soberly. "I hope she will be very happy here."

Mercy looked away. Seeing Mr. Kingsley more often might once have been a thrilling prospect. Now it would only serve to remind her of her disappointment. She would do her best to forget about him, romantically speaking. After all, they both worked for Mr.

Drake now. She would treat him with the detached politeness of a colleague and nothing more.

Mercy drew herself up. "Come, Alice. Let's let Mr. Kingsley get back to work. I am sure he has many important things to do elsewhere in the hotel."

He recoiled in apparent surprise, then said, "Pardon me; I will trespass no longer."

He swiped up his tools, turned, and strode from the room. Mercy watched him go, stomach filled with regret. She had not meant to hurt his feelings, but that was exactly what she'd done.

Jane sat on the front steps of the innkeeper's lodge, petting the stable cat, Kipper, that she'd adopted as a pet. Her father alighted from an arriving coach and walked across the courtyard toward her, face sober.

"Morning, Papa. My offer of a room here still stands, you know. Then you wouldn't have to take the stage or hire a fly every time you wanted to visit."

His expression remained fixed as though she'd not spoken. "Jane, there is something we need to talk about."

"Of course, Papa." She noticed his pale face. "Is everything all right?"

"Yes, except guilt has been plaguing me. I should have told you from the start."

"Told me what? Papa, what is it? Come and sit down." She patted the step beside her.

He sat down heavily, surprisingly winded from the short walk. "Now tell me."

He nodded. "You asked me if Rani and I were blessed with children."

"Yes?"

"As I said, we didn't expect to have any. She was past forty, so we thought it unlikely. But we . . . did have a child." He looked at Jane, then away, worrying his lip.

Jane's heart hammered. She had a half brother or sister in India? Or had the child died shortly after birth, as so many did? Is that what he was trying to tell her? She drew in a shaky breath and asked tentatively, "Did the child live?"

He slowly nodded. "He did."

"He? You had a son, Papa? As you long hoped you would?"

He nodded. Pulling at a chain around his neck, he fished out a locket from beneath his shirt. He opened it and withdrew a small ribbon-bound lock of black hair. Jane saw that each half of the locket held a miniature portrait: an old one of Jane herself, and the other of a dark-haired, dark-skinned woman. Before she could feel touched by this evidence that he had carried her portrait with him all these years, her eyes fastened on the second image and all other thoughts fled. How strange to think of her father married to such an exotic-looking woman, so different from Jane's mother or Jane herself. This would have been her stepmother, had she lived. Jane supposed, in a way, she still was.

"This is Rani. Painted around the time of our wedding." He lifted the ribbon-bound hair. "And this is a lock of our son's hair from his first haircut."

Jane reached out and gingerly stroked the curl. "How dark it is," she said in awe. "How thick!"

He nodded and returned the hair to the locket, snapping shut the two halves. "Not as dark or as thick as Rani's, but just as beautiful."

Jane swallowed. "Where is the child now?"

He avoided her eyes. "With Rani gone, my heart was no longer in India. But I hesitated to bring the child back with me. How would he be received? Not well, I imagined. Here in England, we are not so accepting of people with darker skin and foreign-sounding names and ways. That prejudice alone I could have borne and done my best to shield him from . . ." He sent her a sidelong glance. "But then there was you to consider."

"Me?"

"Come, Jane. How would you have felt had I shown up in Ivy Hill with a mixed-blood child—not a servant, but a son?"

"I hardly know, Papa. But please tell me you did not leave behind another of your offspring to cross the ocean again? Do you think life would be so difficult for him here? That people would be cruel?"

"You tell me. Do you really believe people in Ivy Hill and Wishford would accept a dark-skinned child?"

"I am not sure about Wishford, but I think people in Ivy Hill would. I know Mercy would. And Miss Matty."

"And you?" he pressed. "How would you have reacted had I returned with your brown half brother?"

Brother . . . The word banged around her heart. "I would have been shocked, of course. But I would *not* have rejected him. Nor you, because of him."

"You rejected me because of his mother," he quietly reminded her.

Jane shook her head. "Not because of who she was. Because the choices you made and the way you made them hurt me. But he is an innocent child."

He looked down, distractedly scratching Kipper's ears. "I was worried when Rani became with child at her age. Not only for her health, but because I found the prospect daunting. I knew I had not been a perfect parent the first time around. I had thought I might enjoy being a grandfather someday, but . . ."

Jane shook her head, the old pain returning. "I am sorry I cannot oblige you, Papa. I am not able to carry a child to term."

He flinched. "I am sorry, Jane. I had no intention of raising a sad subject. I was not certain, of course, but I assumed that if you'd had a child, you would have written to me to announce that news, if nothing else."

"Yes, I would have." Eager to change the subject, Jane said, "You still haven't answered my question, Papa. Where is the boy now? How old is he? What is his name?"

"Timothy!" Her father pushed himself to his feet, a smile breaking over his tanned face. Jane turned and saw Sir Timothy crossing the street toward them, an answering smile lighting his handsome countenance.

"Good day, Mr. Fairmont. I heard you were back and had to come and see for myself."

The two men shook hands, and Jane's father clapped the younger man's back.

"Yes, here I am, alive and well. Well enough, at any rate, and delighted to see you."

Timothy added, "As you have not yet called on us, I have come with specific instructions from Mamma to bring you back with me to Brockwell Court. She wants to hear all about your adventures." Timothy looked from him to Jane. "But if I am interrupting . . . ?"

Jane opened her mouth to reply, but her father answered before she could. "Not a bit of it. Of course I'll come. By the way, I was sorry to hear your father passed on. I hope your mother is in good health?"

"Indeed she is, sir."

"And you are newly married, I understand. To Sir William's youngest, no less. I am very happy for you both."

"Thank you." Timothy turned to her. "Jane, will you join us, or are you busy?"

"You two go ahead. But do greet Rachel and your mother for me."

"I shall."

Sir Timothy led her father away toward Brockwell Court as the two men continued to talk.

Jane's unanswered questions would have to wait.

CHAPTER

NINETEEN

The next morning dawned bright and sunny. Mercy rose eagerly, looking forward to the first day of her new life in her new home. She stepped to the window and pushed it open to enjoy the sweet spring breeze while she dressed and pinned her hair. Voices reached her from below, drawing her back to the window in idle curiosity. Down in the stable yard, she saw Mr. Kingsley talking to pretty Esther Dudman again. Her heart sank. What was she doing there? Joseph laughed at something she said and smiled at her, and his smile stole Mercy's breath.

She turned away, determined to get on with her day. She would not waste time mooning like a love-sick calf over a man who clearly admired someone else. She wouldn't.

A short while later, Mercy and Alice breakfasted together in the schoolroom. The room was spacious and tidy, with an old desk, bookshelf, table, and chairs. In one corner stood an ornate puppet theatre that looked brand-new. Noticing her looking at it, Alice said, "Mr. Kingsley made that for me. Is it not wonderful?"

"It is, indeed," she murmured, impressed despite herself. Then she pushed the man from her mind again and began their first lesson.

Midmorning, Mercy gave Alice half an hour respite. The girl was no longer used to sitting still for long periods and had quickly grown restless. Her focus would improve in time, Mercy was sure.

But for now, she encouraged her pupil to go outside and take some fresh air. Alice eagerly agreed and dashed downstairs. Mercy, meanwhile, followed at a more sedate pace, heading toward the kitchen to find a second cup of tea.

Mr. Kingsley passed by with a saw and piece of trim. "Good morning, Miss Grove."

"Mr. Kingsley," she acknowledged politely, but did not stop to talk.

He paused, then turned back to her. "Miss Grove . . . have I done something to offend you?"

Mercy hesitated. It was on the tip of her tongue to say, *"No, nothing,"* and walk away. But she longed to know the truth.

She took a deep breath and stepped nearer. "I realize we had a . . . friendly . . . relationship when you volunteered at Ivy Cottage," she quietly began, "but now that we are both in Mr. Drake's employ, I feel a little professional distance might be a good idea."

He studied her, a slight frown creasing his forehead. "Why?"

She endeavored to keep her voice even. "I would not want anyone to misunderstand our relationship." She added to herself, *Me, most of all.* "After all, you did tell me that Esther is more than a friend to you, that she is practically one of the family."

His brow cleared. "She is. She is my sister-in-law."

"Oh?" Mercy blinked in disbelief. "Which of your brothers is she married to?"

"She is not married . . . yet. She is my wife's sister."

Mercy stared at him. "Your wife's sister?"

He nodded.

"Oh," Mercy murmured, embarrassment singeing her cheeks. She swallowed a guilty lump and acknowledged, "She is . . . quite beautiful."

"Yes. And very like Naomi." He winced, running a hand through his hair. "When I look at her . . ." Emotions washed over his face, but he shook his head and said no more.

Mercy felt a momentary stab of jealousy to hear him praise the woman's beauty. But then she recognized the pain in his shadowed expression, and her petty feelings deepened into concern. She said gently, "I imagine it helps her to see you as well. Someone else who remembers and loved her sister."

He glanced up at her from beneath a fall of sandy-brown hair, and for several moments their gazes held. "You know, you may be right."

Mercy added, "Perhaps that is why she comes all this way to visit."

He glanced away and said, "Oh, I think there is more to it than that."

"Oh?" *What did he mean?* Mercy wondered. Did he have feelings for her, and her for him, in-laws or not?

He opened his mouth, then closed it again, thinking the better of whatever he'd been about to say. "I hope you will forgive me, Miss Grove. I find it difficult to talk about my wife, but I should have told you who Esther was earlier."

"Yes, I wish you would have. Well. Thank you for explaining now."

He gave her a tentative smile. "We are all right then, you and I?"

"Yes, we are." Mercy returned his smile and walked away, her step suddenly lighter. A dozen more questions circled through her mind, but she decided she had enough answers for the time being.

When her father did not return to Ivy Hill the next morning, Jane asked Ted to harness a horse to the gig, determined to travel the few miles to him.

Reaching the Wilton inn shortly before noon, she approached the booking desk and asked the innkeeper where she might find Winston Fairmont. The man's gaze skimmed over her and, apparently deciding she looked respectable, said, "Number three. He has a gentleman visiting at present. But there's a bench in the passage if you'd like to wait."

Jane thanked him and took herself upstairs, pausing when she reached the landing.

A little boy, perhaps five years old, sat alone on the bench, swinging his feet. In one hand he cradled a leather ball. In the other, a biscuit. His skin was a beautiful shade of generously creamed coffee. He wore a collarless shirt of unbleached linen and loose cotton trousers.

Hearing her footfalls, he glanced in her direction, then quickly away again. But not before she saw his eyes—large, dark, and beautiful. Jane's heart began beating a little faster.

"Good day." She stepped nearer and asked quietly, "What are you doing out here all alone? Are you lost?"

He shook his head. "Waiting."

"My name is Mrs. Bell. May I know your name?"

He kept his shy gaze on his toy. "Jack Avi."

"Pleased to meet you, Jack Avi. Whom are you waiting for?"

He shrugged. "Bapu."

She twisted her gloved hands. "And where is your . . . bapu?"

The boy pointed across the passage to a closed door marked *3*. *Of course.*

Jane sat on the bench. Just to be sure, she clarified, "Mr. Fairmont is your papa?"

"Um-hm."

Jane's throat tightened. "He is my papa too."

The boy looked at her directly then, his big breathtaking eyes fastened on hers.

He lost his grip on his ball, and it rolled away. He hopped down after it and scooped it up. Returning to the bench, he inadvertently laid a hand on hers as he wriggled himself back into position beside her. He left his hand there.

Jane's heart squeezed. "May I wait with you?"

He nodded and offered her a bite of his half-eaten biscuit.

The door next to her father's creaked open, and a woman's dark face appeared, her eyes lined with kohl, bangles on her wrists. She was draped in a colorful flowing tunic as exotic as her looks.

"Jack Avi," the woman called in an accented voice, gesturing the boy toward her.

"Who is she?" Jane whispered.

"My *ayah*."

"*Ayah?*"

"Nars . . . ?" He scrunched his face, searching for the right English word. "My nurse."

"Oh!" Jane should have guessed. Her father would not have left the boy unattended when he visited Ivy Hill alone.

The boy hopped down again, responding to the summons, and disappeared within the room. The woman closed the door behind him.

For a few moments, Jane sat there alone, her heart rate slowly returning to normal. Then her father's door opened and Dr. Burton stepped out.

"Oh, Mrs. Bell. A pleasure to see you again. Your father did not mention you were expected."

She rose. "He did not know. I just came over to visit him. Is he well?"

Her father appeared in the threshold, cravat missing but otherwise fully dressed. He waved a dismissive hand. "Oh, Burton here was just giving us all a once-over. Checking for insidious foreign fevers under every bush. Man is a nervous mother hen. We are all perfectly well. Hello, Jane. What a nice surprise."

Jane smiled at the physician. "Thank you for coming all this way to see him, Dr. Burton."

"Well, he wasn't about to come and see me, was he?" Dr. Burton frowned at her father, then turned to Jane. "We heard voices in the passage. Have you met his . . . ?" The physician let the words trail away, a rare flush reddening his neck as he realized he was about to divulge a patient's secret.

Jane reassured him, "Yes, I have just met his son. My little half brother. How strange to say the words! Is he healthy? He certainly appears to be."

"He is, yes. As far as I can tell. Though I am no expert on *insidious foreign fevers*." He glared at her father, sardonically repeating his words, then turned back to Jane. "Well, I will leave you. Enjoy your visit."

"Come in, Jane." Her father held the door for her, and Jane stepped inside.

"I hope you don't mind my coming to see you," Jane said. "You left without answering my questions about your son. I was too curious to wait any longer. I just met him. Jack Ah-vee. Am I saying that correctly?"

"Yes. A good English name and a good Indian name. Half and half, like he is."

"He is a handsome lad and speaks beautiful English. I briefly saw his nurse as well. I am surprised she would travel so far to care for the boy."

He nodded. "She was Rani's maidservant and stays with us for her sake. Rani was very kind to her when her own people were not."

Jane murmured, "Good of her."

He nodded. "It's a godsend to have her help caring for Jack Avi now that his mother is gone."

Jane added, "And someone to watch over him when you came alone to see me."

"Yes. I hope you don't think it terribly deceptive of me. I wanted to get the lay of the land first, to gauge your reception of me before I complicated matters by introducing my son."

"I understand. I am glad you decided not to leave him in India."

"Are you? That's good, Jane. For so am I."

"Will you bring him to Ivy Hill? Gabriel will want to meet him. And Miss Matty, and . . . oh, everyone!"

"Perhaps not everyone," he said more cautiously. "But yes, I shall. I had planned to bring him to meet you soon, but I am having English clothes made for him—a suit like mine and two skeleton suits for play. The tailor should have them ready any day now."

"I wouldn't have cared about that."

"No need for him to stand out more than he has to. Nor do I want anyone to mistake him for a servant." He took a deep breath, then changed the subject. "Now, shall we take tea together? I must offer you some refreshment after coming to Wilton to see me."

"I would enjoy that. Might Jack Avi join us? And his . . . *ayah* . . . if she would like."

"Priya does not like to venture down to the public dining room. She draws too many curious stares. Nor is she comfortable sitting at the same table with the *sahib*. But I shall have tea sent up and we may all partake together. I have a small table there and can bring in two more chairs."

Half an hour later, the four of them sat in one corner of her father's room, a tray of tea things and a platter of bread and butter, muffins, and fruit on the round table before them. Jack Avi sat on one side of Jane, and her father on the other. The nurse sat a few feet away from the rest of them, looking ill at ease.

Winston Fairmont, however, beamed happily. "How wonderful to have my son and daughter at the same table with me. My family all together."

He did not mention the two wives he'd lost, but Jane could not help but think of them. She wondered what her mother would have thought to meet Jack Avi. She also wondered what Rani had been like, and what she would have thought of her husband's daughter.

Jane became aware of the silent nurse studying her face and shifted uncomfortably under her scrutiny.

"Why does she stare at me?" Jane whispered.

Her father asked the woman something in a quiet, musical language Jane did not understand. The woman answered, her dark eyes returning to Jane's face.

"Priya says you have my eyes. She also says your mother must have been a beautiful woman."

Jane's heart warmed to the nurse. She smiled at her. "Thank you, Priya. She was."

On her way back to Ivy Hill, Jane stopped at the Fairmont. She hoped she would not get the new governess into any trouble by interrupting her teaching, but she could not wait to share the news with her close friend.

Mercy and Alice sat on a bench in the garden together, sketch-books open and pencils busy when Jane arrived.

Mercy smiled and waved. A groom hurried forward to take charge of the horse and gig, while the porter helped Jane alight.

She thanked the men, then said to Mercy, "I hope you don't mind me showing up like this."

"Not at all. You are very welcome."

"May we talk, just for a few minutes?"

"Yes. Alice was just asking if she could pay her daily visit to the kittens, so I can easily spare half an hour."

"Wonderful."

Mercy led the way to the front door. "Do come in. Though how strange it must seem for you—that I should be welcoming you into your former home!"

Jane chuckled. "I cannot deny it. My childhood friend, living here as a governess. Never would I have guessed."

"Nor I. Well, come up and see the schoolroom and my bedcham-ber. I know Mr. Drake has already shown you the rest of the hotel."

Yes, and Jane was in no hurry to repeat the discomfiting experi-ence. She was glad for this chance to see Mercy, however, and to assure herself she was well.

She followed Mercy up one pair of stairs, then another. They passed attic storage rooms that, according to James, still held Fairmont family portraits, books, and other memorabilia. Some-day, when she had more energy and perspective, she might brave a look through the relics. Perhaps with her father. But not today.

Mercy opened the door to the old schoolroom. For a moment Jane closed her eyes and breathed the still-familiar smell of plas-ter and musty books. "Oh, the hours I spent in here, though all I wanted was to be out-of-doors riding Hermione."

"Were your governesses kind to you, Jane?"

"Yes, but I only had the one. Miss Morgan. She read me stories—*that* I remember enjoying."

"We had several," Mercy said. "Most didn't stay long. But I liked Miss Dockery the best. I hope to emulate her firm yet kind ways."

"I am sure you shall." Jane looked around. "The schoolroom is much as I remember it."

Mercy nodded. "I brought over the globe and maps from my former school, but otherwise I have changed little."

Jane walked forward, her gaze pinned on the puppet theatre.

"This I don't recognize." She ran her hand over the five-foot-high wooden structure and tentatively parted the velvet curtains. Then she examined the four puppets: king, queen, prince, and princess. "How I would have loved this as a child."

Mercy nodded. "Alice is enamored with it as well."

"A gift from Mr. Drake, I imagine?"

Mercy hesitated. "Mr. Kingsley, actually. Or at least, he built it and carved the puppets. Mr. Drake likely paid him for his time though."

Jane turned to study Mercy and noticed her fidget.

"Mr. Kingsley still works here a great deal, does he not?"

"Um-hm." Mercy gestured toward the door. "Come, let me show you my room, then we can go back downstairs for tea."

Over tea and cake in the coffee room, Jane began. "I have news. I have a little brother. Well, a half brother. I just met him. I still can't believe it."

Mercy's mouth opened in astonishment. "Oh, Jane! Nor can I! Tell me everything."

Jane happily did so.

When she finished, Mercy slowly shook her head. "How strange to learn you are not an only child after all." Mercy pressed her hand. "I am so happy for you, Jane. I hope I shall meet him."

"I will make sure you do. Perhaps at church, if not before."

"And how wonderful that your father and brother shall be here to celebrate your wedding." Mercy added, "How go wedding plans, by the way?"

"Fairly well, I think. The wedding breakfast will be at The Bell. I know it won't be as smart as Rachel's wedding, but I hope people will enjoy it. I wonder if the dowager Lady Brockwell will even attend such a humble affair."

"I would think so. And you know Rachel and Timothy wouldn't miss it. Nor would I."

"Thank you. That reminds me," Jane said, "I spoke to Rachel a few days ago."

"Oh? How is she?"

"Well. Happy. Surprised to hear about you."

Mercy ducked her head. "The Brockwells are no doubt scandalized."

"I wouldn't say that, but taken aback, yes."

Mercy sipped, then said, "I suppose everyone thinks it was wrong of me to leave Ivy Cottage to become a governess."

"No, my dear. Not everyone. And those of us who have met your sister-in-law are among the most understanding." Jane grinned at her friend, but Mercy barely returned it.

"My parents are not happy about the situation but have apparently accepted it."

Jane felt her eyes widen. "Have they?"

Mercy nodded. "Aunt Matty wrote to assure them of Mr. Drake's respectability and to hint that grandchildren might be more quickly forthcoming if the newly married couple had more time alone."

Jane slowly shook her head, another grin overtaking her. "Everyone knows you are clever, Mercy. But I didn't realize you shared that trait with your aunt."

"I do indeed."

Jane took a long sip, then set down her cup and rose. "Well, I think we've reached the end of our half hour, and I don't want to get you into trouble with your *respectable* new employer."

Mercy rose as well and walked her out. She asked, "By the way, have you spoken any further with Victorine?"

"No, but I have invited her to join me for breakfast tomorrow. I will let you know how it goes."

CHAPTER

Twenty

The following morning, Jane was sitting at the booking desk when Victorine entered the inn.

Jane rose. "Good morning, Victorine. Thank you for coming."

"Thank you for inviting me."

"How are things going at the shop?"

"Fairly well, I think. The vicar's wife recently came in and bought a hat, and Miss Featherstone has asked me to make her a daydress."

"Good. I am glad we are keeping you busy here."

Outside, a horn blew, and a moment later, two arriving passengers hurried through the side door, headed for the dining parlour, one of them consulting his pocket watch.

Victorine stepped aside as they passed. "Your inn is very busy too."

"Yes, thankfully. It keeps us in business."

Jane's attention was then drawn to her mother-in-law, Thora, entering the hall, toddler Betsey in arms. The girl's thumb remained firmly in her mouth, though Jane knew Hetty and Thora had tried everything to dissuade her.

"Morning, Thora. Betsey is still sucking her thumb, I see."

"The girl is as stubborn as I am." Thora gently pulled Betsey's hand away with a pop, and the child immediately replaced it. "Good thing she's adorable."

"Yes, she is," Victorine agreed with a warm smile.

Jane turned to include her in the conversation. "Thora, may I introduce Victorine, Ivy Hill's new dressmaker? Victorine, this is Thora Talbot, my mother-in-law. And her granddaughter, Betsey."

Victorine reached out and gently brushed a lock of hair from the girl's face. "She is so pretty. I like her ginger hair."

"Thank you. I quite agree. How goes the new shop? I'm afraid I haven't much use for fashionable gowns now that I am a farmer's wife. But I do like to support our local women in business, so I shall stop by sometime. When I don't have Miss Touch-Everything-Sticky-Fingers with me."

Victorine smiled again. "You would be most welcome, Mrs. Talbot. Betsey too."

"Thank you. Well, don't let us keep you two. Betsey and I just stopped by to visit Mrs. Rooke, who promised us shortbread." Thora waved Betsey's hand at the women and then continued down the passage.

Jane glanced subtly at the clock, then turned to her guest. "Come, let's sit in the coffee room and chat. What can I offer you to drink? Tea? Coffee?"

"Tea would be lovely."

They sat near the door, and Jane ordered tea and toast for two.

No sooner had the tea arrived than Jack Gander passed the coffee room, hesitating in the doorway. He brightened upon seeing her with Victorine.

"Ah, Jack." Jane turned to her companion. "Victorine, please allow me to introduce my friend, Mr. Jack Gander."

Victorine dipped her head in acknowledgment, but Jane did not miss the widening of her eyes. Jack Gander was a very handsome man with dark hair and eyes and a striking smile. He cut a fine figure in his red coat, a narrow shoulder belt emphasizing his athletic build.

"Jack is a guard with His Majesty's Royal Mail," Jane said. "We are all very fond of him. And Victorine is our new dressmaker, only recently moved to Ivy Hill to set up business in Mrs. Shabner's old shop."

"A pleasure to meet you." Jack stepped closer and studied her face. "You look familiar to me, madame. I have seen you somewhere before."

Victorine gestured out the window. "My shop is across the street from this coaching inn, which you pass on your route. If you have seen me, I should not wonder."

"No, I meant somewhere else. Before you came to Ivy Hill."

She shifted uneasily. "Where?"

"London, perhaps?"

"I have been to London several times, but it is unlikely our paths would have crossed in such a large city."

"True, but I know I have seen your face before. I can't recall where at the moment, but never fear, it will come to me."

"Is that a threat?"

"A threat? Heavens, no! Why would you say that?"

"I think you mean to frighten me, perhaps."

"Not at all. That is the last reaction I want from you." He smiled at the dressmaker. "In fact, I must tell you that I am impressed, madame. Leaving everything and moving to a strange new place to start your own business. It is quite a risk, one many people would not take."

She shrugged off his attempt at flattery. "Life is full of risks, thrilling and terrifying at the same time—rather like a tightrope act."

Jane chuckled at the metaphor, but Jack's smile fell away.

"Tightrope act . . . ? Like the one at Astley's Amphitheatre?" He leaned nearer, eyes alert. "Perhaps that is where I've seen you before."

"Me . . . with Astley's! What an imagination you have. I have attended their shows but have never performed there. Good heavens!"

He stilled, then said quietly, "I did not accuse you of performing there, only of seeing you there. *Did* you perform there?"

"No! What a notion."

His gaze remained on Victorine, his brow furrowed with doubt. "Then where have I seen you?"

"I don't know."

"Well, I travel a great deal. I must have seen you somewhere in passing."

Again Victorine shrugged. "Perhaps. If it helps, I have never seen you before in my life."

"Really?"

She nodded.

Jack drew himself up. "Then forgive me. I hope you don't think me impertinent. Still, a pleasure to meet you, Madame Victorine. And now, duty calls." He bowed. "Good day, ladies."

A few moments later, they heard the telltale blast of Jack's horn as he signaled the five-minute warning to his passengers.

The dressmaker asked, "Is he the reason you invited me here at this particular time?"

Jane could not tell if she was angry or not. "He said he wanted to meet you. He's a good man, Victorine."

The dressmaker sipped her tea, then looked up at Jane. "I was telling the truth when I said I had never seen him before." She bit back a small grin, blue eyes sparkling. "I think I would have remembered."

CHAPTER

Twenty-One

When Mercy entered the schoolroom the next morning, she drew up short, stunned to see a framed slate hanging on the wall. It had not been there the day before. It was smaller than her old one in the Ivy Cottage schoolroom, but . . . Mercy walked forward, studying the frame, the familiar hue of the slate.

Behind her someone cleared his throat, and she whirled in surprise, her eyes widening at the sight of Mr. Kingsley in the doorway.

"I asked our local slater to recut the broken one," he said, "and then I made a new frame for it."

It *was* the same one! Last she had seen the slate, he and Mr. Basu had carried it in two pieces up to the Ivy Cottage attic. "How did you manage it?"

"Your aunt let me take it from the attic. I hope you don't mind."

"Of course not."

"I know it's not as big as before, but I thought it might still be useful."

"It certainly will be. I've missed having one. Thank you, Mr. Kingsley. That was exceedingly thoughtful of you."

"You're welcome." He stepped nearer. "Miss Grove, I . . ."

Alice entered the schoolroom. "Good morning, Mr. Kingsley. You are just in time."

"In time for what?"

"I am going to perform a puppet show. You can be the prince."

He grimaced. "I don't think I'm qualified. Now, if you wanted a big bad wolf or a woodcutter . . ."

"Please?"

He hesitated, sending Mercy a pleading look. "What part is Miss Grove to take?"

Mercy sat in a chair placed before the puppet theatre. "I am to be the enraptured audience."

"Ah, a difficult part indeed if I am to be one of the players."

"Just do your best, Mr. Kingsley," Alice admonished in a grown-up voice that sounded very much like something Mercy might have said.

The tall man made a comical face and knelt behind the theatre.

Supplementing the four puppets with a mismatched collection of dolls, Alice began her own adaptation of Perrault's *Cendrillon*, performing all the female roles: stepmother, sisters, fairy god-mother, and Cinderella, while Joseph dutifully manipulated and voiced the prince.

"I am very much in love with the beautiful person who owns this little slipper," said he, reading from Alice's script. "I proclaim throughout the land that I shall marry her whose foot this slipper fits. . . ."

He was no great actor, but Mercy enjoyed listening to his deep, masculine voice anyway.

When they finished, Mercy clapped appreciatively.

Alice popped up and bobbed a curtsy. Joseph Kingsley rose more slowly, his knees cracking. He gave a sheepish little bow. "And now I really must get to work."

Mercy was sorry to see him go. "Thank you again for the wall slate, Mr. Kingsley," she said. "And for performing the part of the prince so admirably."

"If you are pleased, then it was worth the mortification."

She smiled at him. "I am indeed."

Jane's father brought Jack Avi to The Bell that afternoon. He needed to go to Wishford to see his lawyer, Mr. Coine, so Jane took Jack Avi out to Lane's Farm. She had already broken the news to Gabriel but was eager for the two to become acquainted. She also planned to take her brother to Angel Farm to meet Thora and Talbot.

When they arrived, Jane helped the boy down as Gabriel limped over to the gig, leaning on his stick.

Jane said, "Gabriel Locke, may I introduce Jack Avi Fairmont. My brother." How strangely wonderful to say the words!

Gabriel sank to his haunches before the boy. "Hello, Jack Avi. I am very happy to meet you."

"Gabriel . . . like the angel?" Jack Avi asked.

"I can claim no similarities to an angel, I'm afraid."

Seeing confusion cloud his little brow, Gabriel amended, "Yes, like the angel. Though some people call me Gable, which you would be welcome to do, if you like." He held out his hand to the boy.

"Gable." The boy grasped his large hand and lifted it up and down. "I shake you like an Englishman."

Gabriel grinned and asked, "And how would you greet me were we in India?"

The boy pressed his palms together and bowed. "But we are not in India, Bapu says. Now we are Englishmen."

"Father wants Jack Avi to be accepted here," Jane explained. "Hence the new suit of clothes."

"Very smart. You look like a little country squire."

The boy straightened the buttons and grasped the lapels of the small wool coat. "It is good, yes?"

"You look very handsome," Jane agreed, running a hand over his thick black hair.

The boy looked at Gabriel again. "You are my sister's husband?"

"I hope to have that honor very soon now, yes."

"Then you like this." Jack Avi lifted the chain around his neck and opened a locket very much like his father's. He held it near Gabriel's face. "You see? My *didi*, Jane. And my *maaji*."

"I do see. Two beautiful women. So you had seen Jane before you ever met her in person?"

"Yes." Jack Avi nodded, then added matter-of-factly, "My *maaji* died."

"I know. I am sorry."

Gabriel shared a look with Jane, then he rose to his feet. "Jack Avi, have you ever ridden a horse?"

"No, sir."

"Would you like to learn?"

He nodded vigorously, dark eyes wide. "You have a horse?"

Gabriel chuckled. "That I do."

He pointed to Gabriel's cane. "Did you hurt yourself riding one?"

"Um, yes, actually."

"Then maybe Didi should teach me instead."

Jane was afraid Gabriel might be offended, but he laughed out loud. "You are a very clever boy, and no doubt right."

He ruffled her brother's hair. "For now, though, there is a pony I would like you to meet."

The boy smiled. "Yes, please, Gable, sir."

Mr. Drake and Alice were in the habit of spending an hour together before dinner. Having some time to herself, Mercy picked up a discarded newspaper in the sitting room and sat down to read it. Mr. Drake had left his office door open, and through it she could see the two seated across from one another. Alice sat swinging her legs, her little slippered feet rising up and down, trying to contain herself as she waited for him to finish something he was writing, his brow furrowed in concentration, quill scratching away.

Apparently unable to wait any longer, Alice said, "Miss Grove has me learning all the monarchs of England. Shall I recite them for you?"

"Excellent. But perhaps later, Alice. All right?"

She nodded. "The kittens have grown so much already. Would you like to come out and see them?"

"I would, but I have to finish this order and get it into the post."

Alice said, "I had a bad dream last night. A fox came and devoured all the kittens. I was ever so glad to awaken and discover it was just a dream. I don't suppose I could keep the kittens in my room?"

"I'm afraid not, Alice. It is a hotel, after all, and not everyone likes cats."

"Really? I can't imagine anyone not liking cats! That reminds me. Mr. Kingsley told me a funny story called The King of the Cats. Have you heard it?"

"I believe I have, yes. A long time ago."

"Oh."

The little legs slowed, then ceased swinging all together. "All right if I go outside?"

"Hm? Yes, if you like. But I thought we were going to play chess . . . ?"

She shrugged. "Maybe later?"

"Very well." He watched her go, setting down his pen at last. Noticing Mercy in the sitting room, he expelled a heavy sigh and gestured for her to join him.

As she approached, he groaned. "I know, I should have given her my undivided attention. But good heavens, Miss Grove, the girl does talk a great deal."

Mercy nodded and said gently, "Yes, in my experience females have more to say than males. It would be a gift to actually listen."

His lips thinned. "I do sometimes have work to do, Mercy," he said. "And a business or two to manage."

"Of course you do. I wasn't suggesting you need to be constantly at Alice's beck and call. But I had thought you set aside this time before dinner to spend with her?"

"I had, but business got in the way."

"I understand. But when you look her in the eyes and listen to her, it proves that what she thinks and says and worries about is important to you."

He sighed again. "And now I have guilt. Thank you."

Mercy looked down. "Forgive me. I did not mean to lecture or interfere. It is not my place. I am not a parent, after all."

"No, Mercy, forgive me. I really do appreciate your advice and *your* listening to *me*." His gaze returned to his work, but he looked up at her again. "Was there something else you wanted?"

She bit her lip, then grinned. "Later. For now, I shall have mercy on your poor, overworked ears."

The next day being warm and sunny, Mercy and Alice went outside for another stroll through the gardens. Botany book in hand, Mercy pointed out various species of birds and plants as they walked. "There's a swallow flying past. And there's a painted lady butterfly on the blackthorn bush, the one with all the white blossoms. And see that small purple blossom? That's a pasqueflower."

Alice asked, "Do you have a favorite flower, Miss Grove?"

"It would be hard to say. I like so many. But I suppose this time of year, I like lily of the valley best. They grow along the garden wall at Ivy Cottage."

A flash of movement caught Mercy's eye, and she glanced over. A tall man and a petite woman were sitting beneath the sweet chestnut tree between the garden wall and stables. The man turned and pointed at something in the distance, and Mercy clearly saw his face. Joseph Kingsley.

The woman held a basket. She lifted its cover and offered it to him. Mercy could hear her soft feminine voice and the lower rumble of Joseph's reply, though she could not distinguish the words themselves.

"Who is that with Mr. Kingsley?" Alice asked.

Mercy kept her voice neutral. "His sister-in-law, Esther."

"Looks like they are having a picnic. Shall we join them?"

"No, my dear, we've not been invited. But it is a perfect day for one."

"May we have a picnic sometime? You and me and Papa?"

Mercy's heart thumped. It was the first time she had heard Alice refer to Mr. Drake as Papa. She pressed the botany book to her chest and said evenly, "Good idea, Alice. But I think you and Mr. Drake should have a picnic together one day, just the two of you. Wouldn't that be lovely?" It would not be appropriate for Mercy to picnic with the man as though his—

Ringing laughter reached her ears, followed by Joseph's chuckle, warm and husky. Mercy glanced back in time to see Esther give his arm a playful swat.

Mercy told herself not to jump to conclusions again. It was a perfectly innocent encounter. Instead, she directed Alice's attention to the next plant, and they continued their walk.

Later that afternoon, Mercy saw Mr. Kingsley in the passage. She was torn between wanting to pass by unnoticed and stopping to talk. Should she mention she had seen the two together, or would she sound jealous if she did so? *Just forget about it*, Mercy told herself. Then she shook her head, knowing that was impossible. She would only keep torturing herself with doubts.

He smiled when he saw her. "Miss Grove, how are you keeping?"

"I am well. And you?"

"Excellent. It is a lovely day."

"Yes, Alice and I went for a stroll through the gardens earlier. We saw you outside, enjoying a picnic with Esther."

Mercy watched his face for any sign of guilt or sheepishness, but he answered without hesitation.

"Yes. Esther has taken to delivering a midday meal for my brothers and me. I've told her she doesn't need to, but she says it gives her something useful to do."

And an excuse to come and talk to you, Mercy guessed. "Very thoughtful. Is she enjoying her visit?"

"Actually, she is staying in Ivy Hill now. Did I not mention it?"

"No."

He nodded. "I must say, what she brings is far more satisfying than the fruit and cheese I usually toss in my toolbox."

Mercy hesitated. "You could eat in the coffee room sometime, you know." She felt forward just saying the words, but he didn't seem to notice her hint.

He shrugged. "Oh, I don't usually stop that long on a workday. A quick bite is all I need."

Would the man never ask to court her? Apparently not. "I see. Well, em, have a good day, Mr. Kingsley."

"You too, Miss Grove."

Later that day, Jane walked to Ivy Cottage to ask Matilda Grove to join them at the inn. There was someone her father wanted his old friend to meet. Mr. Basu opened the door to her, and for the first time Jane looked into his face, *really* looked. She noticed his eyes were shaped differently from Jack Avi's but were similar in color, while his skin was somewhat darker.

Jane wondered how the man would respond to meeting Jack Avi and vice versa. But that would have to wait for another time.

She smiled at the man. "Hello, Mr. Basu. Is Miss Matilda at home?"

He nodded and showed her into the family sitting room.

Inside, Matilda was sitting alone with a book. She removed her spectacles as Jane entered. "A caller, how lovely."

"Would you come with me to The Bell, Miss Matty? There is someone my father would like you to meet."

"Of course. How intriguing. Just let me fetch my reticule and best bonnet."

Jane escorted Miss Grove down Potters Lane to The Bell. When they arrived, they found Winston Fairmont waiting in one of the private parlours, a pot of tea and four cups on the table nearby. Jack Avi, Jane noticed, was hiding shyly behind his father's legs.

Her father began, "Miss Matilda, my old friend . . ."

"No older than you are, Win," Matilda replied with a saucy grin.

"Very true. Thank you for coming. There is someone special I'd like you to meet."

"So Jane said, but that was all she would tell me."

Her father laid a hand on Jack Avi's head and gently drew him forward. "This is my son, Jack Avi Fairmont. Jack Avi, I'd like you to meet my dear friend, Miss Matilda Grove."

Matilda's expression grew solemn. She walked forward and bent toward the boy. "I am pleased to meet you, Jack Avi."

Matilda studied the boy's face, eyes shimmering with surprising sadness. Then she straightened and her grin returned. "He has your nose."

"Yes, poor lad. Thankfully, he looks a great deal like his mother."

Jane saw Matilda's thin throat convulse. "She must have been beautiful."

"You would like to see her?" Jack Avi extracted his locket again.

"Yes, let me put on my spectacles, and you may show me." Matilda extracted a pair from her reticule and sat down on the high-backed bench. The boy scrambled up beside her, offering her a look at his prized miniature portraits.

She adjusted her eyeglasses and bent to look close. "There's Jane. How young she looks. And your mother . . . Ah yes, you are very like her, Jack Avi."

Her father watched Matilda's face and quietly asked, "You seem . . . unhappy. Do you disapprove?"

"Disapprove? You know me better than that. Disappointed, maybe, but not disapproving."

"Disappointed . . . why?"

"Oh . . ." Matty hesitated. "Only that you stayed away so long." She removed her spectacles and took a deep breath. "Well, we shall have to make up for lost time. I shall enjoy talking with young Mr. Fairmont as well as *old* Mr. Fairmont." She winked. "I see you've already ordered tea. I shall order something to go with it." She rose and turned to the boy. "Which is your favorite, Jack Avi: biscuits, cake, or sponge?"

The little boy nodded vigorously. "All of them."

Miss Matty smiled. "All three it is."

Jane followed her out into the hall. "I'll go, Miss Matty. You stay." She looked at the woman's face in concern. "Are you all right?"

"Yes. Just surprised."

Jane pressed her hand. "I know exactly how you feel."

That afternoon, Mercy knocked on the open door of Mr. Drake's office. "Mr. Drake, may I ask you a favor?"

"Of course. And it's James, if you please. I have taken to calling you Mercy, you may have noticed."

"I have."

"Do you mind?" he asked.

"No, but as you are my employer, I don't think I ought to call you by your given name."

"We were friends first, remember. At least I hope we are."

She opened her mouth to argue, then gave up. "Very well."

He gestured for her to sit. "Now, what did you want to ask me?"

She sat down, clasping her hands. "I've discovered that neither the scullery maid nor the boot boy can read. In this day and age! I wondered if I might teach them? I realize they have their own work to do, and I have mine, but even half an hour a day might go a long way to . . . What? Why are you smiling?"

He slowly shook his head, impish grin remaining. "You can take the teacher out of the school but not the schooling out of the teacher. . . ."

"Is that a yes?"

"The boot boy, yes. I happen to know he has time to spare. But you'll have to ask Mrs. C. about the scullery maid. Even if she agrees, heaven help the poor girl stay awake for lessons. I gather she is up at four in the morning and falls in bed exhausted at ten."

"But I may ask Mrs. Callard?"

"You may."

Mercy smiled. "Thank you."

His gaze lingered warmly on her face. "Completely worth it, I assure you. You have the loveliest smile."

A cold wind blew over the Salisbury Plain that night, and the temperature dipped to winter-like levels. Mercy huddled under the bedclothes and fell asleep reading, her candle lamp still burning on the side table. The cold woke her in the wee hours, wind howling around the windowframe, her feet like ice. She rose, wrapped a shawl around herself, and pulled on stockings. Seeing the kindling and coal already laid in the hearth, she used her candle to light the fire. It leapt to life.

Thank you, Mr. Kingsley. . . .

She dove back into bed and pulled the covers over her head, willing the room to warm and sleep to overtake her once more.

The next time she awoke it was to loud rapping. Were workmen hammering next door? She lowered her covers. The window glowed with a halo of morning light, but . . . why was her room so dark? She felt groggy with sleep, unable to make sense of what she was seeing.

Then she began coughing.

"Miss Grove?" a man called. "Miss Grove!" Her bedchamber door burst open.

Mercy opened her eyes wide in alarm. Mr. Kingsley appeared through the smoke. Was she dreaming? Why was her room full of smoke?

He ran to the window and pushed it open. Cold air rushed in.

He returned to the bed. "Miss Grove, let's get you out of here."

She tried to sit up, but her limbs felt detached from her muddled mind and were slow to obey.

He threw aside the bedclothes and bent low, scooping her up in strong arms. Stupefied and embarrassed, Mercy tried to wiggle from his grasp. What was he doing? She was in her nightclothes!

He carried her out though the passage and into the nearby

schoolroom, where he lowered her onto a chair. "Stay here. I'll make sure the fire is out."

Sitting there breathing clean air, Mercy's mind cleared.

He returned quickly and knelt to look into her face.

"Are you all right? I arrived early to bring you something. When I came upstairs, I saw smoke coming from under your door and feared the worst. Are you sure you're all right?"

"Yes, I'm feeling better already."

"Thank God."

A scuffle step brought their heads around. There stood James Drake, holding Alice by the hand. He adroitly tucked the girl behind his back, as though to shield her from an inappropriate scene. Emotions crossed his face in rapid succession as he tried to work out why his daughter's governess was in the schoolroom in her nightclothes, his builder on his knees before her.

"My fireplace," Mercy sputtered, hoping to quickly dispel the suspicions etched in the tense lines of his face. "Mr. Kingsley saw smoke escaping from under my door. He got me out so I wouldn't be overcome by it."

Hearing this, Alice's head popped out from behind Mr. Drake, her eyes wide in concern.

Mr. Drake frowned deeply.

Before he could say anything, Mr. Kingsley rose and said, "It's my fault. I should have checked the chimney. Flue probably hasn't been cleaned in years and wasn't drawing properly."

"No, it's my fault," Mercy said. "I should not have lit it and gone right back to bed."

Mr. Drake said, "Are you well, Mercy? Shall I send for the doctor?"

"I am all right."

"And your room?"

"I don't know."

Together they walked next door to survey the situation. Cold wind whipped through the curtains, dispelling the worst of the smoke. A thin layer of soot clung to the furniture nearest the hearth.

"I will ask Mrs. Callard to send a maid to clean this up."

"I can do that, Mr. Drake. But thank you."

Mr. Kingsley turned toward the door. "I will send for the chimney sweep directly."

"Yes, please do." Mr. Drake hesitated, brow still furrowed. "May I ask what brought you up here this morning? Not that I am ungrateful you discovered the smoke when you did."

Mr. Kingsley's face reddened. He hesitated, then gestured out into the passage. "I was just bringing Miss Grove a bookcase. There wasn't one in her room."

Mr. Drake looked past him. "I did wonder why that was left haphazardly in the corridor."

Mercy felt embarrassed for Mr. Kingsley and herself. Growing increasingly more so the longer she stood there in her nightclothes.

Mr. Kingsley said, "I made it on my own time, sir."

Mr. Drake regarded him somberly. "I was not criticizing. Though puppets one week, now this? It's a wonder you get any sleep."

Joseph Kingsley lowered his head.

Mr. Drake drew himself up, then turned to look at Alice, her hand still in his. "Well, Alice, it appears school will be starting late today. What say you to a game of chess while you wait? Miss Grove will need time to clean up and . . . dress."

"Very well. Though I much prefer draughts."

Girl and guardian walked away down the passage.

For a moment, Mr. Kingsley remained where he was. Then he cleared his throat. "I am sorry, Miss Grove. I never meant to embarrass you or do anything improper."

"I know you did not. I am sure Mr. Drake knows it too. But we can't blame him for being a little . . . stern. Coming upon us as he did, impressionable Alice in tow."

He flinched. "Surely not how I imagined this morning."

"Nor I. Well. I had better get dressed. I shall see you later."

He nodded and trudged down the stairs, shoulders slumped. She'd forgotten to thank him for the bookcase and for coming to her rescue. She would do so later . . . when fully dressed.

She didn't see Mr. Kingsley the rest of that day, busy as she was cleaning smoky soot from her room and from herself, and teaching Alice. He did send the promised chimney sweep late in the day, though, and in doing his work, the young man sent another cloud of dust and chunks of soot raining down onto the grate so that Mercy had to clean much of her room all over again.

Finished at last, Mercy asked Iris to help carry in the new bookcase. It fit perfectly. No more digging through a box every time she wanted a book to read. It reminded her that she had yet to thank Mr. Kingsley.

The next morning, Mercy went downstairs, hoping to find him. There he was—broad shoulders, sandy hair—on his haunches before a fireplace.

She said, "Thank you again for coming to my rescue, Mr. Kingsley. I feel a bit like Cinderella myself. I am still finding soot in strange places."

He turned, his face lengthened in confusion. With a jolt, she realized it was not Joseph but one of his brothers—with shoulders equally broad, hair a similar sandy brown, but his face younger and features thinner.

"Strange places?" he echoed, one brow raised in question.

Heat rushed to Mercy's face. How foolish she felt. "Oh, sorry. Just a little joke for your brother. I thought you were him. Joseph, I mean."

He shrugged easily. "No . . . Aaron. In future, just remember I am the younger and handsomer of the two. And definitely not Cinderella." He winked, then added, "Joseph isn't working today. Sent me and Matthew in his stead and told us to check every chimney. Now I am beginning to understand why. . . ."

"Oh." Disappointment sank through Mercy. She hoped Joseph wasn't staying away on her account.

"I don't know how long he'll be gone," the young man said. "Is there any message you'd like me to pass along, when next I see him?"

"Oh. Just . . . thank him for me."

"That I will." He returned to his work.

Mercy walked away, ears still burning. She would much rather have thanked Joseph in person.

Aaron Kingsley called after her, "You know, you might be able to catch him in the stable yard, if you hurry."

"Really? Thank you." Mercy turned quickly to the door and stepped outside.

Terse voices in the stable yard drew her attention. Mr. Kingsley's familiar low tones and a woman's higher voice. There was Joseph Kingsley, standing very near petite Esther Dudman, talking in hushed consultation. Miss Dudman was holding a valise and standing beside a traveling chaise. Mercy recognized it as the one James had purchased for his own personal use—as well as an investment, to let out for hire. Joseph opened the door and offered his hand to help the woman inside. He had mentioned Esther was staying in the area, but apparently she was going away somewhere. For good, perhaps?

Mercy's flash of relief was short-lived, however. For a moment later, Mr. Kingsley climbed in after her and shut the door. Mercy blinked in surprise. The mounted postilion signaled the horses and the equipage lurched into motion.

Mercy stood, feet frozen to the cobbles, as the vehicle turned the corner and rounded the house. She saw Joseph's profile clearly through the chaise window, but he did not see Mercy, clearly intent on his traveling companion. An unmarried man and a woman traveling alone together? Her stomach knotted. Then Mercy reminded herself that Esther was his sister-in-law, and the laws of England did not allow a man to marry his deceased wife's sister. She had heard of such couples traveling to other countries to wed, but surely that was not what they were doing. Where *were* they going, just the two of them?

CHAPTER
TWENTY-THREE

On Easter Sunday, Jane and her father took Jack Avi to church with them. The nurse, Priya, remained behind in Wilton.

As they entered St. Anne's, they encountered George and Helena Grove in the vestibule. Jane introduced her father to the new Mrs. Grove and her little brother to both of them.

Helena smiled. "Oh, George, he looks just as I always imagined your servant boy in India."

George Grove looked embarrassed on his wife's behalf. "Only vaguely," he said. "This lad is far more handsome." He grinned at the boy and added a greeting in a foreign tongue.

At Jack Avi's blank look, her father interceded. "I think Mr. Grove means *namaskar.*"

George looked sheepish again. "Never good with languages, I'm afraid." He shook Winston Fairmont's hand. "Good to see you again, sir."

The Gordon family came through the doors. Mr. Gordon greeted them, but his wife gave Jack Avi a wide berth and quickly shepherded her children away.

Jane took Jack Avi's hand and smiled reassurance into his eyes as they entered the nave. Curious stares and a growing murmur of whispers accompanied them up the aisle, moving through the congregation like wind rustling through wheat.

Thora noticed and sent several gossipers her famous black look, then turned to the Barton boys and pressed a stern finger to her lips.

Jane sat in her usual place beside her, and Thora took her hand in a comforting squeeze. Jack Avi sat beside Jane, and her father on the end. Gabriel sat in his customary place across the aisle. They had decided to wait until after they were married to sit together. She sought out his gaze and was rewarded with an empathetic smile.

Mrs. Barton leaned forward from her place behind them and whispered loudly to Jack Avi, "Is this your first time in a church?"

Jack Avi looked to his father again, who answered in the boy's stead. "No, ma'am. We attended services weekly in India."

The vicar entered, and the Easter service began, a joyous time of praying and singing together. During the announcements, Mr. Paley, likely having noticed the whispers and stares, said, "And what a blessing to have Winston Fairmont with us, and to meet his dear young son. We share your sorrow over your recent loss but rejoice that you have returned to England safely after that infamously long and perilous sea voyage. You must come and have dinner with us in the vicarage soon. I know my sons will be eager to become acquainted with yours."

Jane's heart expanded with fondness for their vicar. Her father nodded his gratitude, and the celebration of Christ's resurrection continued.

After the service, Sir Timothy and Rachel came over to greet her father and to meet Jack Avi. Their example would go a long way to ensuring the boy's acceptance in the village. Even the dowager Lady Brockwell came over and spoke to them. It was a kind gesture, and Jane appreciated it.

Then the Miss Cooks came forward, all smiles. Charlotte said, "We've never had a Hindu visit us before."

Her father replied, "Actually, Jack Avi's mother was a Christian, and I am endeavoring to raise him in the faith. Hoping, as parents do, that when the child grows up, he will embrace it for himself."

"Ohhh . . . yes, very true," Judith crooned, batting her lashes. "I do hope you will visit us while you're here, Mr. Fairmont. Not that you have much need of lace, I suppose?" She giggled.

Charlotte added, "We would so enjoy hearing about your travels, would we not, Judy? Did you ride an elephant while you were in India? So exciting, I'm sure—"

"There you are, ladies." Matilda appeared and gently interrupted the awkward scene. "Mrs. Burlingame has just discovered a stain on her favorite lace collar. We are in need of your professional opinion. . . ."

As she led them away, Jane's father managed to catch Matilda's eye, and Jane did not miss the look of gratitude he sent her.

Finally, Mercy came over to speak to them.

"Hello, Mr. Fairmont."

Her father grinned at her. "Mercy, a pleasure to see you again."

"And you, sir." She turned to Jack Avi, pressed her palms together, and bowed slightly. "*Namaskar*. Did I say that correctly?"

He nodded. "You did."

Jane said, "Jack Avi, this is my dear friend, Miss Grove. We have been friends since we were your age."

The boy's face puckered. "You were my age, Didi?"

Jane smiled. "Hard as that is to believe, yes."

"A pleasure to meet you, Jack Avi." To Jane, Mercy added, "I would have liked Alice to meet your brother, too, but she stayed home with Mr. Drake. She is not feeling well."

"I am sorry to hear it. Jack Avi, Miss Grove is a teacher."

The boy asked, "Will you teach me? I am almost old enough for school now, yes?"

"Yes, very soon now. Though I'm afraid I am teaching only one pupil at present."

Again the little brow puckered in confusion. "Only one?"

"For now."

Jane pressed her friend's hand. "Lord willing, Mercy will have a school again one day."

Mercy nodded. "Yes. Lord willing."

After church, Mercy walked home with her family for Easter dinner—the last of the ham cured before winter, along with spring vegetables, hot cross buns, and traditional simnel cake. Afterward, she returned to the Fairmont and went upstairs to check on Alice.

Mr. Drake had been sitting beside the girl's bed and rose in agitation when Mercy entered. "Thank goodness you're back. She still doesn't feel well and seems warm to me. Though what do I know?"

Mercy sat on the edge of the bed. "How do you feel, Alice?"

The girl whispered, "My stomach hurts."

Mercy laid her palm over her brow. It did feel a little warm to the touch.

Mr. Drake asked, "Do you think we should send for the doctor?"

"Not yet. It's probably nothing serious, maybe just something she ate."

"I hope you're right."

"Don't worry, I've had a lot of experience with minor childhood maladies in my years with the girls school."

His green eyes softened. "For which I am grateful. And very glad you're here."

That night, Mercy opened her eyes with a start. Mr. Drake leaned over her bed in his dressing gown.

He winced. "I did not mean to wake you. I only wanted to check on Alice again." He set his candle lamp on the side table.

Mercy recalled then where she was—in her nightclothes and shawl, lying atop the counterpane on Alice's bed. Poor Alice with her hot skin and upset stomach.

Mercy whispered, "I did as well, but she asked me to stay with her. I did not intend to fall asleep." Feeling self-conscious, she tugged higher the neckline of her nightdress.

Mr. Drake sat on the opposite edge of the bed and tenderly felt Alice's forehead and cheeks.

"Better, but she is still too warm."

Mercy sat up. "I shall go for water and cloths."

"Shh . . . stay as you are. I shall fetch them."

He returned in a few minutes with a basin and face cloth. Gently he dipped it in the water, wrung it, and dabbed it to Alice's neck and cheeks.

Mercy whispered, "I can do that, if you like."

"I don't mind." He continued his ministrations, then rewet the cloth and laid it over Alice's forehead. He looked at Mercy. "How are you feeling? I hope you are not ill too?"

"I don't think so. Just a bit tired."

He tentatively stretched out his hand. When she didn't object, he laid his palm over her forehead. "You feel cool."

His fingers gently traced down one cheek before lifting. "I shall bring you a blanket before I go."

"Thank you, but perhaps I should return to my own bed."

"Stay, if you would. It would ease my mind. I will return at daybreak to relieve you."

"Very well."

He pulled a spare blanket from the wardrobe and spread it over Mercy. Gently lifting her plait of hair over its edge, he murmured, "I did not realize your hair was so long."

Surprise and embarrassment heated Mercy's cheeks.

Perhaps realizing the intimacy of what he'd done, he sat there awkwardly, silence hanging between them.

Then he rose. "Well. Good night, Mercy."

She licked dry lips. "Good night . . . James."

By morning, whatever had been ailing Alice had passed, and she was soon her smiling, energetic self again. Mercy, however, was slower to recover from her vigil. For two days, whenever she saw Mr. Drake, she felt herself blush, recalling the feel of his hand on her face. Her hair . . .

Mercy Grove, stop acting like a schoolgirl, she scolded herself. It had only been a gesture of concern and nothing more.

CHAPTER

Twenty-Four

On day one of the Brockwells' house party, Sir Cyril and his sisters were the first to arrive, followed closely by Nicholas Ashford, who carried a single valise. Among the Awdrys' many trunks, valises, and bandboxes, Rachel noticed several gun and bow cases, quivers, and fishing tackle.

Expression eager, Sir Cyril asked, "We will be shooting, I hope? Fishing? Boxing?"

His pretty sister, Arabella, rolled her eyes. "And what are we ladies supposed to do if you men spend the entire time shooting up the countryside and wrestling like lads?"

"I said boxing, Arabella," he replied. "Although wrestling would be diverting as well. And as far as the ladies, hang me; what do I know about female amusements? I suppose you will sew cushions or a sampler or something."

His athletic sister, Penelope, groaned.

Sir Timothy smiled at the tall woman. "Actually, we were thinking of an archery tournament for all of us, if you might offer lessons first?"

"I could, yes," Penelope agreed, face brightening.

Rachel knew archery was not Timothy's favorite sport, but he'd suggested it because he recalled Penelope excelled at it. What a kind and generous husband she had.

Arabella did not appear encouraged by the prospect, so Rachel added, "And we will also have music and dancing."

Justina said, "Though I'm afraid we are short one gentleman to even our numbers. We had hoped our brother Richard might join us, but alas, he sent his regrets."

"I can sit out," Penelope said. "I don't mind."

"But you don't play, Penelope," Arabella reminded her. "One of the ladies will have to accompany us on the pianoforte."

"I shall," Justina offered.

"But you so enjoy dancing, Miss Brockwell," Nicholas protested. "And I had hoped to dance with you again."

"As had I," Sir Cyril added with an awkward little laugh.

Oh dear, Rachel thought. *This will be an interesting few days.* "Never fear," she said. "We have hired musicians, so everyone will have the opportunity to dance."

The Bingleys arrived, Horace apologizing, blaming his sister for taking forever at her toilette and packing enough clothing to outfit an infantry.

Sir Cyril guffawed. "Now, that's an infantry I should like to see."

At Sir Cyril's urging, they began the afternoon with shooting. His man and Timothy's valet loaded guns for the gentlemen, while Penelope prepared her own. The other ladies declined to participate and watched from a safe distance, parasols poised against the sun. Rachel was thankful for the fine weather and a pleasant breeze filled with birdsong, at least until the shooting began.

She flinched as the first shots rang out and hoped the men would be careful where they aimed.

After Nicholas had an unsuccessful round, Sir Cyril clapped him on the back. "Bad luck, Ashford."

Nicholas replied easily, "Haven't had much opportunity to shoot, I'm afraid."

"No matter," Timothy assured him. "There are other abilities more important."

"Are there?" Sir Cyril asked, as though sincerely in doubt.

Horace Bingley watched Penelope shoot with skill, clearly impressed. "You're a crack shot, Miss Awdry."

"Thank you, Mr. Bingley. Actually, I'm off the mark today. Something awry with the barrel, I think." She proceeded to take apart her gun, checking the firing mechanism and chamber before reassembling and reloading. Horace Bingley watched her with wide eyes, mouth loose in amazement.

"I say, Miss Awdry. You are quite a woman."

She sent him a sidelong glance. "Is that good or bad?"

"Good! Excellent, actually."

Next on the schedule was archery. For the inexperienced, Penelope gave a general demonstration of the stance, arrow positioning, aim, and technique, then suggested they try it for themselves.

Horace Bingley's first shot went wild, missing the target altogether, as well as the straw bales behind it. *Thwunk*—right into the gardening shed. The next shot sliced through the privet hedge, glancing off a statue and landing with a *plunk* in the fountain.

"Take pity, Miss Awdry," he beseeched.

Penelope set aside her own bow and tutored Horace one on one.

Sir Cyril employed his bow with skill, taking focused shot after shot, each sinking into the target with a satisfying *whap*. His sister Arabella stood nearby, idly twirling her parasol. She had no interest in this sport either and was content to watch.

Meanwhile, Sir Timothy took great pleasure in helping Rachel. He stood behind her, stretched his left arm parallel to hers, his hand beneath hers on the grip, then wrapped his right arm around Rachel's shoulder to help her pull back and take aim.

She looked up at him with a coy smile. "I thought you said you were not fond of archery?"

"I never attempted it with my beautiful wife before. Now I find I am enjoying the sport very much indeed."

Overhearing him, Arabella teased, "That's enough, you two lovebirds."

To her credit, the pretty young woman seemed to harbor no

resentment toward Rachel for marrying the man that she—at least according to Lady Barbara—had once hoped would take an interest in her.

"And here we are, left to fend for ourselves, Justina," Miss Bingley pouted, bow hanging limply in her hands.

Justina struggled to pull back her bowstring and sighed. "It is more difficult than it looks."

"Mr. Ashford, you seem to have the way of it," Miss Bingley called to him down the line.

It was true, Rachel noticed. Nicholas fared better at archery than he had with guns.

"Have you done this often?" Justina asked.

He shrugged. "Not in years, but I had a target behind the house growing up and practiced a great deal. Far quieter than guns, which wore on my mother's nerves."

"Could you come and show us what we're doing wrong?"

He set aside his bow and walked over to join the two young ladies. "I will do my best."

Much as Timothy had done with her, Nicholas stood behind Justina—though not as close—and placed his hand beneath hers on the grip. He reached around her shoulder and helped her pull back the bowstring and take aim.

"Elbow up. That's it."

Perhaps noticing the somewhat intimate position, his Adam's apple rose and fell, and his cheeks were soon tinged with pink.

Justina released the arrow, and while it missed the center, it did strike the outer ring of the target.

She beamed. "I did it!"

Miss Bingley waved to him. "My turn."

Nicholas helped her as well, patiently and attentively. But Rachel saw no hint of the blush she had seen when he'd stood so close to Justina.

Finally, Horace Bingley insisted Penelope had wasted enough time on him and should shoot a round herself.

He watched the tall woman in amazement as she did so. "Again,

Miss Awdry, you astound me. You are an Amazon! What skill! Do you excel at all sport?"

"Not all."

"Yes, she does," Sir Cyril spoke up. "Pen is just being modest."

"An admirable quality in an admirable woman," Horace breathed.

My goodness, Rachel thought. At this rate, Penelope would be married before Justina was even engaged.

After dinner that evening, the gentlemen joined the ladies in the drawing room far more quickly than Rachel had expected. She had thought Sir Cyril would wish to remain in the dining room to drink port and swap tales of hunting and fishing exploits long after the ladies withdrew. But Sir Timothy had been eager to rejoin his wife, and Nicholas also seemed keen to join the ladies, so Sir Cyril acquiesced. Even Horace Bingley, always ready to share boisterous stories with the gents, added his voice to those preferring not to keep the ladies waiting.

As the men settled themselves in the drawing room, Rachel overheard Nicholas say to Timothy, "I admit, I used to have an erroneous view of the life of gentlemen landowners. Now that I've lived in Thornvale for several months, I have begun to see the role as much more demanding than I ever imagined. I also realized that since Mr. Fairmont left the country and Sir William's ill health limited his participation, you have shouldered more than your fair share. Not only managing your own estate, but serving the parish as well: almshouse board of governors, village council, magistrate. . . . I don't pretend to have your experience, but if there is anything I can do to help, please don't hesitate to let me know."

"Thank you, Mr. Ashford. That is insightful and kind of you. I will keep your offer in mind."

Justina looked from the two men to Rachel, then leaned closer to confide, "How good to see those two talking so companionably when they were once adversaries for your affection. How wonderful if they might be friends like your father and mine—the master of Thornvale and of Brockwell Court—once were."

Rachel nodded. "I agree completely."

When they had all taken seats, Justina began, "As you gentlemen have subjected us ladies to a day full of sports, you must now attempt one of the feminine arts you tried to consign us to, like sewing a cushion or sampler."

Sir Cyril laughed. "Ha, ha! Good joke, Miss Brockwell."

"I am perfectly serious."

His smile faltered. "I have never held a needle in my life and don't mean to start now."

Nicholas said, "I don't mind, Miss Brockwell."

"I shall give it a go as well," Mr. Bingley added.

Sir Cyril smirked at the younger men. "Skilled needlewomen, are you?"

Nicholas shook his head. "Not at all. I've had to sew on a few buttons here and there, and repair a tear when need be, but that is the limit of my experience."

Horace nodded. "The same for me. When I was on my grand tour, my manservant fell ill. I had to learn to do many things I'd never done before."

"Not shoot archery, apparently," Cyril quipped.

"No. Not that."

"How interesting, Mr. Bingley," Penelope said, and Rachel believed it was the first time she had ever heard the woman enter a social conversation of her own volition.

Penelope continued, "Did you meet with any adventures? Danger? Wild animals?"

"All of the above, Miss Awdry."

"Mostly misadventures, if I remember right," his sister teased.

Penelope said, "I would like to hear more about it sometime."

"Then indeed you shall. But later, I think. After whatever Miss Brockwell has in mind for us."

"Yes. Do go on, Justina."

"Never fear, Sir Cyril, I shan't arm you with needle and thread, which would likely be more dangerous in your hands than guns and arrows."

He chuckled. "Very true."

"But each gentleman must trace a silhouette."

"Oh, I would love to have my silhouette drawn," Miss Bingley enthused. "Excellent idea, Justina."

To prepare for the "shade party," Justina and Rachel hung a large piece of white paper on the wall and set a chair before it, positioning a candle lamp nearby to cast the shadow of the subject's silhouette onto the paper.

When all was ready, Justina asked for a volunteer to go first.

Horace Bingley replied instantly, "I shall be the first to draw if Miss Penelope will oblige me by sitting for me."

"Me?" Penelope faltered. "I . . . don't think I have ever had my likeness taken."

"Then you are overdue. It shall be my honor to take the first, though I doubt I can do you justice."

Uneasy with all the attention, Penelope rose with clasped hands and moved toward the chair.

Mr. Bingley showed surprising artistic aptitude, positioning Penelope and the light just so and tracing the outline of her head, face, neck and shoulders. Later, he even created a miniature version by hand, though they had no pantograph to reduce the image mechanically.

As he filled in the outline with lampblack, Rachel looked over his shoulder and decided the likeness was both recognizable and flattering.

"Well done, Mr. Bingley. I am impressed."

"As am I . . ." Penelope breathed.

Next, Timothy drew Rachel's profile. She was relieved that the novelty of the first drawing had passed. Now people began to mingle and help themselves to coffee or tea, so less attention was given to each artist and his subject. The low murmur of voices in the background hopefully meant that people were occupied with their own conversations and not listening to Timothy's flattery.

"I don't need a pantograph," he said to her. "For I know every one of your features by heart. How blessed I am to have such a dear, beautiful wife."

Rachel looked into his face, and tingles of pleasure needled her stomach. After eight long years of pining for this man, she was struck anew with wonder that he was now her husband. "Thank you, my love."

Sir Cyril next traced Justina, more comfortable studying her shadowed profile than he ever seemed looking at her directly. Thankfully, no eye contact was required to draw a silhouette. He created a fair likeness, and Justina thanked him, though Rachel guessed she would have much preferred if Nicholas had been the one to do it, to look at her so keenly and sit with her in such close proximity.

Instead, Nicholas drew pretty Arabella—a pleasant task, Rachel did not doubt.

As they were short one gentleman, Sir Cyril—emboldened by his success with Miss Brockwell—volunteered to draw Miss Bingley's silhouette. Somehow he botched the drawing though, making her nose bigger, her cheeks plumper, and her shoulders slumped forward in unflattering lines.

Miss Bingley glanced at it and instantly looked crestfallen.

Nicholas rose to her defense. "You're blind, man. Miss Bingley is much prettier than that!"

Sir Cyril looked sincerely chastised. "I apologize, Miss Bingley. Pray do not be offended. I am no artist, clearly. You don't look that bad in real life. . . . That is not what I meant. You don't look bad at all. Dash it, I am making a muddle of this. Perhaps we ought to have sewn cushions instead—I could not have performed more woefully."

Arabella laid a hand on her brother's shoulder. "Not every activity needs to show off your skills, Cyril."

He gestured toward the failed silhouette. "And more's the pity."

He went on, "Truly, Miss Bingley, I am sorry. Here, you draw me next. Give me a hook nose and crone chin. I deserve it."

Miss Bingley managed a smile. "Very well, Sir Cyril."

A fresh sheet of paper was hung, and Sir Cyril sat before it, even aping a funny face to encourage her worst depiction. Instead, the image Miss Bingley traced was of a handsome, dignified gentleman.

Regarding it, he shook his head. "You are too kind. This cannot be how you see me. Not after my crude attempt."

She shrugged. "It is how I see you."

And Sir Cyril looked at Miss Bingley, really looked at her, as if for the first time, his gaze holding hers and not shying away.

CHAPTER

Twenty-Five

The next day dawned sunny and mild, so the whole party went out for a long country walk.

Horace Bingley leapt the stile between two fields and challenged Sir Cyril to a foot race. The two dashed ahead across the meadow, but Timothy and Nicholas remained behind and helped the ladies over the stile.

Justina tripped and fell, and Nicholas quickly took her arm and helped her up. "Are you all right? You are not injured, I hope?"

"Only my pride."

"It was nothing, Miss Brockwell. Don't give it another thought. No one noticed."

"You did."

"I am all too aware of your every movement, I fear."

She looked up at him at that, and he looked down.

"It is still so embarrassing!" she lamented, reddening.

"You think a mere stumble over rough ground embarrassing? That is nothing. I once knocked an entire glass of port onto a lady's white silk gown. My mother did not speak to me for a fortnight."

Justina chuckled.

"And at school, instead of Nicholas Ashford, the other lads called me No-class Ashford or Clumsiness Ashford. They also abused my surname . . . but I cannot repeat that to a lady."

"You are making all that up to cheer me."

He gave her a self-deprecating grin. "If only I were. Although if I cheered you, then my mortification is nothing."

"How kind you are, Mr. Ashford."

He offered her his arm over the furrowed ground, "Just in case," and she took it.

Sir Timothy stopped to talk to a neighbor who was surveying an adjacent field with his dog. While the two men talked, Penelope bent low to pet the dog, heedless of its mud-splattered fur. Rachel walked ahead, thinking to catch up with the other women. As she neared them, she overheard Arabella and Miss Bingley's conversation.

"Look at the pair of them," Arabella said, nodding toward the two racers ahead, bent over huffing and puffing. "Mr. Ashford is twice the gentleman our brothers are." She sighed. "But there is no use in admiring him. Not when he looks at Miss Brockwell like he does."

Miss Bingley looked from the men to Nicholas and Justina, walking arm-in-arm, and back again. Rachel saw her expression transform from disappointment to decision.

"I don't know, Arabella. I think your brother has several excellent qualities."

"Has he indeed?" Arabella's eyes shone with knowing light. "How shrewd of you to just now notice."

And for the rest of the day, Miss Bingley stayed close to Sir Cyril Awdry. She was the first to laugh at his jokes and agreed with whatever he said.

Rachel wondered how Justina would feel about her good friend turning her attentions to the man many people expected her to marry. She thought of herself and Jane at that age, both in love with Timothy. She thanked God yet again that those uncertain, turbulent days were behind them.

The next day was spent in lawn bowls and preparing for a formal dinner followed by the promised music and dancing. The ladies donned their best gowns for the occasion, and Jemima, Rachel and Justina's lady's maid, was kept busy curling and coiffing their hair. Even Penelope's hair was subjected to hot irons, though Rachel wished she could provide a more flattering gown for the tall woman to wear.

Her mother-in-law had surprised her by remaining in the background during the party, letting the younger people spend time together and Timothy and Rachel serve as chaperones without her interference. At Rachel's insistence, Lady Barbara did join them for the final dinner but then bid them good night, not staying for the dancing. Rachel did see her speak briefly to Sir Cyril, asking after his mother, but was thankful not to overhear any prodding. Nor did she take Justina aside to persuade her to encourage Sir Cyril's attention. Perhaps she had finally resigned herself to leaving the outcome in God's hands. Whatever the case, Rachel was pleased with the way things had gone and congratulated herself on a successful house party.

Later, after the dancing ended and the musicians were packing up, Rachel and Timothy bid everyone good night and started upstairs. They had just reached the first-floor landing when Rachel heard voices in the hall below. She looked over the banister and was startled to see Justina and Sir Cyril speaking together.

". . . came here with the express purpose of asking for your hand, Miss Brockwell. I know it has long been assumed by our families. I have already made my intentions toward you clear, and I am a man who does not shirk his duty."

He ducked his head and continued, "But I am not such a dullard not to realize you've been reluctant. Your brother believes it is because of your age. Lady Barbara assures me you will accept me in time. In fact, she suggested I take advantage of the social occasion to declare myself before everyone." He chuckled uncomfortably. "But I could not put either of us in such an awkward situation. Nor was I confident enough to risk humiliation. This is one contest in which I have little skill."

His gaze flickered to Justina's face, then away again. "So here we are. I shall not argue with whatever answer you give. It is your decision. What shall we tell our families, Miss Brockwell? Will you marry me, or will you not?"

Wanting to intervene, Rachel started toward the stairs, but Timothy forestalled her with a gentle hand. "Shh," he whispered. "Let her decide for herself."

Rachel knew he was right and reluctantly allowed Timothy to lead her down the passage. Justina would refuse the man, would she not? At least Rachel hoped she would.

Ten minutes later, Rachel was sitting before the mirror in her narrow dressing room, brushing out her hair, when Justina knocked on the door and let herself in. She flopped down on the chaise longue and covered her face with her hands.

Rachel turned toward her in concern. "What is it? We saw you talking with Sir Cyril. Did he take it badly?"

"I am engaged."

Rachel's heart sank. "To Sir Cyril?"

"Of course—who do you think?"

"But I . . . I thought you would refuse him. I thought you preferred someone else."

Justina moaned. "I had no idea it was coming. It had been such a pleasant night. I was tired and happy, my mind full of Ni . . . of other things. When Sir Cyril asked for a moment of my time and walked beside me into the hall, I felt no trepidation. Never guessed what he intended.

"'It is after midnight,' he said. 'You do know what that means? It is your birthday.'"

Rachel drew in a sharp breath. She'd forgotten.

"I know," Justina said. "It had quite slipped my mind too. I know we planned to have a small family celebration later, after everyone had gone, but I wasn't thinking about that yet. My thoughts were full of the party."

The girl lifted her hands and stared at the ceiling. "I should have guessed. For once he wasn't smiling that foolish smile of his. He looked sincere and even nervous. He acknowledged our families' expectations, but said it was my decision."

Justina sighed. "I said I would marry him. I think he was as surprised as I was when the words came out of my mouth."

"But, Justina, if you have doubts, or your inclination lies elsewhere . . ."

The younger woman shook her head. "It's too late. I've given him my answer. I feel better, truth be told. Indecision is so tiresome. I shall enjoy being mistress of Broadmere, and Arabella and Penelope will be dear sisters. I will miss you and Timothy, of course. And Mamma. But on the whole, I think I shall be very content. Sir Cyril is more feeling than I credited. I did not do him justice before."

"And Nicholas . . . ?"

Justina hesitated, then sat up, drawing back her shoulders. "I know you want your cousin to be happy, but I should not worry about him if I were you. Everyone admires him. He'll have no trouble attracting a wife who deserves him. A woman with a strong mind, less easily persuaded by others."

"Justina . . ."

"I am all right, truly. Please try to be happy for me."

"I will of course be happy for you, if this is really what you want."

"It is. Mamma will be so pleased."

After Justina swept from the room, Rachel sat there, heart and stomach twisting. Then she went into the bedchamber and confided in Timothy. He had not expected the news but was not upset by it as she was.

As Justina had predicted, Lady Barbara was thrilled. They could hear her exclamations of delight echoing down the corridor.

The next morning Rachel rose from bed, a headache pinching her brow. She was sitting at the dressing table, massaging her temples, when Jemima came in to help her dress and arrange her hair.

"Are you feeling poorly, my lady?"

"Just a headache. I am sure it shall pass."

"Can I bring you something for it?"

"No, thank you. I know you have other ladies to attend to this morning."

"True, and I had better hurry. . . ."

Timothy had left for an early morning ride, so Rachel descended the stairs alone. She hoped Nicholas would be down already, so she could relay the news of Justina's engagement to him in private.

When she reached the breakfast room, she was relieved to find him standing at the table, his back to her. He turned when she entered, a smile on his boyish face.

"Nicholas. I am glad to see you up early," Rachel began, then noticed the ribbon-tied bouquet of anemones in his hands.

"Good morning. I understand it is Miss Brockwell's birthday, so I dashed out for these. I wanted to mark the day."

Rachel opened her mouth to warn him, but he raised a finger to his lips. "Shh." He set the flowers at Justina's usual spot at the table, then stepped eagerly to the covered dishes on the sideboard.

Rachel's stomach clenched. "That is very kind of you, Nicholas, but I must tell you that—"

Miss Bingley and Penelope Awdry walked in together, talking amicably. Rachel restrained a sigh. She pasted on a smile and greeted her guests, offering to pour them coffee. Horace Bingley entered, his face lighting up when he saw Penelope. Rachel had not expected to see him so soon; he was not known to be an early riser. Horace piled his plate high and sat directly across from Penelope. His sister, Rachel noticed, hid a grin behind a sip of coffee.

A few moments later, Lady Barbara sailed into the room, countenance glowing. A weary-looking Justina trailed more sluggishly behind her, shadows under her eyes, followed by Sir Cyril. Lady Barbara did not usually come down for breakfast, preferring a tray delivered to her room. But today was no ordinary day. Dread twisted Rachel's stomach as she braced herself for the announcement to come.

"Good morning," the dowager said cheerfully. "I trust everyone slept well?"

The others politely nodded their agreement. Rachel said nothing, for she had slept poorly indeed.

"Good." Lady Barbara motioned Justina and Sir Cyril forward. "It is a pity not everyone is present, for we have happy news to share." She looked pointedly at Sir Cyril.

Sir Cyril cleared his throat and announced, "Miss Brockwell and I are engaged."

Nicholas stiffened. Miss Bingley's mouth slackened in surprise and, if Rachel was not mistaken, disappointment. They all remained suspended in awkward silence for several moments. Horace sent his sister a worried glance, then dutifully offered his well wishes. Taking his lead, Penelope and Miss Bingley murmured their congratulations as well.

Justina, Rachel noticed, avoided looking at Nicholas. Her gaze fell upon the colorful bouquet at her place. "Oh, anemones, my favorite! How kind of you to remember, Sir Cyril."

The man chuckled uneasily. "They are not from me, I'm afraid. Capital idea, though."

"Congratulations to you both," Nicholas said, his voice strained.

Justina looked at him then, and realization flickered in her eyes. Blinking, she turned and stepped to the sideboard, blindly scooping things onto a plate. Then she sat and halfheartedly poked at her food.

Arabella Awdry entered last, and Lady Barbara lost no time in announcing the news again to her.

"Excellent! Mamma will be delighted," Arabella exclaimed. "And what a beautiful bride Justina shall be."

Justina smiled wanly in reply, but one glance at Nicholas told Rachel the thought pained him. His shoulders sagged, and he ate not a single bite.

A few moments later, Justina rose. "I . . . find I am not hungry after all. Too much rich food and excitement last night. Please excuse me."

Lady Barbara frowned but made no protest.

After breakfast, guests began to disperse, some strolling outside to take the air on the beautiful morning, while others went up to their rooms to oversee the packing of their belongings.

Stepping into the hall a short while later, Rachel saw Nicholas opening the front door, valise in hand.

"Nicholas, wait. You must say good-bye at least."

He winced and turned back. "I apologize." He bowed. "Thank you for your hospitality and for including me in your party."

Rachel walked near and lowered her voice. "I am sorry things did not turn out as we hoped."

"Me too." He inhaled, then heaved a weary sigh. "Well, I'd better dash. My mother hoped I'd return in time to take her to the Wishford market, but I fear it's too late."

Searching his face, Rachel said softly, "Perhaps it is not too late."

He held her gaze a moment, his mouth curved into a sad smile. Then he turned and walked out the door.

Rachel watched him go with a heavy heart. Suddenly Justina was at her side, silently slipping a hand into hers. Rachel glanced at the girl's resolved profile, her gaze fastened on Mr. Ashford's retreating figure.

Rachel whispered, "Are you sure?"

Her young sister-in-law nodded, even as her chin trembled.

Then the two women watched Nicholas walk down the long drive until he disappeared from view.

CHAPTER
Twenty-Six

Four days after Mr. Kingsley and Esther departed together, Mercy went downstairs during Alice's recess for a cup of tea. She saw Mr. Drake standing at the window overlooking the stable yard and crossed the hall toward him.

He glanced over at her approach, then gestured outside. "Joseph is back from his trip."

"Oh good." Relief and worry wrestled within her. Had Esther returned as well?

Mercy joined him at the window. Beyond the dusty chaise, Mr. Kingsley and Esther stood talking beneath the sweet chestnut tree, half hidden by its branches. Back to the window, his broad shoulders suddenly expanded as he embraced the petite woman.

Then he angled his sandy head and kissed her passionately. Shock ran over Mercy, her heart banging painfully in her breast. *Sister-in-law indeed.* Apparently they had grown even closer during their trip.

Mercy turned away, unable to watch a moment longer. She stood, back resting against the hard wall, hand to her chest, trying to catch her breath. What a fool she had been to let herself care for Mr. Kingsley so deeply. To imagine admiration in his eyes when all along a passion for another woman—a forbidden woman—burned in his heart.

Had he ever admired her, or had he simply felt sorry for Miss Grove, the plain spinster? The thought cut deep. Tears blurred her vision, but she blinked them back.

Mr. Drake turned to her, face grim. "I am sorry."

If he spoke words of pity or tried to comfort her, she'd never be able to hold back the tears. "Please," she whispered, "I just need a moment alone."

His expression softened. "Of course. But if you need anything or want to talk later, let me know." He pressed her hand and strode away, leaving her to her solitary misery.

Mercy told herself she had no right to feel betrayed. Mr. Kingsley had made no promises to her, no declarations. But his actions, his many kindnesses, the fond way he had looked at her . . . she had taken each as a sign, a gift, to be treasured and remembered. *Foolish creature.*

"Miss Grove?"

Mercy looked up at the sound of his voice. She blinked to bring the approaching figure into focus. Joseph Kingsley.

She drew in a shaky breath. Had he seen her spying from the window? Rushed upstairs to try to explain?

She turned toward the window once more . . . and stared in disbelief. The man and women still stood there, locked in an embrace. The man shifted, and she saw more of his face. Not Joseph. His younger brother, Aaron.

A strangled cry of mortification and relief escaped.

"What is it?" Joseph asked. "What's wrong?"

In a moment he was by her side, looking out the window to see what had caused her singular reaction.

He said nothing, but a glance at his profile revealed the tightening of his jaw. The frown. Was he jealous? Did he feel betrayed as she had a moment before?

"You . . . do not approve?" she whispered.

"Of kissing in broad daylight for all the world to see when he's supposed to be working?"

"I meant of them as a couple."

He grimaced. "I told him to wait until he had more to offer her, until he had saved up for a house and could better support her. He spends every farthing he earns before it reaches the bottom of his pocket. But apparently he didn't listen, which I imagine is no surprise to anyone but me."

He looked at her. "I'm sorry if seeing that shocked or scandalized you, Miss Grove. They apparently missed each other a great deal while we were away, but I will talk to him about being more discreet in future."

Her mind wheeled, absorbing the truth like a dry sponge. "No, I am not scandalized. I thought . . . Never mind. I was just surprised." She drew a shuddery breath. "Did you . . . have a good trip?"

"Not sure how good, but we accomplished what we went for. Esther had received urgent word that her mother had suffered a fall, caused by a broken step."

"Oh no." Mercy knew the woman was Naomi's mother as well, and therefore his mother-in-law.

He explained, "I escorted Esther to the house in Basingstoke and attended to the step while she attended to her mother."

"Was she badly hurt?"

He shook his head. "Thankfully it turned out to be just a sprained ankle. Nothing broken. We celebrated Easter together while we were there."

"Good."

He tilted his head and regarded her, concern etched in the lines of his face. "Are you certain you're all right? You looked so upset when I came upon you just now."

Dare she tell him? How humiliating. How . . . revealing.

She managed a wobbly smile. "I am all right. Now."

He stepped closer, and his Adam's apple traveled up and down his muscled neck. "I wonder, Miss Grove, might you have dinner with me sometime?"

Hope flared, but Mercy hesitated. "I . . . would, but I usually dine with Mr. Drake and Alice. He likes to hear what we studied each day."

"Ah." Disappointment flashed across his countenance, and he looked down.

"But I sometimes return to the coffee room for a cup of tea after Alice has gone to bed."

He looked up at that. "Do you indeed?"

She nodded. "Not every night, but now and again."

He thought. "I have a family obligation tonight, but I might wander back here tomorrow evening, if you think you might be having a late-night cup of tea?"

She grinned. "Yes, I think there is every chance I shall be thirsty by then."

Mercy enjoyed taking her evening meals with Mr. Drake and Alice. The coffee room possessed a casual atmosphere, its tables filled with coachmen, off-duty staff, locals, and a few regular guests who preferred it to the more formal dining parlour. Greetings were exchanged from table to table, and diners had quickly grown accustomed to seeing Mr. Drake eating with his adopted daughter and her governess in their midst. There was nothing private or suggestive about the arrangement. The three of them were often drawn into conversations and good-natured laughs with the others. Mercy had become comfortable with the situation and contributed to the conversation when she could.

But the day after Mercy's discussion with Mr. Kingsley, Mr. Drake stopped by the schoolroom and announced, "I thought we would dine in one of the private parlours tonight, if you don't mind. I have invited two guests to join us. A dancing master and his wife, traveling by post chaise to London. They seem most interesting and amiable."

"Oh. Of course," Mercy reluctantly agreed. "Though I would be happy to dine on my own while you entertain your guests. You needn't feel obligated to include me."

"Not at all. I think you would enjoy talking with them and vice versa. Shall we say seven o'clock?"

Mercy nodded. "Alice and I will be there."

At the appointed hour, Mercy and Alice dressed for dinner and walked downstairs together. They entered the private parlour, set with lovely old Fairmont china and silver, and lit by candelabra.

Mr. Drake introduced them to an attractive couple in their mid to late twenties—a dark-haired man and a pale-blond woman.

"Mr. and Mrs. Valcourt, please meet my daughter, Alice. And her governess and friend, Miss Grove."

If they were surprised to be introduced to the governess, they had the good grace not to show it. But then again, some people would probably look down on a humble dancing master.

Mrs. Valcourt was so beautiful and well dressed that Mercy initially felt intimidated. But the woman's manner was so thoroughly unaffected and friendly that Mercy's unease quickly fell away. When they all moved to take their places at the table, Mercy noticed a slight mounding of Mrs. Valcourt's abdomen and guessed she might be expecting a child.

Together the five of them sat down and began the meal. Conversation flowed easily with the charming couple, married nearly four years. They lived in Devon but were passing through, taking in a few sights, including Stonehenge, on their way to town. Mrs. Valcourt explained that they visited London occasionally to meet with the publisher who printed her husband's books of dance music and instruction. Pride and affection shone in her eyes as she described his accomplishments, but Mr. Valcourt dipped his head modestly.

"Only three books, Julia. I am no John Playford."

She patted his hand. "Not yet."

Mr. Drake congratulated him, then said, "I don't suppose I could persuade you to give Alice here a dancing lesson? I would be happy to cover your usual fees, of course. I don't believe she has had any instruction in dance, has she, Miss Grove?"

"I'm afraid not. Though is she perhaps a little young?"

"Never too young to start and never too old." Mr. Valcourt smiled. "I would be delighted, assuming Miss Alice would like to?"

Alice nodded shyly, cheeks dimpled.

The dancing master looked from Mr. Drake to Mercy. "And perhaps the two of you would join us? Easier to teach a figure with another couple or two."

Mr. Drake lifted a casual hand. "Of course. What say you, Miss Grove? Are you willing to give it a go?"

Mercy hesitated. "I am afraid I am not terribly graceful, but if it will help, I will do my part."

Later, after they had eaten their dessert, Mr. Drake asked the servants to move aside tables from the end of the formal dining parlour nearest the pianoforte. The women drank tea and the men coffee while they waited.

When all was ready, Mr. Valcourt said, "Shall we begin?"

He explained a few points of dance etiquette and posture to Alice, then said, "Let's begin with a simple longways dance for two couples. Mr. Drake, if you will dance with your daughter, I shall partner Miss Grove."

"With pleasure. May I have this dance, my fair lady?" James bowed in courtly address to Alice, who giggled and curtsied in turn.

Their playful affection warmed Mercy's heart.

Mr. Valcourt walked them through the steps. Mercy faltered, nervous to dance with this expert. But the handsome man was all ease and encouragement.

He said, "Circle four hands once around. Then first corners change places. Then second corners likewise. Well done, Miss Alice. Now, first couple leads down the center, then back, then cast down one place. . . ."

Mr. Valcourt continued his instructions. Mercy struggled a bit, but elegant James Drake glided smoothly through the steps. He'd likely had dancing lessons as part of his education. She had too but was woefully out of practice.

Mr. Valcourt said, "Now, let's try it to music. My dear, if you will oblige us?"

Mrs. Valcourt moved to the pianoforte. "I don't play often or skillfully, so please don't listen too closely."

Mr. Valcourt smiled his thanks, then turned back to the others. "I will call out the steps the first time. Ready?"

His wife launched into the jaunty introduction, then he called out the first step. After a few minutes, Mercy mastered the simple pattern and began to relax and enjoy herself.

When the tune ended, Mr. Valcourt applauded. "Well done, all of you. Shall we try another?"

"Yes, let's do!" Alice enthused.

"Very well. But first, let's change partners." Mr. Valcourt grinned at Alice. "I want a chance to dance with my new prized pupil."

Again Alice giggled and curtsied.

Mr. Drake moved to Mercy's side without comment.

Mr. Valcourt explained the next dance, and then they walked through the sequence twice without music.

Mercy felt self-conscious dancing with her employer but found she enjoyed the feel of Mr. Drake's smooth hands holding hers, and the way he smiled into her eyes whenever the pattern brought them face-to-face. She also liked the way he bent low to gently take Alice's hands when directed to change places with his corner.

When Mr. Valcourt thought they were ready, he signaled to his wife, who again played while the four of them danced.

Alice beamed brightly through it all, clearly enjoying the attention and the pleasure of moving to music.

The door opened, and Mr. Kingsley appeared in the threshold, mouth parted in surprise. Seeing him, Mercy stumbled, then turned the wrong way, but Mr. Drake gently prodded her in the right direction.

Noticing the newcomer, Mrs. Valcourt stopped playing.

Mr. Kingsley raised a hand. "Sorry. Didn't mean to interrupt."

James released Mercy's hand and asked, "Did you need something, Kingsley?"

Joseph's gaze shifted toward Mercy, then away again. "I was only looking for . . . something. But . . . never mind. Go on with your dance."

With a jolt of guilt, Mercy remembered. They had tentatively planned to meet for tea in the sitting room after Alice had gone to bed. The girl's bedtime had come and gone. Mercy'd had no idea dinner with guests would last so long.

"It's an impromptu lesson," she blurted. "For Alice."

"In fact, you are just in time, my friend," Mr. Valcourt offered. "We could use another man."

"Me? Heavens, no. I'm only the builder."

"You would likely catch on faster than I have, Mr. Kingsley," Mercy said, hoping to put him at his ease. "I have little sense of rhythm."

The dancing master said kindly, "Not at all, Miss Grove. Come and join us . . . Mr. Kingsley, was it?"

"No, thank you. I can't stay. Again I apologize for interrupting. Good night."

He turned and left, shutting the door behind him. Disappointment washed over Mercy. But perhaps it was for the best. Would it not be even more awkward to dance with this man she admired in front of Mr. Drake and his guests? At that thought, she glanced over and was disconcerted to find Mr. Drake studying her with interest and perhaps understanding.

CHAPTER
Twenty-Seven

When Mercy entered the schoolroom the next morning, she drew in a breath at an unexpected sight: a jar of lily of the valley on her desk, just like the ones that grew at Ivy Cottage. She walked closer, admiring the bell-like flowers, and felt her heart warm.

Alice bounded in, wearing a brand-new dress. Mercy asked her, "Did you pick these for me, Alice?"

"No." The girl joined her at the desk and bent her nose to the fragrant flowers. "Mmm . . . they smell good."

"Yes. It's just that I remember telling you they were one of my favorites. Did you happen to mention that to Mr. Drake, perhaps, or . . . ?"

The girl shrugged. "I may have done. Or Mr. Kingsley. I tell them both *everything*."

"I see. Well." Mercy feigned nonchalance. "Thank you to whoever left them."

Alice turned to her. "We could ask them which it was."

"No, thank you, Alice. Never mind." How embarrassing to ask the wrong man if he had given her flowers! She gestured the girl toward the table. "Now, let's eat our breakfast before it grows cold."

Together, they ate the meal Iris delivered: porridge, hard-boiled eggs, toast, and jam. While she nibbled, Mercy's gaze kept returning to the flowers.

After their prayers and lessons, Mercy gave Alice her usual midmorning recess.

"I am going to show Papa my new dress!"

Alice jogged eagerly down the stairs, while Mercy followed more sedately behind her. She reached the office in time to hear James say, "*Another* new dress?"

Joining them, Mercy explained, "Your mother sent it."

Alice held out the embroidered skirt. "Do I look pretty?"

"You were already pretty," he said patiently. "New dress or not."

"I think it's the prettiest yet. I'm going to show Johnny." Alice whirled and ran out of the room.

"Poor Johnny," he murmured, then looked up at Mercy. "I suppose I should have been more effusive in my praise? I confess I fear it will make her vain if I compliment her looks too often."

"I don't think so. . . . Not if you compliment more than her beauty. Praise her when she works hard, or helps someone, or does something selfless."

He nodded. "Sounds like good advice. Thank you. Is that what your father did with you?"

"Perhaps not about my looks, but in other ways, yes."

James blew a breath through puffed cheeks. "Heavy burden, this fatherhood business." He leaned back in his chair, gesturing for her to take a seat.

"True," Mercy allowed. "But you don't need to be perfect." She sat across from him. "My father was not a perfect man, but I never doubted he loved me. I may have been riddled with insecurities about my looks, but thanks to him I never doubted I was intelligent and capable of goodness and kindness as well as accomplishment."

Mercy sighed, thinking of some of her former pupils, now grown. "Heaven help the poor girls who have no notion of their value in a loving father's eyes. Many spend their lives trying to find affection and approval from men in all sorts of damaging ways."

He flinched. "A sobering thought. I am certain I will make many mistakes, but Alice will never doubt how much I love and value her, whether she accomplishes anything in the world's view or not."

Mercy nodded, touched by his words. "I believe you."

He stared into the fire for several moments, fingers tightly clenched around his coffee cup. "And what about a man who has never known approval or affection from his father?"

Mercy looked at him. In his ducked head and slumped posture she saw the dejected young boy he'd once been. She said gently, "I suppose he . . . spends his life buying bigger and bigger hotels."

He gave her a crooked grin at that, and Mercy returned it.

Now that Justina was officially engaged, Rachel accompanied her and her mother back to Victorine's for the first fitting.

Victorine welcomed them, then offered them tea. Lady Barbara accepted and sat on the sofa.

Was it Rachel's imagination, or did Victorine's hand tremble slightly as she poured? Why was she so nervous? Rachel smiled at the dressmaker, hoping to help put her at ease.

Once Lady Barbara and Rachel were seated with their teacups, Victorine helped Justina out of her walking dress and petticoats to better measure her figure. The young woman stood in front of the cheval mirror in her chemise and long stays, slender and lovely, but Rachel thought she glimpsed sadness in her eyes.

Rachel wondered if she should press Justina about the engagement to be sure the girl's heart was truly in it. But she worried interfering would only evoke doubt where, perhaps, none belonged. It would also surely evoke Lady Barbara's disapproval, and perhaps Timothy's too. Clasping her hands, Rachel again resolved to be supportive of Justina's decision. She just hoped it was the right one.

Victorine began draping a long piece of material over one of Justina's shoulders, pinning the front to the neckline of her chemise.

She said, "Now that we've agreed on the design from the drawings, I thought I would begin by making a pattern for the bodice, which will be the most difficult and must fit perfectly."

Lady Barbara wrinkled her nose. "What is that horrid material? Tell me you are not thinking of using *that*."

The material, a garish shade of yellow printed with a haphazard pattern of pineapples and cherries, was singularly unattractive, Rachel could not deny.

"No, my lady. This is simply a remnant left behind by Mrs. Shabner."

As she explained, Victorine pinned a second piece over Justina's other shoulder, then joined and pinned it to the first. "I plan to make a pattern for the gown from this material. I will then use that pattern to cut the actual material. This step will give me a more accurate estimate of how many yards I shall need of the satin, as well as the netting, cording, and lining."

Lady Barbara frowned. "That is not how my dressmaker does it. She drapes the material right on my person and—"

"Mamma, we are not here to criticize," Justina interrupted. "I am sure each dressmaker has her own methods." The girl smiled encouragement at Victorine, then said, "I was thinking, madame . . . What about a layer of white moravian work in cambric at the neckline?"

Her mother frowned again. "We are discussing a wedding gown, Justina, not a new petticoat."

Undeterred, Justina said, "Then . . . how about Vandyke ornaments and net oversleeves? Oh! And scalloped flounces at the hem?"

Victorine hesitated. "Those were not in the drawings we agreed to, miss. I would need to redraw and refigure materials."

Lady Barbara said, "Again, my dressmaker would have no difficulty accommodating her customer's wishes."

Victorine swallowed. "Of course, my lady. Whatever you like."

After pinning the bodice to the desired shape, Victorine measured Justina's arms, hips, and the length from bosom to floor.

She extracted the pins holding the pattern to the girl's chemise, then carefully removed the model bodice. "That is all I should need for now. Besides the . . . advance. I shall send word when I am ready for the next fitting."

Lady Barbara handed her a bank draft. "I would demand a more certain completion date," the dowager said. "But as my daughter has yet to name her wedding day, we shall await *your* pleasure." Sarcasm colored the last words, but they all pretended not to notice.

Later that day, Mercy and Alice sat at one of the inlaid game tables, finishing a game of draughts. Then Alice went outside to play with the kittens, giving Mercy a welcome respite between games. In the adjacent entry hall, James Drake stood near the desk, talking to his clerk.

Two men walked through the front door and, seeing Mr. Drake, broke into broad smiles.

"JD, you old Corinthian," the tall, dark-haired one exclaimed. "How are you, old swell?"

The stout one added, "Still conquering the world one business at a time, I see."

"Rupert and Max," Mr. Drake greeted. "What a surprise."

"It's been too long since you visited us, so we decided to come and visit you. We saw your father at the club. He told us about your little project here. Can't say he approves, you know."

James stiffened. "That's nothing new." He gestured to the soaring reception room. "Just opening a country hotel."

The stout one looked around. "Very grand. But why am I surprised? You are a Hain-Drake, after all, and everything you touch turns to gold."

"There is a bit more to it than that, Max," James said. "But I am glad the Fairmont meets with your approval."

"Will you put us up, JD?" Rupert asked. "Or have you no room in the inn for your old friends?"

"You are very welcome. I have a few completed rooms available, if you'd each like your own."

Rupert said, "Perfect. The last inn put us together with two other gentlemen—and I use that term loosely. Barely room for me and their protruding bellies. Poor Max ended up on the floor."

"Vile place." Max shuddered. He looked around the elegant hall with its lush furnishings once more, his gaze skimming past Mercy as though she were invisible. "But I could get used to this. I might never leave. . . ."

James turned his face away—to hide a grimace, perhaps—and rang a bell on the reception desk.

The porter appeared. "Theo here will show you to your rooms." He handed over the keys. "If you are not too tired from your journey, I'd like to invite you to join me for dinner."

"Of course we'll join you," Max said. "It's why we are here, after all."

"Excellent." James managed a smile. "Shall we say seven?"

As the porter led the two away, James glanced back and noticed Mercy sitting there. He came and flopped down into the chair beside hers.

"Two old friends of mine have just arrived unexpectedly."

"So I gathered." She watched his face. "The surprise is not a pleasant one?"

He glanced up to make sure the men were out of earshot. "Not especially, no. The fellows were pleasant enough companions in my university days, but we have little in common now." He sighed. "Considering how . . . indiscreet they can be when foxed, I think one of the private parlours might be best."

He looked at her. "Though I hope that with you and Alice there, the men will moderate their behavior."

She glanced at him warily, thinking, *Not another dinner!*

Unaware, he continued. "Where is Alice, by the way? Out with Johnny and the kittens again?"

She nodded.

"I should have guessed."

Mercy said, "I understand why you want Alice there. But no one expects the governess to dine with family and friends. I know we usually eat together, and it is very kind of you to include me. However, I think it would be better if only Alice joined you on this occasion."

"I have not included you in our little family dinners out of kindness, Mercy, but because Alice enjoys your company." His green eyes held hers. "And so do I."

Mercy looked away first. "I have enjoyed those meals together as well. But I confess the thought of joining you and your fashionable friends is a daunting prospect."

"You don't give yourself enough credit, Mercy Grove. Don't forget you are a gentlewoman of good breeding and superior education, from an old, respectable family. Not to mention, you have lovely eyes and one of the most beautiful smiles I have ever seen. You are in no way inferior to those two, I assure you."

She looked up at him from beneath her lashes, embarrassed but pleased. "You are generous, Mr. Drake. But my family, though old, is not particularly esteemed, except here in Ivy Hill. I realize you flatter me to bolster my confidence, so I will join you tonight." She gave him a knowing grin. "You must really feel you need reinforcements at dinner, so I will oblige you. And if the conversation turns . . . indiscreet, I will be there to escort Alice up to bed."

"Good point."

Mercy rose. "Is there anything special you would like Alice to wear? She'll be eager to make a good first impression."

"Whatever you think best."

As Mercy walked upstairs, she wondered what she should wear. She decided on the willow green. Most of her gowns were designed to blend in, but on this occasion, she would need all the confidence she could muster.

Iris helped Mercy dress and remained longer to arrange her hair, having caught wind of the special occasion. Alice's hair too was curled with the hot iron, and together Mercy and the maid helped the girl change into a sweet gown of blush pink.

When the time arrived, Mercy walked Alice downstairs, hand in hand. Her own palm was damp, and she held Alice's hand as much to reassure herself as the child. Alice, for her part, seemed more excited than nervous. Her manner displayed increasing confidence in Mr. Drake's affections, though she still felt uneasy about having to make conversation with adults—especially strangers. Mercy didn't blame her. In this instance, she felt uneasy too.

Through the open door to the largest private parlour, Mercy saw the men clustered around a decanter on the sideboard. James turned when Mercy and Alice entered, and noticing, the others turned as well.

"There you are." James's smile encompassed both Alice and Mercy, but his appreciative gaze lingered on her in the green dress. "Come, let me introduce you."

He turned to the others. "Old friends, allow me to introduce two new and special additions to my life. This charming young lady is Alice, my adopted daughter. And this is Miss Grove, her teacher."

Their mouths fell ajar.

James went on to complete the introductions, giving the gentlemen's full names.

"I . . . I don't know where to start!" Rupert sputtered. "Your father made no mention of a daughter."

Max's gaze swept past Mercy, then fixed on the girl. "Alice, is it? How charming you are with your blond hair and green eyes . . ." His gaze shifted to James, flicking from his dark blond hair to his similar eyes. "Come and sit down, Alice." He sent Mercy a curt nod.

She had been dismissed. It was her cue to leave, and only a simpleton would not recognize it.

But Alice reached her free hand toward Mercy. "Miss Grove is to eat with us."

"How kind you are, but I am sure your governess would prefer to take her supper in her own room."

Mercy could not deny it, even though offense crept over her at the man's condescending tone.

"Actually, I particularly invited Miss Grove to join us," Mr. Drake said. "She is more than governess to Alice; she is a valued friend. To both of us."

Rupert's brows rose. "Is she indeed?"

James nodded. "In fact, Miss Grove operated her own girls school before agreeing to come here and continue Alice's education. I am in her debt."

He'd made it sound as though Mercy had given up her school by choice, but she would not correct that misapprehension. Not to these two.

"My, my," Max said. "You must have made quite a tempting offer to convince her to give up her own school to become a governess."

Was that innuendo in his tone? It was difficult to tell. Either way, James didn't take the bait and made do with a nod. "She was very kind to agree. The Groves are the oldest family in Ivy Hill. Miss Grove is respected by everyone who knows her, and she is a close friend of Sir Timothy and Lady Brockwell."

That was going it a bit brown, Mercy thought, trying not to fidget under his stilted praise.

Max and Rupert gave her another look. Max's attention quickly flitted away again, but Rupert's speculative gaze scoured her face, her long neck, and collarbones. Mercy shifted. The way he looked at her made her feel exposed. Wanting. Like a bruised fruit left alone at the end of market day.

Thankfully, at that moment waiters brought the food in, so they were all seated and the meal began.

The gentlemen turned their attention to Alice, asking a few polite questions about her schoolwork, favorite subjects, and books. Max studiously avoided questions of her background, Mercy noticed.

But Rupert asked, "And who is your mother, Alice? Would we know her?"

Max dug a sharp elbow into his side.

Rupert glowered at him. "What?"

Unaware of the tension, Alice softly replied, "My mother's name was Mary-Alicia Smith, but she died."

"Poor thing. How sad. And how kind of you, James, to take her in."

"It was my privilege."

"That reminds me . . ." Max snapped his fingers. "Remember the time JD took in that stray cat at university? His roommate threatened to toss it out the window, so James hid the cat in Rupert's room. What a laugh to hear poor Rupert the next morning, trying to explain all those scratches and red, swollen eyes to the dean."

Rupert frowned. "Oh yes, very funny. How about that house party at Ham Court? JD wagered his entire fortune and almost lost it but then in the last hand won it all back. Poor Fielding. His father nearly disowned him over it."

James grimaced. "I did try to forgive the debt, but the man was too proud to accept."

"How about the time he offered his tutor a hundred pounds to write his exams for him? Too jug-bitten to take them himself."

James squirmed under the duo's attention. While Mercy was relieved to have the attention off of her and Alice, she wasn't sure these were stories about her father that Alice needed to hear.

Dismay puckered James's face. "Come now, you will make Alice and Miss Grove think me an unrepentant reprobate."

"Aren't you?"

His old friends certainly painted an unflattering picture of James Drake as a younger man. Or at least, certainly not as kind and generous as he seemed now.

Alice came to his defense, saying, "I think it was kind of you to take in the stray."

"And thoroughly unexpected," Max said slyly. "Then, and now."

James pretended not to hear his comment and patted Alice's hand.

"Have you finished eating, Alice?" Mercy asked gently. "Perhaps you and I should head upstairs and read awhile before bed?"

"Thank you, Miss Grove. That might be best," James said. "I will be up later to say good night."

He affectionately cupped Alice's cheek. "Up to bed with you, my dear. Before this lot turns you against me."

Alice shook her head, then kissed his cheek. "Never."

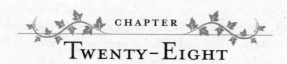

CHAPTER

Twenty-Eight

Later that night, after Alice was tucked in bed, Mercy went back downstairs for a cup of tea, hoping Mr. Kingsley might have returned to the Fairmont to see her.

There he was, sitting in the coffee room. She inhaled a deep breath, struck as she always was by his masculine good looks.

He rose when she entered, a soft smile lifting his face. "Miss Grove, good evening."

"Mr. Kingsley." She curtsied, and he bowed.

When he straightened again to his full height, Mercy took pleasure in looking up at him. Being the tallest of her friends, and as tall as many men, she rarely felt small or dainty. But she felt more feminine in Joseph Kingsley's presence. She liked his competent, strong hands. She liked his muscular arms and broad shoulders. His eyes. His hair. His mouth. *All right, Mercy, calm down. Breathe normally.*

He hailed a passing waiter and ordered tea for them. Then he intertwined his long fingers on the table and began, "How was your day?"

"Interesting. We are studying the history of the British empire, focusing particularly on India."

"I see. I confess I know little about it, though with your brother having lived in India all those years, I imagine you took a special interest in that part of the world."

"True. Though I don't pretend to understand it well. It is such a different culture from ours."

He nodded. "My mother tried to teach us geography, but I'm afraid I was always more interested in how things worked than where they were."

She smiled at that. Tea arrived, and as she poured she said, "Let's see, what else . . . Mr. Drake has friends visiting from his university days. Alice and I had dinner with them too." Mercy wasn't sure she should mention it or not, but she didn't want to keep secrets from this man, and it *had* been an interesting part of her day.

"Ah," he murmured. "I never attended university."

She leaned forward and looked into his eyes. "Neither did I, Mr. Kingsley."

"But you are more educated than I am."

"And you are far more skilled than I am. It isn't a contest. God has given us all distinct abilities and vocations. I thought I knew what mine was, but well, perhaps I was wrong."

"I'm not so sure. I believe you will teach again, one way or another. And for now, you have Alice. To teach, that is. Is it going well with her, now you're here?"

"Yes. I think so."

"I remember how upset you were when I came upon you in Wishford that day. At the time, you did not mention that Mr. Drake was the, um, relative who came forward to claim Alice."

She lowered her head. "No. I was not sure I should say anything, for her sake."

"I understand."

The squeak of wood and voices heralded the arrival of two men in the high-backed inglenook beside their table.

"What do you think?" Mercy recognized Rupert's voice. "Is the girl a result of a past indiscretion, and JD's gone and found religion in his old age?"

"Could be. I had never heard of the girl's mother before, had you?"

"No."

"And what did he mean by insisting the governess join us? Oldest family in the village indeed. I had a governess growing up. She was tolerable, as far as they go, but we certainly never invited her to join our dinner parties."

"Apparently she wasn't the equal of Long-Meg Miss Grove."

Mercy's ears burned. Across the table, Joseph's entire frame tensed. She reached out and placed a staying hand over his tight fist. "Don't," she whispered, shaking her head. "Mr. Drake warned me his friends are indiscreet."

"That's not the word I would use."

"Do you really think JD admires her?" Max asked from the other side, making no effort to lower his voice.

"I hope not." Rupert's tone sharpened. "Surely he doesn't mean to marry the governess! Can you imagine what the old man would say to that?"

Mercy sucked in a breath. Noticing a pulse ticking in Joseph's jaw, she whispered somewhat desperately, "Pay them no heed."

But Joseph rose, his shoulders clearing the back of the inglenook as he scowled down at the men on the other side. "Perhaps you two ought to find another topic of conversation. Or another place to have it."

"What . . . ? Who are you?" Rupert sputtered. "Butt out, fool."

"Rupert, um," Max warned. "That's a big foo . . . er, fellow."

"I am a friend of Miss Grove's," Joseph replied, nostrils flared.

"Ah. Then, a thousand apologies, my friend," Max said expansively. "Rupert here is in his cups. Pray, do not be offended. We meant no disrespect."

Mercy rose and hissed, "Let's go." She crossed the room without looking at anyone, though she felt two pairs of eyes track her exit.

Max's low mutter followed her out the door. "Well, there goes our invitation to return. . . ."

Mercy continued on, stomach churning.

Joseph caught up with her in the hall. "Are you all right?"

"I would have preferred not to make a scene."

"Are you angry with *me*? I couldn't sit there and do nothing while they talked about you like that."

"Yes, you could have. I did."

"You are not me, Miss Grove. I wanted to flatten them both, but at least I resisted that."

"You would have found yourself without a position in the morning, and perhaps I would have as well."

"Do you really think Mr. Drake would choose that sorry pair over you?" He tilted his head and sent her a dubious look. "Hardly."

Mercy stifled a futile rebuttal. He was probably right. She drew herself up. "Well, good night, Mr. Kingsley. Thank you for the pleasant evening, at least until that last bit."

He nodded, eyes glinting. "There was nothing in what they said. Was there?"

"Of course not." She turned and headed for the stairs. As Max had said, Rupert was drunk and spouting foolishness. Surely it was nothing more than that.

When his friends left the next afternoon, James called Mercy into his office. "Come and sit a minute, will you?"

She did so, and he took the chair near hers rather than the one behind the desk. "I wanted to apologize. My boorish friends were rude to you last night, and I am sorry I subjected you to their stories about my past behavior. I know you cannot approve."

"If even half of those stories were true, you have changed a great deal since then."

"I hope so." He fiddled with the wax seal stamp on his desk, then said, "It reminds me of something Jane said to me recently. I mentioned I worry about being a good father for Alice, and she said, 'Just be yourself and Alice will love you.' But I disagreed."

He stared out the window. "I don't want to be my old self anymore. I want to have a far better relationship with Alice than I have with my own father. I can't do that by just 'being myself.' I want to be a better man for Alice's sake. Better than you heard described last night."

Stunned to see him so vulnerable, Mercy instinctively reached toward him, but she stopped herself, clasping her hand in her lap instead. "If it helps, I did not recognize the man your friends described. To change our fallen natures by sheer force of will is incredibly difficult, though I'd say you've made impressive strides already. Thankfully we don't have to rely on ourselves alone. God will help us."

"Mercy, what you propose seems more difficult yet. You know I am accustomed to relying on no one but myself. Even if I could stomach asking God, why would He help me? Why would He care when I have disdained Him all these years—or at best ignored Him?"

"Because He loves you, even more than you love Alice."

He leaned back in his chair, fingers tented. "Well. I will consider what you say. But first, now that Max and Rupert are gone, how about a quiet dinner, just you and me?"

Nervous tension needled her stomach. "I . . . think I have had enough dinners for a while. I will go to bed early, if you don't mind. I am unaccountably tired."

Concern filled his features. "Are you all right? I hope you are not taking ill."

"No, I am perfectly well. Or will be, after some rest." She rose.

"As you wish. I hope you are not . . . displeased with me for some reason? I don't mean to foist my company on you more than is comfortable."

"Of course not. And please don't think this is because of anything I learned about your past." *Only fears for the future!*

"That's a relief. Well, good night, Mercy. Sleep well."

She nodded and walked away, thoughts in a whirl. The previous night's conversation spun through her mind once more, and conflicting emotions bubbled in her stomach. Surely James did not admire her in that way. Most likely he had praised her to his friends only out of protectiveness or kindness. But if not . . . ? Mercy was not sure she was ready to find out.

CHAPTER
TWENTY-NINE

Victorine sat in her workroom, material spread about her, trying not to cry. She was learning that it was one thing to make a gown that looked good from a distance—one made to sparkle and give the illusion of grandeur and elegance—and something entirely different to create a gown that could pass the test of close inspection.

She had once designed and sewn her own court dress after studying fashion prints and newspaper descriptions of ladies at court. She also had experience in creating costumes quickly from secondhand material and making over dresses from the previous year. But to cut and sew something brand-new, with tiny, even stitches perfect enough to withstand the scrutiny of the dowager Lady Brockwell, her quizzing glass held close to each dart and seam . . . ? Impossible.

Victorine pressed a hand to each temple and moaned. "Oh, why did I ever say I could do this?"

She was tempted to tell Lady Barbara that such fine work was best taken elsewhere, and the sooner the better, so the woman could find someone else to make her daughter's dress in time for the wedding. Victorine knew the longer she waited, the worse it would be. If only she could give the advance back and apologize.

But she couldn't. She had already spent the money at the linen drapers in Salisbury—such fine material, along with all the trimmings, was very expensive, she'd learned.

There was no way out. She had to do this. Somehow.

The shop door opened, and Victorine turned to greet a customer. She instantly tensed. There in the doorway stood Ivy Hill's former mantua-maker and milliner—and her present landlady. She had not seen her since signing the lease, and even then the property agent had done most of the talking. The elderly woman wore a frock of yellow-and-blue stripes, and a feathered cap. Fashionable, yes, though perhaps more suited to a younger female.

"Good day, Mrs. Shabner."

The woman dipped her head in acknowledgment. "I wanted to ask how you are getting on here. And see the changes you've made to the shop."

"You are very welcome," Victorine said, forcing a smile.

The woman strolled slowly around the room, pausing to look at the display of bonnets and hats. "You have changed very little." She gestured toward the front window. "May I look at your gowns on display?"

"Of course." She stood awkwardly as the woman studied each one, lifting a sleeve here, pulling back a lining there, inspecting a seam.

"Excellent material and stitching."

Victorine replied stiffly, "Thank you."

"French designs?"

"Yes, I . . . am fond of French fashions."

"Yet you do not wear them." Mrs. Shabner gestured toward the frock she wore. Her oldest. Why had she worn it today of all days?

"I planned to do some cleaning today, so I dressed accordingly."

The woman shifted her gaze to the new gown hanging on a dress form.

Feeling a bit defensive, Victorine said, "Miss Featherstone specifically requested a very simple, inexpensive daydress. It is not finished yet."

"Hmm. Where did you say you spent your apprenticeship?"

Victorine clasped her hands together. "I didn't say. But Madame Devereaux taught me a great deal. And my mother before her."

Mrs. Shabner frowned. "When we met with Mr. Gordon, I thought you had a French accent, but now I don't really hear it."

This again. Victorine said, "My mother was French, so perhaps I sound somewhat like her."

Mrs. Shabner narrowed her eyes. "The name of your shop leads one to believe you are a French modiste. Was that your intention, *Madame Victorine*?"

Her father had often called her Victorine, though it was not her real name. He had a nickname or two for everyone and fondly referred to his wife and daughters as *Mes trois beautés* or *Mesdames Victorine* in flawed French—he never learned to speak it properly.

She and her mother had dreamed of opening a dress shop together one day, planning to call it *Mesdames Victorine*—a nod to his pet name. Instead, her mother took ill with the influenza one winter and died quite young, leaving a gaping hole in their family.

But to Mrs. Shabner, Victorine said only, "I thought the name suited, at the time. Do you object?"

"I suppose not. I admit in my day, I would say most anything to earn a sale, which are difficult to come by in Ivy Hill." The older woman looked around the quiet shop once more. "Have you a girl to help you? The girl I employed has gone off and married, but an assistant is so helpful."

"No. Not yet."

"Then how do you dress yourself?"

She felt uncomfortable discussing undergarments yet knew a seasoned dressmaker would not hesitate to do so. "I have taken to wearing front-fastening stays and frocks as much as possible."

"Ah." Mrs. Shabner surveyed Victorine's old gown again, shoulder to hem. "That color does not flatter your complexion, by the way."

Victorine looked down at the bodice of her old gown. "Does it not?"

Mrs. Shabner shook her head. "Remember, madame, you are a

walking advertisement for your shop." She paused. "How strange to call it yours, but it is now."

"You still own it."

"Yes. Which reminds me, your next rent payment is due soon."

"I will have it for Mr. Gordon next week." *I hope.*

The woman nodded. "Good."

Her gaze landed on the sketches spread across her worktable. "These drawings . . . Are they your designs?" She ran a finger over a front view of Justina Brockwell's gown.

"Yes." A thought struck her, and hope flared. "I don't suppose you would be interested in helping with the project? Miss Brockwell has asked me to make a wedding gown, and a very complicated one at that."

The woman huffed. "I sat in this shop for thirty years hoping for patronage from the Brockwells. And you are here, what, less than two months and they have already asked you to make their daughter's wedding gown . . . ? Perhaps I should have Frenchified my shop name long ago!"

Mrs. Shabner whirled to the door, then turned back, moderating her voice. "It is not your fault, I realize. But still. . . . Now you see why I retired!"

The door slammed behind her, and Victorine flinched, then sighed. "I shall take that as a *no*."

Mercy went outside for a walk the next afternoon. She had not yet seen Joseph that day, but she passed Aaron Kingsley coming back into the Fairmont. She greeted him, then looked beyond him to the sweet chestnut tree. There blond Esther Dudman sat alone on a rug, packing up remnants of a meal into her basket.

Mercy walked toward her. "Good day, Miss Dudman. We have not been introduced. I am Mercy Grove." She curtsied.

The younger woman rose and stepped forward, all eagerness. "I am so pleased to meet you, Miss Grove. Joseph speaks very highly of you."

She spoke with a faint lisp and her front teeth were mildly crooked, though she was still lovely. Mercy was illogically relieved to discover the woman possessed at least some tiny flaw. "And he of you, Miss Dudman."

"That's a name I won't mind shedding, I can tell you." The pretty woman grinned up at her. "Please, call me Esther."

"Then you must call me Mercy. By the way, I hear congratulations are in order. You shall have a new surname soon, from what Mr. Kingsley tells me."

"Yes. Thank you." Esther ducked her head, blushing prettily. "How Naomi would laugh if she could see me engaged to Joseph's baby brother."

"You must miss your sister."

"I do."

"What was she like, if you don't mind my asking?"

"Not at all. Naomi was . . . full of life. Funny. Generous. Rather like Joseph in that regard."

"Oh? How so?"

Esther nodded thoughtfully. "When he was courting Naomi, our father died, leaving debts we knew nothing about. We almost lost our home, but Joseph stepped in and used his life's savings to settle the debt and buy the house. Our mother still lives there."

Ah! Mercy thought. Another reason he'd felt duty bound to hurry to Basingstoke to repair the broken step that contributed to his mother-in-law's fall. "How kind of him."

"I agree." Esther leaned closer. "But between you and me, I think he feels he cannot marry again until he has a proper home to offer someone. Which is a pity, because he would make some lucky woman a wonderful husband. When Aaron and I wed, we're going to save for a house, and as soon as we can, we'll invite Mamma to come and live with us. Then Joseph will be able to sell the house in Basingstoke and buy something nearer Ivy Hill."

Mercy remembered what Joseph had said about Aaron spending every farthing he earned before it reached the bottom of his pocket. It could be a long time before the couple could afford a home of their own. *Was* Joseph waiting until he had a house to offer . . . someone?

Esther cocked her head to the side. "Do you have a few minutes, Miss Grove?"

"Yes. Why?"

"You asked about Naomi. I long to see her portrait again. Will you walk with me to the workshop so I may show it to you? Joseph's working there today, and I know he won't mind."

Is Esther playing matchmaker? Mercy wondered, but she was as interested in seeing Joseph as the portrait, so she agreed. "Yes, I can spare half an hour or so."

"Excellent." Esther held the basket in one hand and linked her free arm with Mercy's. Mercy was surprised but did not pull away.

Together, the two women walked to the Kingsley brothers' workshop. Inside, Joseph bent over a piece of carved moulding suspended atop two sawhorses. He was smoothing it with a piece of dried sharkskin. Sawdust dotted his side-whiskers and the fine hairs of his muscled forearms.

Esther called, "If it isn't the carpenter named Joseph, hard at work."

He looked up with a grin, eyes widening when he saw Mercy beside her. "Miss Grove . . . Welcome. Please don't believe everything my mischievous sister tells you about me."

Esther said, "We were talking about Naomi, actually. Might I show Mercy her miniature? You still have it upstairs, I trust?"

"Of course. And yes, if you like. It's in the drawer of my side table. Don't mind the clutter."

Mercy followed Esther up the narrow wooden steps of the open stairway and through the low door into the room above. Inside, she saw two long single beds. One was stripped bare—where Matthew Kingsley used to sleep before marrying, she guessed—and the other neatly made. A corner stove held a coffeepot, and a plate with a few toast crumbs. But the space was remarkably neat for a bachelor without a servant.

There was also a small desk near the window, and upon it a Bible open to the first chapter of Matthew. She glanced at the page, and an underlined verse leapt out at her: *"Then Joseph being raised from sleep did as the angel of the Lord had bidden him, and took unto him his wife . . ."*

Mercy mused, *Another carpenter named Joseph.*

Esther opened the drawer of the side table and pulled forth a framed miniature portrait. "Here she is."

Mercy walked over to join her there.

"It's sad that, as the years pass, this little painting is becoming clearer to me than my own recollection. It is not a perfect likeness of her, but the artist did a credible job."

In the image, the woman's hair was golden brown, several shades darker than Esther's blond. And her eyes were hazel rather than blue, but still the resemblance between the sisters was striking.

Esther said, "She looks almost bashful in this portrait, but in real life she was a passionate person, laughing one minute and then railing against some injustice the next. She felt things more deeply than I do. How I looked up to her—my big sister. Have you a sister, Miss Grove?"

"It's Mercy, remember. And no, I have only an older brother."

"Then we have that in common, for Joseph has become the older brother I always wanted. The very best of brothers. Kind and protective."

"Yes, I see that."

"Is your brother the same?"

"Not exactly, but he is amiable. He has recently married, so his attention is focused on his wife now, as it should be, I suppose. As you will find out for yourself soon enough."

"Do you mean, when Joseph marries again?"

"No! I meant when you and Aaron marry."

"Oh. Of course. Sorry."

Mercy watched her carefully. "*Will* it be difficult for you if Joseph were to marry again?"

Esther shrugged. "A little, to see Naomi replaced in his affections.

But I love him as a brother and don't want him to be alone for the rest of his life. Naomi wouldn't want that either."

Boot steps on the stairs drew their attention. Joseph appeared, his broad shoulders filling the doorway. "The longer you two are up here whispering, the more uneasy I become." He ducked his head to pass under the lintel. "Pray what are you finding so fascinating?"

"I was only showing Mercy Naomi's portrait. And your bachelor's quarters."

He rubbed the back of his neck. "I have yet to do the washing up, I'm afraid. Was not expecting visitors."

"You keep your things rather tidy for a man," Esther said. "Your future wife will be a fortunate woman." She sent Mercy a sly glance, and Mercy felt her face heat. When she braved a peek at Joseph, she saw his face redden as well.

Mercy cleared her throat. "Well, thank you for showing me your sister's portrait, Esther. Naomi was beautiful, but I am not surprised she should be." She looked at Joseph. "And your room up here is more comfortable than I was led to believe."

He slowly shook his head. "You are just being kind. I know it is humble. Too humble for . . . anyone but a bachelor."

Mercy could not argue with the fact that it would be a step down for her after life in Ivy Cottage. She could easily imagine her mother's shocked disapproval at the notion of her only daughter living in such a place. Although . . . was it so much humbler than an attic room in either Ivy Cottage or the Fairmont?

"Well, thank you again. Now I had better get back."

"Yes," he said. "Mr. Drake will be wondering what became of you."

Mercy hesitated. Was he implying something? "I don't know about Mr. Drake, but Alice will be expecting me, yes."

He held her gaze a moment, then turned and led the way down. "I'll go first, just in case. Be careful. The stairs are steep."

As they descended, a girl of seven or eight with light brown ringlets ran into the shop, waving a piece of paper in her hand. "Uncle Joseph, I drew you a picture."

He lowered himself to one knee. "So you did. Is that giant me?"

"Not a giant. That's you with your saw. And that's me there with the rocking horse you made."

"So it is. Well done, Katrina."

The girl handed him the drawing. "You can keep it."

He cupped the child's face with his hand. "Thank you. I shall treasure it."

On the step behind her, Esther whispered in Mercy's ear, "He's fond of all his nieces and nephews, but there's a special bond between those two. She's the same age as his baby girl would have been, had she lived."

"Oh . . . Then no wonder," Mercy breathed, her heart aching for the man who had lost so much.

CHAPTER

THIRTY

With her father and brother still lodging in Wilton, Jane rode over every few days to see them, when she could find the time between wedding preparations and managing The Bell. On one such visit she learned her father had come down with what he called a "trifling cold," so she brought Jack Avi back to Ivy Hill to spend the day with her. She planned to take him to the farm that evening for a riding lesson with Gabriel.

The afternoon being sunny, Jane walked Jack Avi over to Ivy Green. He wore one of his new skeleton suits—trousers buttoned to a matching jacket—and kicked a ball as he went. The boy had been cooped up too long and needed to run and play outside. She worried, however, that even if they found other boys on the green, they might not want to play with a somewhat foreign-looking newcomer with taffy-colored skin and lyrical accent. Personally, Jane found both charming, but she was his sister, after all.

They reached the green, and two lads were there, kicking a ball back and forth. They noticed Jack Avi, and after watching him kick his own ball for a few minutes came nearer, expressions curious. The boys looked familiar, but Jane wasn't sure of their names.

"Want to play with us?" one of them asked.

"Yes, thank you," said Jack Avi.

The other boy studied his face. "You are very tan."

"And you are very pale," Jack Avi replied with a friendly smile.

The boy shrugged. "Your ball looks new."

"It is." Jack Avi kicked it across the green, and all three lads gave chase.

Jane expelled a sigh of relief.

She noticed Matilda Grove in the rear garden of Ivy Cottage, so she waved, and Matilda waved back, rising from the bench to stand at the gate.

"Hello, Jane."

"Good day, Miss Matty." Looking again to be sure Jack Avi was happily occupied, Jane walked over to talk to her.

Matilda asked, "How is Jack Avi getting on?"

"Well, I think."

"Glad to hear it. Thankfully, younger children are often sweetly accepting. It's not until they grow older that they seem to learn to dislike anyone different from themselves."

Jane nodded, then asked, "How are things here?"

"Oh, I miss Mercy, of course, though she visits on Sunday afternoons when she can. These days I spend quite a bit of time out here in the garden, or calling on friends . . ."

The ball flew past, and the boys came running by. Jack waved at the ladies as he ran after it, then stopped abruptly. Jane looked over to see what had arrested his attention.

Mr. Basu came walking across the green toward them, market basket in hand, with supplies for Mrs. Timmons, Jane guessed. He watched the boys with his usual quiet solemnity, but when he saw Jack Avi, his expression brightened with interest. Jack Avi stood there as the man slowly approached, then said something to him in his native language. Mr. Basu shook his head and gave a low reply.

Jack Avi turned and pointed toward Jane. Mr. Basu looked up and nodded in her direction. Boy and man exchanged a few more words, and then Mr. Basu continued toward Ivy Cottage.

"I wonder if they speak the same language," Matilda mused.

When the man neared, Jane stepped back and Matilda opened the gate for him. "Mr. Basu, I see you met Jane's brother."

He nodded.

"I heard him greet you in his native tongue," Jane said. "Did you understand him?"

The manservant wavered his hand in a so-so gesture.

"A different dialect?" Jane asked.

He nodded.

"Pity."

He bowed and continued into the house.

Jack Avi jogged over to them. "Good day, Miss Matty."

"You remembered my name. I am impressed. A pleasure to see you again, Jack Avi."

He nodded over the fence toward the retreating Mr. Basu. "That man lives with you?"

"He does, yes. Mr. Basu is a faithful servant and friend."

"He looks like my grandfather. I like him."

"Come on, Jack!" one of the boys called, and with a parting smile, Jack Avi ran off again.

Jane said, "You know, I don't think I ever heard where Mr. Basu comes from or how he came to work at Ivy Cottage." Jane was ashamed to realize she had never really given the man much thought before Jack Avi entered her life.

"He was a lascar and came over on one of the East India Company's ships," Matilda said. "From Bengal, I believe. Something happened, and he was denied return passage. On one of her trips to London Mercy found him going house to house looking for work. You know Mercy. She offered him a position here."

"Is he happy, do you think?"

Matilda shrugged. "Content, I'd say. Or he was. I'm afraid life has become more . . . tense in Ivy Cottage lately. For us all."

"I'm sorry to hear it."

"Never mind." Matilda brightened. "Everything set for the wedding?"

"Almost. Thankfully, it's not for a few weeks yet."

"I look forward to it, my dear. I know you will be very happy."

"Thank you, Miss Matty."

"And how is your father? I have not seen him in some time."

"He has come down with a cold, but I am sure he'll be back to visit you again soon."

Matilda smiled. "I look forward to that as well."

Victorine walked up Ebsbury Road, her sewing box in hand, headed for the almshouse. In its sunny front garden, an elderly woman sat in one of two chairs.

The woman squinted and hailed, "Halloo! I have not seen you before, but then again, I can barely see you now." She chuckled to herself. "Silly old eyes."

Victorine stepped into the garden. "Good day. I am . . . Victorine."

"Ah. You're the new dressmaker I've heard about."

"Attempting to be, at any rate. What is your name?"

"Peg Hornebolt. Come closer, my dear."

Victorine walked nearer, admiring the woman's fine grey plaits coiled and pinned atop her head. "I like your hair."

"Why thank you. I did it myself." She patted her hair, then the chair beside her. "Sit awhile, if you can, and we'll have a friendly chat."

Victorine found herself strangely drawn to the kind-faced woman and sat down to oblige her. She said, "I am sorry your eyes are giving you trouble."

"Oh, they are just worn out, like the rest of this mortal frame. Mind is still sharp though, and that's a blessing. Most days."

Victorine asked gently, "How much can you see?"

The woman brought her face near. "Enough to see you are very pretty. And very sad."

"I miss my family, truth be told. But I am well. I just came to see if Mrs. Mennell might need any help with mending or something."

The elderly woman nodded. "I miss my husband and parents too, though they've all been gone these many years. . . ."

The two talked a few minutes longer, then Mrs. Hornebolt

pushed herself to her feet, cane in hand. "Well, I am sure our matron would be glad for your help. Come, I'll show you the way, said the blind woman." She chuckled again.

Victorine grinned and followed her into the almshouse.

Inside a snug parlour off the entryway, they found Mrs. Mennell and a white-haired woman working on a small linen cot quilt. Mrs. Mennell greeted them and introduced her companion, Mrs. Russell.

Victorine bent to look closer at the quilt and saw it was stitched with a repeating pattern of mermaids, ships, and exotic-looking fish. "How delightful!"

Mrs. Mennell said softly, "I am glad you think so. It is a gift for Mrs. Russell's great-granddaughter, whose father is a sailor."

Mrs. Russell said, "I haven't much, but thanks to Mrs. Mennell, I shall have a lovely gift to send for the new baby."

"How kind."

Peg Hornebolt said, "Speaking of kind, Miss Victorine here has come to ask if you need any help with mending and such."

Mrs. Mennell turned to look at her, brows raised. "Oh?"

"At no charge," Victorine hurried to clarify.

The matron considered, then asked, "Have you ever done any quilting?"

"No." Victorine shook her head. Then she grinned and added, "But I would be happy to learn."

Later, back in the shop, Victorine was wrapping Julia Featherstone's daydress in tissue when the shop door opened and a dark-haired man stepped inside. She reared her head back in surprise. It was the first time a man had entered her shop.

The handsome guard swept off his hat. "Good day to you, madame. Remember me? Jack Gander, with His Majesty's Royal Mail."

"What brings you here? I'm afraid I do not make attire for gentlemen. If you need a quick seam repair or button sewn, I can assist you this one time, but otherwise I cannot help you."

He reached up and yanked a button from his red coat, drawing a gasp from her. He held it out, shredded thread and all. "As you can see, I am in dire need of your services. Thank you for making an exception for me." He smiled his charming smile, dash him.

She swallowed, determined to remain officious. "Take off your coat."

His eyebrows rose. "As you wish."

He did so, and she pretended not to be affected by the sight of this man in his shirt-sleeves. She had seen many men attired in even less before, when she had made garments for men as well as women. This was no different, she told herself. In vain.

While she sat at her worktable to sew on the button, he sat on a stool nearby, watching her.

"Are you sure you were not the ropewalker at Astley's Ampitheatre?"

"I already told you, that was not me."

He pressed his fingers to his temple. "But I'm convinced I've seen your face in print or a painting somewhere, and the image is seared on my brain."

"I am in earnest. You probably saw some other brunette. Men so easily confuse females with similar hair and build, I find."

He watched her a few moments longer, then asked, "Why do you not serve men in your shop? Do you not like men?"

"Not at the moment."

He smirked at that and tilted his head to one side. "If you did make gentlemen's clothes, what would you make for me? I rarely see myself in anything other than my uniform."

"Thankfully you look good in red."

He leaned nearer, playful grin on his handsome face. "I am glad you think so."

"However," she added, "I think you would look better in a darker hue, like maroon, more suited to your coloring. Or a deep blue."

One brow rose. "Determined to keep me humble, are you?"

"I doubt such a feat possible."

He grinned.

She knotted and cut off the thread. "There. Good as new."

Before he could rise, she stood, stepped behind him, and settled the coat around his shoulders. She then helped him fit his arms into the sleeves, her hands lingering on his shoulders, under the pretense of smoothing the fabric.

She murmured, "You have a good tailor."

His eyes glinted knowingly. "I shall pass along your compliments."

He rose and surveyed his reflection in the long mirror. "Perhaps you will branch out into gentlemen's attire one day, madame. Ivy Hill has no tailor."

"Oh, I doubt I shall be here that long, unless I earn Lady Brockwell's favor. Besides, ladies' attire is challenging enough, I assure you."

"Well, I hope God blesses your shop here and you remain for a long time to come."

"God?" she snorted. "He and I are not on speaking terms."

"Oh? Why?"

She shook her head.

"Come. Your secret is safe with me."

Which of my secrets? she thought, but said only, "Suffice it to say, I lost someone very dear to me."

"I am sorry to hear it. Someone in your family passed away?"

"I did not say she died; I said we lost her. We have not seen her in over two years. And I think, if God were real, He wouldn't have let that happen." She shook her head again, mouth tight. "I used to pray, but it did no good."

"Maybe it did, and you just don't know it yet."

"*Oh là là!*" she exclaimed, her mother's favorite expression slipping from her lips. "Are you a theologian as well as a guard?"

He chuckled. "The furthest thing from it. But I don't doubt God exists. Riding beneath the night sky as I do, with its moon and stars . . ." He shrugged. "The heavens really do declare His glory."

She considered. "I suppose it isn't that I don't believe He *exists*, but rather than He isn't involved. He's up in the firmament with his stars, too far away to hear the prayers of an ordinary woman like me."

He slowly shook his head, a playful sparkle in his eyes. "There is nothing ordinary about you, Madame Victorine." He reached out and smoothed a lock of hair from her temple.

For a moment they looked into each other's eyes, and then she blinked and straightened. She turned and strode to the door, opening it for him before she divulged all her secrets to this beguiling man. Or kissed him.

He picked up his hat and met her at the door. "I shall see you again soon."

"I doubt you shall have further need of my services."

"*Au contraire.*" He tugged at his top button. "I fear this button is growing loose too."

She frowned. "Don't rip out another. You might tear the fabric next time."

"A small price to pay to see you again."

"Not such a small price," she said tartly. "Next time I shall charge you double."

CHAPTER

THIRTY-ONE

After that night's dinner in the coffee room, Alice went upstairs with Iris for her bath, leaving Mercy and Mr. Drake to finish their coffee alone.

Mr. Drake extracted a letter from his pocket, and said, "My mother writes that she would like to see Alice again, on her birthday, which means another trip to Hampshire."

"Might your parents come here instead?" Mercy asked. "Or have they already been?"

"No. It is . . . difficult for my father to get away."

"Has he a business partner?"

"He has Francis, a cousin. He came to live with us after his parents died and eventually married my sister. Amiable fellow—twice as charming as I am."

"I find that difficult to believe."

"Why, Mercy, you flatter me."

Her neck heated. "I only meant . . ."

"Never mind. I am teasing you. If I have any charm at all, it is despite my father's attempts to drive it from me. He sees humor, kindness, and amiability as weaknesses for a shrewd man of business. But Francis continues to be his charming self, and apparently, so do I." He winked at her.

Eager to correct the notion that she had been flirting, Mercy said, "Everyone speaks of how helpful and likable you are. Jane most of all."

"And you?"

"I have seen your kindness for myself. It is difficult to believe you were raised by a dour father."

"You can judge for yourself when you meet him. I suppose we either embrace our parents' character or strive for the opposite. At least I had a loving and affectionate mother to temper my nature."

"Alice likes her a great deal."

"And the feeling is mutual. Mother would like to come here, but I have asked them to wait. Since the place is not finished, my father would not be impressed. Although, with a house this old, I doubt it ever shall be up to his exacting standards."

"But the Fairmont is lovely as it is, even if a few repairs remain to be done. Surely your parents could see the good and overlook a few minor imperfections?"

"You would think that—because you are a caring, gracious person who sees the good in everyone and everything." He looked at her closely. "I wish you could see yourself as I see you. It is a pleasure just to be in your company."

"Thank you." She dipped her head, discomfited by his praise.

"You will travel with us, Mercy? I should not dread returning to Drayton Park half so much with you along."

"Thank you for the offer, but you needn't take me with you. I can fend for myself here perfectly well. Perhaps I could even take care of some of your duties while you are gone. I am sure your parents would prefer to see you and Alice alone, without an outsider intruding on family time."

"You will not be alone in feeling an outsider there, I assure you."

"But Drayton Park is your home. You spent most of your youth there. And did you not tell me that you and Alice had a pleasant time when you visited over Christmas?"

"Yes, but—"

"Are you worried Alice's education will suffer while she's gone?"

"No. Nor would I expect your lessons to continue while we

travel, unless you wish it. But your presence would be a balm, both for Alice and for me. My father can be . . . well . . . difficult."

Mercy was touched by the boyish uncertainty she saw in his face. "Very well. If you think my company would help."

"It would, yes. Thank you. And do bring an evening dress or two. Perhaps the green one? It suits you—brings out the color of your eyes."

Mercy blinked, taken aback by the personal suggestion.

Noticing her expression, he winced. "Was that inappropriate?"

"Thoroughly."

"Then please forgive me. I meant no disrespect. I simply want you to join us for dinner."

"Mr. Drake, that is going too far. It is one thing to dine with you here, but in your parents' home? It would be rude to presume and terribly awkward."

"You are more than a governess to Alice and me, and you know it. At least, I hope you do."

"Mr. Drake, I am Alice's governess, and in that capacity alone would it be proper for me to travel with you."

He hesitated. "I see. As you wish. I will write to let my mother know to expect you." Then he gave her an impish grin. "But bring your green gown anyway. Just in case."

The next day, Mr. Drake gathered the staff to explain their travel plans. Mercy and Alice stood on one side of him, the housekeeper and clerk on the other. And there, behind the chef, porter, maids, waiters, and horsemen stood Joseph Kingsley, his head rising above the crowd. Not officially on staff, he stood somewhat apart, though near enough to listen to the announcement, since the owner's actions affected him too.

"Two days from now, I am returning to my parents' home near Portsmouth for a brief visit. On this occasion, Miss Alice and Miss Grove will travel with me."

She noticed Joseph's brows lift at that and his mouth tighten.

"As usual, I leave Mrs. Callard and Curtis in charge during my absence. See them with any questions or problems that arise. . ." Mr. Drake continued to talk, but the builder's gaze remained fixed on her.

After Mr. Drake dismissed everyone, Johnny approached Alice and told her about a nest of chaffinch hatchlings he'd discovered. He asked if she wanted to see the blind baby birds.

Alice turned to Mercy, eyes alight. "May I, Miss Grove?"

"Yes. In fact, I would like to see them too. But then we really must begin packing."

The two younger people hurried outside, while Mercy followed more slowly. Joseph Kingsley reached the door before she did and held it open.

"Thank you."

In the stable yard, he asked, "May I talk with you a moment?"

Baby birds forgotten, Mercy stopped and turned to him. "Of course."

With a glance at Johnny and Alice to make sure they were out of earshot, he said, "I was surprised to hear you'd be traveling with Mr. Drake. If you don't want to go, I'm sure he would reconsider. Alice's education would not suffer so greatly in a week, would it?"

"I don't mind going. He is my employer and if he . . ." Mercy paused. She was tempted to lay it all at Mr. Drake's door, but that wasn't fully honest or fair, and she wanted to be both.

She started again. "He does not demand I go, but he does wish it. Apparently, his father is difficult, and Mr. Drake thinks he will be more civil in my company. Which will, of course, make the visit more congenial for Alice as well."

He watched her face carefully. "For Alice."

Mercy nodded. "Yes. Thank you for your concern, but I am sure it shall be a pleasant trip."

"Very well. I felt I needed to ask. If you're certain, I wish you a safe journey." He briefly clasped her hand. "I will pray for you and ask God to protect you from every danger."

"Thank you, Mr. Kingsley. That means a great deal."

He looked into her eyes. "You shall be missed."

The three of them packed up, left final instructions for the staff, and departed two days later in Mr. Drake's chaise. Mounted postilions drove the four horses, and a guard rode on the back.

As they journeyed to the southeast, Mercy watched the passing countryside with interest. She had never been so far south.

Alice soon nodded off, her head lolling against Mr. Drake. He put his arm around the girl, then said to Mercy, "You will meet my sister while we're there. She and Francis have three children—two boys and a girl only a year or so younger than Alice. I should tell you that my mother has already begun to publicly acknowledge Alice as family. In her mind, the more grandchildren, the merrier. My father is less happy about the prospect, but Mother hopes to bring him around."

"How I longed for cousins as a girl," Mercy murmured, feeling wistful at the thought.

He nodded. "Francis is a few years younger than I, but yes, I valued his companionship over the years, at least until I went off to university."

With his free hand, James patted his case beside him. "By the way, I received the papers from the lawyers. This darling girl is now officially Alice Drake. I don't deny her origins may cause some challenges, but I shall harness my great energies into making sure she is showered with affection, education, and opportunities enough to offset what she lacks in society's notion of pedigree.

"And if some dandy chooses not to marry her one day because of her less-than-ideal beginnings, then that will be his loss. I shall retain the pleasure of Alice's company a little longer until a wiser young man recognizes her true worth. Then I shall be left a lonely ol' papa, on my own. I know I cannot keep her to myself forever, as much as I would like to."

Mercy's heart expanded with warmth and fondness when James

spoke of Alice so lovingly. How could it not, when Mercy loved Alice too?

They traveled on for several hours, stopping to change horses at regular intervals along the way. Reaching Southampton that evening, Mercy took in the many ships in the harbor, the tree-lined streets, and elegant buildings.

As twilight fell, they turned down a broad street filled with fashionable shops and inns. There, they stopped at the Drake Arms to spend the night. Pride shone on James's face as he showed Mercy around his first hotel and introduced her to his manager. Then the three of them sat down to a late supper in one of the private parlours. Alice could hardly keep her eyes open, so after the delicious meal, James carried the girl up to the room she and Mercy would share.

"Good night, Miss Grove. Thank you again for coming with us."

She nodded. "My pleasure." But while helping James and Alice was indeed a pleasure, the actual visit to come with his parents weighed heavily on her mind.

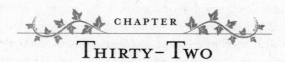

CHAPTER

THIRTY-TWO

After breakfast the next morning, James showed them a few sights around Southampton—the port, circulating libraries, and theatres. Then they climbed back into the chaise to travel the remaining twenty miles or so to his parents' home outside of Portsmouth. James explained that his family had long been involved in shipping—imports and other enterprises facilitated by proximity to the naval port and dockyards. But years ago, his father had built a fine, genteel home for his wife north of the city, in a quieter, more commodious setting.

As the chaise turned up a graceful drive and approached the tall stone-and-brickwork house, Alice patted Mercy's arm and sent her a reassuring smile.

"It's nice. You'll see."

When the horses halted, liveried footmen approached, their shoes crunching over the pea-gravel drive. They helped her and Alice down, bowed to Mr. Drake, and then turned their attention to the baggage.

James gestured Mercy toward the house, and together they walked to the front door beneath a columned portico. Alice took her hand, and Mercy was grateful for the girl's support.

Inside a paneled hall, they were met by a black-suited older man. The butler, she assumed.

James began, "Robertson, this is Miss Grove, our governess and friend. Please ask Mrs. Jenkins to put her in one of the guest rooms—not in the servants' quarters. I want her to be near Miss Alice. Understood?"

"I . . . Yes, sir. Very good, sir." The butler nodded, though Mercy thought she saw a wrinkle of confusion between his eyebrows.

"James!"

They all turned as a handsome woman with silver-threaded blond hair walked forward, wearing a long, practical apron over her dress.

"You are early. You've caught me in my gardening things." She removed her gloves as she approached.

"We made excellent time."

"Alice! Come here, my dear, and let me see how much you've grown."

Alice went forward, shy and eager at once, a suppressed smile dimpling her cheeks.

Mrs. Hain-Drake held out her hands, and Alice offered hers to be gathered in a fond embrace.

The older woman pressed the girl to herself, then held her at arm's length. "I declare you have grown at least an inch since I saw you last. And prettier too."

Alice beamed, and Mercy felt bittersweet pleasure wash over her. Alice's happiness was hers, and she was thankful Alice had more people in her life to turn to for affection and comfort. Yet there was loss in the moment as well. A parent watching the child of her heart leave her confining nest to the arms of the wider world.

"Mother, this is Miss Mercy Grove, Alice's former teacher and now governess. I mentioned her in my reply. I hope you will make her welcome."

"Of course, of course. You are very welcome, Miss Grove. I have asked Mrs. Jenkins to prepare a room for you."

"I would like her to be near Alice, if you don't mind, Mamma. Not up in the attic."

Mrs. Hain-Drake hesitated. "Oh. Well. Whatever you think best,

James. I had planned to put Alice near me. But if you are willing to give up your old room, I could put Miss Grove there, and you could have your pick of the guest chambers."

"Mr. Drake," Mercy demurred, "I don't want to put you out of your room."

"It's no trouble. I don't mind at all. In fact, I insist."

Mercy felt awkward at his adamancy. Alice had traveled here without a governess's company before, so it seemed he was insisting more for Mercy's sake than for hers. An excuse not to see her relegated to the servants' quarters.

His mother turned to her. "Will you join us for dinner, Miss Grove? Or would you prefer a tray sent to your room?"

"A tray would be perfect, Mrs. Hain-Drake. If not too much trouble."

"Not at all."

"Are you certain, Mercy?" James asked hopefully. "You may join us."

"I am weary from the journey, truth be told. An early supper and bedtime are all I want. You enjoy a family dinner with your parents."

"Very good, Miss Grove." His mother nodded, clearly approving her choice.

The matronly housekeeper appeared, followed by a young housemaid. After a terse side conversation with her mistress, the housekeeper turned to Mercy and said, "Miss Grove, Emily will show you to your room. And I will take Miss Alice to hers."

As Mercy followed the housemaid up the stairs, she heard an older man's low voice from below. "James, you made it. Do have compassion on my nerves, wife. Must you cackle like a hen over the mere arrival of expected guests?"

An apologetic murmur rose in reply, though Mercy could not make out the words.

Reaching James's old room, the housemaid began unpacking her small trunk, and Mercy thanked her. As Mercy unpinned her hat and set it aside, she looked around the tidy, masculine chamber and saw scant remnants of his boyhood: a ribbon and a few other awards on the dressing chest, as well as a leather cricket ball signed by several teammates. She noticed a stack of his calling cards on the desk along with a fine writing set, blotter, and wax jack. On a bookcase were volumes on business and economics intermixed with what she assumed were a few old favorite novels, like *Robinson Crusoe*.

Finished unpacking, the maid bobbed another curtsy and left her. Mercy removed the jacket of her carriage dress, then washed her face and hands at the washstand. She had just decided to lie down on the inviting-looking bed for a short rest when a knock sounded at her door.

Mercy assumed it might be Alice or the housekeeper come to see if she had everything she needed. Smoothing her hair from her face, she turned to the door and called, "Come in."

Mrs. Hain-Drake entered, wearing a tentative smile. "Miss Grove, I have come to ask you to join the family for dinner."

"Thank you, but as I said, I am perfectly happy with a tray. Truly."

The woman clasped her hands. "I know you did, but my husband is quite adamant."

"But why? He does know I am the governess, does he not?"

"He wishes to judge that for himself."

Mercy blinked in confusion. "I don't understand." Did he intend to test her knowledge of the classics or something?

The older woman sighed. "It's James's fault, insisting you sleep in his old room, near the family."

Mortification flared. What did the man conclude from those circumstances?

Mrs. Hain-Drake took a step closer. "Come now, Miss Grove. No need for alarm. You are clearly a modest gentlewoman of good character, as he will see when he meets you."

"I hope he doesn't intend to embarrass me in front of Alice."

"He won't. Her cousins arrive tomorrow and the children will take their meals together then, but for tonight Alice will eat in her own room." She returned to the door. "We dine in one hour, Miss Grove. I hope that will give you sufficient time to change. I shall send Emily up to help you."

After the door closed, Mercy remained where she was, thinking. She'd hoped James had exaggerated his father's unpleasant nature, but apparently not.

Soon the maid reappeared to help her change for dinner. Mercy was relieved now she had brought her green evening dress. Though with her stomach churning with anxiety, she doubted she could swallow a single bite.

A few minutes ahead of the hour, she descended the stairs and found her way to the anteroom.

A well-dressed gentleman of some sixty years stood there. His light brown hair had silvered at the side-whiskers and spidery blood vessels webbed his cheeks and nose, but he was still handsome. His eyes were bright green, reminding her of James. Those eyes held a calculating suspicion as they swept over her.

"You are . . . the governess?" He looked past her as though expecting to see someone else behind her.

"I am, sir."

He hesitated, the fire in his eyes fading. "Miss Grove?"

"Yes. And you must be Mr. Drake's father."

"Guilty. Where did he find you?"

"I was Alice's teacher in Ivy Hill. I managed a girls school in my home until circumstances forced me to close it."

"What circumstances?" The flare of suspicion returned.

"My brother married and moved home, so I no longer had the space to accommodate pupils."

"You look nothing like I expected."

"No? And what did you expect, sir?"

"You will forgive me, Miss Grove, but when I was told my son insisted his female companion have his old room near the family, I doubted you were really a governess."

Mercy felt her mouth part as the implications washed over her. She told herself she should not be personally affronted; the man knew nothing about her. But did he really think so poorly of his own son?

She said, "I assure you there is nothing untoward between your son and me."

"Then please forgive my insolence, Miss Grove. I hope you will extend me some understanding. The last time my son came home, he brought with him a girl we knew nothing about and stunned us with the news that he planned to adopt her as his own daughter. Now this time he arrives with a woman we know nothing about, and I have been bracing myself ever since I heard, wondering what he might announce about his relationship with you."

Mercy lifted her chin. "Your son has more honor than you give him credit for, Mr. Hain-Drake. In fact, I am surprised you have not yet visited him in all these months to see his new hotel. He has converted a grand old manor house into a fine posting inn."

"You certainly give your opinion very decidedly. Not like any governess I've ever met."

"I am only lately become a governess, sir, so the expectations of the role are new to me."

"I suppose you did not have a governess of your own growing up?"

"I had several, actually, until my father insisted on educating me alongside my brother."

"Did he indeed? And where is this father of yours now?"

"My parents live in London, sir."

"Where?"

"Mayfair."

His bushy eyebrows rose, impressed. "And what does your father do?"

"Do? He reads a great deal."

"Idle, is he?"

"He is a gentleman."

Once more his measuring eyes swept over her. Then he nodded, reaching some internal decision.

"I am glad you are joining us for dinner, Miss Grove. I want to hear more about you and how my son comports himself in rustic Wiltshire, wasting time on his latest pet project."

"I would have preferred a tray in my room."

"And I would prefer my son to—" He broke off and said instead, "We don't all get what we want, do we."

Mercy wondered what he'd meant to say. Pulling her eyes from the man's challenging gaze, she decided to change the subject. "I was sorry to hear Alice will not be joining us."

Mr. Hain-Drake frowned. "Formal dinners are no place for children."

"How is a child to learn how to conduct herself at formal dinners if she is always excluded from them?"

His eyes narrowed. "Again, I must say, you speak your opinion most assuredly for one . . . so young."

Had he meant to say *for one in service*? Mercy pretended to take it as a compliment. "Thank you."

"My son takes great pleasure in flitting about from place to place, enterprise to enterprise. Turning his back on the family business, even eschewing his rightful Hain-Drake surname. I doubt he will ever grow up and accept his responsibilities."

"Are we talking about the same man, sir? For he is considered responsible and successful by all who know him in Ivy Hill, as well as helpful and generous."

He gave her a wry grin. "Are standards so low in this hamlet of yours?"

"Not at all." Mercy went on to describe how Mr. Drake had helped her widowed friend save her inn and earn a license in her own name, and how he'd generously helped the new Lady Brockwell establish a circulating library for the village.

"And what about the girl?" he challenged. "You have only to look at her to see who her father is. I suppose you view him as above reproach there too? Personally, I don't approve of his way of getting children."

Mercy looked down at her hands for a moment, uncomfortable talking about such things with a man, let alone Mr. Drake's father.

She took a deep breath and replied, "Perhaps not. But at least he did his best to rectify a youthful transgression. When he became aware of Alice's existence, he did not hesitate to acknowledge his duty toward her, which is more than many men would do."

"How you defend my son." Mr. Hain-Drake crossed his arms. "He has worked his renowned charms on you—that is clear."

Mercy shook her head. "I merely speak the truth, sir. I admire your son as a friend and as my employer, but that is all."

The man held her gaze a moment longer. "Pity."

James entered the anteroom with his mother, who now wore a silk evening gown, her hair pinned in a high soft twist.

James looked from Mercy to his father, eyebrows raised. "I see you two have met." He said to Mercy, "I do hope he is being polite to you."

They all turned to her. Mercy hesitated, then smiled at his mother. "What a lovely gown . . ."

After dinner, Mercy declined tea in the drawing room, claiming fatigue, which was perfectly true. She was exhausted after making polite conversation over several courses, not to mention the tense interview with Mr. Hain-Drake beforehand. Mrs. Hain-Drake excused her graciously, and James walked out with her.

In a low voice he said, "I confess I overheard a little of your conversation with my father before dinner. How strange to hear you defending me."

She looked at him in surprise, sheepish to think of all he might have heard. She said honestly, "I have never seen you as someone who needed defending before. I saw only the charming, confident exterior you show the world. But lately I've glimpsed the young boy who feels he will never please his father, no matter how hard he tries, so he pretends to disdain him and avoids visiting his house. And now that I have met your father, I can understand why. But I am sure, deep down, that he loves you."

"Are you?" James shook his head, expression grim. "He has never once said so."

She turned to him, laying a hand on his sleeve. "Oh, James. I know you don't want to hear this, but I have to say it. Even if your earthly father never tells you, your heavenly Father loves you just as you are."

He looked at her, sadness and fondness shining in his eyes. "Dear Mercy, how kind you are to care about my soul. I must say you paint a far different portrait of God from how I see Him." He patted her hand. "By the way, I was proud of you tonight—how you stood up to the old man. He likes you—I can tell." He smiled wanly, as if as weary as she. "Well, good night. Sweet dreams."

"You too, James."

CHAPTER

Thirty-Three

The next morning, Mercy waited for Emily to deliver warm water, then washed and dressed, enjoying the maid's gentle brushing of her hair. Ready for the day, Mercy went downstairs. None of the family was there yet, so Mercy ate a solitary breakfast, serving herself from the covered dishes on the sideboard. When she finished, she rose and stepped from the room.

Seeing a woman coming down the corridor, Mercy stopped and stared. Here was Alice grown up. Or at least what Alice might look like, twenty years on. The resemblance was arresting.

"You must be Lucy," she breathed.

The younger woman smiled. "And you must be Miss Grove."

James's sister was a small, sweet-faced woman with golden hair and a gentle demeanor. Mercy liked her instantly.

"I am very pleased meet you," Lucy said. "I am sorry we weren't here to greet you. We were visiting my husband's elderly aunt, but we rushed home as soon as we could."

A high-pitched squeal and squeak of shoe leather drew Mercy's gaze to the staircase behind Lucy.

Two children ran down the stairs, followed by their father carrying a younger boy and mildly chastising them to slow down and be careful. Alice and Mr. Drake brought up the rear of this procession.

"I don't suppose you can do anything with my three while you're here?" Lucy asked. "They've scared off two governesses already, incorrigible creatures, and now their nurse is threatening to give notice too."

"Now, my dear," her boyish husband said, joining them, "you will give Miss Grove the wrong impression. Lou-Lou and the boys are good children and intelligent. Just a bit . . . high-spirited."

"Then perhaps we should all go outside for a game of tag or battledore and shuttlecock?" Mercy suggested. "Much easier to sit quietly indoors or concentrate on studies if one has taken exercise first."

This suggestion was met with rousing cheers from the three and a smile from Alice.

Mercy turned to the children's mother. "I will go out and watch over them while you have your breakfast. No doubt you will want to visit with your brother."

"Thank you, Miss Grove."

As Mercy walked away, shepherding Alice and the other children out of doors, she heard Lucy say, "She is a gem, James, an absolute gem. Where on earth did you find her, and has she a sister?"

Over the next few days, Mercy observed Alice and her cousins with pleasure. Alice and Lou-Lou—named for her mother, Lucy—walked hand in hand, played dolls, and brushed each other's hair. Even the male cousins, Henry and Harold, included Alice in their activities, introducing her to their dog and puppies, and trying to teach her to play cricket. Together, the four cousins acted out charades, played hide-and-seek, and built a fort of sofa cushions and bedsheets.

One afternoon, Mercy watched from the edge of the lawn as the four flew kites together. Inexplicably, she felt tears heat her eyes. Thinking herself unobserved, she let them flow.

"Mercy?" James's voice resonated with concern. "What is it?"

He stopped beside her, his gaze skimming over the laughing

children before returning to search her face. "What's wrong? Has something happened?"

She shook her head, not trusting her voice.

His eyes hardened. "Has my father said something to upset you?"

"No." She shook her head adamantly and wiped the tears with the back of her hand.

He captured her hand and held it in both of his own. "You're scaring me. Do tell me what's troubling you."

"Nothing. It's . . . I am just happy for Alice."

"You don't look happy."

"Look at them out there. I have never seen Alice so joyful, so free. Do you know Henry wants to give her one of his prized puppies?"

"Won . . . derful," James murmured sarcastically. "And will he train it as well?"

She chuckled. "They get on so well together. Boys or girls, it doesn't seem to matter when they're together. They play games and put on plays and enjoy one another's company."

"That all sounds excellent . . . except for the puppy to train. I still don't understand why you are sad."

"I'm not sad. Exactly. They are cousins, James."

"Yes. So . . . ?"

"Henry told me they even plan to ask your father to take them all fishing—so Alice can learn how. Apparently, Lou-Lou already wrinkles her nose in disgust over hooks and worms, but he still holds out high hopes for Alice."

James shook his head. "They will never get my father out of his office long enough to bait a hook."

"The point is, they have accepted her," Mercy persisted. "Alice is not alone any longer. She has cousins. An aunt and uncle. Grandparents."

He grinned softly. "And a father, don't forget."

"I don't forget. And I am glad of it. But she . . ."

"She what?"

The words *"She belongs here"* stuck in Mercy's throat. Sweet words with a barb that would sting.

Instead, she smiled. Voice thick with emotion, Mercy said, "She is one blessed little girl."

Later that day, Mr. Hain-Drake hailed Mercy as she passed by in the corridor.

"Come and see my office, Miss Grove."

Mercy entered warily, the words *lion's den* going through her mind.

Hands behind his back, he surveyed the room. "I refurbished it ten years ago now, but still I think it's modern enough to impress the learned governess. I also keep an office in one of our warehouses near the docks, but these days I hold most of my meetings here. Francis handles the day-to-day tasks at the port." He grimaced. "Tries to at any rate."

He gestured toward two large windows. "That second window was James's suggestion. He likes a lot of light."

She nodded, then noticed two open doors leading to adjacent offices. She pointed to the larger one, only slightly smaller than the one they stood in. "Whose office is that?"

He glanced at it, shifted from foot to foot, and shrugged. "Francis uses it when he's here."

"And the smaller one?"

"Leonard, my secretary. He's off on an errand at present."

"James said Francis is your business partner?"

He scowled. "More of an . . . assistant. And a poor one, truth be told. But don't repeat that to Lucy. She doesn't like to hear her husband so maligned."

"Is he not . . . skilled?"

Mr. Hain-Drake shook his head. "He's a good man—don't mistake me—and eager to please. But . . ." He sighed. "No business acumen."

"Perhaps in time and with more experience . . . ?"

He slanted her a bemused look. "James told me you saw the good in people, even with evidence to the contrary. I see what he means."

James and his father had spoken of her? Unease swept over her at the thought.

Mercy's focus was drawn to a portrait on the wall—James, as a younger man. His hair a shade lighter, his face leaner, his eyes a bit less cynical.

Noticing the direction of her gaze, he gestured toward the frame. "Commissioned that years ago when James came of age."

She nodded. "It's a good likeness."

He gestured to a smaller frame near it. "That's one of the first buildings he designed. He was only fourteen."

Mercy stepped nearer to study the framed sketch, which resembled a builder's elevation plan more than a piece of artwork. "Excellent. Perhaps he ought to have been an architect."

Again the man scowled. "What he *ought* to have been is my . . ." He let the sentence fade away, unfinished.

Childish shouts drew their attention outside, and they both stepped to the windows to investigate. Below, James, Alice, Lou-Lou, and Henry were playing battledore and shuttlecock, while younger Harold was sitting on the lawn nearby, frolicking with the pups.

Mr. Hain-Drake shook his head. "And now he wants to be a father."

"Yes. I think he will be a good one."

"Do you? I sometimes think we are cut from the same cloth more than he likes to admit. I was too busy building an empire to be involved with his and Lucy's upbringing. Don't misunderstand; they were not neglected. They grew up with every advantage, though you wouldn't know it to see James's bitterness toward me now. Those two had everything they could need. The most qualified nurses, governesses, and tutors, the best education money could buy . . ." He shook his head. "But when James was old enough and I wanted to interest him in the business, he refused me. I doubt he will fare any better in the frustrating business of parenting than I did. Not with his time and energies consumed by his new hotel and the one after that. I am glad the girl has you."

Mercy injected a cheerful note into her voice. "And I am glad Alice has him, as well as her aunt, uncle, cousins, grandmother, *and* grandfather. Perhaps you were not the best father—I cannot say. But you still have time to be an involved and caring grandfather."

"Not much time," he murmured, staring down at the children again.

She gave him a sidelong glance, unsure of his meaning.

Noticing her scrutiny, he said, "They grow up so fast."

At the Monday gathering of the Ladies Tea and Knitting Society, Jane found herself in the strange position of opening the meeting, as Mercy was still away traveling.

The soft-spoken almshouse matron, Mrs. Mennell, did not attend often and usually said little, but today she rose and said, "I know some of you have concerns about Miss Victorine's character, but I have decided she has a good heart. She came to the almshouse last week and asked if she could do any mending for the residents."

Mrs. Barton smirked. "Someone must be desperate for work."

"No, Bridget. She volunteered to do it free of charge."

"Oh."

Around the room, several women pursed their lips, impressed, while others whispered to one another.

Mrs. Burlingame said, "I saw Mrs. Shabner in Wishford recently, and she told me she visited the shop and was impressed with the quality of the designs. And if it's good enough for Mrs. Shabner, it's good enough for me."

Mrs. Barton crossed her arms over her ample bosom. "I still say she tried to pull the wool over our eyes."

Becky said, "You know, she didn't actually *say* she was French, did she? She didn't walk up to any of us and say, '*Bonjour*, I am zee new French modiste, come and spend *beaucoup* money on my Parisian gowns.' She doesn't even have a French accent to speak of."

Jane nodded. "You're right, Becky. I think it was Mrs. Shabner who first said she had an accent, but that is probably because her mother was French."

"Really, you two," Mrs. Barton said. "That is taking charity too far. With a name like *Madame Victorine*, what else were we to think? Next you will tell me she didn't actually *say* she made those fine dresses in her window."

"Well, she didn't, at least not in my hearing," Jane replied. "Though she did alter a dress for Matilda Grove, so we know she is able to sew. And I understand she is making a wedding gown for Justina Brockwell."

Astonished looks were exchanged at that bit of news.

Julia Featherstone stood up. "She made this new frock for me. I asked for an ordinary printed cotton daydress. Nothing fancy. She delivered exactly what I asked for." Julia looked down at her bodice and swished her skirt side to side. "It is very . . . ordinary . . . indeed."

"Humph. And how much did you pay for this very ordinary dress?" Bridget Barton asked.

Julia told her. The sum was surprisingly low.

Bridget raised her hands. "Apparently, you get what you pay for."

As the women talked, Jane was reminded of some of the unkind things her detractors had said about *her* when she took over as The Bell's innkeeper. Her heart went out to the new dressmaker.

And suddenly there she was. Victorine stood at the back of the room, her arms full of fabric. Jane's stomach twisted. She must have slipped in after the meeting started. One look at the woman's pale face and Jane knew she had heard at least some of what was being said about her.

One by one, heads turned as the women became aware of her presence. Most of the women looked sheepish, but Mrs. Barton lifted a stubborn chin.

Victorine said evenly, "If you are unhappy with your new dress, Miss Featherstone, please return it to the shop, and I will give your money back. That goes for anyone else who purchased something from me."

Looking guilt-stricken, Julia said, "I didn't say I didn't like it. I only meant it's not fancy like the gowns in your window."

"I did not make those gowns."

"Aha! It is as we thought." Mrs. Barton elbowed Mrs. Klein beside her. "You were right, Kristine. She's a fraud."

Mrs. Klein winced apologetically. "I didn't say *fraud*. But we were understandably under the impression that your gowns were . . . if not *from* France, at least informed by a familiarity with that country's fashions."

Around the room, heads nodded in agreement.

Victorine said, "The model gowns I displayed *were* made by a French modiste, though one living and working in London. They were given to me."

Thoughts of stolen gowns and the woman wearing an identical dress spun through Jane's mind. "Given?" she repeated. "By whom?" She recalled the London dressmaker the woman had mentioned, and asked, "Are you saying another dressmaker *gave* you these models for some reason?"

"No. Not her. I've mentioned my friend and mentor, Martine Devereaux. She and her husband were planning to retire to France. She had these new gowns made in anticipation."

Victorine looked down at the burden in her arms and slowly shook her head. "She died in her sleep the night before they were to depart. Her husband insisted on giving me two trunks of her things, including the new gowns and hats she'd had made in London."

Jane said gently, "I am sorry for your loss. But don't you think it might have been a *little* deceptive to pass them off as your own work?"

"In hindsight, yes. But newspapers are full of advertisements from mantua-makers and milliners announcing their return from Paris or London 'with a variety of fashionable fancy models.' I did not think I was doing something so very wrong, at the time. Now I realize it was deceptive—especially after you and the Miss Groves met someone who claimed Matilda's gown was made by *her* dressmaker. I was in earnest when I said I'd never met the woman. Even so, I should have told you I did not make these gowns before now, should have told all of you. But I did not, and I apologize."

An awkward silence fell. Some women continued to stare at her, while others avoided her gaze.

Victorine squared her shoulders. "Well. Thank you for hearing me out." She lifted the gowns draped over her arm. "Mrs. Mennell, do you think these could be of some use to the almshouse residents? I have two here and more in the shop. Or should I give them to the church charity guild instead?"

Shock washed over Jane, and around the room women gasped, shared incredulous looks, or sat open-mouthed. A protest sprang to Jane's lips, but she bit it back. She would not discourage the audacious act, not when it would allow Victorine to make a fresh start—as well as restitution.

The almshouse matron blinked, then slowly nodded. "Either would be blessed by such a generous donation."

"Good." Victorine walked forward and thrust the dresses into Mrs. Mennell's arms, then pivoted and strode out of the room.

After she'd left, Jane tried to steer the buzzing conversation to the next topic on the agenda, to little avail. Eventually she gave up and adjourned the meeting early, her thoughts still on the enigmatic Victorine.

On her way back to The Bell, Jane stopped at Victorine's. Faint light seeped through the window. She knocked softly.

The dressmaker opened the door, eyes weary and wary. "Jane. Come in."

Jane stepped inside. Hoping to ease the tension in the woman's tight expression and posture, she teased, "Coming to the meeting like that, your arms full of gowns . . . You sure know how to make an entrance."

That earned a small grin in reply. "Very true."

"You certainly enlivened our meeting."

"No doubt. When you knocked, I was afraid I'd find a whole troupe of angry women at my door ready to rail at me, or at least to demand their money back."

"No, I think they've said all they intend to—and more than enough, no doubt."

Jane looked from the linen tape measure around Victorine's neck to the worktable covered with pattern pieces, tissue, and drawings. "You're working late."

Victorine nodded. "This gown for Miss Brockwell . . . it's more difficult than I imagined it would be."

Jane returned her gaze to Victorine. "Did you even work in a dress shop before coming here?"

She shook her head. "No. Martine and I fashioned costumes of all sorts for years, but this is my first time working in a shop. And my last, at this rate. I have little savings and foolishly thought selling Martine's gowns would buy me more time. I hoped I had learned enough over the years to succeed as a dressmaker. I am beginning to realize I was wrong."

"I am sorry you are struggling. I remember how that feels. When I took over as innkeeper, I was plagued by doubts and unsure what to do and how to make the place profitable."

Jane laid a hand on her arm. "Victorine, I was in earnest when I said to let me know if there is anything I can do to help you. That offer still stands."

"Thank you. That means a lot. But if I can't pay next month's rent, I will have to admit defeat and leave. And after tonight, that is looking rather likely."

Jane found herself studying Victorine's face as she spoke. There was still something so familiar about her. She asked, "Why did you choose Ivy Hill, of all places?"

"I saw an advertisement for a dressmaker's shop for let and had fond memories of visiting Ivy Hill with my family as a girl."

"Where is your family now?"

"Oh, here and there. As I said, my father moves around a great deal for his . . . work. And my sister and I have lost touch. She did briefly live in the area a few years ago—in Salisbury, I believe. She has since moved on, but somehow I feel closer to her here in Wiltshire, silly as that must sound."

Not only was the woman's face familiar, but now her words about her family also had a familiar ring. Jane had a dizzying sense that she'd had a conversation very much like this before. But when . . . and with whom?

CHAPTER
THIRTY-FOUR

Jane should have been thinking about her own approaching wedding, but instead she found herself thinking again of Hetty and Patrick's elopement. When Hetty Piper briefly worked for her at The Bell before agreeing to marry Patrick, Jane had asked about her past more than once, but Hetty brushed off questions about where she was from, saying her family had moved around a lot, and that she had not been in contact with them since Betsey was born. Hetty *had* admitted she missed her large extended family, whom she had not seen in a long while.

At the time, Jane assumed Hetty wished to keep secret from them the fact that she'd had a child out of wedlock. But now she wondered if there was more to it.

She recalled Hetty's discomfort when they'd all sat down together to discuss wedding plans. . . .

"What would Mr. Paley need to publish the banns?" Hetty had asked, her voice edged with worry.

"If I remember right," Thora said, "all that was required was writing down your full name and place of residence."

"Be sure to spell your name correctly," Jane had teased. "Using the wrong name renders a marriage null and void." Jane laughed at the little joke, but Hetty did not smile in return.

"What a lot of bother," she'd moaned instead. "Can we not simply elope?"

Jane had tried to reassure Hetty that a wedding would not be all that difficult, and that she and Thora would help with everything. But in the end, the couple had eloped anyway.

Now Jane wondered anew what had really been the cause of Hetty's reluctance to publicly post their intention to wed.

It had been some time since she had visited Hetty and Patrick in Wishford. She decided to go and see them again as soon as she could.

The following morning, Jane and Thora rode to Wishford in the gig, ostensibly to view Patrick and Hetty's progress on the lodging house. In reality, Jane knew Thora went along mostly because she missed Betsey and wanted to see her again.

When they arrived, the little family greeted them warmly, and Betsey raised her hands, asking Thora to pick her up. Thora happily obliged.

Together, the five of them walked around the property, Patrick showing them the grounds, pride mixed with sheepishness. The yard was weedy and overgrown, and the house did not yet have indoor plumbing. The old privy slumped to one side and would need to be replaced. Everywhere Jane looked, she saw a great deal of work to do. Patrick had become a capable manager but had little experience with repairs or construction. Hetty had always been a hard worker, but with a toddler to keep entertained and out of trouble, it was no doubt difficult to get much done. Thora still watched Betsey on occasion, but Wishford was several miles away and Thora had her own work on Angel Farm.

A little brown mop of a terrier ran into the yard, his tail and entire hindquarters wagging joyously upon seeing Hetty.

Hetty bent low, and the dog bounded over to her. She stroked his long, stringy hair. "Hello, Chips." The terrier sniffed her apron pockets. "Sorry. No treat for you right now."

Betsey, still in Thora's arms, generously offered her soggy biscuit for the purpose. The terrier rose on hind legs, paws raised in supplication, and even turned in a little circle.

Jane smiled. "Did you teach him to do that?"

Hetty shrugged. "Isn't hard. Dogs like these are so clever and eager to please. I had one very like it once."

"Is this your dog, then?" Jane asked.

"No!" Patrick interjected with a mock glower that fooled no one.

His wife's eyes sparkled mischievously. "Not yet."

The tour continued. Patrick showed them where he hoped to extend the building once they had some rental income coming in, as well as the corner plot where they'd erected a fence and planted a kitchen garden. Noticing a loose nail in the garden gate, he pulled a hammer from his pocket and tapped at the protruding nail, only to miss and have to try again.

As they walked around the lodging house, Jane noticed a man of about five and twenty leaning idly against a tree a few houses away, watching them. He smoked a cigarillo and now and again picked tobacco from his teeth. Lank blond hair hung over his face.

"Who is that?" Thora asked.

Patrick glanced over and waved a dismissive hand. "Howard Phillips. His parents own the Crown."

Thora lifted her chin in recognition. "Ah."

Jane had not seen him in some time, but having grown up near Wishford—shopping there and attending church there—she knew who he was.

Thora frowned. "What is he looking at?"

"Probably spying for his parents. Wondering how long until we begin stealing some of their customers." Patrick waggled his eyebrows. "Which won't be long now."

"Now, Patrick," Hetty gently admonished. "Don't instigate a rivalry. You know the Crown caters primarily to people traveling through Wishford. Our lodging house is for people who need a place to live long term. And we had better hope there are enough of them."

He stroked her cheek. "There shall be, my love. Never fear."

Hetty sighed. "The thrills and risks of opening a new establishment, I suppose."

Patrick called to their observer, "You can come over here, Howard, and get a better look!"

"Shh . . . Patrick." Hetty clutched his arm. "Be kind."

"I thought I was being kind. Neighborly, actually."

The young man blew a ring of smoke. "Why should I? I can see your comedy of errors from here. Never held a hammer before?"

Patrick tensed, taking one step in his direction, but Jane quickly moved into his path, brightly changing the subject.

"Speaking of new establishments, have you heard we have a new dressmaker in Ivy Hill?"

With a worried look at her still-glaring husband, Hetty replied, "Only in passing. Mrs. Shabner lives in Wishford now, and she mentioned it. Something about a French modiste, but I confess I paid little heed. Is the shop doing well?"

"I fear Victorine is struggling." *In more ways than one.*

"Victorine?" Hetty repeated, the word disturbing her expression like a stone tossed in a placid lake.

"Yes. Might you know her?" Jane asked.

Hetty blinked troubled blue eyes. "Know her? That's unlikely, is it not?"

"Is it?" Jane watched her face. Surprised by the flash of . . . fear she saw there. At the same time, she became aware of Thora studying *her* with a perplexed frown.

A moment later, whatever Jane had seen in Hetty's face retreated behind one of her pretty smiles. "Why should I know a French dressmaker? Or any dressmaker, for that matter, when all my clothes are secondhand? It only struck me as an unusual name."

"Would you like to come into Ivy Hill and visit the shop with me?"

Hetty shook her head. "I couldn't. Too much to do. Besides, new dresses are not exactly in the budget at present."

Patrick put his arm around her. "But as soon as our lodging

house earns a profit, we shall buy new dresses for you and Betsey both, if you like."

His wife sent him a wry look. "At the moment, I would rather have a long nap, but thank you, my love."

Turning to ask Thora something about the farm, Hetty said no more on the subject of the dressmaker.

Jane swallowed her disappointment. Apparently she had let her imagination get the best of her.

Victorine laid out the pattern pieces on the white satin, careful not to mar its glossy surface. She arranged them one way, then another, trying to make the most economical use of the fine material.

It was more difficult than it looked, and she began to fear she had not purchased enough fabric.

She gathered up the pattern pieces and tried again. Would nothing go according to plan?

The meager savings she'd started with were almost gone. Soon the profits from the shop would have to be enough to support her. But she'd sold only a few hats and gowns, discovered new material was expensive, and now her rent was almost due.

She had thought it would be easier, that this was a role she could easily play. After all, she enjoyed sewing and had made many beautiful costumes—costumes that fastened and unfastened easily, with extra fabric allowance in case a player gained a stone over the long winter or a larger understudy had to take over the role on short notice. But the experience had not prepared her as much as she'd thought for making dresses for daily life, and especially not a fine wedding gown for an exacting customer.

And considering her tenuous position in the village, if she couldn't make this dress for the Brockwells, she feared she would never be asked to make another.

If only she could get through this one challenge, keep up the act just a little while longer, before everyone realized she wasn't qualified and that "Madame Victorine" had never made a wedding dress in her life.

Drawing a fortifying breath, she returned her attention to the pattern pieces and began pinning them to the satin.

But her concentration was quickly interrupted when Jack Gander strode into the shop, something long tucked under his arm. Seeing him, her heart lightened, and a smile tickled the corners of her mouth. But as he crossed the shop to her, she noticed his tense jaw and flared nostrils.

Laying the tube of canvas on the counter, he unrolled it, and her stomach dropped.

He looked up at her, watching her carefully. "I knew I had seen your likeness before, and this proves it."

With his index finger, he tapped the large painted show cloth— one of the many her father had posted on the outside of their tent and caravan wagons. Seeing it stole the breath from her lungs. Had her father thrown it away after she left? It felt like a rejection. But what had she expected?

When she said nothing, he continued, "I wasn't able to find anything on my own, but with the offer of a few sovereigns and a plea for help, I was able to expand my search. I had several other guards and acquaintances searching for anyone who'd heard of, or seen, a beautiful black-haired performer named Victorine or something like it. And yesterday my search yielded this."

She cringed. The image on the advertisement was of a dark-haired woman in a spangled court dress, black and white feathers in her hair. Before her, a white horse "bowed" on one knee, wearing a black collar and cravat around his neck, and black gaiters on each leg. It was a very accurate rendering of them both. Dear old Charger . . .

The text read, *Miss Victor, the raven-haired wonder, dances a perfect minuet with a gentlemanly stallion.* In smaller letters at the bottom was the troupe name: *The Earl's Menagerie and Traveling Players.*

"Where did you get this?" she asked.

"A coachman friend of mine purchased it from one of the troupe's drivers. It was no longer being used because the 'raven-haired wonder' is no longer with the troupe."

She swallowed, unable to meet his eyes.

"You lied to me," he said. "I knew I had seen your face in print."

She braved a look at him. His eyes were cold now, when they had once been so warm. "I did not lie. You accused me of performing for Astley's, and I never did."

"Come on, you knew what I meant."

"I have my reasons for keeping my connection to the troupe private."

Jack's brow puckered. "I realize traveling performers have poor reputations, but that is not cause enough to conceal your past. To deceive an entire village."

"Is it not? Who would engage me to make a fine gown, knowing that I was raised among actors and showmen, and that most of what I have sewn has been theatrical costumes? You know people regard traveling players as equal to gypsies. And actresses, little better than prostitutes."

He flinched at the word.

She added, "I did not set out to deceive people, only to break with my past and start a new life, untainted by prejudice."

She studied his handsome, rigid face, hoping to see a flicker of his former admiration. "Please do not judge me so harshly. You have never had men leer and paw at you as though you were a common trollop." She shook her head, feeling her eyes heat. He wouldn't understand. Men rarely did.

He frowned. "You had better tell me everything, or I will feel it my duty to tell Mrs. Bell you are not who you claim to be and let her decide whether or not to tell everyone else."

She met his gaze, measuring his resolve. "Very well. I clearly have little choice." She took a deep breath and began her tale.

CHAPTER

Thirty-Five

The day after her conversation with Mr. Hain-Drake, Mercy went out on the balcony and sat down to relax in one of the cushioned chairs, enjoying the breeze and the view of the surrounding countryside.

James came out to join her, handing her a glass of lemonade.

"Thank you." She sipped, then said, "Your father showed me his office yesterday."

"Oh? Were you duly impressed?"

"I was. But not in the way you think."

"Then how so? I have not been in there in years, myself."

"That's just it. He is disappointed you didn't go into business with him."

"Only because he wanted to control every aspect of my life, dictate my every step. But I didn't want to be his lackey, like Francis has become. I wanted to succeed on my own terms and on my own merit—not have everything handed to me. That's why I dropped the Hain portion of our surname—to prove I could make my own way in the world without the advantages of our connection."

He looked off into the distance, then continued. "I started my first business when I was still at university. After graduating, I went into partnership with Max and Rupert and eventually sold my share for a considerable profit. I invested the money wisely and used the proceeds to buy my first hotel, but nothing I did pleased or impressed my father. None of my accomplishments could measure up to his."

He slowly shook his head. "So over the years, I came home less and less. The distance helped. My bitterness and desire to triumph over him would fade to the background—at least until a rare visit home when he would again demean my *paltry* endeavors. Then that resentment and desire to prove myself would flare up once more."

"And this visit home?"

James shrugged. "Better than most. Having you here has tempered us both, I think."

"James, I know that on the surface he seems a proud and critical man. But in his office, I got a glimpse behind the mask. He realizes his deficiencies as a parent, the emptiness of his success, and the price he's paid in losing you over it."

"He hasn't exactly lost me. I am here, aren't I?"

"Come, you can't deny there's a wall between you. Your father doesn't know how to go about tearing it down. I think he is afraid to admit he needs you."

"Needs me? My father? I will never believe it."

"Oh, James. Never say never."

Hearing excited chatter and footsteps pass beneath them, Mercy rose and stepped to the railing.

"James, look!"

He joined her there, and together they watched as Mr. Hain-Drake, fishing poles clutched in one hand and holding young Harold by the other, walked with his four grandchildren toward the fish pond.

James shook his head in wonder. "Never say never, indeed."

They left Drayton Park the following day, and the journey back to the Fairmont passed without mishap. Mercy was eager to return, both to start teaching again and to see Mr. Kingsley.

As if reading her thoughts, Alice said, "I can't wait to see Johnny and Mr. Kingsley and tell them about the puppies, and kites, and fishing, and well . . . everything!"

Mercy said, "I understand, but first we ought to put away our things."

Mr. Drake added, "Yes, and then dinner. We're arriving later than I'd hoped and I'm starving."

When they entered the hall, Alice saw the sandy-haired builder kneeling before the wall, reattaching a piece of baseboard. With a giggle, she ran up to him and wrapped her hands over his eyes. "Guess who?"

"I . . . have no idea."

The man stood and turned. Not Joseph, but Aaron.

"Sorry!" Alice blushed furiously and covered her face with her hands.

Mercy hurried to console her. "Don't be embarrassed, Alice. I have mistaken him for his older brother twice now."

"Have you?" There stood Joseph, working in the office nearby. His mouth parted and chin lifted in comprehension. "Ahh . . ." He held her gaze, a knowing light in his eyes. Too knowing.

She feigned nonchalance. "Hello, Mr. Kingsley."

"Miss Grove. Alice. Pleased to see you back. Good trip?"

"Yes!" Alice blurted, and began an exuberant account.

"You can tell Mr. Kingsley all about it later, Alice." Mercy gently turned her toward the stairs. "Now it's time to go up and help Iris unpack. Be sure to wash your face and hands before dinner."

Alice groaned but complied.

Joseph followed them across the hall, and when Alice started up the stairs, he took Mercy's hand and pulled her around the corner into one of the private parlours.

"I have to ask," he said. "That day at the window . . . Did you think it was me kissing Esther?"

She pressed her lips together. "I . . . may have done. You no doubt think me very foolish. But remember, I saw you embrace Esther on the green before, and the two of you in that very spot having a picnic. And you and your brother resemble each other a great deal from behind."

"And that was why you were so upset?"

She thought of how she must have appeared, standing there crying. She looked down—feeling embarrassed and deeply vulnerable—and let her silence be her answer.

He stepped nearer, until his boots entered her field of vision, the masculine brown leather touching the hem of her skirt.

She felt his hand beneath her chin, and he gently lifted her face.

He looked directly into her eyes, his voice rumbling low in his chest. "Mercy Grove, there is only one woman I am longing to kiss."

Mercy's heart banged against her breastbone, in painfully sweet anticipation. Did he mean . . . ? She looked deep into his eyes and felt herself sink into them. She never wanted to leave. Oh, to wake up to those warm brown eyes every day of her life . . .

He leaned near, his gaze locked with hers, then shifting to her mouth. He lowered his head, and her lashes fluttered closed.

A door banged open in the hall, and Mr. Drake's voice called for the porter.

Mr. Kingsley abruptly stepped back, and Mercy barely resisted the urge to reach out and draw him near again. The porter hurried past the open parlour door to answer Mr. Drake's summons. A moment later, the boot boy followed him, waving to Mercy as he passed.

Mr. Kingsley cleared his throat. "Well. I had better get back to work, Miss Grove. But may we . . . talk, later?"

"Yes." She nodded and managed a tremulous smile, then hurried up to her room. She climbed one pair of stairs after another, heart beating hard, her breath coming in shallow draws that had little to do with the exertion of the climb.

Mercy hoped to see Joseph again later that day, but after unpacking, gathering clothes for the laundry, and dining with Alice and Mr. Drake, she was disheartened to learn he had gone home for the evening. Nor did she see him the next day, except in passing, as she was occupied with getting Alice started on her schoolwork again, and in the evening she helped Mr. Drake catch up on the correspondence that had accumulated during his absence.

Mercy was happy to help but inwardly sighed. For she doubted she would have time to talk to Mr. Kingsley the following day either, as she would be busy decorating The Bell for Jane's wedding. She wondered if Mr. Kingsley would attend but had no opportunity to ask him. She certainly hoped he would.

Jane and Gabriel's wedding was fast approaching, and the arrangements were, for the most part, settled. With the wet year they were having, Jane had decided against attempting a courtyard setting for the wedding breakfast, and instead planned to have it inside the dining parlour and coffee room. Mercy and several women from the Ladies Tea and Knitting Society had volunteered to help decorate The Bell for the occasion, while Rachel and her lady's maid, Jemima, would help Jane dress and arrange her hair. Stalwart Mrs. Rooke had planned a fine meal, including a cake ordered from Craddock's bakery.

Even though Jane had been the one to insist on not waiting to marry, now that the day was nearly upon them, the reality of the changes to come began to press on her heart.

As much as she loved Gabriel and wanted to spend the rest of her life with him, she was still nervous about the wedding night and all those nights to come . . . and the likely consequences.

One evening, as they sat together after dinner, Gabriel took her hand and said, "Jane, I know you are worried about losing more children. And so am I. But let's give our marriage, and our marriage bed, to God. Whatever happens, we will get through it together." He bowed his head and prayed aloud, and Jane took comfort in listening to her future husband talk to the Almighty on their behalf in his rich baritone voice. Even so, Jane added a silent plea of her own: *Help me bear more losses, if losses come.*

Two days before the wedding, the Talbots invited Jane and Gabriel to have dinner with them at their house. Over the meal, they discussed each other's farms, and the upcoming nuptials.

"Gabriel's parents and uncle arrive tomorrow," Jane said. "We've decided to put them at The Bell instead of the farm for their visit—in the best rooms, of course."

Thora nodded, then asked, "Is your father still lodging in Wilton?"

"Yes. I've invited him to stay at The Bell more than once, but so far he hasn't accepted. He seems to prefer Wilton for some reason."

"I don't believe I've heard; does he plan to stay in the area?"

"I hope so, but he has not said."

"I'm sure Mr. Gordon, or Mr. Arnold in Wishford, would be happy to find him a house to let or buy—though probably nothing as grand as he's used to."

"I believe he lived fairly simply in India," Jane replied. "I mentioned the possibility of finding more permanent lodgings, but he didn't seem interested, so I didn't press him."

Talbot said, "Well, at least Wilton is much closer than India."

"True."

"Speaking of great distances," Gabriel said, "I'm afraid we won't be able to take a wedding trip. Being laid up as I was, and now amid training the new horses . . ." He regretfully shook his head. "If I leave them for long, all of that work will go to waste. It will be like starting over when we return." He looked at her. "I'm sorry, Jane. I hope you are not terribly disappointed."

"I'm not. As long as I am with you, I will be happy."

"I would like to take you to my parents' house and out to my uncle's farm at some point. Perhaps by Christmas, we can get away."

Walter Talbot cleared his throat and shifted in his chair. "My dear Mr. Locke, you have many horses but only one wife. From one farmer to another, may I say that you won't regret taking a wedding trip of at least a few days. Any inconvenience of leaving will soon be forgotten. I still cherish the memory of my time away with Thora. Having her to myself away from daily chores—it was well worth it, I assure you. My men and I will help tend your animals while you're gone. I don't know much about training horses, but I can keep them fed and cared for, for a few days."

Thora added, "And I would stop by The Bell daily, Jane, and make sure things there go smoothly while you're away."

Gabriel considered, then said, "Very well, you two. You've convinced me. I will accept on the condition that you allow me to return the favor sometime." He parroted Talbot's words back to him. "I don't know much about cattle or sheep, but I can keep them fed and cared for, for a few days."

Talbot grinned. "I shall bear that in mind, Gabriel. Perhaps on a special anniversary." He reached over and took Thora's hand.

Jane's heart squeezed to see the affectionate bond between husband and wife. She thanked God again that she and Gabriel would very soon be husband and wife as well.

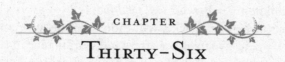

CHAPTER
THIRTY-SIX

Gabriel stood at the altar, handsome in a dark frock coat, walking stick in hand, just in case. Jane stood beside him, holding a bouquet of peonies, sweet peas, and ivy from her own garden. She wore her new dress from London with a veiled bonnet, and Cadi had taken extra pains with her hair.

The church pews were filled with people they knew and loved— their family and friends, along with The Bell staff and many neighbors. In fashionable cities, people generally viewed wedding services as gloomy affairs best inflicted on only closest friends and family, but in Ivy Hill weddings were important social events, widely attended and celebrated with joy.

Mr. Paley stood, facing the expanded congregation, and began the marriage ceremony.

"Dearly beloved, we are gathered together here in the sight of God . . . to join together this man and this woman in holy matrimony . . . signifying unto us the mystical union that is betwixt Christ and His Church . . ."

While the vicar spoke, a flash of memory played through Jane's mind. Of standing beside John, hearing the same words. It seemed a lifetime ago. She thought of Thora, wondering if she was remembering that day as well.

"First, it was ordained for the procreation of children, to be brought up in the fear and nurture of the Lord . . ."

Jane's heart beat hard. She felt several pairs of eyes on her profile at the words. Did those who knew of her childbearing woes look at her in pity? Were she and Gabriel wrong to marry when they knew it was highly unlikely they would ever have a chance to bring up any children? *Lord, your will be done.*

"Gabriel Matthias Locke, wilt thou have this woman to thy wedded wife, to live together after God's ordinance in the holy estate of matrimony? Wilt thou love her, comfort her, honor, and keep her in sickness and in health; and forsaking all others, keep thee only unto her, so long as ye both shall live?"

Gabriel looked at Jane solemnly. "I will."

The clergyman then asked her a variation of the same questions. The words *in sickness and in health* resonated with deep meaning, and she silently thanked God yet again for Gabriel's recovery.

Jane turned to Gabriel and held his dark gaze. "I will."

Later, their vows declared, they both knelt, and Mr. Paley prayed over them. He joined their hands together and said, "Those whom God hath joined together, let no man put asunder."

He then pronounced them man and wife. Finally, the vicar blessed them, read from the Psalms, and closed with an additional blessing for procreation. Jane's ears burned. Beside her, Gabriel squeezed her hand.

Afterward, marriage license signed, Jane and Gabriel exited the church, arm in arm. Gabriel still carried his walking stick, but he barely leaned on it. In fact, there was a decided spring in his step. Jane smiled up at him, and he returned it, warm affection shining in his eyes.

Friends and family bordered the churchyard path, applauding as they passed, wishing them well, and tossing seeds of grain over them in the old tradition.

Reaching the gate, Talbot helped first Jane, then Gabriel into the borrowed barouche-landau decorated with white ribbon and flowers. Then he and Thora climbed onto the front bench and drove them to The Bell for the wedding breakfast. Their guests followed behind them on foot, umbrellas shooting up as a grey drizzle began to fall.

Beside her in the carriage, Gabriel lifted Jane's gloved hand to his lips and kissed it. His deep brown eyes glittered with promises of more kisses to come.

With the weather as it was, Jane's decision to hold the wedding breakfast inside The Bell had been a wise one. Mrs. Rooke and her staff, along with Thora, had put together quite a feast: ham and veal pies, roasted chickens, salads, rhubarb tarts, rolls and butter, and a rich bride cake from Craddock's.

To seat everyone, they had placed the buffet tables in the hall, and added extra tables and chairs to the coffee room and the recently expanded dining parlour. Except for immediate family, seating was first come, first served. Jane had decided not to assign tables in the formal dining parlour for affluent guests, nor consign her more humble friends to the coffee room. As a result, each room held an interesting mix of people. Lady Brockwell and Justina found themselves at a table with Mr. Ainsworth and Mr. and Mrs. Barton, and learned a great deal about the management of cows. Sir Timothy and Rachel sat beside Mrs. Klein and Miss Morris, and before the meal had concluded, Kristine found herself with another pianoforte to tune and Becky with a commission for a new welcome sign for Ivy Hill. James Drake, meanwhile, found himself receiving romance advice from Mrs. Snyder, Mrs. Burlingame, and the Cook sisters.

Jane and Gabriel made the rounds, visiting guests in both rooms, and accepting congratulations from all quarters.

After the meal, the staff removed the tables from one end of the room, setting those chairs in a half circle instead. Then, The Bell's three musicians began to warm up their instruments: Tuffy on his old mandolin, Tall Ted on fiddle, and Colin on pipe.

Jane and Gabriel walked to the center of the gathering and, when conversations quieted, Jane began, "Thank you all for being here to help us celebrate our very special day." She looked up at Gabriel beside her.

He said, "Most of you know about my recent accident—the uncertainty over whether I would walk again. My darling Jane assured me she would love and marry me anyway. Today I stand here on my own two feet and thank God for my recovery, and for the woman who stood by me regardless of the outcome. We also want to thank so many of you who helped us during that trying time with your friendship and offers of help, food, and prayer. We appreciate each and every one of you more than you know." He smiled at Jane and squeezed her hand.

"Now it's time for music and dancing," Jane said. "My groom is not quite ready to dance a jig, but I expect the rest of you are. Who will be the first couple?"

"I will!" Cadi blurted, and only then swiveled around to look for a partner. She grabbed Ned's hand and pulled him up from his chair.

Patrick and Hetty joined them, as did Sir Timothy and Rachel, Mr. and Mrs. Paley, and Gabriel's parents.

Jane asked her father to dance, but he patted her hand and sat down beside Miss Matty. "Sorry, my dear. I am afraid I am not ready to dance a jig either. I think I will sit here instead."

"You can sit here if you like," Matilda teased, rising, "but I intend to dance." Seeing her standing there, Alfred Coine quickly rose to offer his services as her partner.

Winston Fairmont humphed and crossed his arms.

Jane bit back a grin.

Soon, more tables were cleared away and other people joined the dance. At one point, Hetty took Colin's place on the pipe so he could dance with Anna Kingsley, pretty in Rachel's old pink dress. In the corner, Jack Avi held little Betsey's hands and the two danced a jig of their own. Jane looked from face to face, and sweet satisfaction expanded her heart.

She was content to leave the dancing to others as long as there were plenty of couples. She returned to sit by Gabriel's side.

"Happy?" he asked, looking into her eyes.

"Very. You?"

"Yes. Though I shall be happier still when it is just the two of us at home."

Jane's cheeks warmed at the thought. A remnant of worry arose, but she asked God to help her banish it. Then she sent her husband a shy smile. "I like the sound of that."

Mercy watched with pleasure as Aunt Matty danced with the lawyer—her countenance radiant and his boyish as they clapped and skipped through the steps. Mr. Coine's face eventually reddened as the music continued, but rather than stopping, he just pulled a handkerchief from his pocket to mop his brow. Mercy was glad her aunt could enjoy this rare opportunity to dance. She doubted anyone would ask her, especially as the only Kingsley in attendance was Anna. She was disappointed to not see Joseph. She had hoped he would come, but apparently not.

Mr. Drake danced with Alice, using all the skills they had learned from the visiting dancing master. When the two reached the bottom of the line and stood out one round, as the pattern dictated, James stepped nearer Mercy's chair.

"May I have the next dance, Mercy?"

Surprise flashed through her. "Oh, I . . . yes, thank you."

Alice grinned from one to the other.

As they rejoined the dance, movement in the hall caught Mercy's eye. With a surge of excitement, she saw Joseph Kingsley enter, handsome in his Sunday best. He removed his hat and brushed the hair back from his brow. Her mouth suddenly dry, Mercy reached for a sip of punch. She watched as he approached the bride and groom, shook Mr. Locke's hand, and congratulated them both. He next crossed the room to greet his niece Anna and then turned to go.

Mercy was on her feet before she'd consciously decided to move. "Mr. Kingsley . . . I did not think you were coming."

"Miss Grove." His gaze swept over her. "You look lovely, if you don't mind my saying."

Pleasure warmed her. She was glad now she had donned the Pomona-green dress her mother had given her. "Thank you. Are you leaving already? You just got here."

Nearby, the musicians played a final chord, and Mr. Drake escorted Alice back to her chair.

Mr. Kingsley shrugged. "I am not that well acquainted with either the bride or groom. I only stopped by to wish them well. And to see you. . . ."

Mr. Drake approached them. "There you are, Mercy. I've come to claim my dance. Oh, hello, Kingsley. Didn't know you were here."

Mr. Kingsley held her gaze a moment longer, then turned to the man. "Just stopped by to wish the new couple happy. And now I shall wish you both a good day as well." He nodded, turned, and strode away.

The musicians began another tune and couples began forming two lines.

"Mercy?" James extended his hand to her. "The next set is starting."

With a weak smile, she tentatively put her hand in his. As James led her to the bottom of the dance, she could not resist a final look over her shoulder. But Mr. Kingsley had already disappeared from view.

Later that day, Sir Timothy and Rachel delivered the new-married couple home in the Brockwell barouche, the floor and boot filled with gifts, a basket of leftover food, and a portion of the bride's cake to enjoy the following day.

Reaching the farm, Sir Timothy and Rachel helped them carry everything inside. Rachel embraced Jane, and then she and Timothy departed. With a self-conscious smile, Timothy shut the door behind himself. Gabriel walked over and locked it.

Jane said, "I thought you never locked your door."

"Tonight is not just any night. I don't want to risk any joker or well-meaning servant interrupting us."

"Susie?"

"Given this afternoon and tomorrow off."

"I see. Someone thought ahead."

"I admit I have thought of little else these last few days. And nights."

Jane bit her lip, then confessed, "I am nervous."

"So am I." He held out his hand to her. "Come, Jane. Let's get it over with."

"Get it over with!" Jane protested on an incredulous little laugh.

"I mean the first time—the first anxious, awkward time. Then we can relax and enjoy ourselves."

Butterflies tickled her stomach. "Oh dear."

He grinned ruefully. "Sorry. I talk too much when I'm nervous."

She tilted her head and studied him. "You know, I don't believe I've ever seen you nervous before."

"It's my first time for that too."

Again he held out his palm to her, and she put her whole heart and self into his hands.

CHAPTER

Thirty-Seven

Mercy had been sorry to see Mr. Kingsley so briefly at the wedding breakfast. Why had he rushed off? She knew now he had no romantic aspirations where Esther was concerned, but still he did not pursue *her*. Was it only because he had no house to offer her, or was there some other reason?

At least she had been able to talk with Aunt Matty at the wedding. Mercy had missed her while they'd been in Portsmouth.

After finishing their lessons the next day, Alice went down to join Mr. Drake for their evening time together. Mercy stopped in her own room to wash the chalk dust from her hands and tidy her hair. Then she went downstairs as well, hoping for a few private moments with Mr. Kingsley.

She didn't see him anywhere. In fact, when Mercy looked around she was surprised to find only James Drake sitting there.

"Where is Alice?" she asked. "I released her half an hour ago."

"Apparently she forgot our chess game. Again. It seems she prefers Johnny's company to mine."

"I'm sorry."

He shrugged and gave her a crooked grin. "Good training for her adolescent years, I imagine."

She chuckled. "Probably true." Through the window, Mercy glimpsed a flash of pink skirt and went to look outside.

"There she is, by the sweet chestnut tree."

He crossed the room to join her at the window. "I hope she's not planning to climb it. I told her not to."

As they watched, Alice looped her hands around the lowest branch of the gnarled old tree and swung herself up. From there, the branches formed a relatively easy ladder to climb higher.

James unlatched the window and pushed it open. "Alice, I asked you not to climb that tree."

Alice continued climbing.

James frowned in frustration. "Can she not hear me or is she ignoring me?"

"I'm not sure."

He turned on his heel and strode from the room. Mercy followed.

Once outside, he hurried across the lawn. "Alice! Come down."

Alice called back, "But one of the cats climbed up here and can't get down."

"He can get down far easier than you can. That's too high."

"Just a little farther."

He ran a hand over his face. "Why won't she heed me?"

Mercy made no reply, her pulse rate rising the higher the girl climbed.

Sitting on one branch, Alice reached toward the adolescent cat above her and teetered on her perch.

Mercy added her voice to James's. "Alice, be careful!"

"He's scared," the girl called down.

"So am I," James replied. "Alice, stay where you are. I will come up and get you."

Alice's foot slipped, and a second later, she was flailing, then falling. Mercy cried out, heart slamming against her breastbone, and James lurched forward, arms outstretched. In a blur of pink and green, the two collided and fell to the ground, rolling to a stop in a heap of arms, legs, and skirt.

Mercy hurried toward them. "Are you all right?"

Alice rolled off of James, and Mercy noticed blood on his temple.

"James, you're bleeding."

He reached a hand to his forehead, and it came away bloody. "I think I caught her half boot with my head," he said dryly.

Alice's eyes widened at the sight of the blood. "I am sorry, Papa."

The cat scrambled down of its own accord, unscathed.

While James dug for a handkerchief to sop the blood, Mercy quickly examined Alice for injuries. "Does anything hurt?"

The girl shook her head, tears glimmering in her eyes. Mercy guessed her conscience smarted, if nothing else.

That evening—Alice hugged, gently reprimanded, and sent to bed early—James and Mercy sat in his office, him sipping a rare glass of brandy.

"When Alice fell, my heart stopped," he began. "Why would she not obey me? Are my requests so unreasonable? I only asked her not to climb that tree for her own safety. I suppose I should punish her more sternly, but I think hurting me was consequence enough—don't you agree?"

Mercy nodded, eying his bruised and bandaged temple. "She feels terribly guilty."

He frowned. "I don't want her to feel guilty. I want her to listen, to obey a few simple rules for her own good and my sanity. If she doesn't want to spend time with me, that's one thing, but endangering herself is quite another."

Mercy said, "That reminds me of something Mr. Paley said once—that there is nothing like becoming a parent to make one realize what God goes through with *His* children. He longs to spend time with us, mourns when we go astray, has great plans for our future, and would sacrifice anything to rescue us."

James sent her a half smile. "You're not going to let this go, are you?"

She shook her head. "Did you stop loving Alice because she ignored you for a while or disobeyed you?"

"Never."

"Neither will He."

James rested his head in his hands and murmured, "Oh, Mercy."

When he said no more for a few moments, she whispered, "Exactly."

Mercy passed the coffee room later that evening and saw Mr. Kingsley standing near the door. Her heart instantly lightened.

"Miss Grove, good evening," he said stiffly, eyes wary.

She smiled at him. "Mr. Kingsley, I am happy to see you. I was sorry you left the wedding so quickly."

"Were you?"

She nodded.

He studied her face, and his expression brightened. He looked past her and around the empty hall. "Not dining with Mr. Drake and Alice tonight?"

"No. Alice has gone to bed early and Mr. Drake has been invited to dine with the Phillipses in Wishford. So I am on my own."

"Happy chance. Would you have dinner with me, then?"

"I would enjoy that."

He pulled out a chair for her at a table, then looked around the room. "No friends of Mr. Drake's here tonight? Good. That should make it easier to avoid getting into fisticuffs."

He grinned at her, and she returned the gesture.

When they were both seated, one of the waiters soon appeared with printed menus.

"Hello, Lawrence."

"Miss Grove. Mr. Kingsley. You are familiar with our usual offerings, of course. And today, our chef has prepared a few special dishes to tempt you: a creamy white soup, followed by roast loin of pork and parsnips. And almond cheesecakes for dessert."

"Sounds lovely." But Mercy noticed Joseph did not look similarly pleased. In fact, a shadow crossed his face. "Give us just a few minutes to decide, will you, Lawrence?"

"Of course. Take your time."

She studied her companion. "Mr. Kingsley, is something the matter?"

"No. It's only . . . white soup was Naomi's favorite. Just took me off guard." He winced. "I'm sorry. I suppose I should not mention her to you."

"Of course you should. We are friends, are we not? And she is an important part of you."

"Thank you, Miss Grove." He gestured to the waiter. "We are ready now." He ordered the special menu for both of them.

While they waited for their food, Mercy said gently, "Esther told me a little about Naomi. How would you describe her?"

He slowly nodded as he considered his reply. "Bright. Lively. Affectionate. Pretty."

"She sounds perfect," Mercy murmured on a self-conscious little chuckle. "Had she no faults at all?"

He shrugged. "Of course she did. We all do. She was given to moods at times. Not much of a cook, nor good with money. If she met someone in need, she would give him more than we could comfortably spare. Though I suppose that's not truly a fault."

"No. How long has she been gone?"

"Seven years." He winced again and fiddled with his cutlery.

"I'm sorry. Is this hard for you?"

"Not easy. But it's only natural you should wonder. Ask what you like."

She thought of another question. "I understand you have a house in Basingstoke?"

He looked up in surprise.

"Esther mentioned it."

"Yes. Esther and Naomi's mother still lives there. While I, as you know, live in the bachelor quarters above the shop."

"Have no Kingsley females ever lived up there?"

"Laura lived there briefly when she and Neil first married—just until their house was finished—but otherwise no."

"It isn't so bad."

"Of course it is. Small, drafty. Low ceilings." He chuckled. "I walked around with lumps on my head the first few weeks I lived there, until I learned to duck."

Mercy grinned.

A man and woman entered the coffee room, and Joseph stood. "Here are my parents."

He did not seem surprised at their arrival. Mercy, however, was.

She had seen Mr. and Mrs. Kingsley many times about the village or at church over the years, though she was not well acquainted with them. The senior Mr. Kingsley had a full head of chestnut-colored hair, silver at the side-whiskers. He was slightly stoop shouldered but clearly had been a tall man in earlier years. His wife was a handsome woman with bright keen eyes and a toothy smile that reminded Mercy of Anna.

She said, "Joseph, I thought you were not dining with us."

"I had not planned to. But Miss Grove found herself at leisure this evening, so . . ." He let his sentence dangle unfinished.

"Excellent," his mother said. "Hello, Miss Grove. A pleasure to see you."

"Thank you. And you. You are well, I trust?"

"Yes." Mrs. Kingsley beamed and grabbed her husband's hand. "Today this man and I have been married one and forty years."

"Congratulations."

Mrs. Kingsley nodded. "Thank you. Joseph thought we would enjoy dinner at the Fairmont as a special treat to celebrate."

"I see."

The older man added, "And I will enjoy this opportunity to peek at the work he's been doing here for so long. Though something tells me it may not be the work alone that's kept him."

Mercy felt her neck heat at the implication.

"Hush, my dear. You'll embarrass them."

Joseph cleared his throat. "Would you like to join us, or would you prefer a table for just the two of you?"

"Oh, the two of us talk every day." Mrs. Kingsley waved a dismissive hand. "I should like a chance to visit with Miss Grove, whom I see too rarely."

Her son pulled out a chair for her, and the two sat down with them. Lawrence appeared, and Joseph's parents ordered.

"You should have celebrated with us last year, Miss Grove," his father said. "For our fortieth, our sons put on a *ceilidh* for us."

"A *kay-lee*?" Mercy asked, not certain what he was talking about.

"Oh yes." Mrs. Kingsley's expression softened in memory. "Folk music, singing, and dancing, with all our children, grandchildren, and friends gathered around us. My ancestors are Scottish, you see."

Mercy looked at Joseph. "I did not think you danced, Mr. Kingsley."

"Nothing formal like a minuet," he allowed. "But I can fudge my way through country dancing passably well."

"Beware your feet when Kingsleys take to the dance floor, Miss Grove." His mother's eyes sparkled. "Take my word for it."

Mercy smiled. "Sounds like a joyous celebration."

"Indeed it was. Sore toes notwithstanding."

Joseph said, "Miss Grove is governess now to Mr. Drake's daughter here at the Fairmont."

"Yes, I know. I was sorry to hear of your school closing, Miss Grove. I had hoped to send another granddaughter or two your way when they were older. Anna benefited so much from her time with you."

"Thank you, but Anna is clever and disciplined and an avid reader. I can take little credit for her accomplishments. She was a pleasure to teach."

Mrs. Kingsley nodded. "Yes, Anna is a dear girl."

Joseph said, "Mamma here taught all of us boys at home: reading, writing, ciphering, geography, and the Bible."

His mother smirked. "Tried to, at any rate."

Joseph looked at his father. "And from Papa and our uncles, we each learned our craft and profession. Neil followed Papa into stone masonry, but I was always drawn to wood."

His father nodded. "You've got a knack for it, for sure and for certain. That's your carved moulding in the entry hall, is it not?"

When Joseph made do with a modest shrug, Mercy answered in his stead, "It is indeed." She had seen him install it and had admired it at the time. "Your son is very talented."

Three faces turned to look at her, eyes alight with speculation.

Mercy tried to keep her expression neutral. "I am merely stating fact," she defended, wishing she had remained quiet.

Mrs. Kingsley patted her hand with a small, knowing grin. "Of course, my dear. And we agree. Joseph *is* talented. He is a good son and a good man, and we are proud of him."

"Mamma, don't go on so." Joseph shifted uneasily. "Ah, here comes Lawrence with our meals. Just in time too."

After that, the conversation turned to innocuous topics, like the fine food and the weather, to Joseph's obvious relief. Mercy's too.

CHAPTER

Thirty-Eight

Jane and Gabriel slept in late the day after their wedding and enjoyed a leisurely morning in bed. In the afternoon, they each packed a valise and prepared to depart for a brief wedding trip.

Gabriel's uncle had already left that morning, but they would see him again in a few days. Jane and Gabriel planned to first travel with his parents to their home. They met them at The Bell, which allowed Jane to give Colin and the rest of the staff last-minute instructions and to remind them to send for Thora if any problems arose.

Perhaps Gabriel was right and it was time for her to hire a competent manager. She would think about it more seriously when they returned.

They traveled northeast by stage to his hometown of Newbury, where his father worked as a law clerk and his mother sometimes helped in her family's clock-making shop. The new couple spent a pleasant evening talking with his parents over tea and cake, and later slept in Gabriel's boyhood room.

In the morning, Jane and Gabriel walked up a winding path on a hill north of town to see Donnington Castle, its twin-towered gatehouse all that was left of the medieval ruin. Even so, it was an atmospheric, oddly romantic place, and Jane could have explored it far longer if not for the biting breeze. She retreated beneath a wide stone doorway to get out of the wind, and Gabriel lost no time in joining her there to steal a kiss.

Afterward, they walked back into Newbury and strolled around the market town, its streets busy with trade and travelers. They stopped to warm up with a coffee in one of its many inns, visited a bookshop, and then walked along the Kennet and Avon Canal. In the evening, they attended a performance at the theatre.

After a second night with his parents, they bid them farewell and began making their way back south. They visited his uncle's horse farm in Pewsey Vale, and Jane instantly saw why Gabriel loved the place and had spent so much time there. Gabriel took her riding over the trails of his childhood, showing her all his favorite spots, and introducing her to friends and neighbors.

They spent a night with his uncle, then continued south to spend two nights in Andover's lovely White Hart Inn, enjoying a comfortable room, flavorsome meals, and each other's company. The longer they were away, the less they were in a hurry to return. The ties to work and responsibility thinned to a spider's web, while the cord binding them together grew and strengthened.

On the way up to their room after a morning walk, Gabriel took her in his arms yet again. "You know, Mrs. Locke, I'd say Talbot was right. I owe him a debt of gratitude for insisting we take this wedding trip."

Jane smiled and kissed her husband. "I wholeheartedly agree, Mr. Locke."

While she waited for Alice to write her essay, Mercy thought about Mr. Kingsley. She decided she and Alice might go for a stroll later and talk with him while he ate his midday meal.

But as morning waned, the weather took an ominous turn and the temperature dropped. Churning grey clouds covered the sun, until the day darkened to shades of twilight. The wind rose, rattling the schoolroom window Mercy had left ajar and whistling down the chimney flue. A door slammed down the passage, startling them both, though as far as Mercy knew she and Alice were the only ones up there this time of day.

Together they went to the window and looked out. Wind chased leaves, straw, and dust across the stable yard. Men held on to their hats and squinted warily at the sky. The clouds opened, and rain began falling in sheets. Mercy quickly shut and latched the window against the onslaught. The rain thickened and plinked against the windowpanes, then clattered. *Clattered?* Mercy looked again, dismayed to see solid white chunks among the rain. Hail. It bounced like small balls against the roof slates.

In the yard, men now scurried to move not only horses to shelter, but also coaches and chaises into the carriage house or under the stable overhang.

Knowing Alice would not be able to concentrate, Mercy gave up on lessons for the day. "Let's see if there is anything we can do to help batten down for the storm."

Downstairs they found chaos. A fallen branch had broken a bow window in the coffee room, and the sudden, heavy rain outpaced the gutters and cascaded down the recessed basement stairs into the passage below. The kitchen and scullery maids hurried about with mops and buckets, while Mr. Kingsley ran to find something to cover the broken window.

Outside the wind howled and the rain thickened into flurries of snow. It *had* been an unusually wet spring. But hail and snow in May?

Carriages and chaises passing by on the turnpike began stopping at the Fairmont in droves, seeking shelter from the storm. The horsemen worked frantically to keep up, removing horses from their traces, all the while slipping over the icy cobbles. Passengers gripped coat collars tight, held on to their hats, and hurried inside. The ostlers threw tarpaulins over the last chaises to arrive, because the outbuildings were already filled.

The Fairmont was bursting with people who'd decided to stay the night instead of traveling onward. The storm stopped within a few hours, but the roads remained wet and icy.

The chef and his staff flew about, preparing many more meals than usual, and James kept busy talking with his impromptu guests and making sure all were comfortable.

The new roof cisterns had overflowed, causing a leak in the schoolroom ceiling, and Mr. Kingsley helped Mercy move all the books, maps, and papers from harm's way.

Afterward he, Mercy, and even Alice helped out around the hotel, mopping leaks, carrying up extra towels and blankets, gathering glasses and washing tables—whatever was needed. They had to use a few rooms that were not yet up to James's standards, and two university students slept on sofas in the sitting room, a screen set up for some semblance of privacy.

It was after ten before things quieted down and the guests had mostly gone to bed. Alice had gone up as well. The staff were slowly finishing their last tasks and retiring for the night. James, Mercy, Mrs. Callard, and Mr. Kingsley stood in the reception hall, quietly conversing and taking stock of the situation.

"Will we have enough food for breakfast, Mrs. C?" James asked.

"Monsieur is grumbling, but we will make do. There will be more than enough porridge, if nothing else."

Mercy noticed dark shadows under the older woman's eyes.

"Tell him to do the best he can," James said. "I think our guests will understand." He turned to Mr. Kingsley. "Thank you for helping with so many things outside of your regular duties. I appreciate it. Would you mind staying here tonight, in case any other problems arise? It's pitch-black outside, and the roads are still slippery. You don't want to go out in that."

"I don't mind staying."

"All the guest rooms are taken, even the two you are still working in, so . . ."

"No worries. I'll find a corner somewhere."

Mrs. Callard spoke up. "There is one unoccupied room in the attic. The bed is a little rickety and has only a straw mattress, but—"

"That's all right. I don't need much."

The housekeeper regarded the long flight of stairs and took a strengthening breath. "I will go up with you and help you find blankets and a pillow."

"I'll do it, Mrs. Callard," Mercy offered. "I'm going up anyway."

"Would you? Thank you, Miss Grove. I am weary, I confess."

"And no wonder," Mr. Drake said kindly. "You've worked hard today, Mrs. C. You all have. Now get some sleep."

The woman nodded and slipped away.

James handed Mercy and Mr. Kingsley each a candle lamp and picked up one for himself. "I was proud of Alice today. She helped through it all, even though she is not fond of storms."

Mercy nodded. "I was too."

She turned to lead the way upstairs. At the first landing, James diverted toward his own room, while Mercy and Mr. Kingsley continued toward the top floor.

Mercy paused at the linen closet. A few sheets remained, but little else. She would loan him one of her blankets. She also retrieved soap, a brush, and tooth powder from the hotel's stores.

Then she escorted him to the unoccupied room. "It's down here. Though I don't know why I'm telling you—you are probably familiar with every room in the house."

"I have not worked in every room in the Fairmont, Miss Grove, though sometimes it feels like it."

She opened the door and surveyed the small chamber by candlelight. "It is a little dusty, I'm afraid."

"Never mind."

Mercy retrieved a pillow and blanket from her own room, and then they put sheets on the narrow bed.

They had worked together on several tasks during the evening, and at Ivy Cottage in the past, so it seemed perfectly natural to help him now. Only belatedly did she consider that it was likely not proper for her to be alone with the man in what was effectively his bedchamber.

"I'm afraid I don't have a nightshirt to offer you."

"That's all right, Miss Grove. I don't usually sleep in one."

Mercy's eyes flashed to his and quickly away, face heating. Trying to blink away a rogue image of Joseph sleeping without a nightshirt, she backed from the room. "My bedchamber is just down the passage, as you know . . ." She swallowed. "If there is anything you need."

He followed her to the door. "Thank you, Miss Grove."

"There is no basin, but you are welcome to use the communal bathroom."

"I shall. Don't worry, I have all I need. Except . . ."

"Except?"

He leaned close and, when she did not pull away, pressed a gentle kiss to her cheek. "Good night."

Mercy's pulse pounded. She looked up at him from beneath her lashes. Should she give him a good-night kiss in return?

When she hesitated, Joseph leaned toward her again. His eyes glimmering by candlelight, focused now on her mouth . . .

A voice called in a shaky whisper, "Miss Grove?"

Mercy reluctantly turned. There stood Alice at the top of the stairs.

"I'm scared. I had a bad dream about the storm."

Mercy turned back to Joseph with an apologetic smile. "I had better go. Good night."

"Good night."

Padding down the passage, Mercy took Alice's hand, prepared to accompany her back to her room, pray for her, and tuck her in.

"May I sleep with you? Just this once?"

Mercy considered. "I suppose so. It has been quite a night, hasn't it?" She opened the door to her own room, pulled back the bedclothes for the girl, and left the candle on the side table. "I'll join you in a minute."

Guessing Iris had gone to bed long ago, Mercy unbuttoned and unpinned her front-fastening frock, left on her stays, and slipped a nightdress over her head. All the while her heart still pounded and her mind whirled with the memory of Joseph Kingsley's face leaning toward hers, focused on her mouth . . .

Expelling a long sigh, Mercy climbed into bed beside Alice. The girl visibly relaxed.

For several moments, Mercy lay there, her own pulse calming and her mind slowing. He had only kissed her cheek, after all. Yet, what might have happened had Alice not come upstairs? Surely she had not imagined the way he'd looked at her, the intimate register of his voice, the light in his eyes?

Alice whispered, "Miss Rachel let Phoebe and me sleep with her once during a storm at Ivy Cottage."

"Did she? How kind."

"She told us a story about a prince and two girls who loved him."

From personal experience, Mercy guessed. "Did you enjoy it?"

"Mm-hm. Will you tell me a story?"

"I am afraid I am not good at making up stories, but I could tell you a real one, if you like."

"Yes, please."

Mercy thought, then began, "I read once about a man who had a beautiful daughter. He wanted to educate her away from the distraction of suitors, so he built a tall tower on his estate for her to live in. Every level held books and maps and drawings and whatever else he could think of for a subject he wanted her to learn. She would move up a floor as she mastered each one. The tower was like a layer cake. A layer cake of learning." Mercy chuckled at the thought. "Sounds like something Aunt Matty would bake."

"Sounds lonely," Alice murmured.

"Yes. I suppose it was."

"Is that what your father did? Kept you in Ivy Cottage to teach you and protect you?"

"No. He certainly saw to my education, but I was hardly a great beauty who needed to be protected from hordes of suitors."

"I think you're beautiful."

"Thank you, Alice. I think you are beautiful too, inside and out."

The girl closed her eyes and curled into Mercy's side. For

several minutes, Mercy simply relished the sight of her sweet little face by the flickering light, and her trusting, affectionate presence beside her.

Sometime later her door creaked open and she jerked awake. She must have nodded off, candle still burning. Had Mr. Kingsley come? Surely he would not . . .

Instead she saw the shadowy outline of James Drake's frowning face, his expression as dark as the corridor behind him. He huffed an exhale. "Here she is. I might have known." Ire heated his whisper. "Did you mean to scare the life out of me?"

Surprised and chagrined, Mercy climbed from bed and grabbed her dressing gown, slipping it on as she crossed the room to him. She stepped out into the passage, gingerly closing the door behind her to avoid waking Alice. Light from his candle flickered over his unhappy countenance.

"I am sorry, Mr. Drake. I did not stop to think."

"Imagine how I felt, finding her room empty? And on such a night, with so many strangers about?"

"She came up, scared by a bad dream, and asked to sleep with me. I agreed without considering you might look in on her and worry. I was distracted by . . . the events of the evening and wasn't thinking clearly. Next time, I will return her to her room."

He squeezed his eyes closed and drew a deep breath. "I wouldn't ask that. I was only worried. I let myself imagine some harm had befallen her. You needn't turn her away. I'll know where to look next time and will endeavor to remain calm in future."

"Again, I apologize."

He sighed. "Nothing to forgive, Mercy." He laid a hand on her arm. "I apologize for overreacting."

She echoed, "Nothing to forgive."

His eyes made a slow scan of her features. "Do you know . . . you look lovely by candlelight. Such high color in your cheeks. I hope I didn't embarrass you, coming up here like this."

"No, not at all." There were other reasons for her high color, she knew.

He released her. "Well, good night, Mercy."

"Good night."

Early the next morning, Mercy opened her eyes and quickly squeezed them shut again, the sunlight startling after the dark day before. From the stable yard below came the sounds of horse hooves and the crunching of wheels on gravel as chaises were brought out of the carriage house. Birds congregated outside her window, expressing their disapproval over last night's storm in noisy chattering and chirping. Mercy gave up hope of falling back to sleep. Beside her, Alice slept on, peacefully. But uneasy from her encounters with Mr. Kingsley and Mr. Drake, and unaccustomed to sharing a bed with a wriggling child, Mercy had not slept well.

Now she felt groggy, and a headache pinched her temples. Longing for nothing more than a bracing cup of tea, she donned a dressing gown and slipped from the room, tiptoeing barefoot along the silent passage and down the narrow servants' stairs. Light from below seemed a promise of someone already busy in the kitchen and, hopefully, brewing a pot of tea.

But as she descended, she realized the light was from the candle of someone rounding the landing. The top of a head came into view, then broad shoulders in shirt-sleeves and braces. He looked up, and she saw it was Mr. Kingsley coming up the stairs, a cup of something in his hand.

He paused upon seeing her. "Good morning, Miss Grove."

"G-good morning, Mr. Kingsley. I . . . don't make a habit of traipsing about the house in my nightclothes, but I didn't think I was likely to encounter anyone on these stairs so early."

"I just came down for a much-needed coffee." He offered her his cup. "I can fetch another."

"Thank you, but I have my heart set on tea."

"Then let me get out of your way."

He turned his shoulders and pressed to the wall so she could slip past him on the narrow staircase.

Mercy felt self-conscious being so close to him, aware of her bare legs and her hair, which had escaped its pins during her restless night and hung over her shoulder in a single plait.

As she neared, he grinned and whispered, "Lovely feet, by the way."

Heat rushed up her neck even as his boyish grin sent prickles of pleasure through her. His shoulder brushed hers as they passed, and she laid a hand on the spot as she continued to the kitchen.

CHAPTER

Thirty-Nine

The morning of their departure from Andover, Gabriel secured passage on the Royal Mail coach, and Jane was pleased to see Jack Gander on duty as its guard. The three exchanged greetings, and Jack was effusive in his congratulations on their recent marriage.

Sitting together inside the coach, Gabriel put his arm around Jane and drew her close to his side. "I enjoyed every minute. I hope you did too?"

"I did." She laid her cheek on his shoulder and snuggled against him for the journey home.

The last stop before Ivy Hill was Salisbury. Jack kept them entertained with tunes on his horn, then blew the arrival signals as the Quicksilver rattled through the archway into the courtyard of the Red Lion for a brief stop there. He hopped down to assist a passenger alighting, while another passenger on the roof obliged him by handing down the man's valise.

Through the coach window, Jane saw Victorine step from the Red Lion and approach the Quicksilver, a wrapped parcel in her arms.

Seeing her, Jack asked, "May I stow that for you, Miss Victorine?" He tipped his head to one side. "Or should I say Miss . . ." He leaned near to whisper something Jane could not hear.

The dressmaker directed an uneasy glance toward the coach, then replied, "No, thank you. I shall keep it with me."

Inside the vehicle, Jane greeted her politely. "Hello, Victorine." She added, "Jack is a flirt, to be sure, but he is harmless enough."

Victorine shook her head. "There is nothing harmless about that man."

Jane introduced Gabriel, then asked, "Doing some shopping here in Salisbury, I see."

Victorine looked down at the long parcel on her lap. "Yes, I had to purchase more material from the linen draper. I did not buy enough the first time." She peeled back a layer of tissue for Jane to see. "Miss Brockwell chose this from a sample in a magazine. I was relieved they had enough left."

Jane looked at the layers of ivory satin and fine netting. She glanced up and noticed the dressmaker appeared more anxious than triumphant about her purchase.

"It is very dear," Victorine quietly confided. "And difficult to work with, I've found."

Jane reached out a finger to stroke the shimmering fabric but stopped just short of touching it. "It is beautiful."

In the courtyard, Jack Gander blew another signal. Soon the Quicksilver lurched into motion, rumbling out of Salisbury and past Wilton on its way to Ivy Hill. Through the left-hand coach window, Jane saw the sun beginning to set over Grovely Wood and through the right, the distant spire of the church in Wishford.

They passed Fairmont House and began the climb up Ivy Hill. Out the window, Jane glimpsed a blur of fur as some animal ran past. A large animal. A deer, perhaps?

Over the pounding hooves, she heard the horses whinny in distress, a dog bark, and a strange growl.

Alarm snaked through Jane. Was it that wild dog again? Was he chasing the coach horses, as he had chased Gabriel's?

Jane pressed her nose to the glass, trying to see. "An animal ran past. What a strange growl it has!"

"What's happening?" Gabriel leaned close for a better view, his dark brows pulled low. "Is that the same dashed dog who chased Spirit?"

Jane squinted against the dim light. "There are two animals out there. One is a dog. But what is the other one . . . a calf? It is running awfully fast to keep up with four horses."

Victorine looked out as well, her eyes widening. "That's no calf. That's a lion."

"A lion? You must be joking."

Victorine shook her head. "A lioness, to be exact. And I assure you I am not joking."

"A lioness . . . in England?" Jane's heart pounded. Foolishly, she thought of Thora, whom Hetty called *the lioness*. But a living, breathing lion running free in Wiltshire, chasing the horses pulling their coach? It seemed unreal.

Outside, the snarling dog ran after the lion, snapping at its legs.

Victorine muttered something in French. "That stupid dog is chasing her, antagonizing her."

The mail coach crested the rise on the outskirts of Ivy Hill and would soon reach the inn.

Jane panicked. "We're leading a lion right to The Bell! What about the ostlers? The guests? They could be killed."

Gabriel pounded on the ceiling with his stick. "Stop! Stop the coach."

Jane craned her neck to see. The horses strained and jigged in their traces. Again, the dog snapped at the fawn-colored creature. The muscular lion lunged, fangs bared, plunging its teeth into the lead horse's neck. The horse screamed, Jane screamed, and the Quicksilver finally lurched to a shuddering stop in the High Street, just outside the inn's coach archway.

A shot rang out. Jack Gander with his regulation blunderbuss, no doubt. Royal Mail guards were heavily armed to ensure the safety of the mail and their passengers.

In the melee, the frantic outside passengers leapt down, running into the inn and slamming the door behind them. An older, slower passenger reached the door last and found it barred. He pounded on it in desperation.

Jane opened the window a few inches. "Jack!" she shouted, pointing toward the passenger. "Help that man!"

She knew Jack carried a brace of pistols in addition to the blunderbuss and would not hesitate to use them. She prayed he would not end up shooting the horses, or a fleeing passenger in the confusion. *Lord, help us!*

Gabriel reached for the coach door, but Victorine shoved his hand aside. "No. Stay inside." She grasped the door latch.

"What are you doing?" Gabriel protested. "Don't open that door. I'll go."

"Close it after me. Stay inside."

Jane cried, "Victorine, don't! Are you mad?"

"If that fool shoots her I shall be more than mad."

She leapt out nimbly, parcel abandoned, and slammed the coach door behind her.

Gabriel muttered, "That woman is crazy."

"Stop!" Victorine ran forward, hands raised. "Don't shoot her, I beg of you."

"Get back inside!" Jack yelled.

"No. Don't shoot, or you may hit me. If you must shoot something, shoot that stupid dog."

With that Victorine whirled and stalked toward the lioness, whose teeth were still embedded in the panicked horse's neck.

"Sheba—*Arrête!*" she called. "*Maintenant! Arrête-toi!*"

Victorine's stern, commanding voice seemed to slowly penetrate the beast's awareness. The lioness released the horse and turned to look at her. Would it now attack Victorine instead? Jane held her breath.

"I can't just sit here . . ." Gabriel reached for the latch, but Jane threw herself in front of him.

"Oh no. You've barely recovered from one animal attack. I will not lose you now."

He hesitated, and together they stared out the window again. Jane gaped in disbelief at the sight of the lioness sitting submissively on her haunches before Victorine. *How in the world . . . ?*

But then the wild dog jumped at the lion again, teeth barred and snarling. The lioness turned, smacking it to the ground with a lightning-fast slap of her claws. The dog whimpered and slunk away, hiding beneath the old granary.

Then the lioness laid at Victorine's feet, docile as a lamb.

Jane turned to Gabriel, who looked as amazed as Jane felt.

Jack Gander gingerly approached the subdued lion, blunderbuss poised.

Again, Victorine held up a staying hand. "Don't come any closer. She is calm now and will do no more harm if left in peace. The horse will live, I think. If that dog had not bitten her, I don't think she would have attacked the horses."

A wagon rumbled up the hill and halted on the other side of the street.

"Stay back!" Jack yelled, but the driver paid no heed. He and two other men—all strangers—jumped down. Behind the first wagon, another appeared, this one with a large cage on the back. Three more men climbed down from that one.

The oldest man walked forward first, a large burlap sack in his hands. He wore dark clothes and theatrical cape, his auburn hair threaded with silver.

Noticing Victorine, he paused. "Thank God you were here, my dear."

With an uneasy glance at the gathering onlookers, she said crisply, "Yes. Well. You may take it from here. My shop is just across the street there, if you would . . . like to call."

"Very well," the man replied. "I shall see you later."

In the coach, Jane picked up Victorine's parcel and waved out the window, trying to catch her eye, but she retreated, disappearing behind the growing crowd.

The man who had spoken to Victorine laid the sack on the ground near the lioness, and with a single command, the animal lay down upon it. The men then tied her four legs and passed a cord round her mouth. Once she was trussed up safely, the six men grabbed hold of the burlap, lifted on three, and with grunts and grimaces of strain, carried her toward the caravan wagon. The lioness did not resist but rather, once untied, entered the caged den eagerly, clearly relieved to be back in familiar territory, away from snarling dogs, gunshots, and pounding hooves.

Gabriel stepped out and helped Jane down. Her legs were trembling.

The caped man returned to Jack. "Thank you, good sir, for not shooting our lioness. She is worth a great deal, and her loss would cripple our menagerie. I am sorry indeed about the injured horse and will happily pay for its care. In fact, I offer to buy it outright."

"I don't own the horse, man." Jack pointed to Jane. "Mrs. Locke is the innkeeper here and happens to own this particular team."

The man bowed. "Mrs. Locke, allow me to introduce myself. I am J. Earl Victor, owner of The Earl's Menagerie and Traveling Players."

Jane glanced over and saw the same words painted on his wagon. The name seemed familiar, though she did not recall any menagerie stopping at Ivy Hill before.

Mr. Victor squinted in thought. "I believe Frank Bell was the innkeeper here last I visited."

Jane nodded. "My former father-in-law. He's been gone many years."

"Ah. Well." Mr. Victor spread his hands in supplication. "What will you take for this fine horse, far too noble and spirited to live out his days as a downtrodden coach horse."

Jane glanced at Gabriel. It seemed like something he might have said. But would conditions in a menagerie be any better?

"What sort of life do you propose for him instead?" Gabriel asked. "Pomegranate here is a former racehorse, sold as a coach horse several years ago in the hopes it would break his fiery spirit."

"An attempt that has clearly failed. What I propose is a life of valor and adulation equal to his spirited nature." The man held up his hands, emphasizing the words as though they were a newspaper headline. "The proud steed who survived a lioness attack, drawing the attention of the beast to himself to save his three companions harnessed with him, rescuing them from sure death."

"Pomegranate might very well have died," Jane said, "if the lion had not been distracted by a wild dog."

"A wild dog, you say? Better and better. Where is this cunning cur?"

"Under the granary there." Gabriel gestured between the black-smith's and wheelwright's, to a building on mushroom-shaped straddle stones, which kept out the damp and rodents. Beneath it a pair of yellow eyes glowed.

Mr. Victor asked, "Your dog, sir?"

Gabriel shook his head. "A stray, as far as I know. But I have been his victim before when he attacked my own horse. The world is better off without him, in my view."

"Never say so! A valiant dog—a Newfoundland, I hope, or a brute mastiff—who diverted the lion's attention to himself, saving the lead horse and the passengers in the bargain."

Jane smirked. "You have quite a gift for drama, sir, if you don't mind my saying."

"I take that as a compliment. It is my profession, after all. To discover, create, and act out dramas—both of the animal and human varieties—for all to see. Or at least for all willing *to pay* to see." He grinned.

Jane considered. "I would like the horse freed from this life. If Mr. Locke agrees, and you promise not to mistreat him . . ."

"Never, madame! He will become another valued investment to be prized and cared for." He looked from her to Gabriel and back again. "Assuming the price isn't *too* dear."

Together they negotiated a reasonable sum while Gabriel tended the horse's wound. He predicted Pomegranate would heal well but insisted they keep him in The Bell stables overnight before releasing him.

The other men caught the dog, using fresh meat as incentive—meat laced with a mild sedative, which subdued the cur long enough to treat his claw wounds. Then they found a place for him in their caravan.

Jane said, "I am sorry I cannot offer you a place to stay tonight, gentlemen. But I fear several of our guest have been traumatized by tonight's scare and would not sleep well with a menagerie caravan in our courtyard." She gestured toward a painting on the wagon of a lion's head, mouth wide, fangs bared.

"I understand," said Mr. Victor. "Might we leave the wagons on the outskirts of the village for the night? It is late, and we must be on hand to collect the horse as soon as Mr. Locke deems him fit for travel."

"I think that would be all right. I will send word to our local magistrate—Sir Timothy Brockwell—and if he has any concerns, I am sure he will let you know. I trust you can keep the lioness from escaping again?"

He pressed his hand to his heart. "You have my word, madame. Thank you for your kindness. We will return tomorrow to check on Pomegranate. And to . . . thank the young woman who intervened on the lioness's behalf."

"Yes, how fortunate Madame Victorine was on hand."

He nodded thoughtfully, scratching his chin. "Madame Victorine . . . yes. How fortunate for us all."

Tentatively, Jane asked, "I assume she worked for you at some point, and that is why she knew how to subdue the lioness? What—"

Jack Gander surprised her by interrupting. "Excuse me, Mrs. Locke, but perhaps we ought to let her be the one to explain?"

"Oh. Yes. Very well."

Mr. Victor hesitated, looking from one to the other. He said, "Suffice it to say, we have missed her. Well." He doffed his hat and performed a theatrical bow. "Thank you all again. And now I shall bid you good night."

A few moments later the men rumbled away in their caravan wagons.

Only then, Jane noticed, did Jack Gander put away his gun.

Later, after she made sure the passengers were soothed and settled, Jane found Gabriel in the stables, talking over the horse's condition with the farrier. When Tom left, she and Gabriel decided they would sleep in the lodge that night, since it was already so late.

But seeing a light burning in the dressmaker's shop, Jane walked across the street to talk to Victorine, taking the parcel of fabric with her.

When she knocked, Victorine's face appeared at the window, and Jane read disappointment in her expression.

She opened the door. "Hello, Jane."

Jane stepped inside and handed her the parcel. "Victorine, you saved us tonight. How can I thank you?"

"Nonsense. I only saved that poor animal from being shot by an overeager guard. You were never in any real danger."

"I don't know that I believe that. And the other passengers certainly did not. In any case, thank you. How did you know what to do?"

Victorine shut the door behind Jane and set the fabric on the counter. "I used to make costumes for the troupe. I've known that lioness for years."

"Is that man your father?"

"He told you?"

"No. But his surname is Victor. I'm guessing your name is not really Victorine?"

She shook her head. "A family nickname."

"And you said you haven't been to France in years, yet you spoke to that lion in French."

She shrugged. "Sheba was trained by a Frenchman."

"I see."

Victorine sighed. "Jane, it's late and I'm tired. But return another time and I shall tell you everything, if you truly want to know."

"I do, indeed."

A knock sounded behind Jane, and the menagerie owner poked his head inside. "May I come in?"

"Yes, Papa. Please do."

Jane said to him, "I thought you planned to wait and visit in the morning, or I would not have intruded."

"I could not wait any longer." He crossed the room and took his daughter's hand. "Hard enough when your sister left, but to have both of my girls gone . . . ?" He shook his head. "How I have missed you, my dear. Are you well?"

"I am, Papa. Mostly." She turned to Jane and repeated, "Thank you for delivering the fabric, Jane. Will you please return another time?"

As much as she wished to remain and hear the truth, Jane stepped to the door. "Yes, of course. Forgive me. Good night."

CHAPTER

FORTY

The next day, Victorine flipped the *Closed* sign to *Open*, then stepped out of her shop to set up one dress form, displaying a light, summery gown of printed muslin. She had made it herself from pattern pieces she'd found in Mrs. Shabner's workroom. It was a simple style, and the hem was not perfectly straight, but it was an improvement over the gown she'd made for Julia Feather-stone and she was proud of it. She had priced it low, hoping for a sale, hoping it would find a new home more easily than the finer gowns she'd displayed before, which were apparently too formal and expensive for most of the women of Ivy Hill.

Outside the lace-makers' shop a few doors down, she noticed three women clustered at the window. Broad bonnets hid their faces, but she recognized a familiar lavender gown and knew Jane Locke was among them. She hoped she had not seemed rude to her new neighbor the night before. Another woman held the hand of the little girl she had met at the inn. Thora Talbot's granddaughter.

Returning her focus to the display, Victorine smoothed the material over the dress form. As she did, a childish squeal and padding of little feet caught her ear. She looked down in time to see the little ginger-haired sprite running joyously toward her, giggling at her mischievous escape.

She bent low to catch the child, so much like Henrietta that it hurt to look at her—yet she could not look away.

"Whoa there. Where are you going in such a hurry, Miss Ginger?"

"I Betsey."

"That's right—Betsey." The name prompted a nostalgic ache inside her. Her mother's name was Elisabeth, but everyone had called her Betsey, for short. Just as they had shortened her own given name to—

"Eva?"

Her heart banged in her chest, and she rose unsteadily, mouth falling open at the vision before her. The image of the little ginger-haired girl grown up. Her sister.

"Henrietta . . . Thank God. I thought I'd never see you again."

She closed the distance between them, threw her arms around her sister, and held her close.

Mrs. Talbot's voice interrupted the sweet moment. "I take it you two have never met?"

They pulled apart, and her sister gave an awkward little laugh.

Thora skewered her with a pointed look. "Henrietta?"

Her sister lowered her eyes, laying a hand on her daughter's curls as if for comfort. "Yes, that is my given name." She smiled at Eva and explained, "I have been going by Hetty since I . . . saw you last."

Jane looked at her. "And your name is Eva?"

"Yes."

"I knew you reminded me of someone."

Henrietta gaped at Jane in surprise. "Is this why you insisted I come to Ivy Hill today?"

Jane nodded. "I noticed a resemblance between you two, as well as similar stories of a much-missed family who moved around a great deal."

"Ah, I see."

"I don't," Thora said, face puckered.

Henrietta turned to her. "Thora and Jane, I'd like you to meet my sister, Evangeline Victor. Eva, this is Jane Locke and my mother-in-law, Mrs. Talbot."

"Yes, we've met." Eva bent and picked up the toddler. "And this must be your little girl."

"Yes, Betsey Evangeline. Named after my mother and beloved sister, who I've missed so much." Tears filled her eyes, and Eva felt hers burn in reply.

With a sheepish glance at the innkeeper, Henrietta explained, "Jane recently asked me if I knew a Victorine, and it crossed my mind that it *might* be you. But I was afraid."

Eva felt her brow furrow. "Afraid? Why?"

"Afraid to be disappointed if it wasn't. Afraid of what you would think of me if it was."

Noticing Mrs. Prater hovering in her shop doorway across the street, Eva said, "Come inside so we can talk in private."

"Do you mind if Thora and Jane come too?" Henrietta asked. "I've owed them the truth for a long time now."

"If you like."

Inside the shop, Eva set Betsey on the floor and gave her a basket of colorful fabric scraps to play with. The little girl proceeded to happily yank out the remnants one by one.

Eva invited Jane and Thora to sit on the sofa while she brought out chairs from the workroom for her and her sister.

She began, "Henrietta, I have been worried about you since you left Weymouth. Papa believed you when you insisted nothing had happened and you were all right, just determined to leave the traveling life. But I never fully did. Especially when you didn't write again or let us know where you were living."

Hetty clasped her hands, staring down at the floor. "Something did happen. But I didn't want you to find out. How many times had you and Papa warned me never to trust strangers, especially men who came to the show. But Argus Hurst was different—or so I thought. The son of a respected officer. Handsome, charming, gentlemanlike—until he got me alone, that is. Then how quickly his demeanor changed."

She shuddered. "He was far stronger than I, and pitiless in the bargain. A vile, cruel man." Tears welled in her eyes, her expression riddled with regret.

Seeing it, Eva's heart twisted.

"I was such a fool," Henrietta said. "I had flirted with him shamelessly, so when it happened, I blamed myself."

Betsey came over and stared at her teary-eyed mother in confusion. Hetty managed a wobbly smile for the girl and lovingly cupped her cheek. "Mamma is all right, dear one. Don't worry."

"Oh, Hen." Eva groaned. "It was foolish to flirt with the man, but it was *not* your fault. It was his. You should have told me."

Henrietta shook her head. "I couldn't. Argus said if I told anyone, he would come for you next. And I knew if Papa found out, he would probably have killed him, and end up hanged. I had to pretend nothing happened, but I knew if I stayed any longer, I wouldn't be able to keep up the act. I would throw myself in your arms and confess everything. I had to make you and Papa believe that I had taken a new position, determined to give up life on the road. I told myself I was a skilled actress, and it was time to give the performance of my life."

Eva reached out and took her hand. "I knew you were upset and not yourself. But I didn't guess . . . this. Oh, Hen, I am sorry I didn't protect you."

"It wasn't your fault."

For Jane and Thora's benefit, Eva explained, "Henrietta told us her new employer lived in Blandford. We put her on the coach ourselves." She turned back to her sister. "You promised to write as soon as you were settled, but you didn't."

"I'm sorry. I knew Papa would not let me go without some plausible reason. But the truth was, I didn't know where I was going. I just wanted to get away. The stage brought me to the coaching inn here in Ivy Hill. I meant to go farther, but I saw a Help Wanted notice and took a post at The Bell. I gave my name as Hetty Piper. It was all I could think of in my muddled state. I didn't want Argus to be able to find me."

"But we couldn't find you either. I wrote to you at the direction you'd given us, but my letters were returned undeliverable. We even visited Blandford, but no one there had ever heard of you."

"I did write to you, eventually. Did you not receive my letter?"

"Yes, it had been misdirected at first but eventually reached us, postmarked from Salisbury. You wrote that you were moving on to a new place but didn't say where. We were relieved to read your cheerful words, but I was still worried, especially when we returned to our winter quarters and you did not contact us again. Papa was placated by your note. When I asked why you would not let us know where you were living or invite us to visit, he said, 'You read her letter; she wants to live her own life.' But I was not convinced."

"I wrote that letter just before I left Ivy Hill and posted it at a stop along the route. I didn't last long at The Bell."

"Why?"

Thora spoke up. "Because the *lioness* gave her the sack, that's why. Hetty, I'm sorry. I didn't know. . . ."

Henrietta squeezed her hand. "I know. I don't blame you."

She returned her gaze to Eva. "Only when I was leaving did I feel it safe to write to you. I didn't want the postmark to give away my location, because by then I knew I was with child. And I was ashamed all over again." Her voice grew hoarse. "I didn't want you to find me and learn the truth."

"Oh, Hen. You know I love you, no matter what."

Again Henrietta's eyes shimmered with tears, and Eva swallowed the lump in her throat.

Hoping to lighten the mood, Eva rose, picked up Betsey, and sat down with the girl on her lap. "Do you remember that we performed here in Ivy Hill once, many years ago? You would have been very young at the time, but I remember it."

"Did we?" Hetty asked. "Perhaps that's why I was drawn to the place. That and the kindness I saw in Mr. Talbot's face when he offered me the post."

Eva nodded. "We visited Salisbury after receiving your letter, hoping to find someone who knew you and could tell us where you'd gone. But we could find no trace of a Henrietta Victor there. Now I understand why."

"I am sorry to have put you to so much trouble."

"I am just so glad to have found you at last—and here of all places."

Hetty went on. "I ended up in Epsom, expecting never to come back to The Bell. But when I did, I had already given my name as Hetty Piper, so it was too late to change it." She turned to Jane. "I'm sorry, Jane. Thora. But that's why Patrick and I decided not to post banns and marry in the church here. I would have had to use my real name, which would have raised a lot of questions. If I'd married Patrick under my assumed name, the marriage would not have been legal. I confessed everything to Patrick, and he agreed eloping would be the best course, though we were sorry to disappoint you, Thora."

"Ah. I understand now . . . Henrietta."

"Hetty is fine." She smiled awkwardly. "Or Hen, if you like. My family often calls me Hen, and you're family now, if you'll still have me."

Thora took her hand. "Of course I will. We will. You and Betsey are part of us and always shall be."

Henrietta looked back at Eva, wiping away a fresh onslaught of tears. "My goodness. That is quite enough from me. Your turn, Eva." She managed a lopsided grin. "Or should I say, 'Madame Victorine.'"

Eva grimaced. "I think a bracing pot of tea is in order first."

They paused as she boiled water in her tiny kitchen and brought out a tray of steaming tea and a few crumbly biscuits. "I am sorry I don't have more to offer."

As Betsey ate the biscuits and the women sipped their tea, Eva looked to her sister and began. "I don't know if you were old enough to remember, but Mamma and I used to talk of opening a dressmaking shop one day. After one disappointing season, Papa considered selling out to an interested buyer—to settle down, as Mamma had long hoped. So for several weeks, she and I sketched dress designs, hats, advertisements . . .

"We planned to call our shop *Mesdames Victorine*, one of Papa's nicknames for us. But the offer fell through, so instead, he bought more animals and we began traveling as a menagerie as well as players. That was the winter Mamma took ill and died of the influenza. Papa buried his grief by keeping busy, adding more shows and more acts. But nothing was the same without Mamma."

Henrietta nodded her agreement.

"After you left, Hen, I longed to settle down too, but I didn't want to leave Papa. He had already lost Mamma and you. But then Martine and Pierre announced their retirement."

Eva looked at Jane and Thora and explained, "They were our troupe's longtime leading actors. Papa didn't have the heart to replace them in their roles, so we gave up performing Shakespeare."

Henrietta nodded again, eyes wistful. "They were like family to us. How I miss them."

Eva said, "Martine and Pierre were planning to return to France to enjoy their remaining years together among their long-missed friends and family. Martine had beautiful new gowns made in anticipation. Unfortunately, they waited too long to take their chance."

Henrietta frowned. "What do you mean?"

"I'm sorry to tell you. Martine died just before Christmas."

Her sister's eyes widened. "Oh no! Poor Pierre."

Eva nodded. "Yes. He is devastated, as you can imagine. He was the one who insisted I take the new things Martine had made. A beginning, he said, to start my own dressmaking business, as he knew I longed to do someday."

"When I saw an advertisement for a dressmaking shop for let in Ivy Hill, I didn't know if it was foolishness or fate. But seeing you now, I think it was fate that I come here."

Henrietta reached over and squeezed her hand.

Eva continued. "Papa was sad to see me go, but he understood. I decided to let the shop on a trial basis. To make a go of it in three months' time or return to the troupe. I knew if anyone connected me to our family's troupe, it would hurt my reputation and my business, so when people here called me Madame Victorine, I did not correct them."

Hetty slowly shook her head, a small smile on her face. "Look at the pair of us. Both using names not our own." She glanced from Thora to Jane. "I blame our father. He's the one forever giving people nicknames."

"True," Eva said. "By the way, he is here in Ivy Hill, the whole troupe with him."

"No!" Henrietta paled and rose in agitation. "I'm not ready to face him, to tell him about me, about Betsey . . ."

"He'll understand," Eva soothed. "As I do."

"No, I can't. Not yet!"

"Hen, if I had not come here, would you have ever sought us out? Or were you planning to hide from us forever? To keep Betsey from us?"

"No. I had thought I would let you know where I was after Patrick and I had been married a few years. Then, learning I had a little girl would be less upsetting."

A knock sounded, and Henrietta jumped.

The door creaked open, and their father tentatively poked his auburn head inside. "Ev . . ." Seeing Jane and Thora, he cleared his throat. "Um . . . Victorine?"

His gaze landed on the redhead beside her and his mouth fell agape. "Henrietta!"

Her sister twisted her hands, face tight with anxiety. "Papa . . ."

He strode in, ignoring the others, and took his youngest child in his arms. "Henny Penny, my dear girl. Thank God."

Little Betsey watched this exchange in confusion. A few moments later, she tugged on her mother's frock and tried to wedge herself between them.

Their father looked down in surprise and loosened his grip. "Hello there . . ." For a moment he said no more, just studied the child, then returned his gaze to his daughter's face.

Henrietta ducked her head, flushing as red as her hair.

"No need to ask who this is," he said, tears thickening his voice. "She is as beautiful as her mother."

"I'm sorry, Papa," Henrietta whispered hoarsely.

"My dear girl, I am just so relieved you're all right." He held her at arm's length, brows bunched in question. "You are all right, are you not?"

Hetty managed a tremulous smile. "I am now."

CHAPTER

Forty-One

When Jane arrived at The Bell the next morning, she was surprised to see Sir Timothy, Rachel, and Mr. Victor sitting together at a table in the coffee room.

"Jane!" Rachel waved. "Come and join us."

Jane walked over and greeted each person. Sir Timothy rose and pulled out a chair for her.

Mr. Victor smiled warmly. "Good news, Mrs. Locke. I have received permission from your kind friends here to perform and display our menagerie in Ivy Hill."

Jane looked from him to Timothy, her brows rising. "That is good news," she said, wondering if the showman was going to ask to use her courtyard.

Mr. Victor continued, "Our show tent is in sad disrepair after that terrible hailstorm, but Sir Timothy has graciously invited us to set up the menagerie in the old tithe barn." He pointed out the window to the big stone building at the corner of the High Street and Potters Lane.

The cavernous tithe barn was a relic of the fourteenth century, when Brockwell Court was an abbey. With its dirt floor and soaring timber-supported roof, it would be an ideal place to display animals and set up a stage.

Jane nodded. "Sounds perfect."

Mr. Victor folded his hands across his waistcoat and leaned his head back, eyes half closed in memory. "It reminds me of the time we came to Ivy Hill years ago. We were not allowed to perform here at the inn, but another sir—Sir William Ashford—invited us to perform at his house instead. Even set up a makeshift stage at Thornvale and hosted a performance of Shakespeare's *A Midsummer Night's Dream.*"

"I remember that." Rachel chuckled, adding, "On the condition that he be allowed to play Puck."

"That's right!" Mr. Victor agreed. "And an excellent Puck he was."

"Sir William was my father," Rachel said gently. "Unfortunately, he and my mother have both passed on."

"Oh no." The man winced. "I am sorry to hear it. And sorry for your loss."

"Thank you."

Mr. Victor studied Rachel's face. "I remember your mother. She was a lovely, gracious woman. I can still picture her, a daughter by each hand, beaming up at her husband on stage . . ."

Rachel smiled softly, eyes bright with unshed tears.

A thoughtful silence followed, then Mr. Victor sent Sir Timothy a knowing look. "Now I begin to see why you are being so accommodating, sir. But whatever the reason, I am grateful."

Mr. Victor rose and rubbed his hands together. "Well, I have a great deal to prepare. We plan to open the menagerie in two days' time." He put on his hat and tipped its brim. "I shall hope to see you all there."

On Sunday, Mercy went to Ivy Cottage after church to spend time with her family.

As they finished their meal, Matilda glanced at Mercy, then took a deep breath and said, "I would like to invite the Fairmonts to dinner, Helena. When it is convenient."

"Do you mean . . . Mr. Fairmont and his son?"

"Yes."

Helena's lips tightened. "Matilda, I gather you two are old friends, but I don't think that would be completely appropriate."

"Surely you are not worried about my reputation—not at my age!"

"I am thinking of the Grove family reputation as a whole."

Aunt Matty gaped. "What on earth do you mean?"

"I mean, I am not sure a formal dinner with the Fairmonts would be . . . quite the thing."

Offense flashed through Mercy, but thankfully George spoke up.

"My dear, if my aunt wishes to entertain friends here in Ivy Cottage, then—"

"It is our home now, my love. And we have to consider our standing in the community as well as hers. Not everyone is as accepting as we are about Mr. Fairmont's foreign offspring."

Mercy noticed the cords in her aunt's neck tighten and laid a calming hand on hers.

"Ah." George considered, then with a glance at his aunt, suggested, "Perhaps we might simply invite the Fairmonts to call. Serve them tea and cake in the sitting room. No formal occasion that would require you to be there, Helena. No one can object to that."

"Can they not? Well. I do agree an informal call is the less-objectionable scenario."

George sat back in his chair, head tipped back. "I, for one, look forward to chatting with Winston Fairmont. Swapping tales of our adventures abroad . . ."

Helena gave him a brittle smile. "My dear, if your aunt wishes the Fairmonts to call on *her*, it would be impolite for us to intrude."

"Not at all," Aunt Matty said. "You are very welcome to join us, George. And Helena too, if you like."

"No, no," Helena said. "I would not dream of intruding. You enjoy your visit alone." The young woman inclined her head as if she had just bestowed some great favor.

Matilda sent Mercy a telling look. "Then indeed I shall, Helena. Thank you."

The young woman waved a magnanimous hand. "Tea is expensive, but . . . never mind. You and your guests drink all the tea you like."

The entire village of Ivy Hill buzzed with excited anticipation over the coming menagerie. People gathered on the street to watch the caravan wagons unload, hoping for a glimpse of an unusual animal, and exclaiming over the strange calls and sounds spilling from the tithe barn whenever its doors were opened by members of the troupe—some of them as strange and colorful as the animals themselves.

On opening day, Jane and Gabriel met the Talbots, Patrick, and Betsey at the inn, and they walked over to visit The Earl's Menagerie & Traveling Players together. Hetty and her sister had left early to help their father set up but promised to join them later.

The exterior of the tithe barn was hung with large painted show cloths advertising fabulous acts and exotic animals with the name of the troupe below.

A hawker stood on the corner, calling out enticements to passersby. "Come be amazed by the learned pig who figures sums. Marvel at the Arabian steed dancing a perfect minuet with his lovely partner. And for the first time ever, see the famous lion that attacked the Quicksilver, and the mastiff that quelled it!"

To one side of the double-wide doors stood Becky Morris, painting a new sign capitalizing on the recent stage attack.

Noticing them, Becky waved and called, "Almost finished."

Jane walked nearer. "My goodness, Becky. I didn't realize you could draw animals too."

The young woman shrugged. "I worked from a sketch Mr. Victor gave me. Is it accurate? You were there, after all."

Jane regarded the image more closely: A fierce-looking lioness with its jaws around the coach horse's neck, a snarling mastiff at her heels. In the Royal Mail coach, a trio of frightened faces pressed to the window, Jane's clearly depicted among them. On the Quicksilver's roof, each terrified passenger clasped a carpetbag or umbrella, as if determined to fight off the beast with whatever weapons were at hand.

Thora peered closer. "Is that meant to be you, Jane?"

"Apparently."

"You look scared out of your wits."

"I was. Well, we'll leave you to finish, Becky. Wonderfully done."

They approached the money-taker, a slender woman wearing a jeweled turban and oriental dress of blue-and-white muslin shot with silver. They paid their pennies and in return were handed copper tokens. Jane held hers in her palm, staring down at it. She remembered finding a token just like this among John's things, engraved with the words *The Earl's Menagerie*. She had given it to Gabriel as a memento, assuming the two men might have attended together, as Jane had never been to a menagerie.

Standing near her now, Gabriel ran a gentle finger over her palm. "I still have the one you gave me."

She looked up at him. "Did you go to the show with John? You never said."

"No. I hesitated when you first asked, because I didn't know who else John might have gone with. But now, I think he simply went alone. He really was fond of menageries and fairs of all kinds." He took her hand, still clutching the token. "Let's enjoy this in his memory, hmm?"

Jane met his gaze with all the love she felt and nodded her agreement.

Inside the tithe barn, they were welcomed by the "Earl" himself in corresponding magnificence, his waistcoat spangled, as were the voluminous trunks he wore over skinny, stockinged legs, like Shakespearean garb of old.

He beamed at Jane. "Welcome, Mrs. Locke. Welcome, one and all."

She thanked him and looked around in wonder. On one end of the large structure, benches were set up around an open area and wooden stage. In the other half of the barn, pens and large cages displayed a variety of fascinating animals from foreign lands. Among them were the lioness in her cage, Pomegranate tethered nearby, and in a smaller cage, the mastiff, snarling obligingly at all who came near.

Together Jane and her party walked through the menagerie together, reading the placards naming each creature: a hyena, an albino zebra, a coatimundi, an anteater, a spotted cavy, a collection of colorful birds, a gigantic boa constrictor, and a pair of *rackoons* from North America.

As they strolled, they listened to the hyperbole of the menagerie's hawkers: "See a pair of extraordinary and rare pelicans of the wilderness; the only two alive in the three kingdoms. Considered to be the greatest curiosity of the feathered tribe . . ."

They paused now and again to greet a neighbor or to exchange exclamations of wonder and delight. Jane visited briefly with Joseph Kingsley, there with a niece and nephew, as well as several members of the Ladies Tea and Knitting Society. Mrs. Barton stood transfixed, fascinated by an ox-like African antelope called a gnu. "Have you ever seen the like? I am glad my bossies aren't here. They might feel quite inferior by comparison."

Jane saw Sir Timothy, Rachel, and Justina strolling around with a grinning Sir Cyril and his sisters. Sir Cyril shaped his fingers into a gun like a little boy might and pretended to shoot the gnu. Justina rolled her eyes.

Beyond the animal displays stood two enclosed booths plastered with colorful advertisements. The first offered a fortune-telling African parrot.

"Come and learn what your future holds from the Great Ferdinand, a rare and mystical talking bird. Living and breathing. No tricks. Only a penny! Walk up!"

One broadside displayed some of the wonderful fortunes that awaited: *True love. Good news. Riches await. Travel the world.* But apparently the parrot's proclamations were sometimes less positive. George and Helena Grove exited the booth, her face pinched white, and he did not look much happier.

Through the canvas flap, Jane heard the parrot squawk, "Bad news. Fool and his money. Bad news."

The second booth offered the opportunity to test one's mettle against an "unbeatable" domino-playing dog.

There they met James, Mercy, and Alice leaving the booth. Alice called excitedly, "The dog beat us all. Even Miss Grove!"

After sharing grins and greetings, their party walked on.

Strategically placed near the exit door, a glass blower wearing an astounding glass wig made teacups for threepence and tobacco pipes for a penny. Thora bought Talbot a pipe, and Hetty and Jane each a teacup.

Eventually, a loud horn blast pronounced the beginning of the stage show. Musicians in colorful costumes appeared on the wooden platform and played festive music on horn, bassoon, drum, and cymbals. Mr. Victor joined them on a strange-looking instrument—a tenor serpent, Jane believed—and there was Hetty playing her pipe. Thora pointed her out to Betsey, but the little girl did not seem to recognize her mother, who in truth looked quite different in her costume and face paint, a pert hat covering her ginger locks.

"Hetty *Piper* . . ." Jane murmured, struck anew by the significance of the name the young woman had chosen for herself.

The Earl, as master of ceremonies, stepped forward to announce the first act. "Just as royal balls across the kingdom begin with a courtly minuet, our show now begins with a minuet unlike any you've seen before. Be amazed as England's raven-haired wonder dances with her gallant partner, Charger."

Eva Victor strode in through a side door in a stunning costume— a white court dress spangled with paste gems and tulle, black and white feathers in her hair. She adopted an elegant pose and turned expectantly toward the door. In pranced a magnificent Arabian stallion wearing evening attire: black collar and silk cravat around his gleaming neck, and on each leg, black gaiters sparkling with paste gems.

The white horse paused before Eva, bent one knee, and "bowed" to her. The crowd roared with approval. The unusual couple in striking black and white began to perform the dance, a series of courtly bows, side steps, and mincing progressions toward one another and away again, while the musicians accompanied them on their instruments.

"Marvelous . . ." Jane murmured, wondering how long it had taken to train the horse to perform the intricate movements.

"Is that our dressmaker?" Justina Brockwell whispered in her ear.

"It is."

The girl's eyes widened. "Thank heavens Mamma isn't here. She would have a fit if she knew she had hired a show person to make my gown."

"No doubt."

The minuet ended with a final bow, beautiful black-haired woman and majestic white horse side by side. The two exited together to much applause.

The portable stage was pushed forward by four workmen, and the show commenced with the learned pig, doing sums. The musicians played another song between acts, but Jane noticed Hetty was no longer among them. She guessed Hetty might be preparing for a different role and waited eagerly to see what came next.

Eva returned to the costume wagon to wipe off the exaggerated lip and cheek rouge and to change back into an ordinary walking dress and pelisse. She hoped the entire village had not recognized her. Thankfully Papa had remembered not to call her by name.

Slipping back in through the side door a short while later, she looked around for Jane but instead saw Jack Gander standing nearby, clearly waiting for her.

"Well, that was a surprise," he said. "I did not know you planned to perform again."

"Just once, for old times' sake. To oblige Papa."

"The horse was magnificent, and so were you."

She shrugged. "I suppose everyone recognized me and there is an end to my dressmaking business, such as it was. If my lack of skill didn't ruin me, my performance certainly will."

"I'm not so sure. Some people recognized you, but they were no doubt impressed, as I was."

"It was nothing. An act like mine takes little skill."

"Did you make your costume, and all the others?"

"I did."

"Then you are skilled indeed."

"Making costumes and creating fine bespoke gowns are two different things, as I have learned—though I still have a great deal to learn about the latter."

"And you will. I believe you can accomplish anything you set your mind to, Miss Victor."

"Thank you, Mr. Gander. And what about you? You are clearly an excellent guard and accomplished horn player. Are you happy in your chosen profession?"

"I have been, yes, for the most part. But meeting you—seeing you make a brave new start in life, a new profession—it makes me think about my own future. I admire you, you know."

She sank into his dark eyes as he spoke, pulse rate accelerating at his words. His nearness.

On stage, her father announced that the audience was next to be treated to a heartwarming theatrical, written years ago by his eldest daughter.

Eva cringed. "You *don't* want to watch this."

He grinned. "Yes I do, especially if you wrote it."

The set was a simple one: a propped-up "cottage" wall with a working door and unglazed window. An artificial tree stump stood in front of it.

The play began with their trained terrier, Fritz, running out the door and around the stage, tongue lolling and tail wagging. He wore a little pack strapped to his back and tiny cap on his head. People laughed and applauded to see the adorable creature, as they always did.

Her father narrated. "Once upon a time, there was a young scamp who longed for adventure. He left his small village to seek his fortune abroad. Being poor, he learned charming manners and tricks to earn his bread."

Fritz rose on his back legs and danced in a circle, jumped over the stump, turned a flip, and then "bowed." Again the audience applauded, and a trio of players acting as villagers put coins in Fritz's pack.

"People loved his tricks, and he earned more gold than he ever would have had he remained in his provincial village. He had no family to put claims on him, no wood to chop, or taxes to pay. 'This is the life for me,' he sang, as he pranced along to the next town."

Again Fritz took a joyful lap around the stage.

"Years went by," her father said. "He kept performing his tricks, but he was not as young or charming as he used to be, and the coins were harder to come by."

Fritz repeated his tricks but now with exaggerated slowness, even affecting a limp. People in the audience murmured "Aww . . ." or laughed again.

"Occasionally someone still gave him a coin, but none invited him to sup with them or share a downy bed. He sometimes stood at their windows, watching those tranquil scenes of hearth and home, and began to wish he could join them."

Fritz leapt atop the stump near the window, propped his paws on the sill, and looked inside, whining piteously. More murmurs of sympathy arose from the crowd.

"Then one day, as he stood weary and lonely on the corner, a kind old lady came and sat by him."

Henrietta, now dressed in cape and grey wig as an elderly woman, stepped out the door. She sat on the stump, fed Fritz a treat, and petted him.

"She shared her meal and a token of affection. She asked if he ever grew lonely as she sometimes did. He swallowed his pride and admitted he did."

Fritz barked in reply.

"But that night, the lure of the road called to him, the hope that perhaps in the next town, he would find the happiness that eluded him."

The "old woman" opened the door, gesturing him inside, but Fritz remained where he was.

The narration continued, "Hers was a humble cottage. Its larder meager. Her life a quiet one. Nothing adventurous about it at all. He should thank her and move on. As he had done for years. As was his way." Mr. Victor paused for dramatic effect, then added, "Instead, he took a deep breath and accepted her invitation."

Fritz ran and leapt into Henrietta's arms, licking her face.

A murmur of satisfaction swept through the crowd.

"And there he stayed. He might not have adventure or fame, but he had a family and claims upon him, and a place to call home. Happy at last, he sang, 'Now *this* is the life for me.'"

Fritz gave a final bark, then Henrietta bowed and exited, Fritz still in her arms, and the crowd applauded.

Eva leaned near Jack and said sheepishly, "Not exactly Shake-speare."

"Maybe not, but it was sweet. I liked it." He reached out and ran a finger along her cheek. She sucked in a startled breath. Then he showed her a lingering smear of face paint.

"Oh. Thank you." Feeling awkward, she said, "We used to use a trained monkey in the role. But he developed some, er, embarrassing habits."

Onstage, the show continued with a performance by the French lion keeper.

Eva glanced over at Jack, disconcerted to find him looking at her and not the stage. She said, "You're supposed to be watching the show."

"I'd rather watch you."

He looked at her closely. Too closely. His steady gaze made her uneasy. He leaned near and asked, "Is that what you—"

An eruption of applause drowned out his words. With a look of mild exasperation, he took her hand and gently led her out the side door. The crowd and music faded as the door closed behind them.

He said, "I was asking if that was what you longed for when you wrote that play—to settle down in one place? To have somewhere to call home?"

She shrugged and looked away. "To live in one place longer than a few months? It seemed an unattainable dream when I was young. To know everyone in town and be greeted by name. To have neighbors who cared for us, and friends beyond the members of our troupe . . ."

"I can understand that. I am weary of living constantly on the road as well."

"Are you?" she asked in surprise.

He nodded.

"What will you do?"

"I'm not sure. Yet."

Together they strolled between the caravan wagons, past performers hurrying in and out, and workmen moving props. Night had fallen, but moonlight and flickering torches mottled the darkness. Several troupe members waved to her or called greetings as they passed.

An older woman engulfed Eva in a hug. "Hello, love. So good to see you performing again. Your father must be over the moon. Will you be coming with us when we move on?"

The woman surveyed Jack head to foot and waggled her eyebrows. "Or has something here tempted you to stay?"

"I have made no plans beyond tomorrow, Maria. But good to see you again." She pressed the woman's arm and walked on.

Jack lowered his voice. "What will you do now? Have you decided?"

"Finish Miss Brockwell's gown if it kills me. After that, I don't know."

"I don't know what my future holds either. But I'm glad our paths crossed."

She glanced at him shyly. "Me too."

He leaned close and pressed a gentle kiss to her cheek. "I can relate to that poor mongrel. I admit I sometimes get lonely, searching for elusive happiness up and down the line."

He laid a hand on his heart and recited, "'He sometimes stood at their windows, watching those tranquil scenes of hearth and home, and began to wish he could join them. . . .'"

"Jack, don't." Eva writhed in embarrassment to hear him repeat her clumsy words.

He continued, "But he kept moving to the next town, singing, *'This is the life for—'*"

She rose on tiptoe and silenced him with a kiss.

His arms instantly went around her. Pulling back just far enough to look into her eyes, he grinned and said, "I thought that might work," and kissed her again.

CHAPTER

Forty-Two

Matilda scheduled the Fairmonts' visit for Sunday afternoon so Mercy could be there without taking time away from teaching Alice.

Mercy arrived shortly before their guests and helped her aunt tidy the house—and her hair—for the occasion. George and Helena were just leaving when the Fairmonts walked through the gate. A dark woman in flowing tunic and long scarf followed behind father and son. Helena stared at the nurse, her pretty face puckered in distaste.

"George, my boy," Winston Fairmont greeted. "Good to see you again."

"You too, sir."

He eyed George's hat and stick. "Are you not joining us?"

George glanced at his wife. "Unfortunately, we are just on our way out."

"Prior engagement," Helena sweetly lied.

"Pity. I would enjoy swapping tales with you of our experiences abroad."

"I would enjoy that too, sir. Another time, perhaps. You do know my father always credits you with my desire to go to India."

"Blames me, I think you mean," Winston said shrewdly.

George smiled his boyish smile and shrugged. "He simply never

understood its appeal, not being the adventurer you and I are."
George tipped his head back. "Ah . . . Just thinking about India, I
can almost smell the exotic spices. The curries . . ." He closed his
eyes as though to savor them.

Winston Fairmont raised his nose. "I can as well," he said obligingly. Then he introduced his son and nurse.

George nodded vaguely to the woman but warmly greeted Jack
Avi. He said to Winston, "Handsome lad. Clearly India was more
profitable for you than it was for me."

Mr. Fairmont's hand rested fondly on his son's head. "My time
there certainly brought its heartaches but also its treasures."

"The latter eluded me, I'm afraid," George replied. "So I am
happy for a fresh start here at home. Much as you are, I imagine."

"Oh, my days of fresh starts are behind me, I think, but you
are a young man yet, George, and have every opportunity to make
the most of the coming years. I hope you won't take that blessing
for granted."

"I shan't, sir."

"Well, another time, then, as you say."

George nodded. "Enjoy your visit. Good day."

The couple walked down the steps, but before the door closed
behind them, Mercy heard Helena hiss, "Why on earth did he
bring that woman here . . . ?"

Mr. Fairmont turned to Mercy and Matilda, wincing apologetically. "I did not plan to bring Priya. But they were cleaning our
rooms at the hotel, and I didn't want to leave her sitting alone
outside."

"No, of course not. No trouble at all. You are all very welcome."

"Priya doesn't expect to be included. How uncomfortable that
would make her. But if she may sit quietly somewhere with her
sewing, she will be content."

Mercy pointed toward a chair in the hall. "She may sit here, if she
likes. But are you quite certain? We are happy to have her join us."

Mr. Fairmont gestured for the woman to be seated, and she did
so with apparent relief. As Matilda led the way across the hall,

he explained, "I know it may seem unfeeling to you, Miss Grove. But believe me, she will be happier on her own. She doesn't speak English and abhors attention, which she is receiving far too much of since arriving in England. She has learned some of the language Rani, Jack Avi, and I spoke in India, but it is not her first language, and I am but a poor translator, I'm afraid."

Mercy slowly shook her head. "How lonely she must be. Can she be happy, I wonder?"

"If you knew her background, how she had once been treated . . . My wife saved her from the streets, trained her as her maid and, later, nurse to our son. Yes, Priya is happier now. Or at least content."

Matilda paused at the sitting room door and said, "The more I hear about your dear wife, Win Fairmont, the more I like and admire her."

He smiled wistfully. "Thank you. I quite agree."

Aunt Matty rubbed her hands together, face alight. "I know you came expecting tea, but I hope you are hungry."

"Oh?" he asked. "Am I to be treated to one of your famous cakes?"

Jack Avi piped up, "Biscuits and sponge?"

She shook her head. "Not this time."

Winston Fairmont sent her a sidelong glance. "Matilda Grove, what are you cooking up now?"

Mercy wondered as well.

"Me?" Matilda batted innocent eyes. "Not a thing!" She gestured toward the rear door. "Come out into the back garden."

They followed Matilda outside, where a makeshift table awaited. "Please, be seated."

Mercy looked at her aunt, brows raised. Her aunt gave her a mischievous grin in reply. Helena had forbidden a formal dinner for the Fairmonts in Ivy Cottage. Though, come to think of it, they were not *in* Ivy Cottage at present, nor was there anything formal about the setting.

After the four of them sat down, Mr. Basu came out with a large platter bearing a beautifully braised fish with a savory mustard oil sauce. Next came bowls of curried vegetables, lentils and rice, and a basket of some type of fried bread.

Mr. Fairmont's eyes widened. "Do my eyes deceive me, or is that *luchi*?"

Mr. Basu nodded and bowed, a spark of delight in his eyes.

"That's what I was smelling," Winston Fairmont murmured. "Chili pepper, yes? I knew it."

Aunt Matty said, "I thought you might be missing Indian food, though Mr. Basu tells me there are many styles of cooking in that country and he fears this Bengali meal may be too spicy for your liking."

"Spicy food? How I've missed it. That is one thing we don't have here in England."

They began to eat, Matilda timidly, and Winston and Jack Avi with relish.

Mercy put an experimental morsel in her mouth. It tasted savory and exotic but soon transformed into fire on her tongue. She waved a hand over her lips and reached for her water glass.

"Mmm . . ." Winston Fairmont closed his eyes to savor a bite. "This is absolutely delicious. What do you think, Matty?"

"Um-hm. . . ." She nodded, tears streaming from her eyes.

Jack Avi said, "This is good. Ayah would love it."

"Yes, we must fill a plate for Priya," Mr. Fairmont said. "She can't miss this meal, not having suffered through English food this long."

Mr. Basu bent and spoke quietly in her aunt's ear.

Matilda smiled at him and then said, "Mr. Basu has invited Priya to join him in the kitchen, where she is even now enjoying this . . . unforgettable meal."

Mr. Fairmont beamed. "Excellent. Thank you, Mr. Basu. Very thoughtful. A skilled cook and a gentleman. I approve."

Later, Mr. Basu brought out sweet dishes, a folded pastry sealed with cloves, a pudding sprinkled with nutmeats, and a bowl of spongy balls floating in sweet syrup, garnished with saffron.

Mr. Basu pointed out each by name. "*Lobongo latika, payesh, chena rasgulla.*" It was one of the rare occasions Mercy had heard him speak without being asked a direct question.

Finally, he brought out tea.

Matilda grinned and whispered to Mercy. "I said we were having tea, and we are, see? As far as the rest, no one needs to be any the wiser."

After relishing the meal and good conversation, Mr. Fairmont thanked the Miss Groves and Mr. Basu effusively for the invitation and the meal. When they took their leave sometime later, Mercy noticed Mr. Basu hand Priya a covered dish and then bow to her. She bowed in turn and murmured a few melodic words in reply.

As Priya walked away, Mercy whispered to him, "Do you and she speak the same language?"

Mr. Basu nodded, a rare smile lifting his mouth.

"Oh good!" Aunt Matty said. "How pleasant that you understand one another."

"I agree." Mr. Fairmont's fond gaze returned to Matilda. "An understanding friend is a great blessing."

Rachel had kept a close eye on Justina in recent weeks, sensitive to her moods and concerned to see her so melancholy. Her young sister-in-law had yet to set a wedding date, but nor did she express any misgivings or second thoughts about her engagement to Sir Cyril.

In church that Sunday, Rachel saw Nicholas Ashford, but he did not come over to talk to her or Justina. After the service, Rachel whispered, "Justina, there's Nicholas. Shall we go over and say hello?"

For a moment, Justina's eyes brightened, but then the spark faded. "There is no point in my going over. But you may greet him, of course."

Rachel caught his gaze across the nave and smiled at him. His lips rose in reply, but his eyes remained sad. Rachel could not blame him. She was sad too and regretted raising his hopes with the house party, only to see him disappointed in love once again.

CHAPTER

Forty-Three

On Monday, the Brockwell women returned to Victorine's for a second fitting. From Jane, Rachel had learned the woman's name was actually Eva Victor, but she decided it was not the best time to announce that fact to her mother-in-law.

Justina stood before the long mirror in her shift and stays, while the dressmaker brought forth the satin underdress. Rachel again noticed the absence of her sister-in-law's usual cheer and smiled encouragingly. Justina met her gaze in the mirror, expression weary. The dressmaker had yet to add the layer of netting or fine embroidery or cut out Vandyked oversleeves. She said she first wanted to be sure the basic gown fit well.

Rachel held her breath as the satin slid over Justina's head and fluttered around her ankles in a pool of ivory. Miss Victor raised the gown over the young woman's slim hips and guided her arms through the sleeves.

Rachel could see in an instant that the gown was too large for Justina's slender figure, and far too long in the bargain. It hung on her like billowing window curtains.

Miss Victor's face crumpled. "I am sorry. I don't know how it happened. I will need to take this in, here and here. And shorten the hem, and—"

Justina regarded her reflection in the mirror, hands outstretched. "No. It's perfect."

Miss Victor shook her head. "Excuse me, Miss Brockwell, but it clearly does not fit you."

"I know."

Lady Barbara huffed. "I told you this was a foolish idea, Justina. We should have gone to London, as I wanted."

Justina turned toward her mother. "As you wanted, yes, but not as *I* wanted. Don't you see? It doesn't fit. It would suit someone else perfectly well, but not me."

"*That* gown would suit no one, but—"

"Not the dress! The marriage. The man. I can't do it, Mamma. I wanted to please you, but I don't love Sir Cyril, not even a little. I can't go through with it."

Justina's voice cracked, and tears filled her eyes. "I am sorry, Mamma. I wanted to be the one to make you happy and proud, but the truth is, I am miserable."

Lady Barbara frowned. "You are being dramatic, Justina. Sir Cyril is an amiable, handsome man with a title and fortune. What more could you ask for?"

"Much more."

"Sir Cyril has a pleasant disposition and excellent character—a very eligible match for you."

"He barely looks at me, Mamma. I don't think he even likes me."

"Of course he does. He asked you to marry him."

"That's what I tried to tell myself when he proposed. But the truth is, I think he likes Miss Bingley more than me."

"Nonsense. You are twice as pretty as Miss Bingley, as is your dowry."

"I am not so sure about that, but it does not matter. What matters is I am convinced he does not love me, nor can I love him."

"How do you know? You have no romantic experience on which to base such a conclusion. If you spurn this chance, how do you know you would ever admire another worthy man?"

"Because I . . . I already admire another worthy man."

The dowager's eyes flashed. "Ah. And here we come down to it. Mr. Ashford, I suppose. You deem him worthy of you?"

"I do, but there is no point in arguing about it because he has not made me an offer or even asked to court me. How could he when you told everyone I was practically engaged to be married long before I was!"

Lady Barbara's voice dropped dangerously low. "Must I remind you that you already accepted Sir Cyril? Plans are in motion."

"I was wrong to do so. I don't wish to hurt him, or disappoint you, but I've changed my mind."

"You would throw away this offer of marriage from a good man from a titled, respected family on the thin hope of an offer from a lesser man?"

"He is not lesser in my eyes."

The dowager threw up her hands. "It is too late, Justina. Mr. Paley begins reading the banns on Sunday."

Justina lifted a resolved chin. "I am sorry, Mamma. I cannot do it."

"Justina, you do know that to break off an engagement will cause a great deal of talk? Not to mention the fact that Sir Cyril could sue us for breach of promise?"

"He won't, Mamma. If anything, he will be relieved. I think he was only marrying me to please you too."

"Justina, really. That is ridiculous."

"And as far as talk? I can bear that far easier than a lifetime of marriage to a man I cannot love or respect."

"Easy to say, Justina. But what will Mr. Ashford think of you after this? You will be considered a jilt."

"I don't care. And if he disapproves, he is not the man I think him."

Lady Barbara turned to Rachel. "What have you to say about this?"

Rachel blinked, surprised to be asked. "Having married for love myself, I can testify to its joys. Justina is my dear sister now; how could I want any less for her?"

"And you think she will find happiness with Nicholas Ashford, the man you rejected?"

"Happiness may be fleeting, but joy? Unconditional love? Yes, I think Justina has every hope of finding those with Mr. Ashford, who I believe admires her very much. He may not be highly ranked or polished, but he is noble-hearted, honorable and successful, and from an old family. Not without blemish, I grant you, but a good family nonetheless. And he is master of Thornvale, which is much nearer than Broadmere, don't forget."

Lady Barbara slowly shook her head. "But think of poor Lady Awdry! Neither of her daughters married, one with little prospect of ever being so, and now her only son to be thrown over! If life were fair, Justina would marry Sir Cyril and leave Mr. Ashford free to marry one of the Miss Awdrys, especially as Timothy disappointed those hopes once before. If you insist on breaking things off, I doubt she will ever speak to me again!"

"Oh, Mamma. We cannot make decisions based on the Awdrys' matchmaking needs. Besides, I think Horace Bingley admires Penelope Awdry."

"You mean Arabella, surely."

"I do not. I would never have credited Horace with such excellent taste, but he astounded us all at the house party. Penelope most of all."

"Good heavens. What next?" The dowager rose. "Please do nothing hasty, Justina. Promise me you will think it over tonight."

"I have already—"

Rachel laid a staying hand on Justina's arm. They had come so far, and Lady Barbara seemed on the cusp of agreement.

Comprehending Rachel's warning, Justina amended, "I shall, Mamma. If you like."

Justina turned to the dressmaker, who had remained silent and inconspicuous during the battle of wills. "I am sorry, madame. I hope you will be able to salvage the dress and sell it to someone else. I hate for you to lose all that time and expense."

The dressmaker managed a stiff smile. "Thank you, but don't

give it another thought, Miss Brockwell. It is not your fault. I wish you happy, whatever you decide."

Lady Barbara said, "Rachel, would you and Justina mind walking home? I will follow shortly in the carriage, but Madame and I have some business to discuss first."

That sounded ominous.

"Mamma . . ." Justina began to protest, but Rachel took her arm, fearing further argument would hinder the fragile agreement between them.

"Come, Justina. Let us go home." She all but pushed her sister-in-law out the door. Miss Victor could fend for herself. At least, Rachel hoped she could.

Justina burst out of the shop like a bird from a cage and nearly bowled Nicholas Ashford over.

"Oh! Miss Brockwell. Forgive me." He took her by the elbows to steady her.

Rachel followed more sedately and closed the door behind them.

"Nothing to forgive, Mr. Ashford," Justina said. "I am the one who knocked into you. I wasn't looking where I was going in my excitement."

He did not, Rachel noticed, instantly release her arms.

"And what has you so delighted, if I may ask?" He smiled, though his eyes remained wary. He nodded toward the shop she'd just exited. "You are pleased with your wedding dress, I presume?"

She beamed. "Not at all. It does not fit nor suit me. Not in the least."

His brows rose. "And this pleases you?"

Justina nodded, eyes sparkling. "The wedding is off. Or soon will be."

His eyes widened and his mouth parted. "Because of a dress?"

She shook her head. "Because the bride and groom were not suited. It just took me a while to admit the truth of it once and for all. But now I have, to my mother's disappointment. You must think me terribly selfish, not to mention a shameful jilt."

"On the contrary, Miss Brockwell, I think you exceedingly brave. Not to mention beautiful."

He seemed to realize he was still touching her and regretfully removed his hands, offering his arm instead. "May I walk you home?"

Justina hesitated. "I . . . would like nothing better, Mr. Ashford, truly. But I had better not. Not until I have had a chance to speak with Sir Cyril."

"Ah. He does not yet know?"

"Not yet. I have only just convinced Mamma of my change of heart. Though it wasn't really a change. Amiable as Sir Cyril may be, he never won my heart."

"Do you think another man might succeed in doing so . . . someday?"

Justina smiled. "Yes, I think there is every hope he shall."

Eva was sorry to see kind Justina and Rachel leave her shop. She clutched damp palms and faced Lady Barbara.

The dowager began, "Well, madame, I assume you were an accomplice in this little farce of my daughter's. No one could have unintentionally missed the mark so badly."

If only that were true, Eva thought, opening her mouth to correct the misapprehension, but Lady Barbara went on undeterred.

"I want you to know that I don't appreciate your part in today's drama, and you will certainly not be receiving any more commissions from me. Nor will I be paying for this"—she twirled her hand toward the discarded heap of material—"waste of my time and yours. I will have the advance back as well."

"But I spent it on material, and . . ." With a glance at the woman's stony face, Eva changed tack. "Of course, my lady. As soon as I can."

"By the end of the week, if you please. Unless you wish me to make my disapproval of you and your services known to all of my large acquaintance."

Eva swallowed. Did it matter? She was ruined at all events. But honor dictated she pay the woman back. "I shall repay you, my lady. And I apologize for . . . everything."

The dowager studied her through narrowed eyes, as if gauging her sincerity. Then, satisfied, she turned on her heel and stalked out.

After the door slammed, Eva stood there, slowly shaking her head. She had failed to make Miss Brockwell's gown. Now what? Perhaps it was time to set aside her dream for good and return to the troupe, a failure.

The next day, Rachel and Sir Timothy accompanied Justina to Broadmere to make the unhappy call. Rachel went for moral support, and Timothy in case Sir Cyril threatened to sue the Brockwells for breach of promise, though he did not seem the type to sue a family friend. They hoped.

Rachel and Timothy waited at the far end of the great hall as chaperones, while Justina and Sir Cyril sat in facing armchairs at the opposite end. Justina spoke for a few minutes in low, solemn tones. Rachel could guess the words but not hear them.

Sir Cyril expelled a long breath and sank back against the cushions. Crestfallen? Dejected?

Then his louder voice reached them. "It is as I expected. Your mother seemed far more in favor of the match than you were. In truth, I was surprised you accepted me."

"You don't mind, then?" Justina asked.

"No, Miss Brockwell. You have not injured me. My mother will be disappointed, of course. But perhaps she and your mother may console each other."

Justina rose. "Thank you for understanding."

Sir Cyril walked her back to the waiting chaperones, his expression grave. "Well, Brockwell, I don't want my mother and sisters to suffer from any more gossip than necessary, so I hope we can resolve this quietly. Thankfully, our vicars have not yet read the banns."

Timothy nodded. "I will talk to Mr. Paley as soon as we get back."

"I appreciate that. And I will talk to our clergyman as soon as I bid you farewell."

He turned to Justina and took her hand. "I wish you happy, Miss Brockwell."

"And I you, Sir Cyril. Good-bye."

He bowed over her hand, then met her gaze. It was the first time Rachel had seen the man look her in the eye.

CHAPTER
FORTY-FOUR

Although Jane still rode to The Bell every day, she slept at the farm now and was slowly moving her belongings from the lodge to the farmhouse.

She thought Jack Avi would enjoy visiting the menagerie while it was in town and planned to ask her father if she might take the boy there the next time they came to see her. The Earl's Menagerie had proved so popular, drawing visitors from surrounding villages and even populous Salisbury, that Mr. Victor had gained permission to extend the troupe's stay in Ivy Hill.

But Jane's father did not stop by The Bell or the farm as she'd expected. As far as Jane knew, he had not returned to the village since he'd shared a meal at Ivy Cottage with the Miss Groves. As the days passed without seeing her father or brother, Jane grew concerned. She hoped he and Jack Avi were well. Priya too. She decided to ride over to Wilton and see them.

When Jane arrived at the inn and went upstairs, she again found Jack Avi in the corridor, this time kicking his ball back and forth down its length. She decided she would take him outside to play again, if nothing else.

"Hello, Jack Avi."

The boy beamed. "Didi!"

"Where's Bapu?"

The boy pointed across the passage to her father's door left ajar. Jane looked into the room and saw Dr. Burton bent over the bed, a long tube to his ear, listening to her father's heart. Her breath hitched. Was he ill?

She stepped back and for a few moments just stood there, unsure whether to go in or wait outside. Before she could decide, the door opened wider and Dr. Burton stepped out.

"Ah, Jane. I am glad to see you."

With a glance at Jack Avi, out of earshot down the corridor, she asked, "How is he?"

The physician grimaced. "Not as well as I would like, but as I said, I have little experience with foreign fevers."

Jane's stomach clenched. "He has a fever?"

Dr. Burton looked at her in surprise. "Not now, no. But he suffered two serious illnesses while in India and they've taken their toll on his heart, especially. Has he really not told you any of this?"

"No."

"Then I should not be the one to do so."

"I am glad you did. What should I do? Shall I take him to London? Is there someone with more such experience you could recommend?"

He looked up, squinting in thought. "Actually, let's not inflict another journey on him just yet. The man has already traveled enough for two lifetimes. My son Franklin is also a physician, as you may recall. These last several years he has been with a teaching hospital of some renown—Guy's Hospital in London. He is planning to visit me next week. Let's have him evaluate your father before we decide what to do next."

"May we move him to Ivy Hill at least? I would like to care for him there."

"Yes, a good idea if you can convince him. It will also be easier for me to oversee his treatment there. A room at The Bell, are you thinking?"

"Yes, if he can manage the stairs."

"He should be able to. For now."

"Anything else I can do?" Jane asked. "Medicine, a special diet?"

He considered. "Nothing beyond good food and plenty of rest for the present. He is still well able to care for himself. Later, I think it would be wise to ask Mrs. Henning or perhaps Sadie Jones to serve as chamber nurse. There are some things a man doesn't want his daughter helping with."

Later? How much later? Jane wondered, stomach sinking. "Yes, I understand. And thank you for coming here to see him, Dr. Burton."

"I suppose he didn't want to burden you, but I have to say I'm glad you know."

Jane nodded. With another glance toward her little brother, she asked, "Jack Avi is in good health, I trust? And his nurse?"

"The boy is perfectly hale, yes. I must assume the nurse is in good health too, though she won't let me anywhere near her."

"I see. May I go in and talk to my father?"

"Let me make sure he is fully dressed." He ducked his head back into the room, murmured something, and then stepped back out, holding the door for her.

Jane stepped inside. "Hello, Papa."

He took one look at her face and grimaced, muttering something under his breath. "Burton blabbed, did he?"

Jane said gently, "You should have told me yourself."

He looked away from her. "I did not want you to accept me back into your life only out of pity."

"I can understand that concern, initially. But you've been here for some time now."

He shrugged. "I didn't want to worry you. You were busy with the inn and wedding plans."

"Not too busy for you, Papa," she said, then prompted, "Dr. Burton mentioned you'd been seriously ill?"

He nodded. "The Indian climate can be dangerous. Thousands of soldiers and men with the East India Company succumbed to bilious fevers, dysentery, small pox, typhoid. . . . I escaped all but minor illnesses when I lived there as a young man. But the last few years have been a trial. I was laid low with malaria and other fevers more than once. And Rani and I were both afflicted with cholera last year. As you know, she did not survive. I did, but apparently all those illnesses have weakened my constitution. And my heart."

"So Dr. Burton mentioned. He wants his son to have a look at you next week. He trained at Guy's Hospital in London."

Her father waved a dismissive hand. "I have already been to the hospital in Madras and consulted native healing men as well as company doctors. There was little anyone could do, beyond prescribe a return to *my* native climate."

"Is this why you came back when you did?"

"No. At least, not primarily. Receiving your letter after so many years of silence seemed like a clear sign to me. Time to go back. At least for a visit, to see my dear daughter again. If she would still have me."

"Of course I will, Papa. I do. I am glad you're here, and I'm sorry for hanging on to my resentments so long. It was petty and foolish of me. What if you had died there and never came back?" Tears filled Jane's eyes at the thought.

"But I did come back. My dear . . . You see now why I didn't want to tell you? There, there."

He patted her hand. "I also confess to you that I thought of leaving Jack Avi in India with his aunt and uncle. It seemed cruel to rip him away from the only country and people he has known, especially when there is a real chance I might not live long enough to see him grow up."

"Oh, Papa, don't say that," Jane murmured, heart aching.

Her father drew himself up, and for the first time she noticed how bony his shoulders were, how thin he was.

"But I could not do it. I had already lost my beloved Rani. I could not bear to part with our child too."

"Of course you could not. I am glad you brought him with you. I thank God for you both. Now, no more talk of not seeing him grow up." Jane wiped away her tears. "We will consult the best doctors and take excellent care of you—nutritious food, plenty of rest. Now you're here in England, you will improve, Papa, I know it. You will be here with Jack Avi—and me—for many years to come."

He gave her a lopsided grin. "From your lips to God's ear, my dear. From your lips to God's ear."

After Jane helped her father and Priya move into rooms in The Bell, she left them to rest and get settled.

Jane boosted Jack Avi up onto the gig's bench. "You are going to spend the night with Gabriel and me, Jack Avi. How does that sound? And perhaps tomorrow, I shall take you to the menagerie to see the lion and many other wonderful animals."

"What about Bapu?" he asked.

"He is having dinner with his old friend Lord Winspear tonight. Adults only."

"And my ayah?"

"Priya is going to enjoy a rare night of leisure. Mr. Basu plans to cook for her again."

"And what shall we eat?" her brother asked.

Jane patted the basket on the bench beside her. "I have asked Mrs. Rooke to prepare some of your favorites: pigeon pie, sponge, and biscuits."

He raised a triumphant little fist. "Yes!"

Jane got an unpleasant whiff. "When was the last time you had a bath, Jack Avi?"

He shrugged and wrinkled his nose. "I don't like baths."

"Well, I think it's time for one. I'll fill a nice warm tub for you and help you wash your hair."

He expelled a long-suffering sigh.

Later, when Jack Avi sat in the bath, Jane set a small wooden boat Gabriel had carved, mast and all, upon the water. The boy's dread of bathing vanished. "If only it had a sail!"

Jane said, "I shall fashion one for you."

"Would you? Thank you, Didi."

She washed and rinsed his hair and, when the water began to

cool, helped him step out, wrapping a large towel around him. "How good you smell!"

"Now I get pigeon pie, sponge, and biscuits?"

She chuckled. "Yes, now you do."

After they ate, Jane helped Jack Avi into a nightshirt and read him a story. When it was almost time for sleep, he knelt beside the bed and clasped his hands, praying in his musical tongue she wished she understood.

"What did you pray for, Jack Avi?" she asked. "If it is not private."

"I said, God bless Gable, Didi, Ayah, and Mr. Basu. And please make Bapu better. And thank you for pigeon pie and biscuits."

Jane smiled and kissed his sweet-smelling hair.

Sometime during the night, Jack Avi got into bed with them. He climbed over Gabriel and wedged himself between them.

"Bad dream," he mumbled. "Lion chasing me . . ."

"You're all right, Jack Avi," Jane soothed. "You're safe."

Gabriel turned on his side, facing them, and stretched his strong arm over them both. In the moonlight filtering through the window, she could see Gabriel's eyes were open, resting on her. Jane stroked Jack Avi's hair, and in moments he was asleep. Jane reached for Gabriel's hand, and the two looked at each other over the little boy. Tears heated Jane's eyes, but they were not sad tears, exactly. The moment was achingly poignant, and she did not want it to end.

CHAPTER

Forty-Five

Mercy continued to meet with the boot boy for reading lessons, but he was not progressing as quickly as she had hoped. They met in the servants' hall belowstairs, at a time when the room was not otherwise in use. After a frustrating quarter of an hour with a lesson book, Mercy set it aside.

Hoping an article with local flavor might spur the adolescent's interest in reading, Mercy spread the hotel's copy of the *Salisbury and Winchester Journal* before him and traced her finger along the lines of print.

"Let's try this, Bobby."

He arduously sounded out each word. "'The cap-ture of a lioness in Wiltshire has captured the pub-lic's imm . . .'"

"Imagination," Mercy supplied.

"'And is being re-counted in newspapers na-tion-wide. Reports praise the fi . . .'"

Mercy read the more difficult words, "'Financial prowess of the menagerie owner in purchasing . . .'"

"'. . . the in-jured coa-ching horse,'" Bobby continued. "'The horse with its wo . . . wounds, the re-cap-tured lioness, and the dog have all become part of the show.'"

Mercy restrained a weary sigh of relief and smiled at the boy. "Well done, Bobby."

She looked up and noticed James Drake leaning against the doorframe, cup of coffee in hand, a tolerant grin on his handsome face.

Seeing his employer, the boy jumped to his feet. "Thank you, Miss Grove. Better get back to it."

"See you tomorrow, Bobby."

Mr. Drake raised his cup. "Came down for coffee. Thought I'd see how you were getting on."

Mercy expelled the sigh she'd held back in the boy's presence. "Slowly."

"I heard him, Mercy. He's no orator, but he *was* reading. You are doing a good job. I think some boys are slower to catch on. I know I was."

"Thank you. I appreciate your encouragement."

He tilted his head in thought. "I know you miss teaching, Mercy. I've been wondering, could you not find another place in the village to teach?"

She looked at him in surprise. "Even if it were possible, it would interfere with my duties as Alice's governess. I hope you are not trying to get rid of me."

"Of course not. Just thinking of you, of the future."

Mercy had thought he might have overheard Mr. Paley giving her the disappointing news in the churchyard several months before, but apparently he had not.

She explained, "I did ask Mr. Paley if I might use the church. But the churchwardens refused my request. They might eventually allow Sunday school classes, but not general education."

"Then what about the circulating library?" he suggested. "Would your friend Rachel allow you to teach there? Perhaps you might give reading lessons, if nothing else. It would perfectly complement her business by creating more patrons for her library."

She looked at him, impressed. "That is an excellent notion. I cannot believe I did not think of it myself. I have been so busy grieving the loss of my school, and feeling sorry for myself, that I have been blind to a rather obvious option."

He shrugged easily, lips pursed. "I don't say it would be the same as having your own school. And I suppose any classes you taught would have to be outside of library hours. But it would be something—after you've finished with Bobby, that is."

Mercy nodded. "I will discuss it with Rachel when next I see her. For the . . . future, as you say. Thank you, Mr. Drake."

"You are very welcome." Again his gaze lingered on her face. "There, you see? I've earned another of your lovely smiles, which is all the thanks I need."

Dr. Burton's son Franklin, a man of perhaps five and thirty, seemed competent and knowledgeable about Asiatic illnesses, having served a term with Indian Medical Services as well as several years with London's renowned teaching hospital. He examined Winston Fairmont while his father looked on, and Jane waited nervously in the corridor for his verdict.

Examination completed, the younger physician invited Jane to join them as he wrote out a prescription for a tonic of his own composition to help alleviate the lingering effects of the fever, offering to oversee its preparation by the local apothecary. He also prescribed a low dose of digitalis for her father's heart and several days of bed rest while they waited to see how he reacted to the course of treatment.

"It is not a cure, mind you," Franklin Burton said to him. "But I believe it will make you more comfortable and improve the functioning of your heart, which will, in turn, extend your life."

Her father groaned. "Bed rest? I shall go mad with boredom."

"Don't fret, Papa," Jane soothed. "We will keep you company and keep you entertained—though quietly. In fact, Matilda Grove is waiting downstairs, if you are feeling equal to a visitor."

"I don't want everyone in the village gawking as if I'm some foreign creature in a menagerie, but Matilda, yes. A visit from that old friend is always welcome. As is your company, Jane. I hope that goes without saying."

Colin came up to assist her father into clothes more suited to bed rest: a pair of loose "pajama" trousers he'd brought back from India over a fresh nightshirt, with a long banyan jacket belted snugly around him. While Colin helped her father get settled into bed, Jane went downstairs, returning a few minutes later with Matilda. Jane held the door for her, and Miss Matty went inside and took the chair beside the bed.

"I shall bring you tea in a few minutes," Jane said, and turned to go, leaving the door ajar to allow her to enter with a tray more easily.

When Jane came back upstairs a quarter of an hour later, she heard the low exchange of conversation. As she neared the open door, Matilda's words made her pause in the corridor.

"You do know I once hoped you and I would marry, when we were young?"

"No. . . ." Her father sounded as astonished as Jane felt.

"Did you never realize I was in love with you?" Matilda chuckled. "No, I suppose not. Not when your heart was always in India."

"But I thought you were being courted by that Essig fellow."

"Oh, he admired me. But I didn't care for him, so I turned him down."

"I did wonder."

"I doubt you had time to wonder about me," Matilda said mildly. "Not when you were bent on making your fortune abroad. After your brother died and you returned, I foolishly raised my hopes again, but then your parents introduced you to Jane's mother and that was that."

"I am sorry, Matty. Sorry I . . . disappointed you."

"Oh, never mind. It's all a long time ago. I am not that foolish young girl any longer."

Voice husky, he replied, "You will always be that foolish young girl to me, Matty Grove."

"And *you* will always be that rascal who got away, Win Fairmont."

Jane turned and tiptoed back downstairs. The tea was still warm, but it would wait.

After a few weeks in the area, attendance numbers at the menagerie began to fall. Eva's father gained permission to store the hail-damaged tent and a few extra wagons in the tithe barn, while the troupe traveled more lightly to the neighboring counties of Hampshire, Berkshire, and Somerset. Eva knew part of the reason her father remained nearby was to be closer to her and Henrietta— and because he hoped Eva would choose to travel with them when the troupe finally left the area for good.

Eva was tormented by indecision. Her three-month trial had passed, and she had failed. Perhaps she *should* just leave with the troupe. It would be easier than trying to win over the village women who now knew she had not made the model gowns she'd displayed and others who were disappointed in her skills as a dressmaker. No doubt everyone would learn of her shortcomings if she stayed much longer. But Eva didn't want to leave. She liked it in Ivy Hill. Her sister and niece were nearby. She was fond of Jane, Mercy and Matilda, the Paleys, Mrs. Mennell and the almshouse residents, and so many others. And then there was Jack . . .

While the menagerie had been in the village, people had come to Ivy Hill from surrounding towns, and all the businesses on the High Street had profited. Eva herself had sold two hats and received an order for a straw summer bonnet with cherries on it, like the one she'd made for Miss Bingley.

But now the tithe barn was quiet, and the High Street as well. Eva reduced the shop's hours and spent more time at the almshouse— quilting, mending, and chatting with the residents, or reading to Mrs. Hornebolt, whom she'd begun to look on as something of an adopted grandmother.

She also rode with the carter, Mrs. Burlingame, over to Wishford to visit Henrietta and help as the couple worked on their lodging house—caring for Betsey, painting walls, and cooking meals. What a pleasure to prepare their mother's favorite ragout of burgundy beef, or her *sole meunière* in Hen's sunny kitchen.

And how satisfying to spend time with her sister again, to dote on her darling niece, and become better acquainted with the husband and father who clearly adored them both.

Eva enjoyed every minute, even as she realized she could not put off her decision much longer.

CHAPTER

Forty-Six

Jane was glad she'd convinced her father to move to The Bell, nearer to her and the old friends who cared for him. His being in Ivy Hill allowed Dr. Burton to check on him often. And the vicar, Mr. Paley, visited regularly as well.

Cheerful Miss Matilda came to sit with him every afternoon, bringing baked goods, medicinal barley water, and conversation. Her visits always did her father good.

On a drizzly June morning, Jane left the farm and rode into town. She stopped at the circulating library to borrow a book for her father, then continued on to The Bell. As she was going up the stairs to deliver it, she met Matilda coming down, head bowed to watch her step.

"And how did you find him this morning, Miss Matty?"

The older woman looked up, and Jane saw tears glistening in her eyes.

"Oh, Jane . . ." she murmured, reaching out to grasp her free hand.

And in Matilda's glittering eyes and forlorn expression, Jane saw a depth of grief that startled her.

"What is it? Is he worse?"

Matilda hesitated, then inhaled deeply and forced a smile. "Oh, I am probably imagining things. It is just so hard to see him weak like this. No doubt he will be right as a trivet in no time." She squeezed Jane's hand—hard—but Jane felt more desperation in the gesture than reassurance.

Matilda took her leave, and Jane continued to her father's room, a cord of concern tightening her chest.

"Good day, Papa."

Her father sat atop the made bed, dressed comfortably and freshly shaved. "Jane. How are you? You have just missed Matilda Grove."

"Yes, I saw her leaving. How are you feeling?"

He leaned back. "Dashed tired, truth be told."

Jane spread a lap rug over him, then sat on the chair near the bed. "I brought you another book. Rachel tells me it was one of her father's favorites."

He accepted it, his gaze caressing the cover, expression softening. "William's favorite, ey? Then I shall relish it."

"Colin mentioned Dr. Burton was here this morning. What did he say?"

"The father or his son? Neither offers much hope, unfortunately. My heart is weak and will eventually give out. I may experience a period of renewed vigor first or I may not. The timing is difficult to predict, and there is little they can do to affect the outcome."

"What about the digitalis?"

He shook his head. "Yet to produce any noticeable improvement."

"Then what about Mr. Fothergill? He must have something else you can take, some strengthening elixir among the many compounds on his shelves?"

"Jane, there is not a pill for everything, however badly we—or the apothecary—might wish it were so."

He extended his palm to her, and she laid her hand in his. "Whatever happens, it will be all right, Jane." He hesitated and then added, "If you will do one thing for me."

"Anything."

"When I'm gone, will you take care of Jack Avi?"

Jane's heart pounded as waves of emotion washed over her. She was not ready to lose her father after so recently being reunited.

She forced a bright tone. "Of course I will, Papa. But that will be years from now, Lord willing."

His head moved side to side on his pillow. "Jane . . ."

She interlaced her fingers with his. "I don't want to lose you, Papa—not when I have only just got you back!"

"I know, my dear, but just in case, humor me. I will rest easier once Jack Avi's future is settled."

"Then don't fret. No matter what happens, Jack Avi will be well cared for. I will make sure of it."

He nodded, but a worry line lingered between his brows. "Will you raise him as your own, Jane, not just as a guardian or even his sister? He needs a mother. You need a son. And God is a gracious provider. Now that you're married to Mr. Locke, he shall be his pa—"

"Jack Avi *has* a papa."

"A boy needs a father, Jane. One young enough and *present* enough to teach him to ride and play cricket and be a good man. A gentleman."

"He is learning that from you."

"He is still so young. He'll need parents, Jane. A mother and father, ideally, but—"

"Shh. . . . Don't fret, Papa. If the worst happens, as you fear, then I will raise Jack Avi and love him as my own."

"Good." He sighed. "Then talk to that husband of yours, and if he agrees, I will ask Alfred Coine to draw up the requisite papers. But I should warn you, Jane, not everyone will like it—you raising him as your son. Such prejudice exists."

"I will do my best to shield him from that."

"Can't shield him forever. Teach him to face it with courage. Remind him who he is."

Jane nodded. "I will make sure he remembers that he is the beloved son of a respected gentleman."

"Well, that too, yes. But I meant a beloved child of God, who loves us all without respect to color or country of origin."

"I perfectly agree, Papa. And I am . . . sure Gabriel will too."

She wasn't completely sure, of course, as she and Gabriel had never discussed the matter. Would he be willing to raise Jack Avi as his own son? Regardless of prejudice or a longing for a son of his own? She swallowed a nervous lump at the thought of the conversation to come and managed a smile for her father.

"Now, enough talk of your demise," she said. "A few more weeks under Dr. Burton's care and Mrs. Rooke's stout English cooking and you will be your old self again, with that renewed vigor Dr. Burton mentioned."

He gave her a crooked grin. "Your optimism is charming."

"I want you to live a long, long time, Papa, so I can make up for all the years I was cold and silent to you. That was wrong of me, I know now. Wrong of me to withhold forgiveness."

"Do you forgive me, Jane? For leaving you the way I did, without warning? For selling your beloved horse and childhood home without giving you a chance to claim any treasured possessions?"

"I do forgive you, Papa. Will you forgive me for my unjust resentment? For cutting you out of my life?"

"Forgiven long ago." He laid his free hand atop hers. "Now, don't be sad. Thanks to our risen Savior, I know where I'm going when this life ends. No need to feel sorry for me."

"I don't. I feel sorry for me. And for Jack Avi."

"He'll be all right. He has his dear *didi*."

Tears welled in her eyes, but she blinked them back.

Her father's eyes glistened as well. "How I missed you, Jane."

She managed a shaky smile. "I missed you too, Papa."

And she knew she would miss him again, all the more, when the time came.

Jane returned to the farm. After dinner that evening, she walked hand in hand with her husband to the sitting room.

"Gabriel, I have something to tell you. I am not sure how you will feel about it."

"That sounds ominous."

She took a deep breath and began. "My father is not in good health. . . ."

"I know, Jane. I am sorry. I'm sure this is difficult for you."

"Yes, but there is something else we need to talk about." She ran her tongue over dry lips.

His brows lowered in concern. "Shall we sit down?"

She nodded, and they sat on the sofa together. Jane angled her body to face him. "My father is concerned about the future, about what will happen to Jack Avi if he . . . doesn't recover. He wants us to care for Jack Avi after he is gone, to raise him as his . . . parents."

She clasped her hands tight across her abdomen and waited.

When Gabriel said nothing, she looked up at him, trying to read his expression. He seemed to be waiting as well.

"And . . . ?" he prompted.

"And what? That is the situation."

He leaned back, relaxing. "I had already assumed that would be the case. It makes sense—you are the perfect person to raise him, should the worst happen. And as your husband, of course I would share that responsibility and privilege."

"And you wouldn't mind?"

"Mind? Do you mean, because some people might realize he isn't my natural son?"

She chuckled. "I don't think anyone would assume he was."

Gabriel remained serious, brows raised. "Really? I think he looks quite a bit like me. Dark hair, dark eyes . . ."

She wasn't sure if he was joking or not, but it gave her the courage to add, "My father also said that he was glad you would be the one to teach Jack Avi to 'ride and play cricket and be a good man. A gentleman.'"

Gabriel gazed upward, eyes distant, as though trying to imagine the scene. Did he find it disappointing compared to the hope of having his own natural-born children?

He nodded soberly. "I don't know how qualified I am to teach Jack Avi to be a gentleman, but the rest . . . ? With pleasure and honor."

Jane smiled, relief and love flooding her chest. "Foolish man . . ." She leaned near to kiss his cheek. "There is no one more qualified."

Mercy and James sat in his office, discussing the possibility of engaging someone to give Alice lessons on the pianoforte. Mercy, unfortunately, had never learned.

Something caught his eye behind her. "Father . . . this is a surprise."

Mercy looked over her shoulder. There in the open doorway stood Mr. Hain-Drake.

James rose. "I wish you had let me know you were coming. We are in the midst of some work in the hall and have yet to tidy up."

The older man waved away the concern as if it were a midge. "Doesn't matter."

"You would not approve of my 'pet project' at any rate—is that what you mean?"

His father frowned. "That is not what I mean. Don't put words in my mouth."

Mr. Hain-Drake nodded to Mercy. "Miss Grove, a pleasure to see you again."

"And you, sir." Mercy stood. "Excuse me. I will leave you two to talk."

"No, please stay," James said. "We may need a referee."

Mercy hesitated. "I don't wish to intrude."

"It's all right, Miss Grove. If James wants you here, I won't protest. I have not come to argue with my son."

James gestured to a chair. "Then please be seated."

He sat behind his desk while Mercy and Mr. Hain-Drake took the armchairs across from him.

James looked at his father. "How strange to be on this side of the desk during one of your formal reprimands." He interlaced his fingers.

Mercy thought, *And how strange to see James Drake nervous.*

Mr. Hain-Drake leaned forward in the chair. "I never intended to demean your hotel here or the one in Southampton. I suppose I hoped to show you that the Hain-Drake interests are an even bigger opportunity you might turn your hand to. But my indirect attempt to sway you clearly had the opposite effect from the one I intended."

James asked, "Why would you even want me involved now? You have Francis."

"Francis . . ." his father muttered and shook his head. "A good boy—affable, willing—but he lacks focus."

"Then hire a competent manager."

The older man's nostrils flared. "I don't want a manager, I want you—my son—at the helm of the Hain-Drake corporation."

James frowned, perplexed. "*You* stand at the helm, and always have. What is it? Has something happened?"

The man's eyes flashed to Mercy, then back to his son. "I am ill. I don't tell you that to garner sympathy, which I doubt would be forthcoming at any event. More likely you will see it as another ploy to manipulate you. But it's not. It's plain fact."

James's expression tightened. "What does Dr. Larson say?"

"It's cancer. Advanced."

"And his prognosis?"

"Not cheery. A few months. Half a year, if I'm lucky."

James squeezed his eyes shut. "I am truly sorry to hear it, sir."

"Are you?"

"Yes. But still, I . . . There must be someone else who can take over the business."

"James, if it were only the business . . . only my livelihood, I would not press you. But there is your mother to think of. Your sister. Your niece and nephews. All of them depend on Hain-Drake enterprises for their future security. I can't in good conscience leave Francis at the reins. He'll run the whole operation into the ground before I'm a year in my grave, smiling all the while, happily unaware."

"Surely he's not as incompetent as all that."

"I exaggerate, I own. But he isn't you, James. You've got the

Hain-Drake ambition, the talent. You are as capable as I am and twice as personable. I have every confidence that, after a few months working beside me, you would lead the Hain-Drake interests into a long and successful future. Is it wrong to want to leave a legacy? To have something I began, something bearing my name, to live on after I'm gone?"

"No, sir. But you astound me. For you have never praised my abilities before."

The older man looked him in the eye. "You're wrong. I have. Just not in your hearing."

James held his gaze a moment longer. His Adam's apple rose and fell. "I appreciate your confidence, Father. Truly. But I own two hotels."

"Sell them. Or as you advised me, hire a competent manager."

Mr. Hain-Drake stood, not quite steady, and grasped the chair back for support. James rose to help, but his father stayed him with a commanding hand and fierce look. "I am not an invalid yet."

At the door, he turned back. "I will leave you to think it over, to consider my offer from all sides. But remember this. You are my primary heir, James. Of course, I will provide for your mother and leave something for Francis, Lucy, and their children. But the bulk of my holdings, business interests, and property are in your name. You would be a foo—"

His gaze darted to Mercy before he lowered his head and said, "Please don't reject my request. But whatever you decide, know this." He looked at James and his voice grew rough. "I am proud of you, son, and have been for a long time."

He turned and strode from the room, but in the hall, he faltered, and his waiting manservant was beside him in an instant, taking his arm. Mercy was surprised Mr. Hain-Drake did not shake off the underling. Instead, he leaned on the younger man's arm as they crossed to the front door and disappeared from view.

Mercy turned back to James, watching his face with concern.

He sat looking stricken and amazed at once.

Elbows on the desk, he laid his head in his hands. The urge to wrap her arms around him tugged at her, but she resisted. He was not a little boy in need of comfort, however much he looked like one at the moment.

James glanced up. "I don't know what to say. Did he sound sincere to you, or am I fooling myself?"

"I believed him thoroughly sincere."

"I can hardly believe it. Words I had come to accept that I'd never hear from the man."

"He is proud of you, James. He is."

Tears brightened his green eyes into glittering emeralds. "I am only sorry illness is what brought him to say it."

Mercy's heart squeezed. Unable to resist any longer, she rose and stepped to his desk, laying a comforting hand on his shoulder. Still staring blindly ahead, he reached up and laid his hand on hers.

"Thank you for staying." His voice wavered between emotion and humor. "I would have thought I was imagining things were you not here as witness."

"What will you do?"

"I am not certain. I must think. But first I will insist he get the best medical care available. Or I will send someone to him."

Mercy nodded her understanding while questions arose in her mind. If James moved back to his parents' estate, taking Alice with him . . . would she ever see either one of them again? Would he ask her to continue on as Alice's governess in far-off Drayton Park? Could she really leave Ivy Hill, leave Aunt Matilda, Jane, and Rachel, to remain a lowly governess among veritable strangers?

It would be foolish to do so. And what about Joseph Kingsley?

CHAPTER
FORTY-SEVEN

The next day, James wrote to his father's old friend, Dr. Larson. He also wrote to a well-reputed physician he knew and asked if he would be willing to visit his father to spare the ill man the exertion of another trip, offering to pay him handsomely for his time.

Later that evening, Mr. Drake, Alice, and Mercy relaxed together in the quiet sitting room. Mercy read a book, while Mr. Drake and Alice played a game of draughts.

He looked from Alice to her and said, "How pleasant this is."

Mercy met his gaze and returned his smile. "Yes."

Game finished, Alice rose and sat next to Mercy on the lushly upholstered sofa near the fire. She patted the space on her opposite side. "Come and sit with us, Papa."

"Very well."

He rose and joined them on the sofa, Alice between them. The girl was already holding Mercy's hand and now grasped Mr. Drake's hand too.

Alice exhaled a wistful sigh. "How happy I am when we are all together. I wish it could always be like this. Don't you?"

Awkwardness prickled over Mercy. How much the girl assumed. But was it any wonder? She felt Mr. Drake watching her and glanced over, meeting his gaze above Alice's blond head.

She expected him to gently demur, to remind the girl she would not need a governess forever, though of course Miss Grove would always be a friend.

When he said nothing, Mercy opened her mouth to say something along those lines.

But Mr. Drake spoke before she could get the words out. "I agree it would be very nice, Alice."

Alice beamed up at him, then turned to include Mercy in the same gratified grin.

Iris knocked and popped her head in. "Time for your bath, Miss Alice. The tub is filled and ready."

Alice groaned but rose dutifully. Mercy made to rise as well.

Mr. Drake said, "Stay a moment, Mercy, if you would."

Once child and maid had gone, silence stretched between the two adults, broken only by the impatient ticking of the mantel clock. Mercy swallowed, feeling ill at ease now that Alice no longer sat between them, and wondering if he would move to another chair or if she should.

He shifted on the sofa to face her. "You see how attached Alice is to you."

"She is attached to you too. How sweet to hear her call you Papa."

"Yes, thank God. But I wonder if you see the situation as I do."

Confusion flared. "What do you mean? Do you fear it will become more difficult for Alice the longer I continue teaching her? For we both know I cannot remain her governess forever, especially if you move to Portsmouth."

"True." He considered, then added, "At least in Portsmouth, no one knows Alice as the daughter of Lieutenant Smith. Life might be easier there. She—we—could have a fresh start."

Had he already decided to move? Dread filled Mercy, and she silently formed an argument that would convince him to allow her to remain longer, even as a part of her knew that for Alice's sake, the cord should be cut as quickly as possible. Especially if he planned to return to his parents' home.

Voice low, he said, "You see how happy she is now. I hate the thought of hurting her. Or you, of course. Will you put me out of my misery, Miss Grove?"

Mercy held her breath. Here it was. He was asking her to let Alice go.

Mercy clasped her hands, hard, then said, "If you think it will hurt Alice more in the long term for me to remain, then I shall leave directly—end your misery and start mine." She chuckled feebly, hoping humor would cover her disappointment.

"I am not asking you to leave. I am asking you to marry me."

Mercy gasped. Had she misheard?

Whatever he saw in her expression made him wince. "I am far from perfect, we both know, but I hope you are charitable enough to allow that marriage to me would not be a completely miserable state."

When she remained silent, he looked hurt, and said, "Miss Grove, I know ours is not a love match, at least at present, but I would endeavor to make you happy, I promise you."

Mercy stared at him, unable to find any sensible words in her stunned mind.

He pressed on, "What better solution is there? You love Alice and she loves you. I have no wish to be the cause of pain to either of you."

She swallowed. "But to marry?"

"Yes. You deserve better than the life of a governess, a temporary position followed by an uncertain future. I had hoped an offer of marriage would seem a more appealing prospect, but my injured pride aside, I can see that it might not seem so, considering all you know of me."

Still she hesitated, thoughts jumbled. An immediate refusal died on her lips. Was he not right? Would she not give anything, or almost anything, to remain with Alice forever? Was this not what she longed for?

"I thought of asking you earlier," he said. "But we were not well acquainted then. Now, after living in close quarters and caring for

Alice together, I thought we had grown fond of one another. At least, I am certainly fond of you. Surely in time our relationship might grow into something . . . more. I already respect, admire, and care for you. And hopefully, you will be able to forgive my past indiscretions and come to respect and care for me as well."

She blinked, mind whirling. Where to start? "But your parents . . ." she blurted. "They know me as a governess."

"My parents like you already. They would be surprised but pleased, I think." He tilted his head to regard her more closely. "Is it marriage in general you disapprove of, or me in particular?"

"I am not opposed to marriage. Though I had thought it unlikely . . . until recently."

"That's right. . . . You were recently considering a proposal from that dry crust of an academic old enough to be your father. Surely marriage to me would not be as bad as that."

"He was not as old as my father—but his age is not why I refused him."

"Then, is there someone else?"

Was there? Did Mercy want to bring up Mr. Kingsley now, considering this opportunity to remain in Alice's life—to be her mother by marriage? Especially when it was by no means certain that Mr. Kingsley would ever feel himself in a position to marry again and ask for her hand?

But to marry a man she did not love, who seemed to shift his attentions from one woman to the next, while his heart remained untouched, as Jane herself had once mentioned?

But Mercy was fond of James, and they *were* friends . . .

A marriage of friendship. Would it be enough? Mercy was not sure.

He drew himself up. "Well, I see that I have stunned you." He rose and turned to her. "I will give you time to think it over. I am going to Drayton Park tomorrow for several days, to talk to my father's physician in person and see that he gives a second opinion. Might you give me an answer when I return?"

Mercy nodded and rose on wobbly legs.

He stepped forward, hesitated, and then took one of her long hands in his. "Until then." He pressed her fingers and quickly released her.

Mercy walked from the room into the reception hall, stopping midstride when she saw Joseph Kingsley standing there frozen, coat on, toolbox in hand. For a moment their gazes held. He said nothing, his veiled eyes difficult to read. Had he overheard?

Face heating in embarrassment, Mercy turned and crossed the hall, ascending the stairs without a word. He did not call after her, nor follow. Reaching her room at last, Mercy dropped heavily onto her bed. On the side table, she noticed her vase of faded lily of the valley, flowers dried and fallen to the floor.

What had happened? How had she gone from being a confirmed spinster to having three men express interest in her in recent months, and two actually ask for her hand? She should be grateful. Happy. Instead she felt sick to her stomach. *Oh, God, what should I do?*

In the morning, Mercy rose and dressed with care, feeling uneasy. She wanted to talk to Mr. Kingsley and find a way to bring up Mr. Drake's proposal, assuming he had overheard at least part of it. But what to say? She tried to recall her conversation with Mr. Drake—specifically what she had said. She remembered him asking her if there was someone else. And she had hesitated—not mentioning Mr. Kingsley, not saying a word. She had been too stupefied by his offer and the possibility of becoming Alice's stepmother.

Her reflection in the mirror did not please her. Her face looked pale, her eyes wide and worried. She turned to the bookcase Mr. Kingsley had made for her, running her fingers over the polished surface and smooth beveled edge, knowing his hands had done the same.

She took a deep breath and went downstairs, looking for him where she had seen him working last—in the passage beyond Mr. Drake's office.

But when she got there, she found only Aaron Kingsley at work, high on a ladder, reaching up to reposition a cornice piece. She hoped she would not startle him and cause him to fall.

"Mr. Kingsley?"

Manner friendly and open, Aaron said, "Good morning, Miss Grove. Did you need something?" He descended the ladder, a boyish smile on his face.

"I am sorry to disturb you. I am looking for Joseph. Can you tell me where to find him?"

Aaron shrugged. "He isn't here. He asked me to finish this project for him. Surprising, really, when he wanted to do most of the rest of the work himself, or at least oversee it. But now I'm tasked with finishing what he started. Won't take long. He was nearly done—had been for some time, truth be told. He was dragging his feet to complete it." He looked at her, eyes sparkling. "You wouldn't have any idea why, would you?"

When she hesitated, he went on, "At all events, I shall finish the last of it in a day or two, I imagine."

Mercy felt lightheaded. "Joseph is . . . not coming back?"

Aaron shook his head. "I don't think so. He's gone to start another project he's been putting off."

She blinked, mind scrambling to make sense of the news. To bring his work at the Fairmont almost to completion and then leave so abruptly after the scene of last evening? It could not be a coincidence.

She swallowed the lump in her throat. "Where has he gone?"

"Wilton House. Is there a message you'd like me to give him?"

Mercy hesitated. There was so much she longed to say to Joseph Kingsley, but nothing she could convey through his brother.

She shook her head. "No, thank you. Well. I will leave you to your work."

Mercy returned to her room, using the few minutes before Alice would arrive for lessons to compose herself. If she had thought she looked pale before, now a ghostly countenance greeted her in the mirror—the mirror Joseph Kingsley had thoughtfully found for her.

What had she done by remaining silent? And what should she do now?

Jane and Jack Avi went for a ride together—Jane on Athena and Jack Avi on a brown pony named Penny. They trotted down the hill, then carefully crossed the turnpike to reach the Fairmont. A chaise and four waited on the drive, horses harnessed and postilions preparing to depart.

She said, "This is where Bapu and I used to live, Jack Avi."

Jack Avi's eyes widened. "It's big."

"Yes."

He pursed his lips. "I like the farmhouse better."

Jane smiled at the boy.

James Drake came out the front door and handed a valise to one of the men.

He lifted a hand. "Good day to you, Jane and Jack Avi."

The two had briefly met at the wedding, but Jane was pleased James remembered her brother's name.

"Are you here to visit Mercy? I'm afraid I am about to leave for Portsmouth, but—"

"No. We're just out riding. I wanted Jack Avi to see the place. We won't keep you."

"I have a few minutes. How goes married life?"

"Very well, thank you. Gabriel is his old self again. And we just bought two thoroughbreds at the auction in Salisbury."

"Good for you. I was sorry to hear your father is . . ." With a glance at Jack Avi, he said, "Under the weather."

"Thank you, James. We hold out every hope of recovery."

Alice came outside, armed with a carrot. She asked if she could feed the pony and, when Jane nodded, tentatively approached the animal. She stroked its mane and offered Penny the treat. The two children laughed to see the long orange stick hanging from its mouth like a cigarillo.

"May I lead the pony to the horse trough for a drink?" Alice asked.

"All right," Jane replied. "But please come right back."

James turned to watch the children go off together, his expression wistful. "Look at the pair of us, both adding to our families in unexpected ways."

Jane nodded, thinking he might ask more about Jack Avi or her father's condition, but he did not. He seemed distracted.

She asked, "Everything all right with Alice?"

"Hm? Oh yes, she's happy and healthy."

"And how is Mercy?"

He looked up to consider the question. "Confused, I would say, right about now."

"Really? Why?"

"I asked her to marry me."

Jane felt her eyebrows shoot high. "That would explain it! Good heavens. Has she given you an answer?"

"Not yet. I'll be gone for a few days. Hopefully that will give her enough time to decide."

Jane glanced around, making sure no one was near. "You show excellent taste in asking her, but I had thought Mercy's affections lie in another direction."

"Do you mean the professor? She has already refused him."

"No, someone else. But I had better not speak out of turn."

He cocked his head to the side, expression serious. "Perhaps you had better."

When she hesitated, he said, "If you are referring to Joseph Kingsley, I believe he once admired her, but nothing came of it."

"Maybe he is shy. And remember, there is Alice to consider as well."

He frowned. "It was never my intention to put Mercy in an awkward position, nor to use Alice to manipulate her into accepting me. If I thought there was anything between her and Kingsley I would not have proposed. Truly."

"I believe you, James."

He took a step closer to her horse and lowered his voice. "We recently saw him kissing another woman, so I assumed his affections were now engaged elsewhere and Mercy's were free."

Jane stared at him. "Mercy saw this too?"

He nodded.

Jane searched her memory, surprised Mercy had not mentioned it. "I see . . ."

Alice and Jack Avi reappeared around the house, talking companionably. On the drive, a postilion mounted the lead horse.

"Well, safe journey, James. I will look forward to hearing what your future holds."

He nodded. "So will I."

Mercy came out to join Jane, Alice, and Jack Avi, and together they waved Mr. Drake on his way. From her vantage atop Athena, Jane watched her friend's face, uncertain if she should reveal what James had told her, especially with Alice there.

"Everything all right, Mercy?" she asked instead.

"Hm? Oh, yes. That is, I hope so. You haven't seen Joseph Kingsley today, have you?"

"No. I have not seen him, though Mr. Drake was just telling me that you and he recently saw him"—with a significant look at Alice, Jane finished—"*with* someone else."

Mercy must have read between the lines. "Did he? Oh! I wonder if that is why he . . ." She looked down, thinking, and let the sentence dangle. Then she said, "That was not Joseph we saw, by the way. It was one of his brothers."

"Oh? Mr. Drake thought it was."

"I did too, at first. I did not think to let Mr. Drake know we were wrong. Perhaps I should have."

"Yes. Perhaps," Jane murmured, unsure how much to say.

Something in her tone must have given her away, for Mercy tilted her head and asked, "What else did Mr. Drake tell you?"

"That you have a decision to make."

Mercy's face puckered. "Oh, Jane. Mr. Kingsley left. Abruptly. Right after Mr. Drake . . ." Glancing over and finding the children still distracted by the pony, Jane whispered, "Proposed. He's gone to work on some project at Wilton House, his brother said."

Athena stomped a restless hoof. "Shall I return with the gig and take you there?" Jane offered.

Mercy shook her head. "No. How forward that would be. I don't know if he's angry or hurt, or if he decided to simply make way for Mr. Drake. If he's left to avoid me, I won't chase after him."

"But if there has been a misunderstanding . . . ?"

Mercy shook her head. "Mr. Drake may have misunderstood, but I knew the truth and still I did not refuse him. If Mr. Kingsley is angry with me, I couldn't blame him. Oh, Jane, I don't know what to do."

Jane shifted in the saddle. "How do you feel about Mr. Drake?"

"We are friends. I am fond of him."

"And Mr. Kingsley?"

"I think I love him. But neither man has said he loves me."

Jane studied her in surprise. "Oh? Something you told me led me to believe Mr. Kingsley had."

Mercy shook her head again. "He has never said the words, but his looks, his many kindnesses—fitting out my room here on his own time, rescuing me from the smoke, defending me to Mr. Drake's friends, making me a bookcase out of oak . . ."

Jane felt her brows rise. "And you say he hasn't told you he loves you?"

Mercy nodded as realization dawned. "You're right. He has. But I don't know that Joseph will ever propose, and Mr. Drake has. Would I not be a fool to refuse him?"

Jane reached down, offering her gloved hand, and Mercy grasped it.

"I can't tell you what to do," Jane said. "But you, Mercy Grove, are the furthest thing from a fool."

CHAPTER

Forty-Eight

The next day, Thora came by and asked Jane if she wanted to go with her to visit Patrick, Hetty, and Betsey. She did indeed. They stopped by the dressmaker's shop to see if Eva wanted to join them, but she was busy with two out-of-town customers and couldn't get away.

Jane left Colin McFarland in charge, as she had done with more regularity since marrying Gabriel—although she knew the younger man still felt at loose ends when left on his own, especially if a problem arose with a guest, staff member, or supplier.

The Bell had been Jane's focus for most of the last year. She had poured a great deal of her energies, waking hours, and sometimes her sleeping hours into it. But the truth was, her heart wasn't there any longer. Her heart was with Gabriel Locke, and their horse farm, and their future.

She sighed and wondered again if it was time to hire an experienced manager, at least until Colin had more experience himself.

They rode in companionable silence, Thora now and again casting curious glances her way. Finally she asked, "Everything all right?"

"Hm? Oh yes."

"Difficult dividing your time between the inn and the farm, I imagine."

Her former mother-in-law knew her so well.

"Yes. But I am well, just a little tired."

Jane hesitated to bring up the subject that had been on her mind for weeks. She took a deep breath and launched in. "I know you don't approve of employing outside managers, and I agree family is best. But now that you and I and Patrick are all married and busy elsewhere . . ."

Thora grimaced. "Someone with fancy ideas moving in and changing everything, hiring a *fine* cook and wasting money on foolish falderals?" She sent Jane a wry glance. "Oh, wait. You've done all that already."

"I did not," Jane protested on a laugh. "Not the fine cook part."

Thora chuckled, and they rounded the bend into Wishford.

Jane considered and then said, "Of course, we would have to find someone like-minded and trustworthy, who would serve The Bell and make improvements gradually and only after consulting us."

"Someone like that would expect high wages, Jane."

She sighed again. "I know."

Jane looked toward the town as they approached and noticed a menacing column of smoke spiraling into the sky. Alarm twisted through her. It was probably just someone burning rubbish, she told herself.

She found her thoughts returning to the day before the coach contest, when she and Sir Timothy had been out riding and smelled smoke near Fairmont House, only to discover Mr. Drake's new stable building in flames. Sir Timothy had suspected arson, occurring as it had, right before the contest that would decide which hostelry should win the Royal Mail contract.

In the end, however, Mr. Drake had been content to let it pass as an accident—a cigar dropped by a careless builder, perhaps, or a stray spark from a lamp. Jane had never been fully satisfied by that explanation but had been so consumed with the pending contest and her struggles with The Bell, that she'd pushed it to the back of her mind.

"Look, Thora. Something is burning."

Thora frowned. "I don't like the looks of that."

She urged the horse to greater speed. "Maybe someone's brush fire got out of control."

The church bell clanged a warning signal as they turned up the first side street, following the column of smoke to its source.

Jane's heart pounded and her stomach clenched. *Oh no. Please, God, no. . . .*

For there at the end of the lane stood Patrick and Hetty's lodging house, one side engulfed in flames.

Several hours later, the fire had been put out, the water brigade disbanded, and neighbors began returning to their homes. Jane stood talking quietly to Talbot and Gabriel, who had come from Ivy Hill with several other men to fight the fire when word had reached them.

Jane noticed Patrick slump down on a tree stump a safe distance from the charred lodging house, exhausted, face and hands smeared with soot.

Hetty walked over and sat beside him, stretching one arm around his shoulders. The stray terrier came and sat at her feet, and she idly reached down and stroked its ears.

Thora stood at the edge of the property, bouncing Betsey in her arms to keep her safely away from the rubble. The girl chattered happily, blithely unaware of the tragedy surrounding her.

After giving the couple some time alone, Jane excused herself from the men and went over to speak to them. "I am so glad you are all right."

"That was what I was just telling Patrick," Hetty said with surprising pluck. "It's a setback, but at least none of us were hurt. That's what is most important."

"True," Patrick agreed, though he looked weary and defeated.

Talbot and Gabriel joined them. Talbot said, "We'll have to give it a day or two for the smoke to clear, and then we can go in and begin assessing the damage. Decide how best to proceed."

Gabriel added, "We could ask the Kingsley brothers to come over and take a look."

Two local magistrates, Lord Winspear and Sir Timothy, strode down the street with Wishford's current constable.

Approaching Patrick, Sir Timothy began, "We have good news and bad news."

"I've had enough bad," Patrick said. "I'll take the good."

Timothy nodded. "Very well. Mr. Phillips from the Crown has offered to pay damages."

Patrick's face stretched long with incredulity. "Mr. Phillips? Why would he?"

Instead of answering directly, Timothy turned to Jane and asked, "Do you recall the fire at the Fairmont before the mail coach contest? The damage to Mr. Drake's new stables?"

"Of course."

"Mr. Drake deemed it an accidental fire, but I was never fully convinced." He returned his gaze to Patrick. "We have just learned that Howard Phillips set both fires. He was overheard bragging about it in the public house after too many pints."

"No . . ." Jane breathed.

"Thunder and turf," Patrick exclaimed. "Why?"

Lord Winspear explained, "He heard his father grumbling about the Fairmont, and more recently Mr. Bell's lodging house. Complaining about the new competition. Mr. Phillips says he was only worrying aloud, never thought his son would do anything like this. He meant only to spur him to work harder to help make the Crown more profitable. But apparently that sounded like too much work to Howard. So he decided to deal with their competitors by setting fires."

Patrick muttered, "That little—" But Hetty shushed him just in time with a hand to his arm.

"What will happen to him?" Jane asked.

The older magistrate grimaced. "Prison or transportation, most likely. This is beyond the scope of the petty sessions and will likely be settled at the county assizes."

THE BRIDE OF IVY GREEN

"Poor Mr. and Mrs. Phillips."

"I agree," Timothy said. "It's a bad business."

Hetty nodded. "Bad for business, indeed."

The Talbots drove Patrick, Hetty, and Betsey back to The Bell, where Jane offered to fill baths and insisted they take the best room. They tried to protest, but Jane held firm, urging them to wash and rest, and saying they would talk more in the morning.

The next day, Patrick joined Jane at breakfast, eyes still red from the smoke. He carried Betsey with him to give Hetty another hour of much-needed sleep. How much marriage and fatherhood had changed him already.

Over toast and eggs, he fed Betsey from his own plate and asked humbly, "Jane, may we stay another night or two?"

Jane hesitated. "You could, but . . ."

He straightened, his expression growing more formal. "Forgive me. I should not have presumed. Are you expecting a full house tonight? If there are no rooms available, then we—"

"No, it isn't that. You are more than welcome to stay here. But not just for a few nights." She swallowed. "Patrick, would you please stay here . . . permanently?"

His brows rose. "What do you mean?"

"I would like to make you my partner. Fifty-fifty. I would stay involved for a year or two until the horse farm is up and running, but then you could use the profits to buy my share. After that, The Bell would be yours and Hetty's. As you've long wanted."

"Jane, are you sure?"

She nodded. "I know you had your heart set on managing your lodging house, so I will understand if you don't wish to come back here."

"A charred little lodging house compared to a large coaching inn? I am not an idiot, Jane."

"I know you are not, Patrick. I would not offer The Bell to you if I thought you were."

"But I thought you were determined to keep the place?"

"I was. Then. But my heart is not in it any longer. I want to pour my energies into helping Gabriel establish our farm and stables."

Patrick rolled his table napkin as he considered. "We already own the lodging house, such as it is. I suppose we could sell it or rent it out."

Jane nodded. "And with Mr. Phillips offering to pay for repairs, you won't be out anything. Or at least not much." She raised a hand. "But if you don't want to live here, or if Hetty prefers to remain in Wishford . . ."

"I will have to ask her what she wants to do."

"Yes. You two talk it over in private and let me know what you decide. If you agree, then we can meet with Mr. Coine and make the arrangement official."

"I wonder what Mamma would say," Patrick mused.

"She'll like having Betsey closer."

"That's true. And Mr. Locke? What does he say to all of this?"

"He said it is my decision."

"Wasn't he the one who convinced you to save The Bell yourself?"

Jane nodded. "He was. And he was right. At the time, I needed The Bell, and I think The Bell needed me. Working to save the inn brought me back to life after John's death, gave me a purpose. But I don't need to be the innkeeper of Ivy Hill any longer." She rose and grinned. "I am looking forward to being the horsewoman of Ivy Hill instead."

From her window, Mercy saw Mr. Drake's chaise arrive in the stable yard a few days later, returning from Portsmouth. Mercy looked in her mirror one last time and prayed, "Am I doing the right thing, Lord?"

Or was she a fool to refuse this second offer of marriage and perhaps her last? For she had neither seen nor heard from Joseph Kingsley again. And what about Alice? Had God not brought the girl into her life for a reason? Could she—should she—let her go?

Yet when Mercy thought about accepting James, Joseph's face appeared in her mind's eye and her heart ached.

Mercy gave James a few minutes to get settled and then went downstairs. She let herself into his office and closed the door.

He looked up, hope flaring in his expression. He set down his pen and rose.

"Welcome back." She gripped her hands together and began, "I am sorry to welcome you home with bad news, but . . ." Seeing his smile fall, she rushed on. "Howard Phillips set fire to Patrick Bell's lodging house while you were gone. He also confessed to setting the one here at your stables."

"Really?" His brows lowered. "I thought there was something odd about that young man. Is everyone all right?"

"No one was hurt, thankfully. But poor Mr. and Mrs. Phillips."

"Yes . . ." He nodded, eyes distant in thought.

"How did things go with your father?" Mercy asked and sat down, knowing even as she did so that she was beating around the bush.

He considered. "Very well, I would say. He took great pride in showing me his books and all his properties."

"I am glad to hear it. Does that mean you've decided to move back to Portsmouth?"

"I suppose that partially depends on you. Have you reached your decision?"

So much for beating around the bush. "I have." She drew in a shaky breath. "I am honored by your proposal, Mr. Drake. And tempted to accept. But that would be wrong for us both. You may not believe it now, but I am convinced you will meet someone and fall in love, more deeply than you ever loved Alice's mother, because you will have the rest of your lives together and not just a few stolen weeks."

He looked about to object, so she quickly added, "And I . . . love someone else."

"Joseph Kingsley?"

"Yes. How long have you known?"

James sat down. "I knew he admired you when you first came here. Couldn't miss how the man's gaze followed you wherever you went—and the stilted way he spoke of you, which said more about his high regard than any flowery speeches would have. But I assumed you didn't return his interest, since nothing came of it in all that time, day in and day out, the three of us in the same house. And then we saw him kissing that blond woman. I could see you felt betrayed, but I assumed you were finished with the man and vice versa."

"That was Aaron Kingsley, not Joseph. I mistook the one for the other, as you did, at first."

He reared his head back. "Are you quite certain?"

"Yes, in fact Aaron and Esther are engaged to be married."

"Oh." He ran a hand over his jaw. "Well then . . . why hasn't Joseph proposed to you? What is the fool waiting for?"

Mercy sighed. "He may admire me, but he thinks he is not educated enough, nor able to provide a comfortable home. Not *worthy*, I believe was the word he used."

James nodded. "I can understand that sentiment. You are a woman of inestimable worth, Mercy Grove, and the man you marry will have a great prize in you."

"Thank you. That is very kind of you to say."

"Not kind. True."

She looked away from his too-direct gaze. "I believe Joseph overheard your proposal, and that is why he left the Fairmont. He knows how fond I am of Alice and probably assumes marrying you is the answer to my prayers."

"But it isn't, is it?" he asked gently.

She shook her head. "I'm sorry."

He inhaled deeply. "Bad news for me, but good news for him."

"I am not sure he would agree."

"Well then, my dear Miss Grove, the power to convince him lies upon your lips."

Mercy's eyebrows shot up. What was he suggesting . . . ?

He raised a hand. "I meant, a word from your lips would be

enough to spur him to action." He tipped his head to one side, grinning impishly. "Though now I think on it, a kiss would spur him to action as well, if not better."

Heat rushed to Mercy's face.

He rose, green eyes glinting. "You are charming when you blush, Miss Grove. In fact, I had better summon Kingsley before I am tempted to take my own advice."

He dragged his gaze from her face and stepped to the door.

"But he's gone," she blurted. "Left to begin another project at Wilton House."

He turned back. "True, but on my way through Wilton I asked him here to collect his final wages. I believe he is inspecting his brother's work just around the corner." He grinned and swept from the room.

James certainly recovered quickly, she thought. With every receding footfall, Mercy's heart pounded hard.

She heard him call down the passageway, "Kingsley? Miss Grove would like a word with you in my office. Don't keep her waiting any longer, man."

Mercy flushed anew, and her pulse raced in anticipation. Would Mr. Kingsley think her too forward or presumptuous?

Joseph tentatively entered the room, hat in hand, questions written on his handsome face.

Her mouth went dry. "Close the door, if you would, Mr. Kingsley."

He kept his gaze on her as he slowly reached back and shut the door. He stood there, studying her with wary expectation. Was he afraid she was about to tell him she and Mr. Drake were marrying? Or would he feel betrayed that she had briefly considered James's offer, and rebuff her?

Mr. Drake's words ran again through her mind. *"The power to convince him lies upon your lips . . ."*

Joseph took a deep breath, as if bracing himself. "You wanted to speak with me, Miss Grove?"

The words lodged in her throat. She pressed her lips together and slowly moved forward, legs trembling and stomach knotted. She walked directly to him, then a half step closer, looking up into his face, gauging his reaction. When he didn't step back or pull away, she rose on tiptoes, lifting her mouth toward his. She flashed another tentative glance into his eyes, saw them widen and focus on her mouth. He seemed to be holding his breath. She leaned closer and pressed her lips to his. Slowly, softly, one second, two, three . . .

Then she lowered her feet to the floor and whispered, "That is all I wanted to say."

He released a ragged breath, his gaze fastened on hers. He lifted his hands and framed her face. "You're not marrying him?"

She shook her head. "I told him I could not."

"But it would give you the desire of your heart."

Again she shook her head. "*You* are the desire of my heart."

Light flashed in his eyes. He laid his forehead against hers and breathed, "Thank God."

He wrapped one muscular arm around her small waist and drew her close, the warmth of his body enveloping her. She laid a hand on his chest and felt his strong heartbeat. He cupped her cheek with his free hand and leaned down, pressing gentle kisses to her temple, her forehead, and finally her mouth. Then he angled his head the other way and kissed her deeply and firmly.

Again he laid his forehead against hers, catching his breath. Drawing back slightly, he looked into her eyes. "Mercy Grove, will you marry me? I will try to deserve you."

"Silly man. You already do. In fact, you deserve someone far better"—she gave him a teasing smile—"but I shall have to do."

CHAPTER
Forty-Nine

Mercy shared her joyful news with Aunt Matty, Jane, and Rachel. While she was at it, she also asked Rachel if she might teach reading at the circulating library, and her friend was quick to agree. Afterward, Mercy wrote to her parents to announce her engagement, asking them to come and meet Mr. Kingsley when they could. Meanwhile, she and Joseph met with Mr. Paley, who agreed to begin reading the banns as soon as possible.

Then Mercy made a decision. She sorted through her gowns, picked an old favorite, and went to see Eva Victor. When she neared the shop, she saw that the display window held hats, bonnets, and one pretty but simple daydress. On the wall hung a new small sign, adding her given name:

VICTORINE'S
MISS E. VICTOR, PROPRIETOR

Mercy let herself in and saw the dressmaker standing at the shop counter, packing a straw bonnet in a bandbox.

She looked up when Mercy entered. "Miss Grove, how are you?"

"Better than ever. I have just become engaged to marry Joseph Kingsley."

"That is excellent news," Eva replied, her hands in constant motion. "I am truly happy for you." She added a layer of tissue and covered the box.

Mercy smiled. "So am I." She looked again at the sparse display window, with its hats and single dress. "I understand you donated several things to the almshouse while I was out of town. Did you give away every one of your mentor's gowns?"

The woman waved a dismissive hand, then tied a string around the bandbox. "I decided it was time to display only things I have actually made myself."

"Well done. I applaud you." Mercy studied her face. "Eva, you're not leaving are you?"

Her hands finally stilled. "Honestly, I am not sure."

"I hope you stay." Mercy lifted the gown over her arm. "In fact, I came to ask if you might smarten this up for my wedding. It is one of my favorites, though it is rather plain."

Eva's mouth loosened. "I am surprised you would ask me, knowing what you know of me."

"My dear Miss Victor, none of us is perfect, and everyone deserves a second chance. I know it isn't the same as a commission for a new gown, but I hope it demonstrates my support, my . . . friendship."

Tears brightened Eva's eyes. "It does indeed."

And Mercy decided then and there that even if the gown ended up worse for the effort, she was glad she'd asked her.

Eva stepped around the counter and lifted Mercy's gown. "Let's see what we have here . . . Ah, yes. Simple but elegant. I could easily envision a few embellishments to the neckline and sleeves. Perhaps a ribbon at the waist."

"Nothing too showy, if you please."

Mercy had no wish to look the part of a fashionable London lady. She was a modest village woman of one and thirty years, soon to be a teacher again and a carpenter's wife. All roles she was overjoyed to fill and the only ones she longed for.

Mr. and Mrs. Grove wasted no time in traveling to Ivy Hill to meet Mr. Kingsley. After the quiet, awkward meeting, her parents granted their blessing.

Later, in private, her father told Mercy that he would have preferred a more learned man for his only daughter, but if she really loved him, he was happy for her and would not object. Her mother was unexpectedly gracious and accepting, not once bringing up Mr. Hollander.

The Grove and Kingsley families were already slightly acquainted, both having lived in Ivy Hill for decades, but they had never taken a meal together. Joseph's family invited Mercy and her parents to join them for dinner. The Kingsley home was not ostentatious in the least, but it was large, expertly crafted, and exceedingly well maintained.

When they arrived, the Kingsleys were all warmth and welcome. Mercy's father took to them immediately, while her mother seemed a bit overwhelmed by the boisterous brothers. After the meal, however, she and Mrs. Kingsley found a quiet corner for a pleasant conversation.

The next day, when Mercy and her parents sat down to discuss wedding plans, her mother began, "Mercy, Ivy Cottage is a bit small for a wedding breakfast. That is why your father and I married in London, out of my parents' house. However, if we limit the number we invite—"

"No, Mamma, I want everyone to be there. Everyone who wishes to be."

"Anyone who wishes may attend the wedding itself at church, of course, but fit everyone into our snug cottage, especially considering the size of the family you're marrying into? Impossible."

"That is all right, Mamma. I do not wish to have the breakfast in Ivy Cottage."

"But it is your home—or was, for many years. And just because a few things have not gone your way this last year does not negate the pleasant life we've given you here."

"You are right, Mamma. I have much to be thankful for. But it is

George and Helena's home now. I would like to have my wedding breakfast on Ivy Green. It is where I've always imagined it, in my heart of hearts, when I allowed myself to daydream that I might one day marry. I picture the gates of the back garden thrown wide and everyone I love spilling out onto the green—friends, family, children running and laughing. A banquet table and musicians . . ."

"Mercy, do be sensible. Consider what happened the day of Jane Bell's wedding. Matilda told me she originally wanted to hold her wedding breakfast in The Bell courtyard, but it rained, so everyone had to squeeze into the dining parlour and common coffee room!"

"And we managed perfectly well. It was lovely. But just because it rained on Jane's day does not mean it will rain on mine."

"Mercy, we live in England, and it has been an outstandingly wet year. One must expect it to rain."

Mercy supposed her mother was right. An outside wedding breakfast was a risk. But it was what she had always wanted—and now all the more, since she felt like a guest in Ivy Cottage, and not a warmly welcomed one.

Her mother continued, "Perhaps we could look into hiring the Fairmont. There would be sufficient room there, I imagine, and we could engage their cook—a French chef, I believe you said? I doubt Mrs. Timmons is up to the challenge herself. Would Mr. Drake accommodate us at a reduced rate, your being in his employ? Matilda did mention in her letter that he counted you as a friend and not merely a governess."

Generous Mr. Drake was unlikely to be offended by such a request, but Mercy did not want to ask him, nor would Mr. Kingsley be keen on him hosting their wedding breakfast, considering the man had proposed to her.

"Mr. Drake is busy learning all about his father's extensive business affairs. He has more pressing matters to deal with at the moment than my little wedding breakfast."

"Little? Hardly. It sounds as though you wish to invite everyone in the county! Oh, that you had been half as popular with gentlemen of good fortune as you seem to be with everyone else."

"Mamma. Mr. Kingsley is a successful builder."

"I know, my dear. We hear good reports of him. Still, I can't help but wish Mr. Drake had been the one to ask for your hand."

Mercy decided it would be wisest not to tell her he had.

Her mother went on. "I brought with me the handsome veil of Mechlin lace I wore at my own wedding." She lifted the bandbox beside her chair and extracted the item within. "The bonnet is not the latest style, but perhaps with some alteration . . . ?"

"It's lovely, Mamma. I would be honored to wear it."

"Now, as far as your gown . . ."

Mercy lifted her hand. "Don't worry, I have already spoken to our new modiste about it."

She did not wish to rob her mother of any pleasure but feared if Catherine Grove were involved, she would end up wearing a dress with many flounces and bows, more appropriate for a far younger bride—or even her young bridesmaid, Alice.

"Victorine's? I saw the shop when we arrived. Very well. I am relieved to hear you have the situation in hand, for your father and I must soon return to London for several important social events. We will return before the wedding to see to any last-minute details. And of course, we will take care of ordering the food before we go . . ."

They went on to talk over the menu, her mother making notes and lists of tasks for each of them. Then she spent the next two days talking with their cook, the baker, the florist, and the vicar.

On the morning of their departure, her mother asked, "Are you sure you don't want me to meet with the modiste before I go? We want you to look becoming on your special day."

"No, Mamma. You have done so much already, for which we both are very grateful." Mercy kissed her cheek.

Satisfied with the arrangements, Mercy's parents prepared to take their leave. Her father kissed her forehead.

Then her mother gathered her close and whispered, "I am so happy for you, Mercy. Truly."

Mr. Drake again traveled to Drayton Park to spend another few weeks with his father and meet with his lawyers. He took Alice with him this time but promised to return for the wedding. The staff managed as well as possible, but the Fairmont suffered without its host.

Mercy did what she could to help keep the place going during his lengthy absence, assisting the clerk in the office and answering guest questions. Mr. Kingsley stopped by on his way home from Wilton almost every night to have supper with her, talk about their respective days, and to kiss her good-night.

On three consecutive Sundays, Mr. Paley read the banns, and Mercy thrilled to hear her name paired with Joseph's, even as the attention embarrassed her. The warm July weeks passed quickly, and Mercy happily counted down the days until she would become Joseph's wife.

As promised, Mr. Drake and Alice returned from Portsmouth about a week before the wedding. After greetings were exchanged and valises stowed, Mr. Drake asked Mercy and Joseph to meet him in his office.

When they arrived, he congratulated them again. Then he smiled from one to the other. "Now, I would like you both to join me for a tour of the Fairmont." His gaze rested on Mercy. "That way, your soon-to-be bridegroom can show off all his excellent work and the many improvements he has made here."

Mr. Kingsley shifted from foot to foot, clearly uncomfortable. "There's no need, Mr. Drake. You have paid me well for my work; you owe me nothing more."

"I disagree, Mr. Kingsley. A man of your skills deserves to have his talents praised in the hearing of the woman he loves."

Mercy began to feel uncomfortable as well and said lightly, "It is all right, Mr. Drake. I am already convinced of his merits, I assure you."

"As you should be. Still, I hope you will oblige me."

Mercy looked at Joseph, who shrugged his acquiescence, though he still looked a little confused. After all, they were both already familiar with the Fairmont. "Very well."

Mr. Drake led them from floor to floor and room to room, pointing out not only the less-visible repairs and structural work the Kingsleys had done, but especially emphasizing Joseph's fine craftsmanship evident in the woodwork throughout the house.

"I can't take credit for all of this, Mr. Drake. Don't forget my brothers also played their part."

"I understand that, Joseph, but I also know that you were the one who worked the hardest and the longest. The one who was not satisfied to simply patch up the place, but saw to its improvement at every turn, crafting balustrades, chair spindles, cornices, and trim to match the style of the damaged originals, carving that fine moulding for the entry hall, the new mantelpieces, and more. Often on your own time. I know for a fact I have not come close to paying you all you're rightly due for your hours and skill."

Joseph waved a dismissive hand. "I don't mind. Wouldn't have been right to charge you for work you didn't even ask me to do. Not your fault another man's 'good enough' is rarely good enough for me.

"Besides, you know I was happy to spend the extra time here, especially these last few months." He looked significantly at Mercy as he said it, and the three shared a smile. "Being in Miss Grove's company was all the reward I wanted."

"Worked out well for you, I agree," James replied. "You have been richly rewarded with the hand of a fine woman."

"Exactly, sir. Which only proves my point—nothing further is required, in praise or pounds. You have been good to Mercy and me, and we appreciate all you have done for us both."

Mercy nodded. "He's right, Mr. Drake."

James shook his head. "I have done very little. You deserve so much more." His plaintive green eyes fixed on her, eyes so like Alice's, that Mercy's heart squeezed. She did love him in a familial way, she supposed. After all, he was a part of Alice. And Mercy could not look at the one without seeing the other.

On their way back to the office, James gestured across the hall. "I can see Mr. Kingsley's handiwork, his signature skill, everywhere I look, even if you cannot, because I recall what this old place looked like when I first bought it."

They reached the office. Once there, James opened a leather folder on the desk and pulled out an official-looking document.

"What is that?" Mercy asked warily.

"Consider it a wedding present." He watched her face, adding, "After our tour, do you not think that, with some little alteration carried out by your skilled husband, the Fairmont would make an excellent school, Miss Grove?"

Mercy stared at him, flummoxed. "No . . ." she breathed, heart pounding.

One golden eyebrow rose. "No?"

"No, I mean—you cannot."

"I already have." He pushed the document toward them. "Here is the deed. Made over to you for the purpose of housing your charity school. A place to 'educate most if not all of the parish's children, boys and girls, regardless of their ability to pay.'" He winked at her. "How'd I do?"

He had repeated an excerpt from a letter she'd written to him months ago about the proposed charity school.

"Almost verbatim," Mercy replied, pulse racing. "But I could not accept."

"Of course you can. It is for the school you've long dreamed of creating. And you and Mr. Kingsley might live here if you want, as schoolmistress and manager of grounds or whatever title you like. Together you can oversee the school and hire additional teachers and staff as needed." He tapped a second document in the folder. "You will see that I have also included an annuity to help with ongoing expenses, and I have verbal commitments from Winspear, Brockwell, and Bingley to help fund the school as well. And if more is needed, I have no doubt that, with your passion and campaigning skills, you will raise it without fail."

Mercy's chest tightened. She felt warm and lightheaded. "Mr. Drake. This is . . . inconceivable. Far beyond anything I could have imagined or asked for. I don't—"

"Mercy Grove," he interrupted, face suddenly solemn. "Not only did you ease my reconciliation with my father, but you have also given me my daughter, the greatest, most precious possession of my life. I know the sacrifice it was, when you gave me Mary-Alicia's letter, confirming my identity as Alice's father. I didn't understand it then, but I do now. I know what your honesty cost you when you came to see me that day. When I think of someone showing up and taking Alice from me . . . the loss, the bereavement . . . Now I understand what I took from you."

"You didn't take her from me. She is your daughter, Mr. Drake. And Mr. Coine said you likely would have won a custody case even without that letter."

"Perhaps, but regardless, you spared me both the uncertainty of my claim and an expensive and drawn-out court case during which Alice and I might have been separated for months, if not longer. Now I can look her in the eye and tell her without a doubt that she is my daughter. And though I don't deserve her, I am her father. I hope—I pray—to be worthy of that title. Difficult though it will be."

"But not impossible," Mercy said. "For nothing is impossible with God." She held up the deed. "As this proves."

She glanced at Joseph, saw him standing there, shoulders tense and expression somber.

She shook her head. "Though I still cannot accept it."

"Miss Grove, I know a building can never take Alice's place. Yet you lost not only Alice, but also your precious school at Ivy Cottage, as well as your dream of opening a much larger charity school. It is in my power to restore at least that dream to you. Please don't deny me."

Mercy glanced again at Joseph, who had yet to say a word. "I should like to speak to Mr. Kingsley in private before I decide."

"Of course. I will step out. Take your time. But I hope, Mr. Kingsley, you will not refuse for pride's sake. Not when you know what it will mean to your wife."

Joseph nodded. "I will consider what you say, Mr. Drake."

When the door closed behind him, Mercy turned to her beloved. "Can you believe it? Is it not amazing?"

"Yes. And for myself, he is right. I would refuse. It is too much. The thought of being beholden to any man for the rest of my life . . . Not to mention the taxes on such a place!" He quirked his lip, attempting to lighten the moment with humor.

"You're right. It is too much. Shall I refuse him?"

He sighed, thinking. "You have already refused him once, when he asked to marry you. . . ."

Mercy dipped her head. "Yes."

"For which I am forever grateful." Joseph looked at her from beneath a fall of sandy hair. "Not having a change of heart now, I hope?"

"Never."

"I know how much you want this school. And what I want most in this world, Mercy Grove, is to see you happy."

She rested her fingers on his chest. "I am happy."

He laid his hand over hers and pressed a kiss to her temple. "Then I'd say both God and Mr. Drake have blessed us beyond measure."

"I agree."

"So the least we can do is take this old house off his hands if he wants us to." He grinned, adding, "And here I hesitated to propose because we would have no house to live in." He wrapped his free arm around her waist, drawing her close. "Well, there's that problem sorted."

Mercy laughed with joy and kissed him.

Mercy and Joseph stood beside Mr. Drake while he made the stunning announcement to his staff. The Fairmont would cease to operate as a hotel and become a charity boarding school, operated by Mercy and Joseph Kingsley. He assured them that the closure did not reflect poorly on their performance, but rather that he would be too busy managing the much larger Hain-Drake interests to give the rural hotel the attention it deserved.

To his credit, Mr. Drake offered positions in Southampton and Portsmouth to anyone willing to relocate. The chef, porter, clerk, and several others accepted. The horsemen and postilions would need to find new jobs, but thankfully Mercy would be able to keep on Iris and Mrs. Callard.

The staff's astonished reactions mirrored her own feelings. Mercy could hardly believe the school she'd long hoped and prayed for would soon become a reality.

Mercy planned to spend the eve of her wedding in Ivy Cottage at her mother's request. But she invited Jane and Rachel to spend the night before that with her at the Fairmont. Her room was too small, so Mercy selected one of the larger rooms on the first floor with a bed wide enough to easily accommodate all three of them.

In some ways, it felt like old times, the three friends sleeping over, staying up late in their long white nightdresses, talking, laughing, and sharing secrets. In other ways, so very much had changed.

After Iris delivered hot chocolate and slices of cake, Mercy told Jane and Rachel her news about the Fairmont.

Jane's mouth fell wide. "I am all astonishment! Of course I am relieved to know there will be a school so close to Ivy Hill. Now we won't have to send Jack Avi away to be educated. But that James would give you the Fairmont . . . ?" She shook her head in awe.

"Do you mind, Jane? It was your home, after all."

"Not for many years. When I think of the former state of the place—abandoned, neglected, falling into ruin—and now . . . ? Repaired and improved. First as a hotel and soon to be a school? It's astounding, really. And if I had to choose between a hotel to compete with The Bell and the school my dear friend has longed for these many years, you know which I would choose. I am not sorry to lose the competition."

Mercy watched her face and asked gently, "Are you not?"

Jane hesitated, and tears brightened her eyes. "I suppose I am a little sorry. Sorry to lose James. He has been a good friend to me, and I shall miss him."

Mercy nodded. "As shall I. And Alice, of course."

Rachel took her hand. "Will you be all right?"

Mercy nodded, tears now filling her own eyes. "I will. Alice is fond of me, I know, and I will miss her, but she will be happy with her father. Those two have bonded more closely than I ever dared hope. And she is attached to his mother, sister, and new cousins as well. Truly, it does my heart good to see her surrounded by such a loving family."

Rachel squeezed her fingers. "Then we will pray that God will bless you and Mr. Kingsley with children of your own—and soon."

"Mr. Kingsley promises to strive toward that end." Mercy's face flushed, and she ducked her head.

Jane chuckled and then rose. "That reminds me, we have a gift for you . . ." She stepped to her valise, returning a moment later with a box tied with ribbon.

Mercy opened it and found inside a lovely, finely embroidered nightdress and dressing gown. She felt her face heat again.

Rachel bit her lip, eyes sparkling. "On that note, I would like you two to be the first to know—after Timothy, of course. We are expecting a child."

"That's wonderful!" Mercy exclaimed, kissing her cheek.

Rachel touched Jane's arm. "I hope that doesn't make you sad, Jane."

"No. I am thoroughly happy for you both."

Jane drew in a long breath. "And I suppose this is a good time to tell you that with my father's tenuous health, he has asked Gabriel and me to care for Jack Avi after he's gone. He wants me to raise him not as his guardian or sister, but as his . . . mother."

Mercy clasped her hand. "How like God to work something so good and right from the sad situation with your father."

Sitting cross-legged on the big bed, the three held hands in a misshapen triangle—heart-shaped, perhaps. They smiled from one to the other even as tears wet their cheeks.

"God has blessed each of us," Rachel said.

Jane and Mercy nodded.

"He has indeed."

CHAPTER

FIFTY

At the following night's meeting of the Ladies Tea and Knitting Society, Jane sat beside Rachel. The new Lady Brockwell attended less frequently since marrying but had made an effort to be there for Mercy's sake.

The women gathered around the bride-to-be, asking about the next day's festivities—if she still planned to hold the wedding breakfast on the green, what was on the menu, and what she would wear.

Jane and Rachel listened with interest as well. The night before, the three of them had talked briefly about plans for the wedding, but Mercy had said little about her dress. Jane assumed Mrs. Grove had insisted on some fancy gown Mercy was not thrilled about, so she had not pressed her for details, focusing on happy topics instead. In fact, the news of James giving Mercy the Fairmont had chased more ordinary subjects from her mind.

Now Mercy patiently answered everyone's questions, bemused by all the attention. She replied that she still hoped to have the wedding breakfast on Ivy Green, weather permitting, assured them they were all welcome, and finished by saying, "And I plan to wear one of my favorite old gowns. I did, however, take it to our dressmaker and asked her to smarten it up a bit."

"Really?" Jane asked, taken aback. "I assumed your mother would insist on a new gown."

Mercy shrugged. "She offered, but I told her I had already asked Miss Victor to help with the dress. She is still working on it as we speak. I will pick it up first thing in the morning."

Jane and Rachel exchanged looks of concern—surprised Mercy had done so when they knew Eva was not as skilled as first believed.

Mrs. Burlingame nodded her approval. "Very practical. I wore my best dress when I married."

"So did I," Mrs. Klein replied.

Mrs. O'Brien raised her hand. "Me too."

"I still wear my wedding dress," Miss Morris announced.

They all looked at the unmarried woman in astonishment.

Becky's dimple appeared. "At least, the dress I plan to wear if I ever do get married."

The women laughed, as she had clearly intended them to.

The meeting continued with talk of other things, including the news that the Earl's Menagerie and Traveling Players had returned to Ivy Hill to pick up the trunks and wagons they'd stored in the tithe barn. The troupe would be leaving Wiltshire the following day.

Later, after the meeting adjourned, Rachel, Jane, Matilda, and the Miss Cooks lingered, talking together in whispered consultation. Mercy was their esteemed leader and friend, of whom they were all deeply fond. There must be some way to do better for her than an old gown refurbished by inexperienced hands.

Eva sat in her workroom, shadows lengthening. She would normally still have plenty of sunlight to work by at this time of day, but the weather had been grey and cloudy since dawn. She would have to light the lamps soon.

Eva thought about Miss Grove's plan to hold her wedding breakfast outside on the village green tomorrow. She hoped it wouldn't rain.

Ah well, she thought. At least if it did and the bride's dress was ruined, it would not be much of a loss.

Eva set down her sewing, pressing her burning eyes closed. Miss Grove's request to embellish her old gown had seemed more feasible than making a whole new dress, so she had agreed. But now, she feared, even this project was beyond her. The temptation to give up rose, but she resisted it. She would not be the one to rain on Mercy's big day.

Her father's troupe had returned to pick up their stored belongings and would be leaving Ivy Hill for good the next day. Eva needed to decide what to do by then—to stay, or to go with them. But first to finish this dress . . . Mercy had come to pick it up a few days earlier, but Eva had to apologize and ask for more time. Kind Miss Grove had not complained.

Determined to stay up all night if need be, Eva stretched her neck side to side, forward and back, then bent to her sewing once more.

A knock on her door startled her. It was past regular business hours. Might it be a potential customer? She doubted it. Especially not on the evening the Ladies Tea and Knitting Society met. For a moment, she considered ignoring the knock. But perhaps it was Hetty or her father. Or Mrs. Mennell come with more mending or news. She hoped Mrs. Hornebolt's cold had not worsened.

She rose, but before she could reach the door, Jane Locke and Lady Brockwell briskly entered the shop, clearly bent on some officious purpose. Eva steeled herself. Had they been sent by the other women to ask her to leave Ivy Hill?

"Good evening, Eva," Jane said. "Did you know Rachel here is an excellent seamstress? Very skilled with embroidery and fancy work."

"Perhaps," Rachel demurred, "but I have never made something as complicated as a formal gown." She turned to her ladies' maid behind her. "So I've asked Jemima to join us. She is a dab-hand with a needle."

Eva blinked in confusion. Were the women suggesting they take over the shop? Replace her? They no doubt could.

The Miss Cooks came in next, armed with lace and needles.

Judith said, "I think this piece would look lovely across the neckline of Mercy's gown."

Eva stammered, "But . . . there is no place for such a piece."

"Oh, you mistake us," Charlotte said, gesturing to Mercy's old gown. "Judy wasn't suggesting adding it to that hodgepodge."

Jane added more gently, "We're here to help you make a new gown."

Eva hesitated. Clearly the ladies had caught wind of Mercy's economical plans for her wedding dress and decided they could do better.

"By tomorrow? You must be mad," Eva said. "Even with the six of us, it would take too long. Have any of you constructed a formal gown from start to finish before?"

Around the room, heads shook no.

A voice from behind called out, "Well, I have. Hundreds of times."

Eva whirled. In the doorway stood Louise Shabner, the former dressmaker of Ivy Hill.

Eva raised her hands. "But when I hinted I needed help with Justina Brockwell's gown, you refused. Insisted you were retired."

"True. This, however, is for our dear Mercy."

"How did you even know to come here tonight?"

Mrs. Shabner gestured across the street. "Matilda borrowed The Bell's fly and rode over to fetch me. She dropped me off and is returning the horse and carriage now."

Seeing the dressmaker, an idea struck Eva. She hurried to her workroom and brought forth the gown she'd begun for Justina Brockwell. The ivory underdress had proved too large and long for the young woman, but it was beautiful material.

"Might this give us a starting point?" Eva produced her drawings and the netting and trimmings as well.

They put the gown on a dress form and Mrs. Shabner studied it. "The center line is off. The darts, the seams . . ."

Mortification singed Eva's face.

Then Mrs. Shabner turned her attention to the design and detail drawings.

"But these are excellent. Lots of potential here."

Eva held up a veiled bonnet. "I made over this bonnet from an old one of her mother's."

"Lovely," Mrs. Shabner breathed, and passed it around for the others to see.

The door opened again, and the elder Miss Grove came huffing and puffing inside. "Did I miss anything?"

"No," Rachel said. "You're just in time."

Soon lamps were lit, and the women set to work.

Mrs. Shabner took the lead on reconstructing the underdress, then creating the netting overlay, working from Mercy's old dress for size. She delegated the simpler but time-consuming seams to the less skilled among them, like Jane and Eva. While the finer needlewomen like Rachel, Jemima, and the Miss Cooks helped with the embroidery.

A few hours later, however, Eva could see the women's initial enthusiasm waning. There was a great deal to do, and progress was slow. The workroom table was covered with material in various stages of pinning and cutting. And the floor was littered with scraps of satin, netting, and cambric. Mrs. Shabner had decreed Mercy would also need a new gored petticoat to support the shape of the dress.

The Miss Cooks were the first to beg off. Judith said, "I am sorry, my dears, but our old eyes and old bones can't continue. I cannot remember the last time we were awake at midnight."

Louise scowled. "Well, go if you're going, you two. Don't stand around distracting the rest of us. We still have a great deal to do."

When the Miss Cooks departed, Rachel showed Eva how to embroider the embellishments. Eva sat down to work, though far more slowly than did Lady Brockwell.

An hour later, Miss Matty fell asleep on the shop's sofa, half buried under a heap of fabric remnants that served as her blanket. They let her sleep. A short while later, Eva found Mrs. Shabner, head down on folded arms over the workroom table.

"Mrs. Shabner," Eva whispered gently. "Why don't you go upstairs and rest in my bed for a little while? It will do you a world of good."

She rose and yawned. "Very well. But only for half an hour or so. Then wake me and I'll help with the trimming."

"I shall."

Eva returned to her chair beside Jane, Rachel, and Jemima and resumed her work. Her eyes had been burning before the ladies had even arrived, and now the inside of her lids were on fire. They began to water, blurring her vision too much to see the tiny stitches. She set her work in her lap and decided to close her eyes, just for a few minutes.

Early in the morning, Mercy walked down Potters Lane toward the High Street to pick up her dress. She had spent the night in Ivy Cottage with her parents. How astounded they had been to learn about the Fairmont and plans for the school. However, Mercy had been disappointed not to spend the evening with her aunt, who had gone to Wishford to visit Louise Shabner for some reason.

Mercy would have liked to pick up her dress a few days earlier, but when she'd called in, a harried-looking Miss Victor had apologized and said she was still working on it. She prayed it was ready now.

Reaching the shop, Mercy knocked softly and tentatively opened the door. The interior was dim, the shutters and curtain still closed, the lamps gone out.

"I'm sorry. I must be early," she whispered. She paused just over the threshold, her eyes adjusting to the faint light. Inside the shop, she was surprised to see several ladies in various postures of repose, asleep, surrounded by mounds of material spread all over the room. There was Jane, Rachel, her maid, and Miss Victor. And . . . was that Aunt Matty asleep on the sofa?

"My goodness," Mercy said quietly. "What are all of you doing here?"

Eva blinked awake and straightened. "Oh heavens. I did not mean to fall asleep."

Rachel rubbed her eyes. "Nor the rest of us, I imagine. It's all right. We're nearly finished."

"You kept working after I fell asleep?" the dressmaker lamented. "I feel terrible."

"No need. It was my pleasure," Rachel said. "I enjoy sewing."

Mercy looked from woman to woman, confused. "I know my old dress was not fashionable, but . . . *all* of you had to help? It must have been in worse condition than I thought."

"It wasn't *so* bad," Jane began. "But—"

From above came the sound of loud snoring.

Mercy looked up the narrow stairs, perplexed. "Um . . . Eva? Is that a man I hear upstairs?"

Eva chuckled. "No, that is Mrs. Shabner. I sent her up to my bed for a few hours sleep."

"She helped as well?"

"Yes, and the Miss Cooks, and your aunt. They were at it until the wee hours."

"Gracious."

Rachel rose, smiling. "Come, Mercy. Let's try on the dress. That way, if we need to take it in a bit more, we'll still have time to do so."

Miss Victor searched for her watch pin. "What time is it?"

"Nearly eight."

"The wedding is in two hours!" Eva exclaimed, gathering up spare material. "Now where is that ribbon sash . . . ?"

Mercy said, "*You* are counting the hours? What about me? I am so nervous."

Jane squeezed her hand. "All will be well."

Mercy met her gaze. "If it does not rain. I almost wish now I had planned to have it at the Fairmont. But I have so long dreamt of having it on the green."

Rachel's lady's maid, Jemima, spoke up. "I will dash to Brockwell Court for the curling irons. I do hope you will let me dress your hair, Miss Grove?"

"If you would like. Thank you."

Rachel smiled. "Oh, yes, Jemima. Excellent idea."

After the maid hurried out, the other women assisted Mercy off with her daydress and helped her step into the new half petticoat. They then positioned her before the long cheval glass.

"Close your eyes, Mercy," Rachel said.

Considering her discomfort with mirrors, Mercy was happy to comply. Even so, she asked, "Why? Is the dress so altered?"

"Just close your eyes."

"Very well."

The ladies helped Mercy step into the gown, then raised it, the fabric gliding with luxurious silkiness over her hips. They guided her arms through the sleeves and began lacing the waist and fastening the buttons.

"Keep them closed," Jane insisted.

"I am, I am."

Someone tied a ribbon around the waist and fashioned a bow. "Wait," Eva said. "The bonnet."

Mercy asked, "My mother's old bonnet, right?"

"Shh . . ."

She heard whispering and rustling. Something was settled upon her head, and she felt a fluttering curtain of lace around her neck and shoulders.

"There. All right, Mercy. Open your eyes."

Mercy tentatively did so, turning first to peer at the women. She noticed them looking at each other with eager, suppressed smiles. Had they pulled a joke on her? She turned toward the mirror, and the tolerant little grin she wore faded. Her eyes widened, and her lips parted. She looked at her reflection in disbelief, then looked again at her friends. Tears blurred her vision.

"Oh no," Rachel said. "Do you not like it?"

"I . . . This isn't my dress. I don't know what to say. It's beautiful. Too beautiful for me."

"Nonsense," Jane soothed. "You are beautiful, Mercy."

She noticed Aunt Matty sitting up, eyes alight. "I agree. Always have been and always will be, my dear. And that dress . . . It's perfect for you."

The gown of fine net over ivory satin nipped in under the bosom in a waist-defining style, which emphasized Mercy's slender torso before flaring out over her feminine, curvy backside. Exquisite embroidery ornamented the hem. The vee neckline, with an inset of fine lace, flattered her delicate collarbones and modest bosom. The lace complemented her mother's veil flowing from a new ivory bonnet. Mercy blinked to better focus. The woman staring back at her looked elegant, graceful, and almost . . . beautiful.

She wondered uneasily how much of her governess's wages this gown would consume, but she said only, "This lace is lovely."

"The Miss Cooks' work. And the women of the Ladies Tea and Knitting Society contributed toward the new bonnet, slippers, and trimmings."

"Slippers!" Eva tapped her forehead in dismay. "I nearly forgot."

She retrieved a pair of dainty satin slippers in ivory and gold and placed them on the floor before Mercy. Mercy kicked off her old shoes and slipped into them.

"There you are. A perfect fit." Eva grinned and added in a French accent, "*Voilà! Cendrillion.*"

Mercy grinned. "At the moment, I certainly feel like Cinderella."

Mrs. Shabner shuffled downstairs and stood on the bottom step, eyes misting. "Beautiful. As every bride should be on her wedding day."

"Thank you for your help, Mrs. Shabner."

The older woman nodded. "Worth coming out of retirement for, I assure you."

CHAPTER

Fifty-One

Her aunt beside her, Mercy walked back to Ivy Cottage in her new dress, hair curled and styled. Excitement tingled her stomach—until she looked up at the grey sky. *Please, God, not rain.*

Aunt Matty opened the door for her and followed her inside, dimples creasing her cheeks. "I want to be there when Catherine sees you."

Catherine Grove sat in the drawing room, talking to Helena. She turned as Mercy entered.

"There you are, Mercy. I wondered where . . ." Her words trailed away, and she stared, mouth parted.

"My dear, you look so beautiful." Tears brightened her mother's eyes, and Mercy felt answering tears fill hers. She could not re-member her mother ever saying so before.

"Your dress is exquisite," Helena said. "Surprisingly so."

"Thank you," Mercy said. "I quite agree."

Her mother rose and stepped forward, taking her hands. "I know I have disappointed you in many ways over the years, Mercy, but I love you, and I am proud to be your mother. Today and always."

"Thank you, Mamma."

Her mother's voice thickened. "I don't want to lose you."

"You won't. You may visit Mr. Kingsley and me whenever you

like. We shall have rooms to spare at the Fairmont, if you don't mind the noise of many children about the place."

Hope flared in her mother's eyes. "Grandchildren?"

Mercy smiled. "Hopefully those too."

After the women left, Eva splashed cold water on her face, put on an apron, and began to clean, determined to restore order after the chaotic late-night sewing session. She had yet to decide for sure, but *if* she was going to quit Ivy Hill, she wouldn't leave the shop in disarray.

She gathered an armful of material and carried it to the back room. Then another. Then she swept the floor. A short while later, Eva stood in the open doorway, sweeping dust outside. She paused, glancing across the street toward The Bell, hoping for a glimpse of Jack Gander on his route.

There came the Quicksilver right on time, Jack standing on the back, proud bearing, handsome. He lifted his horn and played the arrival signal. But all too soon, she knew, he would play the signal to depart.

Her father came striding around the corner from the direction of the tithe barn. "Good morning, Eva. You're up bright and early."

"Yes, I suppose I am." She chuckled to herself, as she had not yet been to bed.

"I've come to ask if you've decided what you will do, my dear." His brow creased into apologetic lines. "I don't mean to pressure you, but the troupe must pull out this afternoon. We have remained too long as it is and shall have to drive through the night to reach the next stop on time."

Eva's stomach sank. "I understand." She hesitated, emotions whirling. Without intending to, her gaze returned to the mail coach. To Jack Gander.

Her father followed the direction of her gaze to The Bell. "I can see why you'd hesitate to leave, with your dear sister right across the street, helping her husband manage the inn. And of course there's sweet little Betsey as well."

His gaze returned to her face. "So I will not presume you plan to return to the troupe, though of course a part of me wishes you would."

"Only a part?"

He pursed his lips in thought. "I have missed you and your sister terribly, I don't deny. And selfishly, I would love nothing more than the comfort of my children near me again. But I have always regretted that you girls never had a real home. When your mother was alive, wherever she was, *was* home. But after she died . . ."

"I know."

"Seeing you and Hen here now, I think you have a home."

"Hen does indeed. I am still trying to find my place."

"Are you? You seem very at home here to me."

"You know, I suppose I do. It is surprising, considering I came here under false pretenses. But I have asked forgiveness of God, as well as the women here. And several have offered me their friendship. I am thankful."

"What did you say of yourself that was so false? Your mother was French, and you grew up eating French food and listening to scoldings in her native tongue when vexed. You *were* called Victorine, at least by me. And you have sewn clothes and costumes for years. You came here with good intentions—to open a shop in your mother's and Martine's memory. Nothing wrong with that."

"Thank you, Papa. Not everyone takes such a charitable view of my selling Martine's gowns as my own. Even so, I appreciate your understanding more than you know."

He pressed her hand. "Well. Take a little more time to consider. I will stop by again after the wedding, all right?"

"Yes, thank you."

Eva returned to the shop, tidying the apartment upstairs as well as the workroom below. A knock sounded, and Eva paused in her cleaning to answer it.

The older mantua-maker stood there, dressed for the wedding.

"Mrs. Shabner. I didn't expect to see you again."

"No, I imagine not." She looked at Eva's apron. "Not going to Mercy's wedding?"

"I hadn't planned to, no."

The woman humphed her disapproval. "Well, I thought it was time you and I talked. In private."

Had her landlady come to evict her? If so, Eva could not blame her.

"When I was here helping with Mercy's gown, I took the opportunity to study your work. Your embellishments on her old gown were second rate at best. I also looked at the daydresses you've begun to make. Simple design. Simple pattern. Imperfect construction. Too much fabric allowance, too wide at the hems, and the ties! La! Have you never heard of a button? And don't get me started on your stitching." She *tsk*ed and shook her head.

Eva looked down at the floor.

"As I mentioned, your drawings for the ill-fated gown for Miss Brockwell were most impressive," she said. "Though your execution left a great deal wanting."

"I know," Eva murmured, hoping acquiescence would end the woman's reprimand more quickly.

"You said yourself that you have had no formal apprenticeship," Mrs. Shabner added. "Quite presumptuous, if I may say so, to hang out your shingle as a dressmaker having never been apprenticed to an experienced mantua-maker. I myself worked as Mrs. Warwick's apprentice for four years. And she would make me unravel every stitch if she found an imperfect one."

Bon sang! Eva thought. Would this tirade never end? If she was going to evict her, could she not get to it already? Eva knew she deserved it, but must the woman heap shame and criticism upon her head?

"You are young and pretty, I grant you. And people *like* you, which is surprising really, considering your rough start here."

"Yes," Eva acknowledged. "I am surprised as well."

"It says a lot about your amiable nature. A dressmaker's ability to develop relationships with customers, to earn their loyalty, is worth a great deal. And you have a talent for design and millinery. Your new bonnets and hats are excellent."

Was this the woman's way of letting her down gently? Trying to soften the blow?

"Do you want me to leave, Mrs. Shabner?" Eva asked. "I have been considering doing that very thing, so if that is what you've come to tell me, I will understand."

"No. I am here to offer you a bargain."

Eva looked up warily. "What sort of bargain?"

The older woman extracted a card from her pelisse pocket and held it up for Eva's inspection.

On it was neatly written *Misses Shabner & Victor, Dressmakers and Milliners.*

Eva looked up, mouth parted. "Are you serious?"

"I am. You would serve as my apprentice, of sorts. But you are not a true beginner, so I think a year will do, if you are agreeable."

"But . . . I thought you were happily retired?"

"Retired, yes. Happy, no. Bored out of my wits."

"Would you live here with me?"

"Yes. Too inconvenient to drive back and forth from Wishford with Mrs. Burlingame, and I have no horse of my own. I should warn you that I've been told I snore. Exaggerated, no doubt. Though now I think on it, my last girl slept with cotton wool in her ears."

Eva bit her lip.

"If the shop does well, I will pay you better wages than the usual adolescent apprentice. So in time, if you prefer, you could afford to rent out the apartment over the circulating library, where our former banker lived. With the two of us working together, I have every confidence the shop will be profitable."

Eva's thoughts whirled. "Do you indeed?"

"Yes." Louise Shabner stuck out her hand. "So . . . have we a bargain?"

CHAPTER
FIFTY-TWO

On a cloudy summer morning, Miss Mercy Grove left spinsterhood behind to marry the man she loved. On that day, she gained not only a tall, handsome husband, but also many brothers, sisters-in-law, nieces, and nephews.

After the wedding in St. Anne's, the bride and groom walked hand in hand down Church Street, followed by friends and family in a festive parade of well-wishers.

Mercy winced up at the sky, seeing the ominous clouds above. Would a rainstorm ruin her wedding breakfast on Ivy Green as her mother predicted? It was too late to move everything to the Fairmont now. *Plop.* A drop of rain hit her nose. *Oh no. Lord, please.*

Joseph squeezed her hand, clearly guessing the direction of her thoughts.

Hopefully their guests could at least eat something before the rain chased them home.

Together, she and her bridegroom led the way past Ivy Cottage and its walled garden, festooned with garlands of flowers and ivy as she'd always imagined. Reaching the adjoining green, Mercy drew up short and turned to gape at Joseph.

He looked as surprised as she was.

There on Ivy Green stood a massive tent bearing patches of

every color of the rainbow. This must be the Earl's Menagerie marquee, Mercy realized. Its canvas sides were tied up to create an open-sided shelter. Mercy had heard the tent had been damaged in the recent hailstorm, but somehow it had been repaired.

Relief and gratitude washed over her, her stomach tickling with delight. She smiled deeply into Joseph's eyes, then looked around for someone from the troupe to thank.

Instead, among the first to follow them onto the green were several women from the Ladies Tea and Knitting Society.

Mercy gestured toward the marquee. "I didn't know this would be here. I thought the menagerie tent was too damaged to use."

"It was," Mrs. Snyder said. "But several of us ladies joined forces with the troupe and the Kingsley brothers and stayed up half the night repairing it."

Mrs. Klein said, "As you can see, our sewing abilities leave something to be desired." She pointed up at the hodgepodge of patches. "Be glad we weren't the ones sewing your dress."

Mercy slowly shook her head. "I can't believe it."

"Oh, Mercy." Mrs. O'Brien squeezed her hand. "You know we would do anything for you. How could we not, when you have done so much for us?"

The bride hugged one after the other, and then walked over to thank members of the troupe, lingering on the far edge of the green. She invited them to join in, but most were hesitant to intrude. They did, however, accept the refreshments brought over to them by Mr. Basu and Agnes.

Beneath one end of the tent, a buffet table awaited, overflowing with platters of food of all descriptions, including a dish of curry, a large cake, and a bowl of punch. The bride cake was decorated with icing and sugar flowers. Aunt Matty had helped make it, under Mrs. Craddock's supervision. The tall cake was a tiny bit crooked but she knew it would be delicious.

On the other end of the tent stood a makeshift platform, where musicians from The Bell played—two of Jane's ostlers and Colin McFarland. Mr. Victor and a few others from the troupe joined in, forming quite the orchestra, if a cobbled-together band playing jigs and ballads could be called an orchestra.

Chairs borrowed from every house in the village ringed the tent. People filled plates and sat down to eat from their laps or at one of the tables spread here and there. Mercy saw several elderly women from the almshouse, dressed in finery that had recently graced Miss Victor's display window. They looked like wealthy London dowagers. Mercy giggled at the cheery sight.

Her husband brought her a plate, and Mercy ate a few bites she barely tasted. She was too happy to savor much of anything beyond the beauty of this moment and this day. Rain speck-speckled the canvas, but the bride and bride cake remained dry.

Hand in hand, Mercy and Joseph walked from group to group, person to person, thanking them for coming and accepting congratulations and well-wishes.

On the gift table, Mercy glimpsed a new wooden sign from Becky Morris:

THE FAIRMONT BOARDING & DAY SCHOOL
PUPILS ACCEPTED, REGARDLESS OF ABILITY TO PAY.
MRS. MERCY KINGSLEY, HEADMISTRESS

Among the other gifts were a large wheel of cheese from the Bartons, hand-sewn gifts from her former schoolgirls, handwritten copies of favorite recipes from Aunt Matilda and Mrs. Timmons, and a lovely potted palm from Mrs. Bushby. Last was an unattractive puce vase from George and Helena, which Mercy was fairly certain she'd seen gathering dust in the Ivy Cottage attic.

George saw her looking at it and said sheepishly, "I know it's rather homely, but I thought you might like a memento of Ivy Cottage."

Mercy was too happy to feel offended. She smiled at her brother. "Thank you, George. I shall keep flowers in it, and it shall look very well indeed."

Something homely from Ivy Cottage made beautiful, she thought. It seemed fitting.

In the distance, Eva heard the church bells ring. She hoped the wedding had gone well. Taking a deep breath, she made her decision. Then she washed, put on one of her better gowns, and walked up Potters Lane, umbrella raised. She had missed the ceremony but was hopefully not too late to join the wedding breakfast.

Reaching Ivy Green, she stopped and stared. The troupe's tent stood there, protecting the tables, guests, and musicians from the rain, patched with a kaleidoscope of fabrics to rival Joseph's coat of many colors. Damaged by hail, the marquee had been one of the things her father had stored in Ivy Hill's tithe barn while the troupe traveled elsewhere, but now here it stood, in makeshift repair. Her father's doing, she guessed.

Eva helped herself to two pieces of cake and then went to find him among the troupe members lingering on the edge of Ivy Green.

Eva handed him a piece of cake. "Thank you, Papa. It looks like you saved the day."

He accepted her offering with a nod of thanks. "The tent you helped fashion years ago saved the day, but I was happy to do my part." He fondly tweaked her chin. "And happier still to be reunited with my beloved daughters."

"Yes. I am so very thankful." Eva looked across the green to where Henrietta sat with her husband and daughter—and a second child on the way. Her father followed the direction of her gaze. Patrick took Betsey from Hen so she could eat and lifted the child into the air to the little girl's glee. Henrietta ate her cake and watched the pair with a fond smile.

Then Eva felt her father's gaze return to her profile.

"Have you made your decision?"

Eva took a deep breath. "I have, Papa. The town's former dressmaker has offered to come out of retirement and take me on as her apprentice. So I am glad you see me as 'at home' here, because I've decided to remain in Ivy Hill. For now."

"For now?"

Without intending to, her thoughts returned to Jack Gander. "Yes."

"I understand. How wonderful to be so near your sister after your long separation." His expression turned wistful. "It's perfect."

Eva said, "I hope you are not too disappointed, Papa. Perhaps you ought to settle down in Ivy Hill too."

"Me? Settle in one place? No, my dear, the traveling life, the show, are in my blood. I am not ready to leave it. Besides, the troupe members need me, as do the animals."

"Of course they do, Papa. But you will visit us, now that you know where we are, won't you?"

"I will indeed. In fact, I think it's time to put Ivy Hill on our annual circuit."

"Excellent idea. And perhaps you can visit us over the winter lull. You'll want to meet your new grandchild, after all."

His eyes misted over again, and he held out his hand to her. "Indeed I shall."

"Miss Victor!"

Eva turned at the sound of someone calling her name.

Miss Morris waved, and Julia Featherstone patted an empty chair beside her at a table filled with members of the Ladies Tea and Knitting Society. "Come and sit with us!"

With a quick squeeze of her father's hand, Eva walked over to take her place at the table.

Sometime later, the rain stopped, and the sun shone amid blue skies.

Mercy sat down to catch her breath and rest her feet from all the dancing. Her cheeks ached from smiling so much. Across the tent, her groom stood talking and laughing in a huddle with his brothers. Her brothers now too.

Seeing her alone, Mr. Drake walked over to join her. "Well, Mrs. Kingsley, I wish you happy."

"Thank you, Mr. Drake. And thank you again for coming back to attend the wedding."

"We wouldn't miss it. Alice made a lovely young bridesmaid, did she not?"

"She did indeed."

"We plan to travel as far as possible today, so we can reach Drayton Park tomorrow. So we can't get too late a start . . ."

"Oh. You're leaving now."

He nodded. They turned as one to pick out Alice among the crowd. There she was, dancing with Phoebe, Sukey, and Jeremy Mullins. She looked charming in her pink dress and crown of flowers in her golden hair, a broad smile on her face.

He said, "I will let her finish her dance, of course, but I'm afraid we must then take our leave."

"I understand."

"I am sorry to cast a shadow on your happy day."

"James Drake, you have nothing to be sorry for, I promise you. I am truly happy for Alice, and for you." She chuckled. "And for me!"

He squeezed her hand, held her gaze a moment, and turned to go.

The set ended, and the musicians called for refreshments and a short respite. Mercy watched as Mr. Drake walked over and bent to whisper in Alice's ear. The girl's smile dimmed a bit, but she did not look surprised or sad. Instead, she searched the crowd, her gaze fixing on her. Mercy lifted a hand, and Alice skipped buoyantly toward her, as though still dancing.

Mercy held out her arms. Alice ran into them, and the two embraced for several moments.

Alice said, "We have to leave, Papa says."

"I know. You have a long trip ahead. Did you have a good time?"

"Oh yes! It was the best wedding ever. I loved the dancing and the cake and the music."

"Me too. And I especially enjoyed having everyone I love here to celebrate with me. I am so glad you were able to share my special day and serve as my bridesmaid. And now I wish you every happiness in your new home."

"Will you come and visit us? And Mr. Kingsley, of course."

Joining them, Mr. Drake spoke up, "You would be very welcome at any time, Miss . . . Mrs. Kingsley. And I mean that sincerely. I am not just being polite."

"Thank you. That is very kind. And I hope it goes without saying that you will always have a place to stay with us when you visit Ivy Hill. You will visit, I hope?"

"I cannot promise, I'm afraid. My father's affairs will keep me occupied for some time, and . . ."

"And?" she prompted.

"And I feel as though this chapter of my life is at an end. I would not change my experiences in Ivy Hill for the world, for here I found my daughter. But I am ready to start anew."

"You found friends here as well, JD. Never forget it."

He grinned at her use of his nickname. "I shan't."

"God bless you, James Drake."

"And you, Mercy Kingsley."

Mercy watched them leave.

Noticing, Joseph came and stood beside her. "All right?" he asked.

She took a deep breath and found that she was. "Yes, perfectly."

He took her hand, and together they walked over to join his brothers.

Seeing them approach, Aaron and Esther made room for them in their circle.

Joseph sent her a rueful glance. "I apologize in advance for my unruly family."

Mercy smiled. "No need. I am blessed to count myself as one of them."

Joseph put his arm around her and said low in her ear, "You, Mercy Kingsley, are my nearest and dearest family. My wife. My heart."

Filled with joy, she reached up on tiptoe to kiss him, to the cheers and catcalls of the Kingsley brothers.

The wedding party continued for several hours, guests relishing each moment and reluctant to see the occasion end.

Jane's gaze swept over the tent—the dancers, chatting guests, laughing children, and radiant new-wed couple. Her heart expanded with aching joy. She was thoroughly delighted for Mercy and Mr. Kingsley. If God blessed them with children, how tall and handsome they would be!

What a memorable wedding it had been, and so touching to see the women of Ivy Hill come together not only to make Mercy's dress, but to repair the tent as well. Jane looked up again at the patched marquee and chuckled. How wonderfully gracious was God's provision to bring the troupe to Ivy Green in time to save Mercy's wedding breakfast.

Eventually, people began to say their good-byes to the bride and groom, and then drift away in twos and threes until only the Kingsley family continued to dance. Hetty joined the musicians so Colin could dance with Anna Kingsley. Then she returned to sit with her husband, daughter, and in-laws. After a time, Eva joined them too.

Finally, the dancing ceased altogether, but the musicians continued to play more softly for their own enjoyment and the pleasure of their listeners.

At a nearby table, the Brockwells sat with Nicholas Ashford and his mother. Another wedding in the near future, Jane guessed. How good to see her dear friends Rachel and Timothy so happy together. Even the dowager Lady Brockwell looked pleased and relaxed surrounded by her family.

Family . . . Bittersweet tears heated Jane's eyes at the thought. She'd had her father back in her life so briefly, and now the doctors said his heart was giving out. He might have a few months, a year at most, they solemnly estimated, all the while acknowledging that it was only an educated guess, and that God's will might dictate otherwise. Jane was deeply grateful that her father had come back to England, to her, for his final days. *Oh, Lord, thank you! And thank you for Jack Avi!* Yet her gratitude was threaded with poignant awareness of impending loss.

She scanned the tent for Miss Matty, guessing she would see the same wistful regret in her expression. The lost years. The what-might-have-beens. Matilda held her gaze, then crossed the tent to her. She extended her hand.

Jane rose and took it, throat tight, and for several moments the two stood there, hand in hand, watching Mercy among the Kingsleys, smiling and laughing, Joseph's arm around her waist.

Matty looked fondly on the couple. "How happy they are."

Jane nodded. She wondered if Matilda's joy for her beloved niece was also threaded with a hint of loss. She and Mercy had always been so close. Had shared a home, a school, everything. And now Mercy had a husband to share everything with instead.

Jane squeezed Matilda's fingers. "I'm sorry my father didn't feel well enough to be here. He is very fond of you, you know."

The older woman nodded. "And I of him, the old nabob." The tears glistening in her eyes belied the teasing tone.

Matilda brightened, saying, "Have you heard the news? Mercy and Mr. Kingsley have invited me to come and live with them. After their honeymoon, that is. Mr. Basu as well. I'm so glad for him. Helena wanted him to start wearing livery and forbade the cooking of curries! Instead, we are both to help with the new school."

"That is wonderful!" Jane beamed, then studied her face. "Or . . . is it? It must seem strange to contemplate leaving Ivy Cottage. It has been your home for, what?"

"More than fifty years. My entire lifetime."

"Are you sad to leave?"

Matilda looked at her, eyes twinkling. "Never been happier about a change in my life. Between you and me, I can't wait."

Matilda's attention was caught by something beyond Jane. Her lips parted in surprise. "Well, knock me down with a feather."

Jane turned to see what had caused such a reaction. There came her father, walking across the green in a summer suit of buff linen and a broad-brimmed straw hat. True, he used a walking stick, and his stride was not as long as it once was, but he looked more hale than Jane had seen him in weeks.

"Winston Fairmont!" Matilda called. "What are doing out of bed?"

He grinned like a mischievous boy. "You all conspired to keep me from enjoying this happy occasion, but I feel remarkably improved today. A second wind, as Dr. Burton said might happen. Whatever the case, I am thankful. For I did not want to miss such an important day in the life of my dear friend, Matilda Grove."

Tears filled Matty's eyes again, but she blinked them back.

He offered her his arm. "Perhaps we might take a turn together, Miss Matty, and taste that grand cake you told me about?"

She gave him a wobbly smile. "With all my heart."

Matilda laced her arm through his, and the two walked slowly toward the others.

For a moment Jane stood watching them go, her heart lifting, her tears slowing. She knew better than to think this changed her father's ultimate prognosis, but she decided she would enjoy every day God gave them together.

She felt a small hand slide into hers and looked down to find Jack Avi standing beside her, gazing up at her with his dark eyes.

"Didi, why are you sad?"

She grasped his small fingers. "These are happy tears. I am happy for my friend, and I am happy Bapu brought you here to meet me."

"Me too. Bapu says you will be my mamma."

Jane's throat tightened again. She whispered, "Is that all right with you?"

He nodded and raised his hands to her. Heart squeezing, she bent and picked him up. Though five years old, he was slight for his age, and carrying him was no burden at all.

Gabriel came over and put one hand on Jack Avi's shoulder and the other on hers. "Hello, you two."

He looked from the boy to Jane, searching her face. "Everything all right?"

She smiled. "More than all right."

"Did you get enough to eat?" Gabriel asked. "I know Jack Avi did. I saw him devour a second piece of cake." He patted the boy's tummy, then his patting turned into tickles.

Jack Avi giggled. "Yes, I'm full."

Gabriel looked at Jane, eyebrows raised in question.

Jane looked from her new husband and future son, to her father and Matilda, and everyone gathered on Ivy Green. She nodded her complete agreement. "My heart is full indeed."

AUTHOR'S NOTE

Thank you for reading *The Bride of Ivy Green*. I hope you enjoyed it, as well as the first two books in the TALES FROM IVY HILL series. Here are a few historical notes I'd like to share with you.

As described in this story, 1821 was indeed an outstandingly wet year in the south of England. On May 26th in Wiltshire, "Snow and hail fell over 5 inches deep."

The lion attack in the book was also based on a true story. In 1816, a lioness escaped from Ballard's menagerie and attacked the lead horse (Pomegranate) of the "Quicksilver" Royal Mail coach as it traveled through Wiltshire. A few passengers fled to a nearby inn, locking the door against the remaining passengers, while the Royal Mail guard attempted to shoot the animal with his blunderbuss. Some accounts say the lioness killed the large dog chasing it, and others say that all three animals survived and went on to be displayed together in the menagerie. The *Salisbury and Winchester Journal* described the lioness's capture this way: "Her owner and his assistants . . . made her lie down upon a sack; and then she was lifted and carried. . . . The lioness lay as quietly as a lamb during her removal to the caravan."

Sometimes truth really is stranger than fiction. I became intrigued by this story a few years ago, when I first began plotting the series and enjoyed weaving a fictionalized version into this novel. Details about the menagerie animals and acts were inspired by the book *The Old Showmen, and the Old London Fairs* by Thomas Frost, if you would like to read more on the subject.

Now for a few acknowledgments. I am thankful for the help of several people who helped me hone this book: Cari Weber (my first reader), Anna Paulson (research and revisions), Michelle Griep (feedback), Karen Schurrer and Raela Schoenherr (editing), Jennifer Shouse-Klassen (dressmaking details), Tony Signorelli of Blue Harbor (a great place to write), Cathy and Rajeev Tandon and Sumita Punia (culture of India), and each and every one of you (my wonderful readers).

Thank you for spending time with me in Ivy Hill, a fictional village that has become very special to me. It is loosely based on the National Trust village of Lacock in Wiltshire, which I've had the privilege of visiting three times now. If you find yourself missing Ivy Hill, you can always visit Lacock yourself—either in person if you like to travel, or via television, since Lacock has been used as a filming location for scenes in *Pride & Prejudice* (1995), *Cranford* (2007), *Emma* (1996), and several other productions. You can also visit talesfromivyhill.com to see photos of the series setting, as well as a helpful character list and full-color village map. Please also visit me online via social media or email. I'd love to stay in touch!

DISCUSSION QUESTIONS

1. In the early nineteenth century, marriage was often considered a duty for young women. However, many of Jane Austen's heroines reject marriage proposals from men society would consider a good match, choosing instead to marry for love. How have views of marriage changed since then? Do you agree with the relationship decisions of Ivy Hill's women?

2. Victorine is not entirely honest when she first comes to Ivy Hill. Characters like Jane and Mrs. Shabner gradually change their opinions of her as more information is revealed throughout the story. How did the slow reveal influence your opinion of Ivy Hill's new dressmaker?

3. Jane struggles to forgive her father. Have you or someone you know ever dealt with a similar situation? What are the risks or rewards of forgiving someone who has caused you pain?

4. Do you agree with the saying "Just be yourself"? James Drake wants to become a good parent to Alice, even as he struggles to reconcile with his own father. He says, "I can't do that by just 'being myself.' I want to be a better man for Alice's sake." Mercy reminds him that we don't have to rely on

ourselves alone—God will help us. Have you seen someone change their life, with or without God's help?

5. Through the series, characters like Mercy and Jane follow circuitous paths toward happiness, struggling through personal loss, professional troubles, and uncertainties about the future. Can you relate? How so?

6. What was your reaction to George and Helena's claiming of Ivy Cottage? How would you have responded in Mercy's situation? Have you ever had to share a home with extended family members? If so, was the experience wonderful or stressful?

7. In this novel, Ivy Hill residents react differently (some positively, some negatively) to characters from India. Do we see similar variations today in how people treat those from other cultures?

8. As the TALES FROM IVY HILL series closes, did any or all of your predictions come true? What about the ending surprised you? Would you like to see more written about any character(s)?

Keep reading
for an excerpt from Julie Klassen's

The Painter's Daughter

CHAPTER

ONE

March 1815
Devonshire, England

Infuriating artists . . . Captain Stephen Marshall Overtree grumbled to himself as he walked along the harbor of the unfamiliar town, looking into each shop window.

He glanced down at the crumpled paper in his hand, and read again his brother's hastily scrawled note.

> *. . . I will let a cottage as last year, though I don't know which yet. If the need arises, you may write to me in care of Mr. Claude Dupont, Lynmouth, Devon. But no doubt you will manage capably without me, Marsh. As always.*

Stephen stuffed the note back into his pocket and continued surveying the establishments he passed—public house, harbormaster's office, tobacconist, and cider seller. Then a stylish placard caught his eye:

CLAUDE DUPONT
Painter, Royal Academy of Arts

~

Portraits by commission, also local landscapes.
Instruction and supplies for the visiting artist.
Inquire within.

Stephen tried the door latch, but it wouldn't budge. He cupped a hand to the glass and peered inside. The dim interior held easels, framed landscapes, and shelves of supplies, but not a single person.

He bit back an epithet. How could he *inquire within* if the dashed door was locked? It was not yet five in the afternoon. What sort of hours did the man keep? Stephen muttered another unflattering comment about artists.

From the corner of his eye, he saw a frowsy woman step from the public house, dumping a bucket of water. He called, "I am looking for Wesley Overtree. Have you seen him?"

"That handsome Adonis, you mean? No, sir." She winked. "Not today at any rate."

"Know where he's staying?"

"One of the hillside cottages, I believe, but I couldn't tell you which one."

"Well then, what of Mr. Dupont?" Stephen gestured toward the locked door.

"Mr. Dupont is away, sir. But I saw his daughter pass by not fifteen minutes ago. Walking out to the Valley of Rocks, I'd wager, as she does nearly every day about this time." She pointed to the esplanade, where a path led up the hillside before disappearing from view. "Just follow that path as far as it goes. Can't miss it."

"Thank you."

For a moment Stephen remained where he was, looking up the hill—thatched cottages and a few grander houses clung to the wooded slope, while Lynmouth's twin town of Lynton perched above. Perhaps he ought to have remained in the coach for the half-mile climb to Lynton. He sighed. It was too late now.

He walked along the seaside esplanade, then started inland up the path. He was glad now he'd brought his walking stick—a thin sword cleverly concealed inside. One never knew when one might meet highwaymen while traveling, and he preferred to be armed at all times. His military training was well ingrained.

The steep path soon had him breathing hard. He'd thought he was in better condition than that. The month of soft living, away from drilling his regiment, had already taken its toll. He would have a few choice words for Wesley when he found him. Stephen should be with his regiment, not at home doing Wes's duty for him, and not here.

He ascended through the trees, then out into the open as the rocky path curved westward, following the cliff side, high above the Bristol Channel—deep blue and grey. The steep downward slope bristled with withered grass, scrubby gorse, and the occasional twisted sapling. Little to stop a fall. If a man were to slip, he would instantly tumble four or five hundred feet into the cold sea below. His stomach lurched at the thought.

His old nurse's recent pronouncement echoed through his mind. *"You won't live to see your inheritance. . . ."* He could still feel the wiry grip of her hand, and see the somber light in her eyes.

With a shiver, Stephen backed from the edge and strode on.

The cry of a seabird drew his gaze upward. Gulls soared, borne aloft by strident wind. Black-and-white razorbills and grey-tipped kittiwakes nested among the rock outcroppings.

He walked for ten or fifteen minutes but saw no sign of the young woman ahead of him. He hoped he hadn't missed a turn somewhere. As he continued on, the temperature seemed to drop. Although spring came earlier on the southwest coast, the wind bit with icy teeth, blowing across the channel from the north, still held in the grip of winter.

He tugged his hat brim lower and turned up the collar of his greatcoat. In less than two weeks he would again exchange civilian clothes for his uniform, return to duty, and make his grandfather proud. But first he had to find Wesley and send him home. With Humphries retiring, someone needed to help Papa oversee the estate. Their father was not in good health and needed a capable spokesman to keep the tenants happy and the estate workers on task. As a captain in the British Army, the role had come easily to Stephen. But his leave would soon be at an end, Napoleon exiled or not.

The role of managing the estate should have fallen to his older brother. But Wesley had again gone south for the winter, in spite of their mother's pleas. His art came first, he always insisted. And he preferred to leave practical, mundane affairs to others.

Rounding a bend, Stephen saw a craggy headland—rocks piled atop one another like castle battlements—with a sheer drop to the lashing currents below. He looked down to assure his footing, but a flash of color caught his eye and drew his gaze upward again.

He sucked in a breath. A figure in billowing skirts, wind-tossed cape, and deep straw bonnet stood atop that high precipice. Wedged between a rock on one side, and the cliff on the other, her half boot extended over the edge. What was the fool woman doing?

She fell to her knees and stretched out a gloved hand . . . trying to reach something, or about to go over? Did she mean to harm herself?

Pulse lurching, Stephen rushed forward. "Stop! Don't!"

She did not seem to hear him over the wind. Leaping atop the summit, he saw she was trying to reach a paper entangled in the prickly gorse.

"Stay back. I'll retrieve it for you."

"No," she cried. "Don't!"

Taking her objection as concern for his safety, he extended his walking stick to reach the paper and drag it back up the slope. Bending low, he snagged a corner of the thick rectangle—a painting. His breath caught.

He turned to stare at the tear-stained face within the deep bonnet. He looked back down at the painting, stunned to discover the image was of the very woman before him—a woman he recognized, for he had carried her portrait in his pocket during a year of drilling and fighting, and had looked at it by the light of too many campfires.

A gust of wind jerked the bonnet from her head, the ribbon ties catching against her throat, and its brim dangling against her back. Wavy strands of blond hair lifted in the wind, whipping around her thin, angular face. Sad, blue-grey eyes squinted against a dying shaft of sunlight.

"It's . . . you," he sputtered.

"Excuse me?" She frowned at him. "Have we met?"

He cleared his throat and drew himself up. "No. That is . . . the portrait—it's your likeness." He lifted it, also recognizing the style—clearly his brother's work.

Instead of thanks, her face crumpled. "Why did you do that? I was trying to toss it to the four winds. Make it disappear."

"Why?"

"Give it back," she demanded, holding out her hand.

"Only if you promise not to destroy it."

Her lips tightened. "Who are you?"

"Captain Stephen Overtree." He handed over the paper. "And you must be Miss Dupont. You know my brother, I believe."

She stared at him, then averted her gaze.

"That is, he let a cottage from your family. I stopped at the studio but found the place locked. Can you tell me where to look for him?"

"I should not bother if I were you," she said. "He is gone. Sailed for Italy in search of his perfect muse. His Dulcinea or Mona Lisa . . ." She blinked away fresh tears, and turned the painting over, revealing a few scrawled lines in his brother's hand.

He read:

My dear Miss Dupont,
 That visiting Italian couple we met invited me to travel with them to their homeland. To share their villa and paint to my heart's content. It was a spur-of-the-moment decision,

and I could not resist. You know how I love Italy! We sail within the hour.

I know I should have said good-bye in person. I tried to find you, but could not. Thankfully, as a fellow artist you understand me and realize I must follow my muse and pursue my passion. Must grasp this opportunity before it leaves with the tide.

We shared a beautiful season, you and I. And I shall always remember you fondly.

Arrivederci,
W. D. O.

Spend a Festive Christmas in Ivy Hill

Can the romance of Christmastime
in Ivy Hill, with its village charm,
kissing boughs, and divine hope,
change the heart of one prodigal . . .
and the woman determined to rebuff him?

~

Return to Ivy Hill and fall in love all over
again in an upcoming Christmas novella from
Julie Klassen.

~

Visit TalesFromIvyHill.com
for information about the series, including photos,
character lists, a map, and more.

Sign Up for Julie's Newsletter!

Keep up to date with Julie's news on book releases and events by signing up for her email list at julieklassen.com.

More Tales From Ivy Hill

Gentlewoman Rachel Ashford has moved into Ivy Cottage with the Miss Groves, where she discovers mysteries hidden among her books. Together with her one-time love Sir Timothy, she searches for answers— and is forced to face her true feelings. Meanwhile, her friends Mercy and Jane face their own trials in life and love.

The Ladies of Ivy Cottage
Tales from Ivy Hill #2